TALES FROM THE FAERIEVERSE

Into The Between

by
Timothy Swiney

This book is a work of original fiction with characters based on mythological figures from various legends and myths from Scottish folklore. Any similarities or resembelance to other characters or works of fiction are the result of a common historical basis. Characters and situations presented in this work are the sole product of the author's imagination.

Published by Skinny Brown Dog Media
Atlanta, GA USA and Punta del Este, Uruguay
www.skinnybrowndogmedia.com

Distributed by Skinny Brown Dog Media
Developmental Editing and Design by Eric G. Reid
Cover Design by Skinny Brown Dog Media

ISBN: 978-1-957506-90-6 -Paperback
ISBN: 978-1-957506-60-9 Hardback
ISBN: 978-1-957506-62-3 Case Laminate
ISBN: 978-1-957506-63-0 eBook

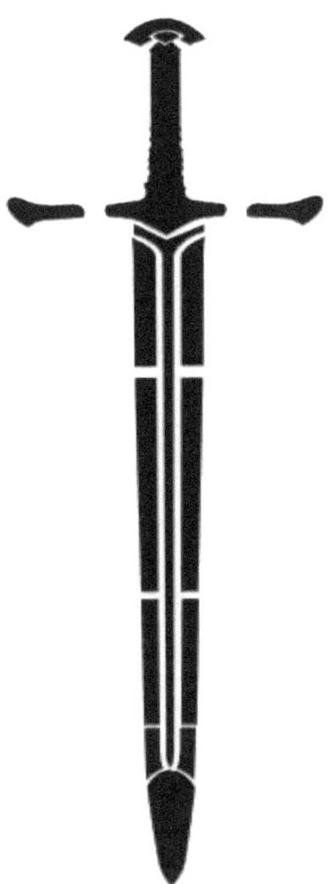

DEDICATION

For Ignacio and Eva,

In the realms where faeries weave shimmering spells, heroes wield ancient swords, and mystical creatures whisper secrets in the wind, I proudly dedicate this book to you. May its pages transport you to worlds beyond imagination, where the boundaries of possibility fade and the extraordinary becomes your reality. Embrace the magic, let your spirits soar, and may this fantastical journey forever ignite the spark of wonder within your hearts. Thank you for being the true heroes of my world.

With love and imagination,
Daddy

AUTHOR'S NOTE:

Dear Readers,

I want to ensure that you fully enjoy the journey through the Faerieverse and become acquainted with the unique characters who inhabit these pages. As you delve into their stories, you may encounter a few names that may initially seem challenging to pronounce. To help you along, I have provided the following pronunciation guide:

Drustan (Druh-stan): The name Drustan is pronounced with the "u" having an "uh" sound, similar to the "u" in the word "hut."

Sluagh (sloo-ah): The word Sluagh starts with the "slu" sound, which is pronounced as "sloo," or "slew." The final part, "ah," is a short "ah" sound, comparable to the "a" in the word "father."

Bean Nighe (bahn nee-yeh): "Bean" is pronounced as "bahn," with the "ea" combination sounding like the "a" in "ban." "Nighe" is pronounced as "nee-yeh." The "ni" sounds like the "nee" in "knee" and the "ghe" is pronounced as "yeh," similar to the "ye" in "yes."

I hope this pronunciation guide assists you in immersing yourself in the Faerieverse. Remember, the most important thing is to enjoy the story, and I appreciate your interest in their lives.

Happy reading!

Within the realm of fairy tales, where gossamar wings grace the air and mischievous spirits dance, enchanting creatures beckon, reminding us that wonder dwells but a heartbeat away.

Timothy Swiney

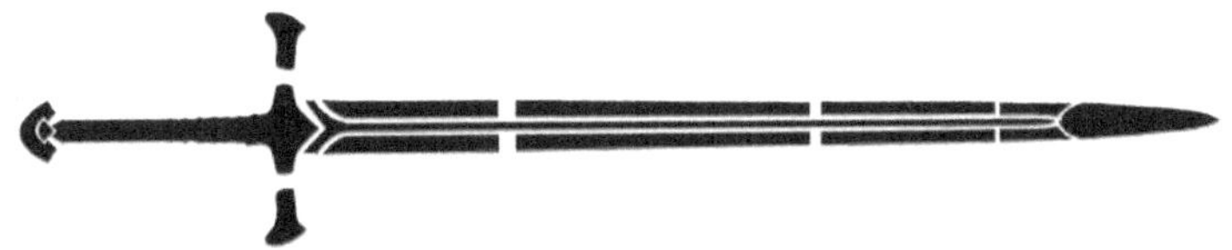

CHAPTER 1

Encounter with the Underfolk

"Hush, boy!" Sibby commanded, her voice sharp as a blade as she stood rooted to the earth, a beacon of vigilance in the heart of the dirt road.

Her son, Drustan, obeyed, his hand slipping to the hilt of the sword at his side. He scanned the land, his gaze sweeping over the rolling hills and distant forests, searching for any sign of danger that might have caught his mother's keen eye.

And then, he saw it - a flicker of movement, a shadow in the trees. Drustan's hand closed around the hilt and he silently unsheathed his sword, preparing for battle.

"What is it, Mother?" he asked, his voice low and steady.

"'Tis a witch at hand," Sibby whispered, her eyes locked on some unseen target.

Drustan's turned his attention back to the plump little woman to find she was now bent over looking at something in the middle of the dirt path they were traveling. He sighed heavily as he stood upright and sheathed his sword. He watched her in amusement, realizing she was only vexed by some meaningless oddity she had found. He had no doubt this peculiarity would be interpreted as a bad omen or some obscure message from the gods.

He walked toward her to get a closer look at the offending object that had captured her attention. "Mother, 'tis only a tree branch."

"Only a tree branch? Open thine eyes, boy!" She scolded. "Look about! 'Tis a willow branch?" She waved her arms all about pointing at the surrounding fields leading up to the forest. "Dost thou see a willow tree?"

Drustan glanced about again at the tall grass on both sides of the road that stretched to the edge of the forest.

"Nay. 'Tis none in my sight," she answered before he could reply. "So, from whence did it come?"

Drustan shrugged. "Maybe the wind blew it here. Or more likely it fell from a farmer's wagon on the way to the village."

It was only a stick and held no interest for him. He could easily have brushed it aside and not given it a second thought. However, he was intrigued as to how his mother concluded from a discarded stick that there was a witch nearby. Over time, he had become accustomed to Sibby's unusual and insightful observations on the mysteries of the world. And there were good reasons she was widely known among the villagers as one of the "cunning folk," possessing arcane knowledge of spells and potions.

Despite the frequent visits from town folk seeking Sibby's skills at foretelling the future, removing curses, and performing healings, Drustan didn't put much faith in the mystic arts or magic. Neither did he believe the dire signs and warnings she pronounced every time she encountered something even slightly out of the ordinary. He did, however, appreciate his mother's ability to profit from the superstitious villagers, and her ability to turn a good tale. So, despite his disbelief Drustan was curious as to what story she was about to spin connecting a discarded twig to the presence of evil witches.

"A witch you say?" Drustan nudged her. He smiled slightly in anticipation of her explanation.

"Dost thou not remember anything I have taught thee over all these years?" She stood up to face him. He was more than a foot taller so she cocked her head upward to glare into his eyes.

"It must've slipped my mind," he shrugged with a slight grin.

"The willow branch, boy! You must remember these things!" She stamped her foot with frustration. "I might as well speak to the wind as to try and teach you about the world!" She pointed at the branch laying at her feet. "The willow branch is too big to have been carried by the wind, and see the out-shoots and have been trimmed away."

"Then must be a walking stick someone discarded along their journey through."

"Perhaps so. Perhaps some poor crippled soul used it to walk." Suddenly, a mischievous grin appeared on her face as she continued, "Or maybe, just maybe, the gods had a hand in it. Perhaps they healed the pitiful wretch right here on this very spot! And he was so overjoyed that he dropped the staff where he stood and danced a jig all the way to Edinberg!"

Drustan stared back at her, not sure if she was spinning another of her fantastic tales that she truly believed, or if she was simply teasing him.

After a moment, she answered his uncertainty. "'Tis a witch, boy!" She snapped impatiently. "I know well the signs, and a willow branch is one of them."

He anxiously awaited her story like a wide-eyed child anticipating a bedtime tale. Of course, he wasn't about to believe a word she said but he did love to listen. As much as he loved to hear her tales, he also loved to tease her about them.

"Young witches … those who have not yet learnt to use the dark magic … those foul fledglings sit upon a willow branch to take flight."

Drustan tried to hold back but he couldn't help but laugh.

Sibby pulled her shoulders back, thrust her hands on her chubby hips and glared at him.

"I'm sorry," Drustan immediately said after seeing her disapproving expression. He did not mean to offend her, but the thought of a crinkled old crone sitting on such a thin stick and flying through the air was amusing. The mental image of such a thing was just too odd for him to accept with a straight face.

"You think I speak in jest? Did I labor for two days and nights to birth such a child to ridicule his old mother?"

"No! No. I'm sorry," Drustan insisted. "I don't mean to disrespect your wisdom. I just don't get it. A witch riding a stick? Really?"

"'Tis as I have spoken."

Drustan truly wanted to hear the details of his mother's tale, if only for the entertainment value, so he continued to prod her. "Why a willow branch? Surely that could not hold the weight of a small child. Why could she not just turn into a sparrow or a crow?"

"'Tis not the branch that makes the witch to fly, nor does it suffer her weight. The willow wand helps her focus her powers so she can take flight. The younger ones will ride upon a willow staff or a bristle broom if one is at hand. As the witch's power grows, then she can shape shift and take flight as a bird or run as a beast in the field. Only the oldest and most powerful witches can fly in their true form."

Drustan picked up the limb and studied it for a moment. He saw nothing unusual or ominous about it. It was of good length for use as a staff for walking. The bark had been peeled away and the buds and small branches had be shaved off so that it was straight and smooth. But it was rather thin, not likely to bear much weight.

"So, if this does belong to a witch, what would she be doing here?" He asked only to indulge her. Though he did not believe her tale, he knew she believed every word she had spoken. So, rather than risk offending her any further he allowed her to continue spinning her tale.

"Mischief making, no doubt. Who knows the evil intentions of a witch, save the witch herself." Sibby replied, then she gave a dismissive wave of her hand and began walking down the dirt road once again. "Let us tarry no longer. We must make haste and be vigilant, lest we be caught unaware."

"Then let us be on our way. I have already spent too much of this day picking flowers with you," he laughed, knowing well that the sack Sibby carried over her shoulder held medicinal herbs they had foraged from the fields and among the trees.

"I know you have other chores," she intertwined her arm with Drustan's as they walked. "But I do enjoy our time together. I am grateful to have your company."

"As do I," Drustan patted her fondly on her hand. "Besides, who would protect you from the witches and goblins if I weren't with you."

"And such a fierce protector to watch over me."

They continued to stroll casually down the dirt road heading to their home. After a while, Sibby disrupted the silence.

"Tell me, my son. I come to believe you doubt thy mother's wisdom in these things. Perhaps you just humor me with thy conversation."

Drustan had no doubt of his mother's wisdom, it was her magical abilities that gave him pause. He had witnessed with his own eyes his mother's uncanny ability to anticipate future events and her skills in the use of herbs and potions to heal many ailments. There was also the steady stream of visitors who would travel great distances to seek Sibby's wisdom and to purchase an elixir for love or fertility. So Drustan did not question her ancient wisdom in the mystical arts. What he did question, however, was how much of her talent was due to secret mystical knowledge verses her ability to spin a good tale. When it came to her magical abilities, Drustan attributed her powers to showmanship and artistic flare rather than to magic and witchcraft.

"No! Not at all!" Drustan protested. "I take your words as the voice of the ancients."

"Then why do you disregard my instructions and warnings? I speak to thee of important things to protect against the evils of this world, and you brush them aside giving my words no more regard than old wives' tales. You hear me speak, but you do not heed nor listen."

"Forgive me mother, it's just —" He paused and struggled for the right words to avoid offending her. The fact is, he saw his mother's warnings as little more than tales to entertain children or puffery to sale her elixirs and charms. But to tell her such would be a terrible insult since clearly Sibby believed herself to be a mage of sorts.

"It's just what? That you don't believe?"

"Uh, well. I wouldn't say I don't believe you." Drustan struggled. "It's just I have never seen a witch, nor any of the magical creatures you speak of. 'Tis sometimes hard to believe such fantastic beings are real."

"Have you seen thy mother's love?"

"Huh?"

"'Tis a simple enough question. Have you ever seen love?"

"Aye. Certainly, I have."

"Truly? And how does it appear? Is love the color of the heather in bloom? Does it possess a delightful fragrance akin to wildflowers and the dew of the morning? Does it taste like the nectar of honey and the cream of the cows? Or is it as gentle as the finest fleece?"

"You know what I mean."

"What of fear? Or hate? Or happiness?" Sibby pressed. "Hast thou seen those as well? Of course not! So how do you know they are real?"

"That's not a fair comparison!" Drustan insisted. "You can't see love or hate, but you can see their effects."

"Exactly, my son. You may not be able to see the witch, but a wise man can recognize her works."

"There's no arguing with you," Drustan sighed.

Sibby laughed. "Not about such things."

"Still. I believe in the things I can touch and grasp with my hands."

"You believe only in things you can punch with thy fists and pierce with an arrow," she scoffed. "I understand the prideful ways of men. You are no different from your father when he was your age. But he has seen the workings of evil and now knows the dark forces lurking around us. There are many things in this world that cannot be seen with unbelieving eyes, and many enemies that cannot be felled by a blade. It would be wise for you to heed your mother's words and learn how to defend yourself against all who would cause you harm."

"Herbs and roots and spells and portions. 'Tis a woman's domain, and not fit for a man."

Sibby stopped and grabbed him roughly by the earlobe and pulled it hard. Drustan yelped as she pulled him down to where they were at eye level.

"Listen to me, foolish boy! Protecting thy family is not just a woman's work. 'Tis thy job to protect your family. Your younger brothers and sisters look up to thee to keep them from harm's way. And the gods willing, someday you will have a wife and children of your own.

You need to know how to protect them! Not just from the wolves in the fields, but also from the devils in the night."

"Aye, I get it!" Drustan groaned. "Now will you let go!"

Sibby released her hold and immediately continued walking along the road. Drustan rubbed his ear and hurried to catch up with her.

"When will you stop treating me like a bairn? I'm a grown man!"

"You're a grown man when I say you are. Count thyself lucky I didn't take that staff to your hind quarters. You're still not too old to put o'er my knee."

She gave a belly laugh at the thought of it all. Drustan towered over her and was as strong as the plow horse. The days when she could turn him over her knee had ended long ago by the time he was ten years of age.

"I have no doubts about that." Drustan acknowledged.

"What are you doing with that thing?" Sibby noticed that Drustan was still carrying the willow branch and dragging it through the dirt as he walked.

"Nothing. It's a good stick."

"Well get rid of it. 'Tis bad luck."

Drustan shrugged and hoisted the branch onto his shoulder, gripping it like a spear. With a mighty throw, he launched it over the field and toward the trees. The willow branch soared high into the air, sailing beyond the pasture and through the canopy of the first line of trees, disappearing into the depths of the dark forest.

"Behold!" exclaimed Drustan. "Did you see how far

it flew?"

Sibby was impressed by her son's natural prowess and athleticism. Drustan was a strong man, gifted with both sword and bow, so it came as no surprise that he was also skilled with the spear. But instead of indulging his self-adulation, she merely rolled her eyes.

"Are ye not awestruck?" Drustan bellowed, raising his fists to the sky in triumph. "Fear me, ye witches and dark gods! Hast thou ever beheld such a great warrior?" He let out a loud laugh, reveling in his own glory.

Sibby opened her mouth, preparing to caution him about being so bold but before she could utter a word an unearthly howl arose from the forest. The sound was so unnatural and horrific it made both her and Drustan freeze in their tracks. A flock of birds arose from the trees and flew away in fright, scattering in all directions to escape whatever had made such a horrid cry.

"What was that?" Drustan's eyes widened as he turned to see his mother's face drained of color and her mouth agape.

Sibby gathered herself and grabbed her son by the arm and pulled him down with her into a squat. "Get down!"

"What was that? A wild boar?"

"'Tis no boar. I have never heard such a wail," she whispered. "I suspect tis something not of this world."

Again, the terrible sound filled the air. It sounded like a combination of a roar and a scream, as if the creature that made it was in both agony and rage. It was the sound one could image a demon might make.

Drustan looked all about, trying to discover from

where the cries came so as to get a glimpse of what creature could produce such a noise. He rose slightly, still crouching enough to use the tall grass as cover. He peered into the woods.

"There!" Sibby pointed into the trees just a short distance beyond where Drustan had thrown the willow branch. "'There in the shadows."

"I don't see anything." Drustan stood taller and squinted his eyes as he searched the area where his mother was pointing. Then he saw it. A dark figure moving within the brush. "What is that?"

He stood completely upright and crept to the edge of the road and into the grass. When he reached the grass, the thing suddenly began to thrash about as it let out another tremendous roar. Instinctively, Drustan dropped back down returning to the cover of the grass. He looked back at Sibby, sitting on her knees in the middle of the road. Her hand clutched to her heart and her face pale with fear.

"Do you recognize what this thing is?"

"Hush boy," she whispered. "Do not draw its eye?"

Getting no answers from his mother, Drustan turned his attention back to the creature and stained to get a closer look. It flailed about again and this time he could see its large black wings flapping about. For a moment, he thought it must be nothing more than a large black bird of some type, but as it continued to flail about, he could see the creature was too large to be a bird. At least it was no bird he had ever seen. Its wings were massive with a dark body. Though he could not make out the physical details, he could see it was the size of a grown man. This was neither a bird nor man, but something else entirely. Something unnatural.

Always curious and rarely showing any fear, and as his mother would say — seldom showing good judgment — he began to creep through the brush and towards the creature. He had to get a closer look.

"What are you doing?" Sibby whispered. "Get back here!"

"I want to see it."

"No, boy!" She urged. But he was already half-way to the edge of woods. "Fool-hearted ox! He'll get himself killed." She grumbled and reluctantly crawled after him.

Once Drustan reached the edge of the woods, he crouched down behind a tree to conceal himself and waited silently. Once he was confident that the creature was unaware of his presence, he continued to venture deeper into the woods. He eased his sword from its sheath and darted from tree to tree, moving himself closer to where the creature lurked.

When he was as close as he dared go, he paused behind a tree and slowly peered around the trunk. He finally saw the thing clearly. It was something he had never seen before and the strangeness of it made the hair on his arms stand up. It had a large black leathery body the size of a man was large black wings. It was face down on the ground and turned away from him so he could not completely see the creature, but he did see that its lower body was pinned beneath a fallen tree. It was trapped and desperately struggling to break free.

Cautiously Drustan emerged from behind the tree to

get a better view. It was a strange and repugnant sight, something more appropriately seen in a nightmare than in the light of day, though the darkness of the forest seemed a suitable place to encounter such a monster. It had large black wings like a giant bat and long spindly arms with finger-like talons. It had the shape of a man, two arms and two legs, and was covered with black leathery skin that hung loosely as if it were barely clinging to the bones. Sparse strands of long white hair covered its head and the gruesome face had sunken cheeks and long jagged teeth protruding from a drawn mouth. To Drustan, this creature looked like a winged corpse that was rotting to the bones. Perhaps it was a man, or the remnants of one, that had been cursed and transformed by some dark magic.

Upon seeing Drustan the creature struggled wildly against the log trying to dislodge itself, but it was still unable to break free. The creature shrieked that same horrible cry then collapsed back to the dirt, its chest heaving up and down in exhaustion. It raised its head and hissed and snapped at Drustan warning him away, but it was clearly unable to continue the struggle.

"What manner of beast is this?" Drustan asked aloud as he heard his mother approach.

Upon seeing the thing, Sibby gasped and grabbed at a tree to steady herself. "What have you done? We should not have ventured to look upon that thing!"

"There's nothing to fear. 'Tis pinned underneath the tree," Drustan assured her.

"Then I have raised a fool, for ye should be terrified!"

"Do you know what it is?"

Sibby eased closer, but only slightly. Looking the hideous thing up and down, she had never encountered one in the flesh but she knew the creature from legends and stories she heard from elders. "'Tis a Host. One of the darkest and most dreadful of all the Fae."

"This thing is a faerie?"

"Aye, the most evil form of Fae. 'Tis one of the Underfolk. They will tear the flesh from a man's bones, then devour his very soul." Sibby scanned the trees above and all about. "We must leave this place now."

"We can't just leave. It's trapped. We need to help it."

"Help it! Are you mad? Would be better to help the devil himself than one of the Underfolk."

"I can't leave it to suffer like this. It is a living thing despite its outward appearance."

"No, 'tis not! It's not a living thing. It is the unsanctified dead, a cursed soul. The soul of someone who in life was so cruel and evil that they were damned by the gods to this existence."

"I don't believe that, mother. Look at it. It's in pain and terrified. Don't let its appearance condemn it." Drustan looked at the creature and felt pity for it. Despite the strange appearance, the creature had an almost human quality in the way its eyes followed him. The thing had one green eye and one blue, and it gazed at Drustan with a human quality and understanding.

"No! We must leave this place!" She protested. "You don't know these things. Where there is one of the Underfolk, there are all. They move as a swarm and feed like locusts on the souls of the hopeless and dying."

"Well, we're neither dying nor hopeless. And I will

not turn away and leave this thing to suffer." Drustan began to study the fallen tree, looking for a means to free the creature from underneath it.

"You don't understand these things," Sibby warned. "The Underfolk hide in the shadows waiting for night-fall and once the sun has set, they will take to the sky as a great horde. Their wings flapping like the sound of thunder as they attack in a whirlwind of claws and teeth; devouring all who draw their attention."

"Uh huh," Drustan murmured in disinterest as he walked around the log and continued to study the situation.

"I warn you, son. Do not tempt fate. Do not let thy name rest on the lips of the dark Fae."

"There's just this one, I see no horde. And you said they seek the dying and those in despair. We are neither. Besides, if the thing should move against us, I have my sword. I will cut it down."

"No! Do not raise thy sword against the Underfolk. 'Tis said, he who kills a Host is cursed to take its place among the horde."

"Is that so?" He asked off-handedly, barely paying attention to her dire warning. "Anything else I should know?"

"'Tis wise to avoid these creatures at all costs. Once you draw the attention of the Underfolk, you are marked. They will seek you out, watching from the shadows for when you are vulnerable. They will hunt you until you draw your last breath."

He hesitated a moment to consider Sibby's urgings. She could be right; perhaps this thing was not something worthy of compassion. It was a dreadful creature and difficult to look upon, but did that mean it was evil and undeserving of human kindness?

Drustan did not doubt that this Host, as his mother called it, was not of this world. It was unnatural. For a moment he considered following his mother's advice and walking away, but then he looked at the one green and one blue eye that followed him. Those eyes were pleading with him, and the creature was terrified and desperate. He could not leave it in such a cruel way; it was not in his nature to ignore the suffering of any animal, even one such as this beast.

"Mother, return to the road and remain at a safe distance. I will set this creature free and then we will be on our way."

"Drustan! I beg you! Let the thing be! No good will come of this!"

"I can't just leave it to suffer." Drustan handed her his sword. "Take my sword and go back to the road. I'll be along shortly."

"I'm not leaving my firstborn child to face that thing alone!"

"All will be well, mother. Like any trapped animal, once this creature is loose, it will flee into the safety of the woods."

"'Tis foolishness," Sibby grumbled and took a step back. She raised the sword in front of her. "Do what you must, but I will remain here should this creature turn on you."

"Might want to take a few steps back, just in case."

Sibby backed away slightly, all the while keeping the

sword high in the air ready to strike if needed.

Drustan walked to the broken end of the fallen tree and squatted down over it. He wrapped his arms tightly around the trunk, took several deep breaths and blew out heavily after each. He took one last deep breath and as he blew out, he pushed up with his legs harnessing all his strength. The veins on his forearms bulged and the seams of his leather pants strained to contain his thick muscular legs.

"Arghh," he groaned loudly as every muscle in his body fought against the weight of the heavy tree. Little by little, the tree began to lift off the ground, and off the creature that was pinned under it. Abruptly the beast bolted from underneath the log, startling Drustan so that he lost his grip and the tree fell back to the forest floor with a dull thud.

Rather that escape into the forest as Drustan had expected, the thing instead lunged at him knocking Drustan backward to the ground and the creature was quickly upon him, perched on Drustan's chest. It looked down at him with its piercing blue and green eyes, cocking its head from side to side in curiosity. It didn't seem to be threatening but was instead struggling to understand why this human had set it free. The thing made clicking sounds from deep within its throat as if it was speaking.

Drustan resisted the urge to fight and instead he remained motionless. The creature was only curious so he knew it would be best not to alarm or provoke it. It brought its face close to his and began to sniff. Its breath cold against Drustan's face like a cold winter draft and it smelled like burning flesh.

"Get away from him!" Sibby rushed toward them brandishing the sword in front of her.

The Host turned to Sibby and hissed to warn her away.

"Stay back!" Drustan raised his hand to stay her approach. "It's only curious. Nor more so than you and I."

Sibby waved the sword in the air but dared not get close enough to the creature to strike at it. "Shoo! Get away!" She waved the sword again.

"Don't make it mad! Let it satisfy its curiosity," Drustan stated calmly in a soft, non-threatening tone.

"That's right," he spoke softly to the creature. "We're all friends here. Nothing to be afraid of."

The creature again leaned down and sniffed Drustan's neck and hair the way a curious dog would. Drustan turned his head and winced from the stench of its foul breath. It raised up and gave him another long look and made some clicking noises. Then suddenly, it spread its massive wings and in a rush of wind flew off into the forest.

Sibby threw the sword to the ground and rushed to help her son to his feet. "Are you alright?"

"I'm fine. It did not harm me. It was just curious."

She spun him around to check for any injury and slapping her hand against his back and shoulders to shake the dirt from his clothing. "Such foolishness! You could have been killed!"

"Yet I wasn't. All is well, mother. We helped that poor creature. Besides, now you have another precautionary tale to frighten your grandchildren on some dark winter's night."

"Jest if you like, but mark my words, nothing good will come of this. That thing knows you now. It has your scent. The Underfolk do not forget; they will be drawn to you now."

"Perchance someday I will need its help, and it will repay my act of kindness."

Sibby grabbed him by the arm. "No. Do not even suggest such a thing!"

She looked around the woods to make sure no one was near, then lowered her voice as if to reveal a secret. "They say that one can call upon the Underfolk. Calling their name in the dark of night — their true name — aye, they will come. But they will not bring compassion. They will bring death and torment to whoever dares summon them."

Drustan retrieved his sword from where his mother had dropped it, placed it in the sheath and slung it over his shoulder. "Let us be on our way."

Drustan took his mother by the arm to steady her as they made their way through the tall grass and back to the dirt road.

"Why not summon them in time of need? Who wouldn't seek such a fierce ally to call upon in time of need?'

"No! Do not entertain such nonsense!" Sibby snapped sharply. "These creatures have no friend, nor ally, not even among the dark demons of the underworld."

Sibby grabbed Drustan by the arm and turned him to face her. She looked directly into his eyes to impress the importance of her warning. "Hear me child, and mark these words as the solemn truth. You must never speak the true name of these beasts, especially after sunset. Never call out to them, even in the most desperate of time. No good can ever come from a dark faerie, especially not from the Underfolk. The dark fae are tricksters and deceivers, and the Underfolk are the most dangerous of all. Do you hear me?"

"Yes, I hear you," he sighed reluctantly.

"They tell of a King who called upon the Underfolk during a time of war. His kingdom was under siege from an enemy and his army was all but defeated. In a final act of desperation, the King called out to the Underfolk. He called them by their true and secret name. She looked all about before speaking the foul name of the beasts. Satisfied that they were alone, she whispered in a hushed voice, "'Sluagh' he cried out to the night sky."

"Sluagh? Is that their name?"

"Hush boy!" Sibby placed a finger to her lips. "They may hear you."

"And they came to his aid."

"Aye. They came. Descending from the night sky in a thunderous whirlwind. A maelstrom of wings and teeth so thick that it blocked out the moon and turned the sky as black as pitch. When the sun rose the next day, no one remained on the battlefield. Both armies, and even the King himself — all were taken up by the horde and never seen again."

Drustan tilted his head to a side and looked thoughtfully into the distance. After a moment of consideration he added, "All save one."

"No. Not one was spared."

"If no one survived, then who was left to tell that

tale?"

He grinned. Even after having an unnatural beast like a sluagh sitting upon his chest and breathing its foul breath into his face, Drustan could not resist teasing his mother about her tall tales. Despite his taunting, Drustan now knew the story of the Underfolk was not simply an old wives' tale. Clearly his mother knew more of the dark world than he had been willing to admit.

"Still you disbelieve? Wasn't but a moment ago that you would have said the Underfolk was a made up tale to scare my grandchildren." Sibby pulled her shoulders back proudly. "Maybe the stench of that beast will linger long enough to remind you otherwise."

"I am still shaking from the experience, but despite the oddity of it all, I knew I could count on you to gloat."

"Mothers do not gloat; I simply revel in the moments when my child learns a valuable lesson."

"Aye, that is called gloating, mother."

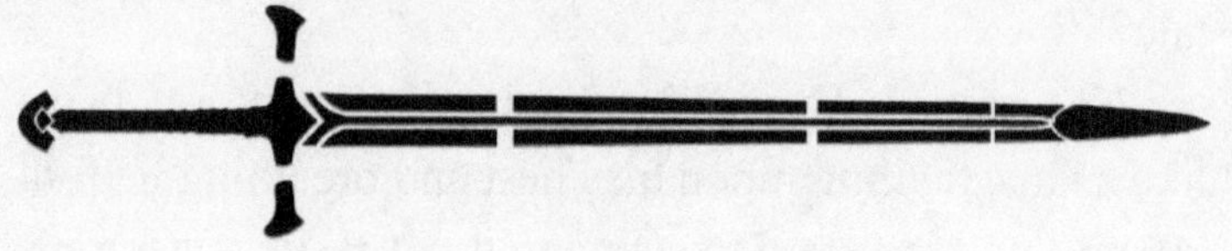

CHAPTER 2

The Face in the Mist

Sibby and her husband nurtured Drustan into a formidable warrior, instilling in him the skills and discipline needed to defend himself and his loved ones against any threat, be it human or otherwise. This was not just because he had a duty as the eldest child to protect his siblings, but also as a precautionary measure, as Sibby feared that the hidden truths of the past could put him and those around him in harm's way. She knew that one day, despite her efforts, the past would return to haunt them.

At Sibby's insistence, Drustan's stepfather Rowan, who was a seasoned warrior in his own right, began imparting his knowledge of combat to the young boy. With Rowan's guidance, Drustan quickly developed a passion for swordsmanship and a natural talent for it. Even at a young age, he surpassed his stepfather in their sparring matches. And once he mastered the sword, Drustan moved on to perfecting his archery skills, becoming a master marksman, even more skilled than any Rowan had ever seen during his time serving in the king's army.

Sibby knew that in addition to honing his combat skills, it was crucial for Drustan to learn the ancient ways of the Druids. For her, the dangers that threatened their land went beyond those of mere mortals and physical combat. She taught him how to ward off dark witches, banish malevolent spirits and defend against the monstrous creatures from the Otherworld. Though he showed little interest in the intricacies of magic and spell work, she persisted in her teachings, determined to arm him with the knowledge to protect himself and his loved ones from the ominous forces that lurked on the fringes of their world. After his encounter with the sluagh, Drustan's eyes were opened, if only slightly, to the value of learning the mystical arts and Sibby seized upon the opportunity to continue his education.

"Answer me, child." Sibby insisted as she snapped her fingers in front of his face. "Pay attention!"

Drustan had been lost in his thoughts as they walked along the dirt path toward their farm. "What?" He shook himself back to reality. "Uh..."

"The thirteen powers of a witch. Come on, Drustan! I've told you this a hundred times."

Drustan hesitated, struggling to recall the teachings of his mother. The thirteen powers of a witch, a subject she had drilled into him, yet one he had paid little attention to at the time. "The ability to curse or bless, to commune with animals, to summon spirits, to tie knots for spell casting…" The teachings slowly came back to him.

He silently counted his answers on his fingers. That was only four. He growled under his breath. Only nine more to go.

"Think, son!"

He struggled to remember. "To control the weather?"

"Aye," she said. "Continue. 'Tis only five."

Drustan's mind raced as he tried to remember more of his mother's teachings, but the words eluded him. He could feel the frustration and disappointment mounting within him as he realized he had not retained as much as he should have. "I'm sorry, mother," he muttered, his voice heavy with regret. "I've forgotten."

"It is crucial that you remember these teachings, Drustan," his mother's voice was stern but laced with concern. "To safeguard yourself, you must not only know the vulnerabilities of your foes, but also their strengths. 'Tis the same as in battle. Knowledge is the greatest weapon in the struggle against the darkness. It may very well be the thing that saves your life one day."

"You speak wisdom, mother," Drustan replied with a hint of remorse in his voice. "I shall strive to do better, to learn and remember all that you teach me. I will not let my own shortcomings stand in the way of my protection and the safety of those I hold dear."

"Do not utter hollow words simply to placate me, Drustan," Sibby implored, her voice taking on an urgent tone. "You must act on them. A sword or bow alone will not be enough to combat the malevolent forces of the Otherworld. You must learn and master the ways of the old ones, it could mean the difference between life and death."

"I understand mother, I will strive to be more receptive to your knowledge. But, truly I have yet to meet a creature that can survive without its head."

Sibby's voice grew stern as she spoke, her words filled with warning. "Your encounter with the sluagh should have been a lesson to you, Drustan," she said, turning to face him, her finger wagging in emphasis. "There are many dangers in this world that are not of mortal flesh and blood. And there are many others that will not stand idly by while you brandish your sword. Beware of arrogance, my son. Remember the moment when you lay vulnerable, at the mercy of a creature from the Otherworld, with death only a breath away. Heed the warning that fate has given you this day."

"Aye, mother. You are right," he admitted. "I will heed your words."

"Now, let us tarry no longer," Sibby said, her tone becoming urgent. She quickened her pace as she continued, "We have already seen signs of witches nearby and encountered one of the Underfolk. We must be on our guard, lest we come face to face with the devil himself. This is a day of ill omens, my son. The wind carries a chill that goes beyond the cold breath of winter."

As they traversed the winding path, the bend in the road revealed their humble abode in the distance. As they drew closer, they spied a grandiose carriage stationed outside their dwelling. It was a magnificent coach, masterfully crafted and lavishly adorned, pulled by two majestic steeds and a finely garbed driver perched atop the coach box, staring ahead stoically. It was evident that this was not a conveyance that one would have arrived from a nearby hamlet. The proprietor of such opulence must be a wealthy lord or possibly even a member of the royal court.

"Who is this that travels in such grandeur?" Drustan commented with surprise.

It was not uncommon for the villagers to seek out Sibby's guidance and assistance, many young maidens would come to her for love spells and the neighbors would often come to her for healing. However, most of her visitors were poor peasants, arriving on foot or on horseback. Occasionally, a wealthy merchant might arrive in a carriage, but those instances were rare. But none have ever arrived in a carriage of such splendor. It was clear that this was not one of the locals, the dust on the carriage and the sweat on the horses indicated that they had traveled a great distance.

Drustan couldn't help but pause and admire the grand carriage, his curiosity getting the better of him. He walked around the carriage, inspecting the horses and gave them a pat. "Good day," he addressed the coachman as he gently stroked the side of one horse.

The man paid no heed to Drustan, instead lifting his nose high into the air as if he were avoiding a displeasing odor.

Drustan couldn't help but chuckle at the coach driver's haughty demeanor. "Well, well, it seems someone has a high opinion of himself," Drustan said with a smirk, not letting the driver's rudeness affect him.

The man remained impassive; his gaze fixed ahead.

Undaunted, Drustan shrugged his shoulders and offered, "Looks like you've had a long journey. There's a horse trough around back at the barn if you need to water your horses."

Sibby, unimpressed by the extravagance of the carriage before her, marched up the steps and onto the porch without a second glance. She paused before going inside and called back to Drustan.

"Drustan, I need you to go to the coop and select a plump and healthy hen. Make sure you handle it with care, and do not bruise the bird while collecting it." Her gaze was intense, and her tone left no room for question.

"Do you think they're here to seek food and rest along their journey?"

"'Tis not supper that brings these people to our door. They are in need of our help. Now, go quickly and do as I ask."

Drustan did as instructed while Sibby made her way inside. As she opened the door she was immediately greeted by her eldest daughter, Gilda.

"Mama, we have company," Gilda announced upon Sibby's arrival.

"So I see, my dear."

Sibby looked at the visitors curiously. They were a young couple. A young man dressed in finery stood behind his wife who was seated in the chair by the fireplace. In her arms she cradled a small child, three, maybe four years of age. At first glance, anyone could see that the child was deathly ill and delirious with fever, but Sibby saw much more. Death hung over the boy like an oppressive shadow preparing to claim him.

"Gilda, bring these weary travelers some cool water and some bread."

"No thank you," the young woman replied. "Your daughter has been kind enough to provide us some water, and we have already eaten."

"You have traveled a great distance to find me. What is it you seek?" Sibby asked them only out of courtesy, she already sensed the dark forces that were at work around them.

"Are you the one known as Sibby, the witch?" The man asked abruptly.

"John!" The woman scolded him. "Forgive my husband, my lady. He meant no offense."

"You address me as both witch and lady. Which one do you seek?" Sibby responded.

"Whichever can save our child," the man implored.

"Please, we beg of you," the woman pleaded. "Our servants spoke of your gifts and we have traveled a great distance to find you."

"We can pay a handsome price," the husband added, revealing a small leather pouch on his belt filled with coins.

"If I can aid your child, I shall," Sibby said, retrieving a white cloth from the cupboard and laying it over the wooden dinner table. "Place the child here."

The man lifted the boy from his mother's lap and gently laid him on the table. Sibby immediately began her examination. She lifted his arm and let it fall, noting that the boy was limp and unresponsive, as if already lost to the Otherworld. She examined his nails, arms, and legs, then opened his eyes and peered into them one at a time.

"How long has he been afflicted?" Sibby asked.

"Since yesterday morning," the mother replied. "He was playing in the courtyard, healthy and happy, but one of our women saw him fall to the ground. When we reached him, he was burning with fever and would not wake."

"Have you seen this sickness before?" The father asked. "Can you heal him?"

"'Tis not a sickness of the body that afflicts thy child, but a sickness of his spirit. The boy has been bewitched."

The couple clutched at each other for comfort in face of the revelation. To tell them that their son was bewitched was worse than saying the boy had the plague. With the plague, it was only his body that was at risk, but with witchcraft, his very soul was in danger.

"Do not despair, the spell can be broken," Sibby assured them.

Sibby returned to the cupboard and retrieved a small wooden chest from the top shelf. It was crafted from ancient oak and adorned with mysterious, arcane symbols. She carried it to the table with reverence, and placed it near the child's head. She lifted the lid to reveal four gray stones, each bearing a unique symbol representing the four elements: earth, wind, water, and fire. She carefully placed one at each corner of the table where the boy lay, creating a sacred space for her magic to take hold.

"Gilda, fetch me the pouch of salt from the kitchen," Sibby commanded her daughter.

The young girl darted behind a curtain and returned a moment later with a small bag of salt. She presented it to her mother, who then began to sprinkle the salt around the table, encircling the boy. As she did, she chanted in an ancient and forgotten language, "*Eldrida vaelyn, dyrnwyn awen.*"

Drustan entered the house, cradling a hen in his arms. As he looked around the room, he couldn't help but feel a sense of unease. This was a most unusual day, he thought to himself. He noticed the couple sitting at the table beside the ill boy and wondered what kind of trouble they had brought to his mother's door.

"Give it to me, Drustan," Sibby said as she held out her arms to take the fowl from him.

Drustan handed her the hen, and then turned to Gilda, "Let's go outside and check on the animals." He led his little sister to the door. His mother always sent the children outside when she had visitors. Though she would freely speak to them of her mystical practices and the services she would perform for those who came seeking her help, she would not allow her children to witness her craft. Sibby didn't want them exposed to the dark forces that sometimes revealed themselves in her practice.

"Drustan," Sibby stopped him before he left the house. "Let your sister tend the animals. I would have you here with me."

Drustan hesitated for a moment, unsure of what to do. He had always avoided his mother's magic, preferring instead to focus on honing his combat skills. But something in her words, and the gravity of the situation before him, made him realize the importance of understanding the mystical arts. He nodded, "I will stay, mother."

He took a step back into the house and watched as Sibby proceeded with her spell work, ready to learn and understand the ancient ways of the Druids.

Sibby held the hen upside down over the child as she resumed her chanting,

"Dràsta mallachd dìomhair,
Cleachd mo chumhachd,
Thoir fios dhuinn,
Càit a bheil an daonna marbh."

As she repeated the incantation over and over, the symbols on the stones began to glow and the room grew colder. Drustan could feel the hairs on his arms stand up as a faint mist formed above the table. The hen in his mother's hand began to squirm and squawk, as if it were in great distress.

Sibby's voice grew louder and more urgent, her gestures more frantic. Drustan could see the veins in her temples bulging and her eyes were closed in concentration. Suddenly, with a final crescendo of her chant, she snapped the hen's neck and the room was filled with a blinding light.

Drustan shielded his eyes and when the light dissipated, he saw that the child on the table was no longer limp and unresponsive. He was sitting up and looking around, confused but very much alive. The parents wept tears of joy, thanking Sibby for her help.

Drustan was shocked and impressed by the power his mother possessed, and he knew that he would never underestimate her mystic knowledge again. He had much to learn and many mysteries to uncover, and he was eager to begin his journey as a student of the ancient ways.

The joy of the child's healing was fleeting. Suddenly, the table upon which the child lay began to quiver, starting off as a gentle tremor, but quickly escalating into violent convulsions. All those present recoiled in terror, except for Sibby. She bellowed her incantations over the deafening sound of the heavy wooden table crashing against the floor. As suddenly as it began, the table stilled, and an eerie silence descended upon the room, as all present held their breath in tense anticipation of what was to come next.

Then, the boy who was still seated on the edge of the table moaned softly. Suddenly he threw his head back, his mouth fell open and a mist rose from the child like a hot breath escaping into a cold night air. This vapor was not the pale white fog like one would see on a cold morning; rather it was dark, almost black, like smoke rising from a smoldering fire. Instead of dissipating, the mist hovered in the air above the boy, gathering and growing denser until it formed itself into the image of a face.

The face twisted and contorted, becoming more and more grotesque until it let out a blood-curdling scream that shook the very foundations of the house. Everyone recoiled in horror, except for Sibby who stood her ground, her voice rising above the discordance as she continued to chant the ancient words.

"I have found thee!" A hideous voice emerged from the mist.

Sibby was momentarily shaken by the words as if she recognized the face that spoke to her. She quickly regained her composure and continued shouting at the swirling entity in defiance. The mist continued to swirl and writhe, forming into a dark, sinister figure, but Sibby's chanting seemed to be having an effect. The figure began to shrink and dissipate, the scream growing weaker and weaker until it was nothing more than a faint whisper.

With one final burst of energy, Sibby screamed the final words of the incantation, and the figure was gone, dissipated into the ether. The room was silent once more, save for the sound of the child's frightened whimpering.

Sibby looked at the parents, her eyes filled with a mix of triumph and sadness. She was relieved for the child and his parents, but her heart was full of dread. She was shaken by the experience and her trembling hands betrayed her inner thoughts.

"What is it mother?" Drustan asked and began to approach.

She glanced at Drustan and saw the reflection of her own fear in his expression. She took a deep breath and gathered her composure, but did not respond. Instead, Sibby walked over to the boy and gently picked him up, cradling him in her arms. "Hush now, child," she said softly. "You are safe now."

She looked at the boy's parents, who were still in shock from what they had just witnessed. "Take your son and go home," she said firmly. "He will be fine now. But be warned, this was not an ordinary sickness. The creature that possessed him was not of this world. It is gone for now, but it may return. Keep your child close and protect him.

Both the father and mother grabbed the little boy and hugged him tightly, sobbing with relief.

"We are grateful to thee," the mother cried to Sibby as she embraced her son tightly.

"What was that thing?" The father asked. "That thing that came from his breath?"

"'Twas a pestilence. The essence of the evil witch who cursed the child."

"That thing was a witch?" Drustan was surprised. He thought it to more demon than any other living creature.

"Aye, the worst kind," Sibby replied. "Even more evil than the sluagh you encountered this day."

"Why would she do such a thing?" The mother asked as she pulled her son closer, her voice still shaking from the ordeal. "What offense could we have committed against this witch that she would harm an innocent child?"

"We have made no enemies. We are good and decent people," the husband added.

"It was not thy sin that brought this evil to thy door, nor the misdeeds of a child. It was the wickedness of the one who cast the spell. Maybe it was envy for your possessions, or the jealousy of one who remains childless. Or, maybe, 'twas nothing more than for her own entertainment. No one knows the mind of a witch nor should you waste your time to understand why evil breeds evil."

"Are we safe now? Should we be afraid?" The mother asked nervously. "What if it happens again?"

Sibby picked up the bag of salt and approached them. She dipped her hand in the bag, pulled out some the crystals, and handed it to the husband, then the mother. Then she took another handful and put it into the young boy's pockets.

"Witches cannot physically abide salt, they will avoid it as much as possible," she explained. "Keep a pinch of salt in thy pockets, and spread some under the beds where you sleep. Make a line of salt along the threshold of every door to your home and along the window sills. It will repel her evil magic and dissuade her mischief."

"That is all? Salt?" The man asked in disbelief. "We need do nothing more?"

"'Tis a deterrent, but only slight. If a witch is determined, she will find a means to strike against you. The only true safety is to find the witch and kill her," Sibby stated bluntly. "But that is a much more dangerous prospect. 'Tis best you leave well enough alone and count your blessings that you have your son well again."

"Heed my warning," Sibby then added. "Do not seek revenge against this witch. She is more powerful than you could imagine. Pray that she leaves you in peace."

"What if she doesn't?" The father asked.

"Keep the salt at hand as I instructed," Sibby answered. "Now, you should go. Tell no one of what you have seen today. Continue along the road as if you were only passing by. After you have gone a distance, turn back and return to thy home from a different direction. Let no one know you came hither."

"We will do as you ask," the woman agreed. "If you ever need …"

Sibby cut her off abruptly. "Just leave and do not look back. Now go."

"We are forever in thy debt, my lady." The child's father said and dropped the pouch of gold coins on the table. "Here, take it. Take it all. We can never thank you enough."

Sibby pushed the leather pouch across the table back toward the man, "'tis not necessary."

Drustan stepped up to the table and seized the bag

of coins. "'Tis not necessary," he glanced as his mother then back to the family. "But we gratefully accept your generosity."

Sibby gave him a stern look of disapproval. She did not like taking money for helping those in need; and the last thing on her mind after her experience was payment.

But Drustan did not relent. As the eldest son, he was one of the providers for the family and he realized that such a payment in gold could feed the family and livestock for an entire year. He would not challenge his mother in most situations and would submit to her authority, but in times like this, he held his ground. He did not shy away from stepping in to accept fair payment for services rendered. Besides, they were now short one nice plump egg-laying hen that needed to be replaced.

Sibby, feeling a mix of guilt and relief, watched as Drustan accepted the payment. She knew that the gold would provide for her family, but she also knew that the true cost of her work was much greater than the value of the gold.

As Drustan escorted the young family from the house and into their waiting carriage, Sibby couldn't shake off the feeling of unease and the memory of the twisted, dark face that had appeared before her. She knew deep down that there was more to this spell than just healing a child's sickness.

"Bless you dear lady," the woman shouted and waved as the coachman snapped the reigns and the coach rolled away.

Drustan stood gazing as the pompous carriage receded into the horizon, the ornate wheels and finely-garbed driver becoming smaller and smaller until they were nothing more than a speck on the horizon. As they disappeared from sight, Drustan turned and walked back to the house. Inside, he found Sibby sitting at the table, her small hands wringing anxiously around each other. Sibby's eyes were glued to the door, as if expecting someone or something to come through it at any moment. Her body language betrayed her anxiety, her breaths coming in short, shallow pants. Worry lines creased her forehead, and her fingers were twisted together in a knot on her lap. The silence in the room was palpable, only broken by the crackling sound of the burning wood in the fireplace.

"What troubles you mother? You helped that poor family, saved the child, and we have enough gold to last for several seasons."

Sibby hesitated to respond, searching for where to begin to answer. She was relieved when Gilda returned and came inside.

"Gilda, gather the hen from the table and burn it on the hillside, well away from the house," Sibby instructed.

"You will waste the meat and not cook it?" Drustan asked.

"Tis tainted and spoiled," she replied then turned back to Gilda. "Quickly, girl! Do not linger! And bring your sister and brother inside before the sun sets."

"Yes, ma'am," Gilda answered and quickly gathered the dead hen in her arms and headed out the door.

"Mother," Drustan spoke discretely as to not be overheard. "'Tis something you are not telling me? Why do you look worried?"

Sibby walked onto the porch and looked at the sinking sun. In would not be long before the sun would reach the horizon and twilight would be upon them. "It will be night soon. Go to the fields and gather your father. We must prepare and be alert this night, lest we be caught unaware."

"Caught unaware? What troubles you, Mother? What do you hesitate to say?" Drustan asked, noticing the distress etched on Sibby's face. As the words left his mouth, he recalled the menacing voice that emerged from the mist, "I have found thee!" He repeated the words aloud, his tone grave with sudden realization. "The spirit knew you!"

"So, it did seem."

"What kind of evil have these people brought upon us?" Drustan began to understand why his mother had expressed little interest in the gold payment for her services. She knew that the price for her interference could be much more costly than a purse full of gold.

Drustan, a mixture of anger and fear in his voice pushed her for an explanation. "Did you recognize the face in the mist?"

"Perchance a face from a time long past," Sibby replied, her voice heavy with thought. She stared into the distance, as if lost in a memory she wished to forget. But she quickly shook her head and pushed the thought aside. "There is no time for explanations. Know her or not, the witch has seen my face, and those who would dare interfere with a witch's dark machinations are not received kindly. We must be vigilant this eve, for she may seek retribution. And let us not forget that the Underfolk are near, danger lurks all around us this night."

"Do not keep secrets from me, mother."

"The truth shall be revealed this eve, my son," Sibby spoke, her voice heavy with the weight of secrets kept. "We shall speak of things that have long been kept hidden, things I had hoped to shield you from. But for now, hearken my call. Gather the young ones and bring thy father from the fields. Time is of the essence, for darkness looms and we must make ready before the night falls."

Drustan nodded and quickly set about his tasks. He knew that whatever secrets his mother held, they were not to be taken lightly. He could sense the weight of them in her voice and the gravity in her eyes. As he gathered the children and hurried his father back to the safety of their home, he couldn't help but feel a sense of foreboding. He knew that whatever was to come, it would change their lives forever.

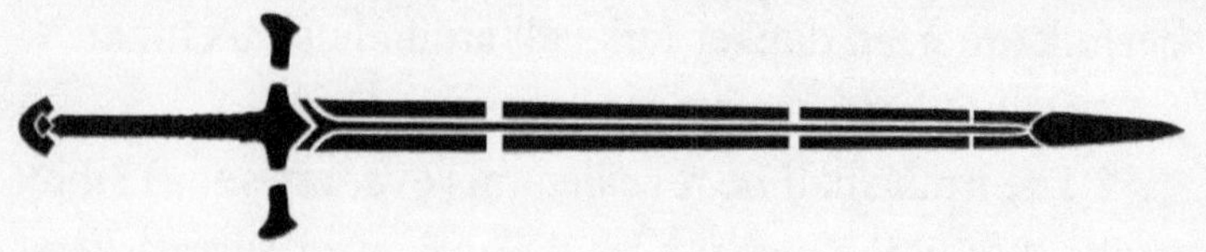

CHAPTER 3

The War Begins

Deep in the Caledonian Forest, hidden among the trees, lay an ancient citadel, its blackened stone walls worn with the passage of time. Vines and ivy obscured its form during the spring and summer, but as autumn approached, the forest's lushness gave way to dried leaves and barren branches, revealing the castle in all its ominous glory. The blackened structure stood out like a warning to all who dared to approach. Despite the appearence, the castle was not abandoned, as the distant chanting emanating from within attested. For within its walls lurked an ancient evil, an powerful witch, known as Mora.

Feared by all who knew of her, Mora was a figure of darkness and legend. She was the subject of tales used to frightened disobedient children. Her name was whispered in the dark corners of village taverns. It is said that her powers were unmatched and her wrath legendary. Her spells and curses could summon the dead, bring forth plagues, and bend the elements to her will. Those who dared to cross her were said to suffer a fate worse than death. But there were also whispers of a prophecy, that a brave hero would rise and vanquish the witch, freeing the land from her reign of terror.

Deep within the decaying castle, the wicked Mora sat upon a grand, ornate throne of ancient oak, the very embodiment of regal power. For she was, in truth, a queen in all but name, the most feared and potent witch in the known world. Her dark presence stretched over the land like a shadow, looming over all who dared to defy her.

Before her, upon the cold, stone floor of the great hall, knelt a coven of twelve witches, each one twisted and corrupted by centuries of practicing the forbidden arts. They were her loyal followers, sworn to serve her and her will alone, until the end of time.

Together, the coven crones swayed back and forth, their bodies undulating like a writhing mass of serpents. They slithered in a twisted heap of flesh, their moans and murmurs rising up in a guttural chant. This was their way of offering their power to their mistress Mora, a way of joining their powers as she began to cast her dark magic. The ancient symbols etched upon the stone floor glowed with an otherworldly light, and the air grew thick with the scent of brimstone and rot. Mora stood up from her throne, her eyes glowing as she channeled the power of the coven's offering. The air around her crackled with dark energy, and the very stones of the castle seemed to groan in protest. The coven continued to chant, their voices growing louder and more frenzied as the magic reached its peak.

In the dimly lit corner of the great hall, a figure lurked in the shadows, observing the coven's dark ritual.

He kept his distance, avoiding the corrupting influence of the witches and the piercing rays of sunlight that dared to sneak through the cracks of the shuttered windows. He watched in silent contempt as they performed their vile ritual, repulsed by their twisted appearance and the overwhelming stench of evil that hung in the air like the scent of burning sulfur from the depths of the underworld. This observer was not a witch, but a vampire, a creature born of darkness. He knew the dangers of playing with such forces and the price of immortality, and he knew that the witches' ambition and cruelty would bring them to their downfall.

Normally, vampires hated witches and this relationship was no exception. He despised what he was seeing, and he despised the one he was forced to call his mistress. He would slaughter the whole coven if he had his wish and could easily do so if it were not for Mora. She was no ordinary witch. She was too powerful, and he was also in her debt. He considered himself her ally and even an equal; but in reality, he was nothing more than a servant to her, a savage killer at her command.

He watched with deep loathing as the brood of witches worked their magic, joining their power to Mora so she could project her spirit across a great distance and conduct her evil mission.

Mora stood motionless, her arms outstretched, and her milky eyes fixed in a trance-like state. Her spirit had left her body, traveling through time and space on a mission of great importance. Guided by the power of her coven, she searched for the sages, white witches and those wise in the ways of the ancient magic. She sought their knowledge and secrets, for they held the key to unlocking powerful magic that had been lost for centuries.

Mora's mission was not only to uncover the secrets of the sages but to eliminate them completely. Sages and white witches were the natural enemy of black witches. They interfered with the workings of dark magic by removing spells and curses, healing the pox and curing other diseases brought by the black witches. The sages believed in using their powers to benefit mankind and maintain the natural order and they believed it was their duty to oppose evil at every turn. This put them in direct conflict with Mora and her coven, who saw their power being challenged and their very existence threatened. Because of these opposing philosophies, a war existed between the white and the black witches with both sides determined to bind or destroy the other.

Then there were the witches known as pellars. These were powerful witches, neither white nor black, whose magic was strong enough to command the elements. Their magic was inborn, given directly by the ancient gods, and not reliant upon spells and incantations. These witches could use their powers for good or evil, and could bring life as easily as death. They were not bound by the same limitations as the white and black witches and could choose their own path. These pellar witches were extremely rare, and they were the witches that Mora feared the most.

The war between the white and black witches seemed to have a new player, and Mora was determined to come out on top. Her spirit-walk had a singular purpose: to hunt down and capture a powerful pellar witch rumored to reside in the highlands. This witch was said to possess magic unrivaled by any other, and Mora was determined to claim it for her own. To find her, Mora and her coven had devised a devious plan. They had placed a curse upon an innocent child of a young family, knowing that the desperate parents would seek out a powerful witch to cure their child. And in the process of providing a cure, the pellar witch would reveal herself. Once exposed, Mora would unleash her full power, projecting her spirit through the victim and destroying her enemy. This war was not just about power, it was about survival and Mora was willing to do whatever it took to come out victorious.

Mora's plan was a masterstroke, one her coven had executed to perfection time and time again. But this time, her quarry was no ordinary witch. It was the one who had eluded her for two decades, the one who had betrayed her and stolen the very essence of her existence, the secret of her immortality and youth. The key to her longevity and power, taken away in a single night of treachery. Now, as the trap was about to snap shut, Mora's long hunt was coming to an end, and the revenge she had sought for so many years was finally at hand.

"The witch works her magic," Mora spoke to her coven from her trance.

"Kill her!" One of the witches screeched.

Immediately, the others began to chant, "Kill the witch! Kill the witch! Kill the witch!"

"Be still!" Mora commanded abruptly. "'Tis no ordinary witch! She wields the old magic!"

The coven grew deathly silent, hanging on Mora's

words. The witches knew what was meant when Mora spoke of the old magic. It was a pellar witch; one who's power came from the gods. The purest and strongest form of magic, even more powerful than their own black arts.

"Isabel!" Mora gasped, recognizing her adversary. She reached her hand out into the air as if to confirm her vision was real. "I have found thee!" Her voice was filled with a mixture of excitement and anger, for she had been searching for her former apprentice for many years, and finally, the moment of confrontation had arrived.

Suddenly, the coven was thrown into chaos as Mora screamed out in pain and fell to her knees. They hastened to her side, their visages mirroring their fear and anxiety at seeing their leader collapse.

Laine, Mora's most trusted servant and her most gifted apprentice, was the first to reach her. She knelt beside Mora, cradling her head in her lap and trying to offer comfort. "Good mistress, what hath befallen thee?" Her voice quavered with concern.

The other witches swarmed around Mora, their expressions a chaotic blend of fear and confusion. The coven knew well the power of the pellars, but they never imagined that one of them could be powerful enough to challenge their leader. They were taken aback by the sudden turn of events, their minds whirling with the implications of this revelation. Their leader, whom that saw as all powerful, was taken unaware, unprepared for the encounter and was suddenly vulnerable.

As Mora sat back on her throne, she reassured them with a calm and steady voice, "I am well, my daughters."

Despite her words, the coven could not shake off their unease, the power of this pellar was not something to be trifled with and they knew it was not going to be an easy battle.

"Good sister, what hath transpired?" Laine asked.

"I know this witch," Mora snarled, her voice filled with malice. "She is the one who betrayed me in the darkest of nights. The one who stole my secrets and fled into the shadows."

Raum, the vampire who had been a silent observer until this point, felt a spark of interest ignite within him. He stepped closer, still concealed in the shadows, eager to hear more of this revelation. The displays of dark magic repulsed him, but the possibility of a powerful enemy who could stand against the witch queen intrigued him.

"She has taken my knowledge and grown strong in the ancient ways, more powerful than I could have ever imagined," Mora spoke, her voice filled with anger. "We cannot strike at this witch from a distance, she must be confronted face to face," she said, her eyes burning with a fierce determination. "This witch owes a great debt and it will be paid. This night, when the moon is at its zenith, we will visit this witch and reclaim what she stole from me!"

Mora's words echoed through the great hall, her voice filled with rage and determination. "Prepare yourselves, my daughters, tonight we will have our vengeance."

The coven of witches listened attentively, their eyes fixed on their leader. Some of them, like Laine, felt a surge of excitement, they were eager to prove their loyalty to Mora and they relished the idea of attacking a powerful pellar witch. They began to chant and sway, preparing themselves for the battle to come.

Others, however, were filled with fear and uncertainty. They knew the power of the pellar witches and had witnessed first-hand their adversary's ability to repel Mora's magic. They whispered among themselves, expressing their concerns and doubts.

"Art thou certain this is wise, Mora?" one of the witches asked, her voice trembling. "We know not what we may encounter."

Mora's gaze was filled with wrath as she fixated on the witch who dared to question her authority. Her white eyes burned with anger and her voice was low and menacing. "You would dare challenge my power," she growled. "You will obey my command, or suffer the consequences. Face the pellar witch, or you will face the full force of my wrath."

The coven was in a state of turmoil, with some members ready to heed Mora's command and others filled with trepidation and fear. Despite their disparate emotions, they were all aware that they had no alternative but to abide by their leader's dictate.

"Now go!" Mora commanded, her voice ringing with authority. Without hesitation, the witches dispersed, each hastening to make ready for the impending conflict.

As her coven scattered, Mora slumped against her throne, her body wracked with exhaustion from her brief confrontation with Isabel. The chamber was silent, save for the soft whispers of the wind as it crept through the windows. But Mora knew that she was not alone, and her voice, infused with dark magic, filled the room. "Come forth, my child," she called out, her voice a low, menacing growl. "Show yourself to your mistress."

Raum emerged from the shadows like a wraith, his movements silent and graceful as he approached the withered hag upon her throne. He had made no effort to hide himself, his only desire to avoid the company of the coven of crones, whose very presence filled him with revulsion.

"'Tis no need to skulk in the corners or lurk in the shadows, spying on us," Mora said with a hint of amusement in her voice. "You are welcome here, my child."

"I do not skulk. 'Tis the company you keep that I choose to avoid."

Mora let out a cackle, her voice raspy and eerie. She relished in the knowledge that her coven's presence caused him discomfort. "You watched our conjuring?" she asked, her tone hinting at a twisted sense of amusement.

"Aye," he replied, his tone stoic.

"And you heard my words?"

"I did," he acknowledged. "This pellar witch. 'Tis the girl from the south who was with child almost twenty years ago?"

"Ah," Mora grinned devilishly, "then you remember her."

"You know I do."

"Good." Mora said with a sly grin, then added, "her son was by her side." She eyed him closely, eager for his reaction.

"Her son?" Raum raised an eyebrow, his voice betraying a hint of surprise. "Do you seek revenge or the child?"

"I will have both," Mora declared, her voice laced with venomous delight. "Does that concern you, Raum?"

"Why should it?" Raum replied, his tone as cold as ice. "I have no interest in this woman nor her son. Do as you please with them both."

Mora cackled with glee, relishing in Raum's apathy. "I assure you, I will."

"So, Isabel is a witch now, is she?" Raum taunted. "Will you take her in, teach her as before, show her mercy and forgive her?"

Mora sneered, "You think me a fool? She would surely stab me in the back the moment I embraced her return to the coven."

Raum shrugged, "I simply remembered your fondness for her. She is but a fledgling witch, in need of guidance."

"She is not just any witch," Mora spat. "She wields true magic, the natural gift."

"How powerful can she truly be?" Raum mocked. "Perhaps she stumbled upon a spell or two, but where could she have gained such power in only half a lifetime? I think you overestimate her abilities."

Mora leaned in closer, her voice a hushed whisper. "It was not I who revealed myself to Isabel. It was she who drove me out of the child. No witch has been able to do such until now."

Raum scoffed, "Pure luck. She stumbled upon a spell and it worked. It was not great power she demonstrated, but mere chance."

Mora shook her head, "It was more than that. I felt

power radiating from her. I saw the confidence in her eyes when she challenged me. She was not afraid, only surprised that it was I who had come."

Raum had no interest in Mora's vendetta towards Isabel. He knew their history all too well, having been there from the beginning, witnessing it all first hand. He had seen Mora's anger when Isabel fled in the night, depriving her of the child she so coveted. But, the thought of Isabel posing a threat to Mora and her coven intrigued him. He loathed the witches and if there was even the slightest chance that Isabel could harm or, better yet, kill Mora, he would do everything in his power to encourage such a confrontation. And so, he prodded her further.

"So, Isabel returns to defy you once again," he taunted. "Do you suspect that this woman's power could rival your own?"

Mora's face blazed with fury, "I have no rival!" She spat, her voice thick with indignance. "I fear no one!"

Raum's lips curled into a sly smirk, "Perhaps," he mused, "But I saw the distress upon thy face when you encountered Isabel. Even your coven could see it. The mere thought of her power was enough to bring you to your knees."

Mora's rage simmered, her pride stung by Raum's words. "This child is not my rival, nor my equal!" she growled. "If you or my daughters doubt that, then thou are mistaken. I will have my revenge, and I will have it this very night!"

Raum's face remained expressionless, but inside, a sense of triumph swelled within him as he watched the fury ignite in Mora. He silently reveled in the thought of her anger consuming her, clouding her judgment and causing her to underestimate Isabel. He envisioned her downfall at the hands of the powerful young witch, a satisfying end to the malignant hag who had caused him so much disdain. He thought to himself, *That's right you diseased hag. Let your rage take control. Take a risk. Be careless and underestimate Isabel. May she grind you into dust.*

With a flourish, Mora reached for a silver chalice on a nearby table and hobbled towards Raum. "Raum, deliver thy tribute," she commanded, offering him the cup. "I must have your blood to strengthen me in the face of my enemy."

It was a familiar ritual for Raum; the price he paid for his own immortality. It was part of their arrangement from the beginning of his rebirth as a vampire. As a witch Mora could sustain herself well beyond her natural life span using magical spells, but such longevity was only a temporary reprieve to stave off death. To live for centuries as Mora had, required more than just an incantation; it took the powers of hell itself.

For Mora, that was accomplished by consuming vampire blood; partaking of the ancient curse of immortality that was known as the dark gift. At times when she felt her own life fading, or her powers start to wane, she would call upon Raum to provide her the dark blood. By drinking of his life force, she was able to hold back death and strengthen herself. The blood did not restore her youth as it did those who resurrected as a vampire, but it did heal her body and sustain her existence for a period. This, along with her own dark magic, was enough to extend her life for centuries.

Raum obediently removed the dagger from his belt and holding his arm above the chalice, he drew the blade across his wrist. The blood poured from the wound, quickly filling the cup. Once the vessel was full, he withdrew his arm and lapped at his wound until the bleeding ceased.

The old witch brought the chalice to her lips and drank. As she did, the blood immediately began to work its dark magic. She began to transform. The white glaze that covered her eyes faded to reveal a green color. Her sparse gray hair thickened and her hunched back straightened. By any standard, she was still an elderly woman of advanced age, but the vampire blood had strengthened her. She was renewed and well-distanced from death once again.

"Ah, I feel my life return; but, the dark gift will not sustain me forever. What news do you bring?" she asked with renewed strength. "Have you found the one I seek?"

"My children search the highlands each night. We move throughout the land, but have yet to find the mother and unborn child you require."

"Find her," the witch screamed at him and threw the chalice. "Else it will be thy skin that I wear!"

Raum was angered by her threat, but he dared not respond. As a vampire, he feared only two things in his existence, the light of day and this evil witch that held him and his clan in her power. For Raum, witches were nothing more than insignificant pests, to be hunted and fed upon for the dark power that flowed through their veins. But Mora was different. He loathed her; her ancient and withered form, her vile coven, yet he could not deny the fear that she instilled in him. He yearned to tear her throat out, to slaughter her entire coven, but to challenge her meant certain death. Her mastery over the elements and the black arts was unparalleled, and he was but a fledgling vampire, inexperienced and powerless in comparison. He longed for freedom from her dominance, but knew that she was his creator, and that her power was absolute. So, he bided his time, waiting for the opportunity to strike and be free from her grasp.

"What of the young man, the son of Isabel?" Raum asked. "If he yet lives, would he not still serve your need? Could he still be your sacrifice?"

"No! The boy will no longer serve my purpose. The child must be unborn and untouched by this world. You must find another, and soon!"

"We will. Have I failed you yet?"

"See that you do not," she warned before turning to another matter. "I have one more task for you, one you will enjoy."

"And what is that?"

"Along the road to the parish of Dunkeld, there is a family who travels by carriage; a husband, his wife, and their young child. Take thy brethren and find them. When you do, tear the boy apart before their eyes then kill the parents."

"This is the family and child you bewitched?" Raum asked.

"'Tis the same."

It was a harsh judgment that Mora pronounced. The young couple whose child she had cursed and tormented had already suffered under her power, but for her it was not enough. They must be punished. She had used the family as bait to find a sage and they had fulfilled their purpose, even more than she had hoped. They were the instruments that led her to Isobel after all this time. Still they must pay the price for insolence. They had defied her, challenged her power by seeking aid from a white witch. Though it was Mora's plan and the reason the family was chosen, such an insult could not be tolerated and the consequence was death.

Raum did not consider the severity of Mora's judgment nor did the immorality of it affect him in the least. He was a predator and humans were his prey. He had no affection or regard for humankind, so to him, killing the parents and their child held no more meaning than would slaughtering a hog.

"We will delight in the feast," Raum said coldly then turned to leave.

"And Raum," Mora called out just as he was about to exit the chamber. "You must find the woman and child soon!"

"It will be done."

With a slight nod, Raum excused himself from the castle. The setting sun signaled his departure, and a sly grin crept across his face as he felt a sense of satisfaction. He had already found the mother-to-be that Mora sought, but he had also managed to keep her hidden. He planned to wait until Mora was at her most desperate, then use the girl as leverage to bargain with the witch-es for his freedom. Also, the thought of goading Mora into attacking Isabel prematurely, without proper preparation, filled him with even more satisfaction. He held onto the hope that if Isabel was truly as powerful as it seemed, she could be the one to finally rid him of the coven's oppressive grip.

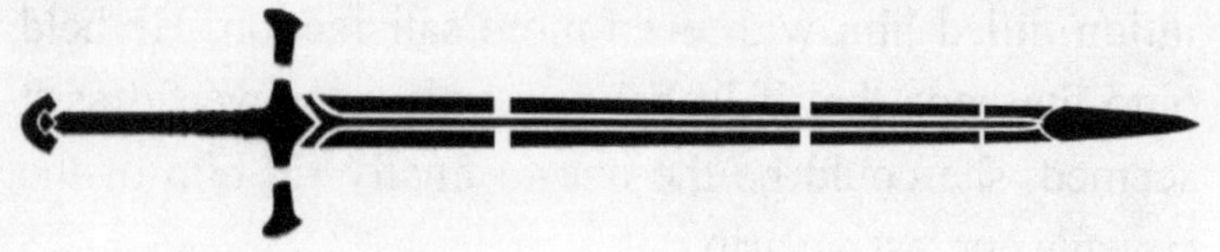

CHAPTER 4

Truth Be Told

Sibby opened the wooden shutters, the cool night air rushed into the cottage as she gazed out into the darkness. The silvery moon was already well above the horizon, casting its pale light over the land. Though not yet full, its radiance was enough to illuminate the fields beyond the wooded fence and offer clear view of any who might approach. As the moon continued its ascent towards its zenith, Sibby knew that the hour of maximum power for a black witch was approaching. If Mora intended to attack, she would do so shortly. She briefly scanned the star-studded sky before closing the shutters and turning her attention back to her husband who sat at the table carving into an arrow with a steady hand.

Sibby knew the weight of these arrows, the gravity of their purpose. She watched as her husband worked with precision, carefully inscribing the ancient incantations along the wood, imbuing each arrow with powerful magic. These were not ordinary arrows used for hunting. They were witch-killing arrows. The shafts were made of oak wood, harvested during a new moon and blessed under the full moon, with magical words inscribed along the length of the spine. The arrowheads were of iron, forged in the fires of a sacred forge and tipped with silver blessed by the Christian priests. The fletching was made of the feathers of white doves, symbolizing the purity and righteousness of their cause.

These arrows and the spells that they bore were made precisely according to the ancient ways. One prick from the tip of a witch-killing arrow would poison the witch's blood, causing immense pain to the victim and eventual death. To be pierced by one would mean certain death. These arrows were the ultimate defense against a witch. There are many ways to combat spells and dark magic, but the most effective means is to destroy the witch. Sibby did not only plan to defend against Mora's dark magic, she intended to defeat it completely. If Mora came for vengeance, Sibby knew it would be a fight to the death; a fight that she intended to win.

Rowan, who had never before taken the life of a witch, harbored uncertainties regarding the true effectiveness of the arrows, despite having crafted them meticulously following Sibby's precise instructions. He recognized her as an authority on all things mystical, but to his knowledge Sibby had never used such magic before nor had she ever had to battle a black witch.

"Do you trust in the power of these arrows?" he inquired. "Will they truly work?"

Sibby met his question with one of her own. "Are you questioning the arrows or the witch we're facing?"

He paused before answering, "Both, I suppose."

"I cannot say for certain, husband," Sibby replied, her voice tinged with worry. "But the ancient texts speak of their power, and I have instilled them with every spell and incantation I know to ensure their effectiveness." She paused in her pacing to take one of the arrows from the completed stack on the table. She ran her hands over the full length as if caressing it. "I feel the power it holds. If this cannot kill Mora, then perhaps she cannot be killed."

"Are you certain it was Mora you saw in the mist? Twenty years have passed, and she was frail and bent with age even then. How can it be the same woman you knew?"

"I saw her as plainly as I see thy face. 'Twas the old woman from years before. She looked the same; old and haggard, but no more so than the last time I saw her. 'Tis she, of that I'm certain. I felt the darkness around her; she uses the blackest of magic to stave off time and to thwart death."

"But why would she come now? After all this time, what would be her purpose?" Rowan asked.

"Vengeance is what I believe," Sibby murmured, her thoughts heavy with the weight of the past. "The night I left, I did so with fear for the life of my unborn son. I had witnessed the malevolence within her, the magic she dabbled in. She tempted me with the allure of the darkness, and I knew she desired my child for some nefarious purpose. So, I fled. No doubt in her eyes, I had betrayed her. I escaped into the darkness of the night and never looked back, yet always looking over my shoulder knowing that one day she would come. The heart of a black witch knows no forgiveness and holds grudges for an eternity. She is here to collect a debt. And I fear she is here for our son."

As they heard the heavy footsteps descending the stairs, Sibby placed her finger to her lips, signaling for silence. It was the sound of Drustan approaching, having put his siblings safely into bed. She didn't want him to overhear their conversation, but neither did she want to keep the truth from him any longer. She had kept the secret for too many years now, and it was time to tell the story of who he truly was. She wanted to speak openly, rather than have the truth be overheard through whispers.

"The children are asleep," Drustan said as he entered the room.

"The doors and shutters are locked?" Sibby asked.

"Aye, I checked twice."

Drustan took a seat next to Rowan, and began admiring the precision and care that had gone into crafting each arrow. He picked them up one by one, holding each up to the light to check for straightness and quality. Rowan watched with a sense of pride as his stepson took such a keen interest in his work.

"Checking my work, son?" Rowan said with a smile, impressed by Drustan's confidence and attention to detail.

"Sorry, father," Drustan said, a hint of embarrassment creeping into his voice. "I didn't mean to question your skills. I was simply marveling at the craftsmanship."

"You were checking my work," Rowan insisted, "and you are wise to do so. Never trust your weapons to another, always remember that; even if it is thy own father's hand you must question."

"I would sooner question my skill at using them, than question your craftsmanship in making them." Drustan replied, but still continued to hold one arrow after another up to his eye to check the alignment. "Perfection," he admitted after checking the last of them.

"I'm glad you approve," Rowan grinned and patted his son on the shoulder.

Sibby paced the room, her mind whirling with thoughts and emotions. She couldn't shake the feeling of unease that had settled in her stomach. She opened the shutter once more, staring out into the night sky, but this time her thoughts were not on the witch Mora, but rather on the conversation she knew she had to have with her son Drustan. She felt apprehensive, a feeling that was all too rare for her. Sibby was known for her boldness and her ability to speak her mind on any subject. But this time, she found herself struggling to find the right words. She knew the conversation was long overdue, but the weight of it felt heavy on her shoulders.

"Sit," Rowan urged, gesturing to a chair. "This could be a long night, and all your worrying may be for naught."

"'Tis a mother's job to worry," Sibby replied, taking a seat beside her husband. "The moon is already high. Perhaps she won't come."

"Why do you think this witch will show up at all?" Drustan interjected.

"The family that came to us was not cursed of their own doing," Sibby began to explain. "They committed no offense to incur this witch's wrath. They were chosen, used as bait to lure a powerful sage. The target of this witch was not that innocent family, it was anyone who dared to help them. This witch's target was me."

"Why? Because you have a kind heart and are willing to help those in need?" Drustan asked.

"Aye. A black witch does not take kindly to those who would interfere with her works. To undo a witch's curse is to challenge her power. I'm afraid that in revealing myself, this has become something more personal."

"The face in the mist, you said you recognized her," Drustan said.

"Aye, from a time long past. And I fear she remembered me too. She spoke of having found me," his mother replied, her voice heavy with sorrow.

"What manner of witch is she that she would seek you out? What malice does she hold against you?" Drustan pressed, his curiosity piqued.

"It is a tale of darkness, my son. One that is even more painful to hear than it is to speak. I had hoped to never utter it again, especially not to you," his mother said, her eyes downcast.

Drustan looked at her warily, sensing there was something she was holding back. "What tale is this?" he asked, his voice firm.

"The story of my youth, I've shared with you all, of how my family was brutally attacked by a Viking horde and I alone survived. But there's a darker chapter to that tale, one I've kept hidden in the depths of my soul, ashamed to reveal it to anyone save my husband."

Rowan remained silent yet reached over and tenderly patted Sibby's hand as a show of support. He knew the truth she was about to reveal, and he recognized how difficult it was for her to share this dark period in her life.

"Speak freely, mother. Lay bare this secret that's been weighing on you."

"As I stumbled through the wilderness, my family taken and my own life hanging by a thread, I searched desperately for a glimmer of hope. And then, amidst the trees, I caught sight of a cottage nestled on the fringe of the forest. Without hesitation, I made my way towards it, and the kindly old woman who lived there took me in and tended to my wounds. As I recuperated under her care, she offered me a place to stay and in return, I offered my service as her helper. I believed her to be a wise woman of the cunning folk, steeped in ancient knowledge. Little did I know, she was a force far more sinister, a black witch, skilled in the dark arts who tempted me to become her apprentice."

"You studied under a black witch?" Drustan was shocked. "But you have warned me so often of their evils."

"I warned you from my own knowledge. They are as black as pitch, my son. But at that time, I was angry and filled with rage. I had witnessed my family, my home, my entire life crushed under the heel of a band of ruthless barbarians. The lure of retribution was a powerful temptation."

"Then you were deceived. Tricked by this evil woman. 'Tis no shame in that," Drustan said. "What matters is that you turned away from the darkness and have dedicated your life to helping those in need and being a good mother. Surely, that brief moment is not the burden that weighs heavily upon you after all these years."

"Deceived, aye, my son," Sibby said with a heavy

heart. "But the path of darkness is one that is easy to fall upon, yet so difficult to escape from. And the weight of that transgression has been a constant companion, a shadow that has followed me throughout the years. It is not a burden I can simply cast off, for it has shaped who I am and the choices I have made. But sadly this is not the truth I must now reveal, nor the burden that weighs upon my soul."

"Then speak."

"It was soon after I came to the witch's home that I found I was with child."

"Yes, you were carrying me. You said that my father was killed in the raid."

"Aye, I was with child. But thy father was not killed as I have said. I told you that to hide the truth, to protect you from the past," Sibby said, her tone heavy with regret. "The truth is, when the raiders came to our home, I was not wed. I was but a maiden, untouched by any man. Your father did not perish in the attack as I had led you to believe."

"But ... I don't understand."

"Thy father was not killed by those who invaded our home, your father was one of them—a Viking warrior who took me as his spoils of war and left me to die in mud." She began to sob as she finally revealed the truth, she had hidden for all those years. She cried not because the memory was still painfully vivid in her mind, but because she feared that her son would find shame in his father's sins.

Drustan sat in stunned silence, taking in the revelation about his true parentage. He had always believed that his father had died bravely defending his family, but to learn that his father was one of the very raiders who had killed his mother's family and taken her as a spoil of war was devastating. He couldn't believe that the man who had fathered him was capable of such atrocities. He didn't know how to process this new information and felt a mix of anger, betrayal and disgust. He couldn't bring himself to look at his mother and struggled to find the words to express his feelings.

"You told me my father was a soldier in the king's army. That he was an honorable man. I've spent my life trying to live up to his heroic legacy." Drustan sounded despondent, lost and confused. "My entire life I stood tall and proud, believing myself to be the son of a great hero. I trained my body, honed my skills and fought with all my might, all in the pursuit of living up to the legacy of my father. Your deception, mother, cuts me deeper than any blade could. All my life I've been chasing a shadow, a mirage of what I thought my father was, only to find out it was nothing but a lie. Now I am left to carry my father's shame and guilt."

"This is not your burden. You are blameless of your father's sins and are the same good man that you were before this moment. But the truth I must tell you now after these many years," Sibby sobbed realizing the pain and confusion she was causing him.

"Why did you let me live this lie. Allow me — no encourage me to honor a man who had no honor? I must look like a fool. To have stood so proudly and arrogantly believing to descended from a hero."

Rage boiled within Drustan as he confronted his

mother for her deceit. The revelation that his father, whom he had idolized as a hero, was in fact a ruthless murderer, was a bitter pill to swallow. He couldn't bring himself to accept it as truth. The horror of realizing his mother's suffering at the hands of his father, twisted like a knife in his gut. He couldn't comprehend how she could bear to look at him, without seeing the monster who had caused her so much pain. Did she see his father in him? Did his very presence fill her with disgust and loathing?

"If this is true, how can you stand to be in the same room as me? How can you bear to look upon me, knowing what my father did to you?" Drustan asked, his voice shaking with emotion.

"This is why I never spoke of it, why I kept the truth from you. What good would it have done?" She reached across the table and took him by the hands but he pulled away. "Listen to me. What they did, what your father did, was unforgivable. But that is not your burden to bear. You are not your father's son, you are mine. You were born of my flesh and I have been blessed to be your mother. When I look upon you, I feel joy because you have been a blessing from the gods. You were the reason I survived."

Despite his mother's heartfelt words, Drustan was consumed by grief and shock. He bolted upright in his chair, his mind and emotions in turmoil from the shocking confession. "Why didn't you just kill me in your womb?" he spat out, his voice raw with emotion. The thought of being the offspring of a monster, a constant reminder of his mother's suffering, was unbearable to him. He felt overwhelmed with anger, disgust, and despair.

"Drustan! Do not speak such evil!" Rowan interjected.

"How could I ever do such a thing?" Sibby gasped at the very idea. "I loved you from the moment I felt you move in my belly, and I have loved you more than my own life since that very day.

"What thy father did to me and my parents can never be forgiven. But because of him I have you, my most precious son. Despite the terrible price that was paid, thy father's actions brought me the greatest gifts in my life—a loving husband, a warm home filled with beautiful children, and the most precious son a mother could hope for."

Drustan sat in stunned silence, his mind unable to fully grasp the truth that had just been revealed to him. Sibby's heart felt like it was breaking, watching her son as he struggled to process the information. She could feel the weight of years of secrets lifting off her shoulders but the cost was too high. She watched as the image of the father Drustan idolized, the one she had encouraged him to believe in, crumbled before his eyes. Drustan's face was a mask of confusion, disappointment and shame, his eyes filled with the turmoil of a shattered identity.

Sibby's heart ached as she watched him struggling to make sense of it all, she wanted to reach out and comfort him but knew that this was a journey he had to take alone. Her eyes filled with tears as she watched him, feeling guilty for not telling him the truth earlier and for letting him idolize a man who was a monster.

His silence was suffocating. The very air was thick

with the stench of betrayal and Drustan felt like he was drowning in a sea of deceit. His pain and confusion were palpable, and one could see the years of trust and admiration being chipped away, replaced with a feeling of worthlessness and disgust.

Sibby reached out for his hand, and again he withdrew from her.

"Why now?" Drustan finally spoke, his voice ragged with raw emotion. "You could have told me this from the start, rather than spin these fanciful faerie tales you so love to tell. Or, you could have never told me at all. So, why now?"

"I never wanted to burden you with this, and would have gladly taken the secret to my grave. But now, the past has come back like a ghost from a bygone era. The old woman who took me in after the attack, she offered me a potion made of juniper, one that would have brought on my labor and taken your life while you were still in my womb. Despite her insistence I couldn't bring myself to do it. You were all I had left, my only family, my only hope.

"But the old woman, she wouldn't let go. Her persistence was like a noose around my neck, tightening with each passing day. I couldn't shake off the fear that she would slip that potion into my food, taking your life before you could even take your first breath. The thought of losing you, it consumed me. It was like a nightmare that I couldn't escape.

"So, I knew I had to do something, I couldn't just sit there and wait for her to act. Finally, I resolved to get away. I waited for the cover of night, when she was deep in her slumber. I took my chance and I ran, never looking back. I left everything behind, including her. I never saw her again until today."

"The face in the mist," Drustan realized, his voice in almost a whisper. "She was the one you saw."

"Aye, 'twas her face I saw in the mist; that evil witch, Mora. She comes for revenge, and I fear she comes for you."

The story left Drustan overwhelmed with a mix of emotions. From an early age, he had been told the lie that his father died defending his family against Viking raiders. He had thought himself the son of a brave warrior, the son of a hero. Now, he discovered that it was untrue. He was born a bastard, the son of a murderer and he had been conceived in a violent attack upon his mother. He suddenly felt disgraced, full of guilt and shame as though he himself had committed the crimes. And now that he understood the reason for the witch's appearance, he felt rage. He struggled for words to express his feelings. Then after a moment, he spoke.

"You should have heeded her wisdom," Drustan mumbled. "You should have drunk the potion and been well rid of me and all memory of the monster who sired me."

"Do not say such things," Rowan protested. "You are my son, not his. You may have been born of his loins, but it is I who has been thy father all these years. You'd do well to remember who raised you."

"And for that I am truly grateful," Drustan said respectfully. "If only you were my true father."

"He is so in every way that matters," Sibby assured

him.

"This history with the witch has long passed," Drustan said. "Do you believe she still seeks revenge for you leaving after all these years? Did you take something that belonged to her?"

"I took nothing. Still she perceived it as a betrayal. The soul of a black witch manifests all the wickedness of man. Of those evils, pride and vengeance are the most powerful. When I refused to destroy my child, I defied her; and when I ran away, I betrayed her. Now, after all these years I believe she comes to take payment for that insult."

"Then let her come," Drustan proclaimed. "Let this be the night the story ends."

Suddenly, the air was pierced by the cackling laughter of the old witch Mora, emanating from outside. The three of them exchanged a look of dread, their hearts sinking as they realized that the moment of reckoning had finally arrived.

"She's here, as I expected," Sibby announced and immediately headed to the door.

"Mother! Do not go outside!"

"Do not fear, son. Our gate and fence are blessed, consecrated so that no dark witch or her evil enchantments may pass."

"Can your enchantments shield you from the sharpened blade of a spear or the swift flight of an arrow?" Drustan asked. "If she cannot breach our gates, then why bother to engage her? Let us remain within, and let her tire of waiting until she leaves."

But Sibby was not so easily swayed, her eyes gleaming with determination. "If not tonight, then she will come again and again, until she is heard," she replied firmly. "Perhaps if I speak with her, she will have her say, and then be gone."

Sibby reached for her trusty walking stick, left by the door, and stepped out onto the porch with Rowan following closely behind. Drustan, not one to be caught unawares, snatched his bow, stuffing a quiver of the prepared arrows onto his shoulder, before joining them outside.

As he stepped onto the porch, his eyes were drawn to the eerie figure of an old woman draped in ominous black robes. She seemed to blend seamlessly into the darkness of the night except for her long, snow-white hair that stood out like a beacon, drawing him closer. To his amazement, she appeared to be floating a few feet above the ground, just beyond the gate.

As he watched, a chorus of crackling laughter echoed through the air, and he cast his gaze skyward. In the moonlight, he saw a group of witches, at least a dozen of them, soaring overhead. They flew in a haunting circle above the home, following the outline of the fence that encircled the yard. It was a scene straight out of a nightmare, and he couldn't help but feel a sense of unease as he watched their sinister dance.

"Huh," Drustan grunted, slightly humbled when he realized that several of the witches were indeed sitting on tree branches while others were upon bristle brooms. For a moment, he regretted scoffing at his mother as she suspiciously examined the willow branch on the road earlier that day.

"My dearest daughter, Isabel," the witch addressed her. "How I have missed thee."

"After these many years." Sibby replied as if she were making an accusation.

"And the child," Mora said, casting an eye toward Drustan. "How he has grown so. Such a handsome young buck he has become."

"Why are you here, Mora?" Sibby demanded.

"I've come to see you, and our boy. You have warded thy gate and fence so that I cannot pass. Would you not invite thy old friend inside?"

"Speak thy peace if you must, but do it from a safe distance," Sibby replied. She stepped off the porch and into the open yard to gain a better view of Mora. Suddenly, without warning, a massive stone came crashing down from the sky overhead. It thumped loudly as it struck the ground only a few steps from where Sibby stood. One of the witches had thrown it at her.

As Sibby recoiled in shock, another stone came hurtling towards her, this one landed even closer. Suddenly, like a hailstorm of fury, a barrage of rocks rained down upon them as the witches cackled with glee.

"Quickly, get under cover!" Rowan yelled, his voice ringing with urgency. He lunged forward, grabbed Sibby, and pulled her onto the covered porch of the house. As they huddled together, the stones continued to fly, pelting the porch and shattering roof boards with a deafening crash.

It was a surreal and terrifying encounter, but Drustan refused to back down. Instead, he stood his ground, his eyes blazing with defiance. With lightning-fast reflexes, he reached for an arrow from his quiver and drew back his bow.

The witch, who was preparing to hurl another stone, never saw it coming. Drustan took aim with deadly precision and released his fingers, sending the arrow flying towards its target with a fierce determination.

The sound of the arrow hitting its mark was like a thunderclap, echoing through the night. The witch let out a blood-curdling scream as the arrow pierced her chest. Suddenly, she burst into flames, a fiery inferno consuming her as she fell from the sky like a shooting star.

It was a sight that was both glorious and terrifying, and Drustan knew that this would be a moment he would never forget. He stood tall and proud, unyielding in the face of danger, an unbreakable force against the forces of darkness.

Even before the first witch had even hit the ground, Drustan was already in motion. With lightning speed, he pulled back a second arrow and launched it at another of the witches. The arrow hissed as it flew through the air, then struck its target. Another witch screamed and fell from the sky in smoldering ash.

Drustan didn't hesitate for a moment. He pulled back his bow once more, and this time he aimed directly at the leader of the coven, Mora. His eyes were cold and fierce, and his voice boomed like thunder as he commanded, "Call them off!" He held his bow fully drawn and aimed at her. The tension was palpable, and the air was thick with the smell of hot sulfur and the crackling of flames.

Mora laughed at him in contempt.

He did not give her a second chance. Without warning, Drustan loosed his arrow, sending it hurtling towards Mora. He was an excellent archer, and never missed his mark. But just as the arrow was about to strike its target, Mora caught it in her hand, the silver tip only a finger's width from her forehead.

The sudden movement caught Drustan off guard, and he lowered his bow in shock. The witch stood there, her hand still gripping the arrow, her eyes locked with his. And in that moment, he knew that he had underestimated her, and that this was not going to be an easy battle.

"Thou art skilled with the bow," she laughed devil-ishly, unfazed by how close it had come to striking her down. With a flick of her wrist, she flung the arrow back at him as if she was tossing a spear.

He barely had time to react, but his reflexes were quick, and he leapt to the side, narrowly avoiding the arrow as it whizzed past him, embedding itself into the front of the house. The near-miss didn't faze him in the slightest, and he remained steady, his eyes locked on his opponent with fierce determination.

He grabbed another arrow and drew back his bow. With his eyes still locked on Mora, he raised his bow toward the sky, released the arrow and struck down yet another of the witches. But Drustan was not done yet. He reloaded his bow again and another witch fell to the ground in ash and smoke. All the while never breaking eye contact with Mora. It was a show of power and de-termination, as he stared into the witch's eyes, daring her to make a move against him.

Mora did not react but with his keen eyesight, Drustan could see her jaw quivering, betraying her show of confidence. Sensing her fear, Drustan realized it was time to strike. With a fierce determination, he grabbed two arrows, nocked them against the bowstring and drew back, aiming directly at Mora.

"Let's see if you can catch two arrows at once," he sneered, as her prepared to unleash his fury.

"What about three?" Rowan added as he stepped next to Drustan and drew his own bow.

"Wait! Do not release thy arrows!" Sibby abruptly said. She walked out to stand in front of the two men facing Mora.

"I do not want this fight, Mora. I have no quarrel with thee." Sibby truly did not want this conflict. Despite her fear of the woman, Sibby owed her a debt. She had taken her in and nursed her back to health. She had given her a home when there was nowhere else to turn. Sibby was grateful to the old witch and felt indebted to her, even though she ended up fleeing in the end.

"Then give me what is mine," Mora replied. "I demand what is due. Only then will thy debt be paid."

"If I had taken anything that belonged to you, I would gladly return it. But I know not of what you speak."

"The boy!" Mora squawked, her voice filled with rage as she thrust an accusing finger at Drustan. "The one who is now a man! He was to be mine! You stole him from me." She spat out the words with venom in her voice, her eyes locked onto Drustan with a look of pure hatred.

"Are you mad with the fever! The son I carried and delivered? What claim could you possibly have on my child?"

"The fruit may be nestled in the basket, but it is the gardener who truly owns it," Mora seethed with fury. "It was I who orchestrated the raid on your home and set his father upon thee. I planted the seed that grew into the boy. He is mine, crafted by my own hand."

Sibby recoiled in horror, "You speak false, you deceitful serpent! Such treachery cannot be true."

"Really, Isabel. You know the truth. Did you think the brute took thee because of thy beauty? Because you stirred desire in his loins," Mora laughed hysterically. "Is that why you clung to his bastard child? To hold onto the memory of his burning desire?"

"You poisonous toad. It was you who did that to my family! To me? I was only a child."

"You weren't no child, you were a woman in full bloom, parading thyself before all the men of the village; burning with desire to be plucked like a ripe fruit. That's why you were chosen. That's why I sent him to thy door."

"Shut your vile mouth!" Sibby screamed back. "Thy tongue is like a festering boil, dripping with vile and rancid lies."

Mora was pleased to see that she was stirring Sibby's calm disposition. "If you had obeyed, you could have been the most powerful witch in the land! Even more powerful than me!"

"Who says I'm not," Sibby growled then raised her staff into the air and pointed it at Mora. "Deche mal!" She screamed in fury and thrust the staff toward the witch. A dazzling burst of light shot from the tip of Sibby's staff, flying like a bolt of lightning and striking Mora squarely in the chest. With a scream of agony, the old witch tumbled backward to the ground.

Rowan and Drustan stood frozen, gaping in disbelief at Sibby's raw power. Never had they witnessed her preform such a feat, nor did they suspect she could wield such power.

"By God's teeth," Drustan exclaimed, his mind reeling with the sudden revelation of Sibby's hidden abilities.

Mora regained her footing and prepared to return fire. She brought her hand up and a green ball of light rose from within her palm. She threw the orb toward Sibby, but Sibby's protective spells prevented the dark magic from crossing her barrier. The orb disintegrated in the air just as it passed over the wooden gate.

"I see you have mastered the old ways well," the old witch said. Then she called out to her witches that still circled above, "Rain down upon them and bash in her head! I want to see her brains spilt in the dirt at my feet!"

Sibby, Rowan and Drustan quickly retreated to the cover of the porch just as another barrage of stones began to fall from the sky. The porch roof shook from the impact of the heavy rocks causing several of the wooden planks to splinter.

Sibby turned to her husband and son. "Loosen thy arrows," she said, "lest they bury us with stones!"

With fierce determination in their eyes, Rowan and Drustan raised their bows, the wood creaking under the tension of their fingers as they drew back the strings. Rowan, with his single arrow, aimed for the sky, targeting one of the witches soaring overhead. Drustan, with his deadly double arrows, aimed directly at the heart of Mora, intent on ending their confrontation decisively.

In a swift motion, Rowan released his arrow, and with a satisfying thud, it connected with its target, causing the witch to plummet to the ground in a fiery inferno. Drustan followed suit, releasing his arrows with pinpoint accuracy. Just as the arrows were about to strike, Mora twisted and contorted, her body transforming into that of a massive black bird. With powerful flaps of her wings, she began to ascend, narrowly missing one arrow as it sailed past her. But the second arrow found its mark, piercing her left wing and causing her to tumble to the earth in a flurry of feathers and pain.

With a final flutter of her wings, Mora transformed back into her human form, her body wracked with pain with the arrow lodged deep in her shoulder, the flesh of her wound sizzling and smoldering. Her cries of anguish filled the air as she lay on the ground, defeated.

"Sisters! I beg of you, come to my aid!" Mora cried out, summoning her coven to her side.

In swift response, two of her witches descended from the heavens, each one seizing Mora by the arm. Together, they lifted her up and bore her away into the darkness of the night. Seeing their mistress wounded and in retreat, the other witches followed suit. Drustan and his stepfather continued their barrage, and were able to claim another witch as they tried to make their escape.

The confrontation with Mora and her coven of witches, which had loomed like a dark cloud on the horizon, ultimately proved to be a crushing defeat. Unprepared and caught off guard, the witches were left with nothing but crude stones to defend themselves against the deadly onslaught of Drustan's expert archery and Rowan's blessed arrows.

The witches fell one by one, their bodies consumed by flames as they plunged to the ground, their ashes smoldering in the wake of the brutal battle. The homestead, protected by Sibby's powerful enchantments, stood unscathed as the coven's attempts to penetrate its defenses proved futile.

In the end, seven of the witches lay in ashes, while Mora herself, only momentarily escaped the same fate. Her body wracked with pain and likely dying, she was carried away into the night by her remaining sisters.

Sibby felt little triumph in her victory. Instead, she was consumed by a deep sense of turmoil. The woman she had once looked upon as a kind mother figure had been revealed as a ruthless and malevolent villain beyond her imagination. Despite her suspicion of Mora's motives many years earlier, Sibby still held gratitude for what the old woman had done for her in her time of need. But now, with the truth laid bare, Sibby saw the darkness that consumed Mora's soul. The one she had believed to be her savior was in fact even more evil than the man who had taken her family and violated her as a young girl.

The thought of someone harboring such malevolent intent, to orchestrate the brutal rape of an innocent young girl and the slaughter of her entire family, was unfathomable. Sibby had found solace in believing that her past was nothing more than a cruel twist of fate or a senseless act of violence. But now, to discover that the attack had been a calculated and targeted assault, with her as the intended victim, was a revelation that reopened old wounds and made them almost unbearable.

Along with her emotional turmoil, an ominous feeling clung to Sibby like a shadow. She had watched as many of the coven witches were consumed by raging flames after being struck by the witch-killing arrows. Yet, unlike her evil followers, Mora had not met the same fiery fate. Despite her severe wound, she somehow survived the initial injury, at least long enough to retreat into the night. Whether Mora had already succumbed to wound or was teetering on the brink of death, Sibby couldn't be certain. But the implications that her adversary had somehow managed to escape and evade death, filled her with a sense of impending doom and uncertainty for what the future held. The knowledge that her enemy still drew breath, somewhere out there in the darkness, meant that she and her family would never feel safe until Mora and her coven were completely destroyed.

She sat there, motionless, at the rough-hewn wooden table, her shawl tightly swaddled around her frame, offering both comfort and warmth. Her tears flowed freely, cascading down her flushed cheeks, as anger and frustration furrowed her brow. Rowan approached cautiously, and with a tender touch, leaned over and placed a kiss on the top of her head. She reached for his hand, pulling it to her chest and patting it gently, a silent acknowledgment that she was alright. Not a word was spoken between them, yet their emotions were communicated clearly. Rowan knew his wife all too well, and in moments such as this, he knew it was best to give her space and time to sort through her thoughts. He would be there for her, ready to listen and offer support when she was ready to speak. She needed to work through this on her own, and when she was ready, she would open up to him, if she so desired.

Drustan returned from the porch where he had been standing vigil against any further threat from the coven. As Rowan headed to the door to resume the watch, he gave his son a reassuring pat on the shoulder as he passed by. "You did good tonight, a brave and true warrior. I'm proud of you, son," Rowan said, his voice low and steady.

Drustan gave him a slight nod, but the praise failed to elicit any sense of pleasure or satisfaction from him. His internal conflict was too overwhelming.

Rowan opened the door to head outside. He paused briefly. "Why don't you warm yourself by the fire?" He told Drustan.

"Aye, for a moment I will," Drustan replied as Rowan stepped outside closing the door behind him.

Drustan took a seat in front of the crackling fireplace and held out his hands to feel the warmth. He couldn't help but glance over at his mother, seated at the table, her face reflecting her grief as if a part of her had been ripped away. He could only imagine the pain she must have felt all those years ago, as a young girl, when the attack was not so far away. Her family murdered, her innocence stolen, and with no one left in the world. She was just a child herself, and suddenly everything and everyone she knew was gone. He felt a mix of emotions toward her: anger over a lifetime of lies she had told to him, but pity and compassion for the circumstance the led her to such deception.

"Mother, I'm sorry," he said, his voice barely above a whisper.

"For what, my child?" She questioned and continued to stare blankly at the table.

"The witch, she destroyed your life. All because of me."

"No, my son!" His mother's voice was stern as she turned to him, her eyes piercing through his own. "Do not think such thoughts. You were not even conceived when that woman laid her evil plans. Do not place such a heavy and false burden upon thy shoulders."

Drustan shook his head, feeling the weight of the recent revelations. "But she did this so I would be born. For whatever evil purpose she intended, I was born of it. I was born of this evil." No matter what sweet words his mother offered, one truth remained. His very existence was the result of an evil witch and her savage mercenary.

"Listen to me, Drustan. What Mora did, what she took from me as a young child, was no fault of yours. And, the gods have given back many times over. You, a loving husband, and all my children. All that I hold dear was given to me in repayment for the evil I endured."

She dried the tears from her cheeks and smiled at him. "The price that I paid many years ago was very high, but given the chance to undo her evil, I would not, if doing so meant I would not have you."

She stood up and brushed the creases from her apron as if she were preparing to go to work. "Now, put such thoughts from thy head. We have more important concerns to discuss. Come, let's speak with my husband."

Drustan followed his mother outside where they found Rowan sitting on a chair, bow in hand, keeping a watchful eye on the night sky.

"Wife," Rowan nodded and greeted her. "All seems as it should."

"For the moment," Sibby replied. "But I fear we are still in danger. Mora is a more powerful witch than I imagined. Only the blackest of witches could be injured by the hexed arrow yet still live."

"Maybe she's mortally wounded and dying. Or she's already dead," Drustan supposed.

"Shall we dare to take that risk?" she pondered.

Having nurtured a bitter grudge against Sibby for nearly two decades, she knew Mora would certainly come back to seek revenge if she still lived. They had been fortunate this time around, as Mora had not expected to encounter such fierce resistance. If she managed to live and to return, she would come much more prepared. Even if Mora were to meet her demise, there was no telling what the remainder of her coven might do. They could scatter like leaves in the wind or return with vengeful intent. Sibby was weighing the potential risks and consequences of taking any further action against the coven and was unsure of the solution.

"Then what do you want us to do, wife? Should we gather our belongings and our family and flee our home? Go far away and hope they do not come after us?"

"No, she would continue to hunt for us; and we will not give up our lives and our home," Sibby answered. "We will fight and make a stand here. Our home is warded and the witches cannot pass beyond our gate or fence."

"Then what, mother?" Drustan asked. "Are we to remain inside the fence from this day forward, corralled like cattle? What about our crops, who will tend the land?"

"Of course not son," she replied.

"What of the children?" Drustan continued. "Will they be safe outside if a witch decides to rain down stones upon their heads?"

"The boy is right," Rowan agreed. "We cannot hide within these walls and wait for them to come to us. We must find her and see that she and her followers can do no more harm."

"We must finish this. I will go seek out this witch. I will find their nest and destroy them all," Drustan stated.

"As will I," Rowan agreed.

"No!" Sibby snapped. "'Tis too great a risk. I cannot have my men folk away while this evil woman threatens our home."

"I will go alone," Drustan spoke to Rowan. "You should stay and protect the family. Our home is protected against the witches' magic, but suppose she should send mortal men against us. Just as she did against my mother's family, she could do so again. You should remain here to protect the family."

"Nay, I said!" Sibby protested. "Neither of you shall go. It is a black witch of which you speak. 'Tis madness to seek out this evil."

"Mother, this is the only way. We must stamp out this evil and crush them completely while they a weakened."

"He's right, wife," Rowan said reluctantly. "We must

seek out this witch while she is weakened. We must find if she yet lives, and if so, she must be killed. But it is I who will go. Drustan, my son, you are the better swordsman and gifted with the bow. There is no other I would trust to defend our home than you. You must remain here and protect the others."

Sibby was a stubborn woman and fiercely protective of her family. However, she knew the decision had been made and now it was a discussion between the men folk. She did not want either her husband or Drustan to face these witches alone, but she realized that they were right about the matter. After all these years, Mora had sought her out to have revenge. If the witch lived, she would return, the next time more prepared and determined than before. The only solution was to kill Mora along with her coven before they had the chance to recover and regain their strength.

"So be it," Sibby reluctantly agreed. "I do not want this, but you are of your own mind and will do this regardless of my objections."

"I leave at daybreak," Rowan said.

"But father ..." Drustan protested.

"The decision has been made, son. There will be no more argument," Rowan announced sternly.

Sibby crept to the window, cautiously opening the shutter and peering outside. She scanned the fields beyond the fence and gazed up at the sky, searching for any sign of danger. Satisfied that all was well, she closed the shutters and fastened the latch. "We should rest now; the dawn will come too soon," she whispered.

The next morning, Rowan awoke to the warm rays

of the sun streaming through the cracks in the wooden shudder. He turned over, expecting to find Sibby by his side, only to discover that she had already risen. He quickly dressed and made his way to the main room, where he found her standing at the window, her expression unsettled.

"What troubles you, my love?" he asked, standing beside her and looking out at the morning mist that hung over the fields.

In the distance, he saw a figure trudging down the dirt road away from the house. He squinted, trying to make out who it was, and soon realized it was Drustan. "What is that foolish boy thinking?" Rowan growled immediately realizing that Drustan had decided to disobey and head out in search of the coven himself.

Rowan gathered his boots that he had kept by the fireplace. As he laced them up, he declared with conviction, "Do not fret, my love. I shall return him safely to you."

"Stay, my husband," Sibby said with resignation. "He is no longer a boy, but a man. It is time we treated him as such. After what he has learned in the past night, he needs to find himself. This is a journey he must make alone."

Sibby watched as her eldest son disappeared into the distance, her heart heavy with sorrow. She sank to the floor, tears streaming down her face. Rowan rushed to her side, lifting her gently and leading her to a rocking chair by the fireplace.

"Do not worry, my love," Rowan reassured her. "We have raised him well. He will return safely to you."

As he tried to soothe her, Rowan's gaze fell upon a bowl of water on the table, a broken eggshell and the yolk lying beside it. He peered into the bowl and saw the ghostly white of the egg resting at the bottom. He knew this was a message from the beyond, a way of divination that Sibby used many times in the past to foretell the future for those who sought her wisdom. She would study the unbroken egg for signs, scrutinizing its color and shape, and the spots that were visible on the shell. Then, she would crack the egg and spill the white into a bowl of steaming water. The shapes of the egg white would reveal more signs and omens, a prediction of things yet to come.

"What did you see?"

"I cast the divination for you. To see your fate if you should set out in search of the coven," she answered, her voice heavy with sorrow. "The gods have answered. You will die if you attempt this quest."

Rowan sank into one of the chairs, his mind reeling. "And our son? Have you sent him to his death in my place?"

The journey ahead for our son will be perilous and treacherous, a path fraught with danger and uncertainty. But alas, it is the road that fate has chosen for him to walk," Sibby spoke with a heavy heart.

"But will he return to us safely?"

"The future is yet to be decided, and it is Drustan who will determine the final outcome," Sibby said mournfully. "But one thing I know for sure, 'tis his destiny that he treads on now. And we must let him brave this path to its ultimate end, come what may."

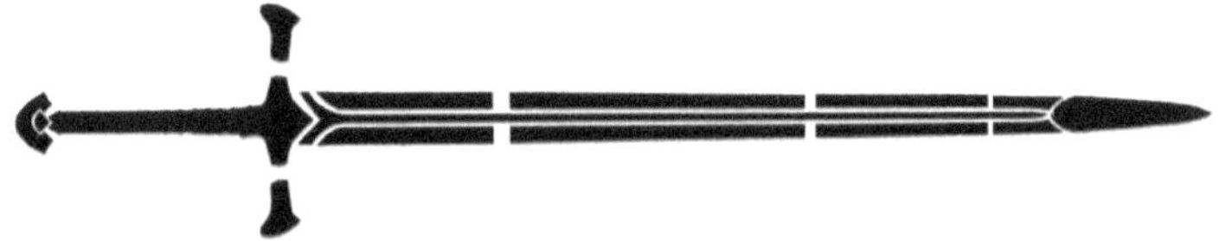

CHAPTER 5

The First Step Toward Destiny

Drustan felt his spirit soar as he ventured forth from the confines of his family home, embracing the serenity of the open road. The revelation of his true lineage and the identity of his father had left him reeling, a tempest of emotions roiling within him. Betrayal and humiliation gnawed at his very soul, kindling within him a burning desire to vanish from the world, to conceal himself and become a stranger to all. The web of lies spun by his mother for all those years still clung to him, a noxious miasma that he knew would take time to dissipate. But it was not solely his anger towards her that had driven him to seek solace in the wilderness; it was the shame that consumed him, a shame that he could not bear to face. All his life he had worn his false heritage as a badge of honor, but now, instead of seeing himself as the son of a fallen hero, he saw himself as a mongrel, the illegitimate offspring of a monstrous savage.

So he welcomed the solitude of the road and set his sights upon the ancient crone who had wrought this cursed existence upon him, determined to unravel the truth of his birth and to reclaim his rightful place in the world. With each step he took, the weight of his past lifted, and he felt his spirit rise as he embarked upon a journey of redemption and vengeance. The wilds of the land lay before him, and he knew that the answers he sought lay beyond the horizon, waiting for him to claim them.

The revelation of his true origins was a bitter pill for Drustan to swallow, and he knew that seclusion was the only way to come to terms with it. So it was with a heavy heart but a fierce determination that he set out to confront the witch Mora, the one responsible for his torment.

The previous night, as he lay awake in his bed, listening to the echoes of his mother's voice in his mind, the witch's taunting laughter ringing in his ears, he knew that the time had come. With the first light of dawn, he rose and donned his gear, preparing to embark on his quest.

When he descended the stairs, he found his mother sitting by the fire, her eyes red-rimmed from a night of tears. Rather than protest his intention, Sibby instead had anticipated his actions. During the night, she had used a very old technique of divination; in order to consult the spirits. Because of that insight, she accepted that it was Drustan's destiny to undertake this journey. Reluctantly and painfully, she gave him her blessing, handed him a handful of coins, and with a tight embrace sent him on his way.

As Drustan left his home behind, he felt a sense of liberation wash over him. The previous night he had been burdened with the knowledge of his father's crime and the weight of it was heavy on his shoulders. But now, he had a purpose, a quest to prove himself and establish his own identity. He wanted to show the world, and more importantly, himself, that he was not his father's son. He wanted to be known as a man of honor and respect, someone who was worthy of admiration.

This journey was his chance to redeem himself, to prove that he was not like his father. He was determined to be a hero, to show bravery and integrity. He knew that if he could succeed in this quest, he would be able to set himself apart from the villainous legacy and create a new legacy of his own.

As he trekked forward, Drustan's mind was awhirl with thoughts and musings. The morning sun was high in the sky when he arrived at the quaint village of Alyth. He had visited this place many times before, accompanying his parents as they traded their crops and purchased supplies for their family. But this was his first time making the journey alone, and he couldn't help but feel a sense of excitement and curiosity as he viewed the village with fresh eyes.

He strolled the streets slowly, taking in all the sights and sounds that he may have missed in his previous visits. At first, he was disappointed to find that the village offered little more to him as a grown man than it did as a boy. The humble peasantry, caught up in the daily grind of survival, offered few new sights to behold. But as he made his way through the village, he stumbled upon a place that had always captured his imagination as a young boy: the local tavern.

He hesitated at the threshold of the tavern, staring at

the closed door with a mix of nostalgia and apprehension. Flashbacks of his first trip to the village as a wide-eyed boy flooded his mind. He remembered the raucous laughter and the clinking of tankards as he sat at a small table near the door, watching Rowan negotiate with the patrons. The carefree atmosphere of that day, when the troubles of the world seemed so distant, lingered in his memory.

As he stood there, lost in his thoughts, the door sprang open and a peasant woman emerged and tossed a bucket full of dirty water into the street. She was older than him, her features worn by years of hard labor. But despite her plain appearance, her low-cut dress drew his gaze to her ample cleavage. He couldn't help but look, like any other young man would.

"Feast your eyes, young lad," the woman chirped and pushed her bosom outward and playfully jiggled them. She let out a boisterous chuckle, her merriment genuine and not meant to mock the young man.

"Well, are you coming in, or are you just going to block the doorway from my paying customers?"

Drustan, embarrassed, looked away and quickly stepped into the tavern. Inside, the place was dimly lit, but it was still early in the day and the patrons were few. The smell of soured ale and wood smoke filled his nose as he made his way to an empty table.

He looked around the room, taking in the rough-hewn tables and chairs, the stone fireplace, and the patrons sitting at the bar, laughing and drinking. This was a place of escape, a place where one could forget their troubles and just be in the moment.

The woman he encountered at the door placed a cup of cool water and a small piece of bread on the table in front of him. "What'll it be, young buck? I have some eggs and bread if you want to eat. There's mutton stew on the fire, should be ready soon. Also, I have a stout ale and wine for drink."

"Eggs and bread, if it is no bother."

"And how will you be paying for that?" she asked with a hint of suspicion in her voice. "I don't need any work done today, but I can find something for you to do if you're short on coin."

"Aye, I can pay," Drustan answered and reached into this pocket. He took the small leather pouch from his pocket and opened it to reveal several pieces of hack-silver. He poured the contents on the table for the woman to access.

She looked at the silver pieces and nodded her approval, then went off to the kitchen to prepare his meal. A short time later, she returned with a plate of eggs and a stale piece of bread.

"You want a cup of wine or ale to drink?"

"A cup of ale, if you please."

She fetched a stein of ale and placed it in front of him on the table. Then she picked up two pieces of the silver and put them in the pocket of her apron. She watched with satisfaction as Drustan greedily dug into his meal.

Two burly men strode into the establishment. Drustan couldn't help but take note of their rugged appearance, which screamed of a life of hard labor and possibly even mischief. They gave him a curt nod as they made their way to a nearby table.

"I'll be with you gentlemen shortly," the tavern maid called out to the newcomers before turning her attention back to Drustan. "Is there anything else you'll be needing?"

"I'm in need of some dried meat for my journey. Enough to last a few days, perhaps a week. And if you happen to have any information that could aid me on my way, I'd be much obliged."

"I have some salted pork I can offer," she replied as she picked up several more of the hack-silver. "As for the information, that will cost too."

"Do you know of an old woman, with long grey hair and her face withered with age?"

The woman let out a hearty chuckle. "You just described every woman in this village, dearie."

Drustan leaned in, his voice low and hushed. "The crone in question goes by the name of Mora — a witch, if you will."

"Do not speak that vile name in here," she snarled abruptly and spat on the floor, an old custom believed to ward off evil.

"So, you do know the woman of whom I speak," Drustan pressed, his voice low and full of intrigue.

"I cannot help you," the woman replied curtly, her eyes narrowing. "Don't bring that kind of trouble into my establishment."

"I seek no trouble, only information," Drustan protested, holding up his hands in a gesture of innocence.

"Well, I don't have any to give," she said, her tone icy. "I'll bring you your salted pork and then you should leave." With that, the woman stormed off, muttering to herself as she disappeared into the back room.

Drustan let out a sigh and leaned back in his seat, his hopes of gaining information on Mora dashed by the woman's refusal to assist him. Despite her curt response, he couldn't blame her for wanting to avoid getting involved. He knew all too well the dangers and repercussions of crossing Mora.

The two patrons at the other table had witnessed the conversation and when the barmaid was out of sight, one of the men leaned over and addressed Drustan. "I couldn't help but overhear your ask about the witch," he said, his tone low and serious.

"You know of her?" Drustan asked, his voice filled with hope.

"Aye, she is well known in our own village," the man replied, his eyes narrowing. "But she resides northwest of here, several days journey."

"Is that where she lives?" Drustan pressed, growing increasingly intrigued.

"No one knows for certain where the witch lives," the man said, his voice laced with caution. "There are rumors that she lives in the forest or somewhere in the north highlands. What business do you have with her?" the man asked, his tone darkening. "She is a dangerous witch, any dealings you have with her would be better off dealt with the devil himself."

"I have personal business with her," Drustan said, unwilling to reveal too much information.

"Personal business you say?" The man raised an eyebrow. "If it's a spell or charm you seek, there are others of the cunning folk around who will help you for a small price. I hear tell of a woman nearby who is gifted with such powers. I think her name is Izzy, or something like that.”

“Sibby,” the other man said. “Her name is Sibby.”

“Aye, ‘tis her,” the man confirmed, his eyes alight with recognition. “She is the one you should seek.”

Drustan leaned forward, his voice low and filled with determination. “Sibby is my mother. She is the reason I hunt this witch Mora.”

The man’s expression turned more serious. “Then thy mother should have warned thee. The witch you seek will only bring misery and death.”

“It is her death I seek,” Drustan growled, his fists clenched tight. “She has brought harm to my family, and I will see her burn for it.”

Both men laughed loudly, but Drustan didn’t flinch.

The other man taunted. “Just how do you plan to do what no other man could?”

Drustan’s eyes blazed with anger. “Do you know the witch’s whereabouts or not?” he demanded impatiently.

The first man leaned in and lowered his voice, his eyes darkening with intensity. “If your mother, the cunning woman, has sent you on this journey, then I trust that you have been warned of the dangers you face. If you are set on this path, then head north. ‘Tis said the witch you seek resides in a dark tower deep within the Caledonian Forest. I know no more than that.”

The second man’s voice trembled with fear as he warned, “Beware, the Caledonian Forest is a dangerous place, full of dark forces and terrifying creatures. Many brave men have ventured into those woods, never to return. Those who do make it out, come back forever changed, forever haunted. I heard of one poor soul from the north who dared to seek out this witch. He was found wandering the roads, days later, his tongue ripped out, and his eyes plucked from their sockets."

"Be warned, lad, and run back to thy home. You will find nothing but sorrow if you continue down this path," the first man insisted.

Drustan's heart raced as he listened to their dire tales, but despite his trepidation he remained undeterred. He had already faced this witch once and had given her a devastating defeat. He did not fear another confrontation, and more likely than not, Mora had already succumbed to her wounds and the remaining coven had scattered to the wind.

"Thank you for the information," Drustan replied and retrieved several of the hack-silver bits and offered them to the two men.

The men accepted the payment with a nod of gratitude then returned to drinking and their whispered conversation.

The barkeep emerged from the kitchen, her arms cradling a small parcel of meat, wrapped in paper and bound with twine. She plopped it down on the table in front of Drustan without ceremony and snatched up the remaining hack-silver, tucking them away in her apron.

"Ye can be on thy way now," she sneered, her tone as sharp as a knife.

Drustan rose from his seat, taking the meat with him. He turned to the two men, giving them a nod of gratitude for their valuable information. He then turned to the barkeep, bowing his head in a courteous farewell before making his way out into the bustling streets.

As Drustan made his way out of the village, he came to a sudden halt at the edge of town. His mind raced with uncertainty as he pondered the gravity of the journey ahead. Each step he took from this point forward would take him further from home than he had ever ventured before, and deeper into a world unknown. He cast a final glance back towards the village, his heart heavy with nostalgia, before steeling himself to face the long, dirt road that stretched out before him.

His heart pounded with indecision. Part of him yearned to turn back and retreat to the safety of home, to be that carefree boy he once was, the proud son of a hero. But he knew that was impossible now. The witch had shattered his illusions, revealing a life built on lies. He could never go back to the way things were before.

Yet, even as fear and apprehension gripped him, Drustan knew he could not back down. He had a duty to protect his family, and a burning desire for revenge against the witch who had taken so much from his mother, and has shattered his own innocence. But greater than those reasons, Drustan hungered for the adventure and for a life less ordinary.

With a fierce determination burning in his chest, Drustan stepped forward. The first step toward destiny. His heart was pounding in his ears. He took a deep breath, steeling himself for the unknown ahead. Each step forward felt like a step into the unknown, as if he were stepping into a cold, dark abyss. But with each step, his confidence and determination grew. He picked up his pace, striding forward with purpose and determination.

Drustan knew that this was the moment he had been preparing for all his life. He was no longer a boy, but a man, with responsibilities and a mission to fulfill. But even as a man, a boy's curiosity and thirst for adventure still burned deep within him. He was eager to explore the world and face his destiny head on. This was his chance to prove himself, to become the hero he had always wanted to be.

With each step, Drustan felt his heart pounding harder and harder. He knew that the road ahead would be long and treacherous, but he was ready for anything. He was a man now, and nothing would stand in his way. He would face his destiny head on, no matter what the cost.

By the time the sun was directly overhead, Drustan stood at a crossroads. The path before him twisted and turned eastward, to continue north he would have to abandon the familiar safety of the road and delve into the dark and ominous woods. He knew the road would eventually turn north again but taking the long route could add precious time to his journey. The decision weighed heavily on him as he struggled to weigh the risks and rewards of his choices. Should he stay the course and wait for the road to turn in his favor, or should he forge ahead through the woods and brave the unknown?

Drustan could hear his mother's voice echoing in his mind, warning him of the dangers that lurked in the woods. She had always warned him never to venture into the woods alone and especially never to be caught in the woods after sunset. But Drustan, driven by a fierce determination and a desire for adventure, disregarded his mother's warnings and ventured into the forest.

He knew his chosen path could be treacherous, but he had his sword by his side and his bow and quiver on his back. He was determined to face any danger that came his way. He knew that he had to be brave, even if it meant disregarding his mother's advice. He had to push forward, even if it meant risking everything. He would face his destiny head on, no matter what the cost. He would not be stopped by fear or caution, for he was determined to become the hero he had always dreamed of being.

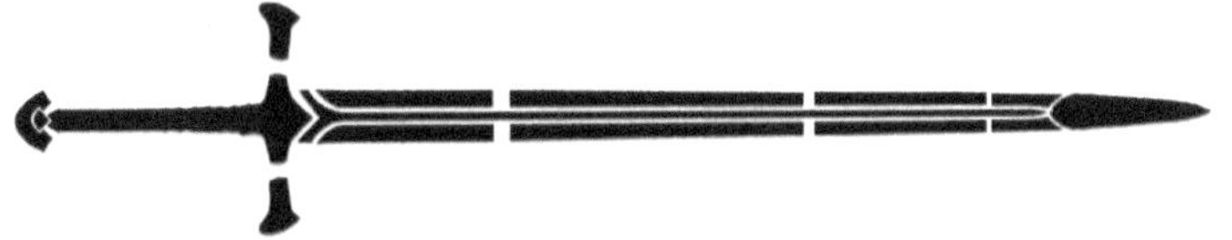

CHAPTER 6

The Bean Nighe

As Drustan ventured further into the depths of the dense, dark forest, the ominous canopy overhead blotted out all but the faintest glimmers of sunlight. The twisted, gnarled trees seemed to loom closer and closer, as if closing in around him, conspiring to trap him within their grasp. His path became increasingly treacherous, with twisted roots and low hanging branches slowing his progress and making passage at times nearly impossible. It was as if the forest itself was coming alive, moving to impede his advance to keep its secrets hidden from him at all costs. Each step forward was a battle, but Drustan pressed on, using his sword to cut through the thick brush and hack away at the twisted roots that threatened to ensnare him. He pushed through the undergrowth, determined to move forward.

As Drustan pushed deeper into the forest, the trees began to thin out, and the ground became softer underfoot. He soon found himself at the edge of a wide, fast-flowing river. Drustan studied the river for a moment, noting the direction of the water flow and the position of the sun. He decided that if he followed the river bank, it would lead him north, towards the Caledonian Forest where Mora's castle was said to be located.

Drustan set off along the river bank, following its winding course as it flowed through the forest. The path forward was arduous, with the river bank often steep and slippery. He had to scramble over rocks and fallen trees, and at times he was forced to wade through the icy water. But Drustan was determined, and he pressed on, using his sword to hack away at the overhanging branches that threatened to impede his progress.

Drustan finally came to a delta where two streams fed into the river he had been following. He paused for a moment, catching his breath and surveying the scene before him. The forest here seemed almost peaceful, as if it had given up trying to impede his advance. The trees were taller and straighter, and the undergrowth was sparse.

As Drustan reached the clearing and the river delta, he was greeted by a warm, golden sunlight that filtered through the trees. He had been traveling for hours and was tired from the difficult passage, so he decided to lay down on the soft grass and rest. The soothing sound of the river and the warmth of the sun on his face soon led to him nodding off. He closed his eyes, letting out a deep sigh as he felt himself drifting off into a peaceful sleep. But his peace was short-lived as he soon found himself in the midst of a vivid and disturbing dream.

In the dream, he was on the battlefield, sword in hand, fighting against a man who he knew to be his true father. The trauma of discovering his true heritage had been overwhelming, and now it was playing out in his nightmares.

The dream battle was intense, Drustan and his father fought with a fierce determination, their swords clashing with a deafening noise. Drustan could feel his anger and disgust towards his father building with each blow, fueled by the knowledge of his mother's pain and suffering. He fought with all his might, determined to rid himself of this nightmare once and for all.

Finally, the man fell to the ground, defeated. Drustan stood victorious, but the victory felt hollow as he looked into his father's eyes and saw his own staring back at him. He awoke with a start, sweating and shaking, his heart racing. The warm sunshine seemed less inviting now, and he felt a chill run down his spine. He knew that the dream was a reflection of his inner turmoil, a reminder of the traumatic truth about his father.

He sat up, rubbing his eyes and looking around. At first, he saw nothing out of the ordinary, just the peaceful clearing and the river flowing by. But then he noticed a figure in the distance. It appeared to be an old woman, washing clothes in the shallow water of the river. She was bent over reaching in the water, her hands moving rhythmically as she scrubbed the clothes clean..

Drustan stared at her in disbelief, his mind racing with curiosity and unease. He had not noticed her before, nor seen any signs of anyone being in the woods except himself. She was just suddenly there. He scanned his surroundings, searching for any indication of where she might have come from or where she might be going. But there was nothing, no path or trail, no sign of a cottage or dwelling. It was as if she had simply appeared out of thin air, a haunting presence in the midst of the tranquil riverbank. He couldn't shake the feeling that she was not just an ordinary woman, but something far more mysterious and otherworldly.

He approached the edge of the bank, intent on getting a better view of her to assure himself that she was not a figment of his imagination. Or worse, that she was not one of Mora's coven who was following him.

As he drew closer he could see she was an elderly woman advanced in age, too old in his opinion to be alone in woods and standing in icy water doing laundry. She was dressed in green ragged clothing and a dingy white bonnet with locks of wispy grey hair protruding from underneath. She was bent over, reaching into the water as she sang a mournful song of sorrow. There wasn't anything very distinctive about her; she appeared just as any elderly woman would, so there was nothing that would cause concern for Drustan to find her there, except for the fact that she was there at all.

"Greetings!" He called to the woman. He hoped that she could give him directions to set him on the quickest path to the castle that lay deep within the Caledonian Forest.

She ceased her song and turned to peer at him for a moment. Otherwise, she paid him no mind and quickly went back to her chore.

"Perchance can you help me?" Drustan asked and he began to wade into the water toward her.

She continued washing, and continued to disregard him. As he drew closer, he saw what made her work so diligently. In her hands was a long white cloth stained with blood. It appeared to be a burial shroud. She beat the cloth against the rocks, washing and scrubbing but the blood remained despite her best efforts. Beside her, a rock protruded above the water and on it laid another shroud; this one was neatly folded and white as snow.

As Drustan laid eyes upon the bloody shroud, a paralyzing fear took hold of him as he realized the identity of the woman before him. She was the Bean Nighe, the washerwoman; a dark faerie and cousin to the banshee. She was a harbinger of death that wandered near streams and washed the blood from the grave clothes of those who were about to die. According to his mother's tales, the Bean Nighe was a death omen, a warning that the one who encountered her would be touched by the hand of death. If asked politely, she would reveal the names of the ones who were marked for death. But her answers were often given in riddles and rhymes, if she felt so inclined to speak plainly at all.

As Drustan looked upon the two shrouds, one covered in blood and the other white as snow and unblemished, he began to back away, feeling the weight of the Bean Nighe's ominous presence. Though she was only a messenger and not the cause of death, she was still one to be feared. Her faerie nature was known to be spiteful and mean if provoked.

Drustan turned to flee, but when he turned, he was startled to find himself face to face with the Bean Nighe once more. The unexpected confrontation caused him to stumbled backward and he fell into the freezing water.

The Bean Nighe's eyes glinted with an otherworldly light as she leaned over Drustan, holding out the two shrouds for him to see. "There are two," she spoke in a voice that was like the whisper of the dead. "One is due, and one must wait. Thou must choose and seal thy fate."

Drustan's heart thundered in his chest as he gazed upon the two shrouds. One stained with blood, the other as white as snow and unblemished. He didn't understand what the Bean Nighe wanted from him. Was she offering him a choice between life and death? He didn't know what to think.

He remembered his mother's tales of the Bean Nighe, that she came bearing tidings of death. But Drustan remembered nothing about being given a choice.

He hesitated, not wanting to know if death was at hand. But as he looked into the Bean Nighe's eyes, he saw that she was not just a messenger of death, but also a guide, offering him a chance to avoid it. He took a deep breath and ventured the question.

"Tell me, good woman," he said politely. "Whose shrouds do you tend? Have you come to foretell my death?

"Two hunters draw nigh, one will live one will die." The old woman answered with a sinister smile. She then turned away and headed across the ford, singing a woeful tune as she disappeared into the woods.

> "When the fire rages and the woods crack,
> Guard thyself he's at thy back!
> One crown of gold and the other of red.
> Blood for vengeance or blood for his head.
> Who will bleed from the choice ye make,
> Run and die, or his crown ye take."

Even after she was out of sight, Drustan could hear her voice and the strange warning she had issued. He stood up out of the water, shivering from the cold and hurried back to the bank. Wrapping his cloak tightly around him for warmth, he sat and considered the meaning of the Bean Nighe's words and her strange song.

She had delivered a warning that he was in danger, and it was clear that he would come into conflict with an adversary, one she called a hunter. But the song and its meaning were obscure. What did she mean by a raging fire or crowns of gold and red? It made little sense to him, but he knew the words were a warning and he had to discover the meaning.

The encounter had been unnerving, but despite the warning Drustan was determined not to let the Bean Nighe's appearance dissuade him from his quest. The Bean Nighe had warned him of danger, but she had not actually foretold his death. Ultimately, it seemed that she had left the matter in his own hands, and his fate up to his own actions. Therefore, he decided that he would heed the warning and be alert; but for now, he thought it best to put as much distance between him and the washer-woman as possible. After all, she was a faerie of sorts, and as such, she had the ability to cause death as much as predict it.

Choosing the western branch of the stream, which fortunately diverged from the path taken by the Bean Nighe, Drustan pressed onward with renewed resolve. His feet splashed through the shallow water as he trudged steadily towards the west. Coming face to face with the legendary Ben Nighe had left him shaken, but he remained resolute in the face of adversity. A task awaited completion, and he would not allow a cryptic warning from an enigmatic faerie to hinder his progress.

As he walked, he kept his senses sharp, scanning the woods around him for any sign of danger. He knew that the hunter the Bean Nighe had spoken of could be anywhere, and he couldn't let his guard down for even a moment. He clutched his sword tightly, ready to defend himself in the event that this hunter should appear.

As the day wore on, Drustan's mind kept returning to the Bean Nighe's words. "Two hunters draw nigh; one will live one will die." He couldn't shake the feeling that the hunter she had spoken of was not just some random predator, but a specific person, someone with a grudge against him. He couldn't shake the feeling that the hunter was someone who he had wronged in the past.

The more he thought about it, the more Drustan realized that the Bean Nighe's warning was not just about the hunter, but also about the choices he would have to make. The crowns of gold and red, the blood for vengeance or blood for his head. He knew that he would have to make a difficult decision, and that the outcome would depend on his actions.

With this realization, Drustan felt a renewed sense of determination. He would not let the Bean Nighe's warning defeat him. He would be vigilant, and he would be ready to face whatever challenges lay ahead. With his sword in hand, he pushed on, determined to reach his destination and complete his quest.

As the light filtering through the dense forest canopy began to fade, Drustan knew it was time to find a suitable spot to set up camp for the night. He had hoped to have returned to the road before nightfall and avoid having to camp in the forest overnight, but the road was still nowhere in sight and he did not want to risk being caught by the darkness while trying to reach it. So his thoughts turned to finding the first secluded and safe place he could to set up camp..

As he trudged deeper into the woods, the ground beneath his feet began to rise and he soon found himself standing before an ancient clearing. The ruins of an old castle or fortress lay before him, their stones and rubble scattered haphazardly across the ground. The remains of a stone floor, cracked and moss-covered, stretched out before him. To one side, the crumbling remains of a wall stood, the tallest point barely reaching his waist.

Drustan's mood lifted as he realized the potential shelter this forgotten place could provide. With a sense of relief, Drustan quickly set to work, gathering dry wood and kindling to start a fire. As the last rays of sunlight danced across the clearing, he carefully nurtured the flames, watching as they grew stronger and brighter with each passing moment.

As the fire crackled and roared, Drustan shed himself of his still-damp clothing and placed them near the flames to dry. Wrapping himself in his cloak, he settled himself against the remaining wall, using it as a windbreak as the cool autumn night descended upon him. The heat of the fire chased away the chill that had seeped into his bones, and he felt a sense of comfort and safety wash over him as he curled up against the ancient stone.

The ruins were eerie and forlorn, but Drustan found

comfort in their solidity, grateful for the protection they provided as he bedded down for the night. He rested his back against the wall, listening to the crackle of the fire and the whispering of the wind through the trees, reflecting on the strange and unexpected twist his journey had taken.

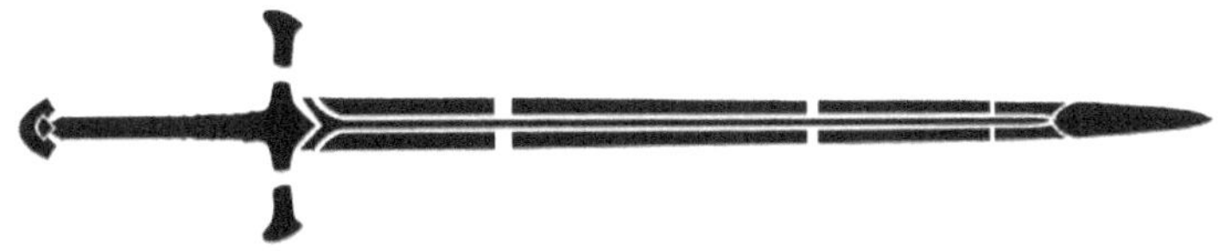

CHAPTER 7

A Life for a Life

"Who dares enter my domain?" The ancient witch Laine spat, her voice a jagged symphony of cracks and rasps. In her gnarled hands she gripped a torch and a dagger. The flickering light danced across her twisted features, casting eerie shadows on the dark stone walls. "Show thy face!"

"Peace, Laine," Raum's voice was smooth and cold as he emerged from the darkness, his fledgling vampire by his side. "She has summoned me."

As he approached the withered old witch, her expression softened with recognition, but her eyes remained narrowed with suspicion. "Where hast thou been?" she demanded, her dagger still aimed in his direction. "Thou wast summoned in the dead of night, and she hath cried out for thee in agony these many hours since."

"I was in pursuit of the young maiden she had tasked me to find," he replied coolly. "I did not hear of her need until I returned to my sanctum at dawn. Once there, I could not leave until sunset."

But Raum's words were nothing more than a well-crafted lie. He had known of Mora's encounter with Sibby as it was happening. After encouraging Mora to make the unprepared assault, he wanted to see the results of his handiwork with his own eyes. So, he had been there watching from a distance, hidden in the shadows. He witnessed Mora's resounding defeat and watched with satisfaction as she was struck by the enchanted arrow. As he watched her being whisked away by her fellow witches, he thought Mora was surely dead.

When he received word of Mora's summons, the only surprise was that she still lived. He already knew what the summons concerned and his delay was intentional. There was plenty of time for him to have safely reached the castle before sunrise, yet, he had chosen not to come, hoping that without the healing power of his blood, Mora would succumb to her wound and die.

Laine was not fooled by Raum's excuse. She could sense the deception in his words, and a hint of malice danced in her eyes.

She had sent word to him as soon as they returned from their confrontation with Sibby, and she had waited impatiently for him throughout the night and day until he finally arrived at sunset. Her anger at him was palpable, but she was relieved to that he had finally appeared.

She stepped closer, holding her torch high to get a clear look at the vampire who accompanied him. The fledgling recoiled at her appearance, her stench overwhelming and repulsive. Laine was the most unsavory member of the coven, as revolting as the depths of hell itself. He pulled out a handkerchief to cover his nose and mouth, while Raum looked on with amusement as the young vampire's disgust for the witch mirrored his own.

"So, I'm here now, take me to her." Raum feigned concern, when in fact he could barely hide the smirk on his face. "Does she still live?"

"She doth suffer greatly, and even now she barely clings to life."

"How can this be that she was so fatally wounded? Has Isabel grown so powerful that she could defeat Mora?"

"'Twas not the pellar witch who wrought this misdeed, but the son. He stood against us, aiming with deadly precision and unleashing enchanted arrows upon our company. His skill with the bow was as deadly as the great horned god Cernunnos. But enough of this talk, ye must make haste to Mora ere it be too late. She is nigh unto death."

"Then we are to be free of her," Jaret, the fledgling vampire who accompanied Raum whispered.

"How dare thee speak such impiety!" screeched Laine in a fit of fury, her rotted teeth bared and drool dripping from her twisted lips as she glared at him with unrestrained rage. "I should burn thee to ashes where thou dost stand for thy audacity."

The vampire cowered and recoiled, stepping behind Raum for protection.

"Control yourself, witch, or it will be you who finds yourself on the pyre," Raum threatened, his voice low and menacing. "Now, take me to your mistress then be gone from my sight. Your foul stench is an abomination, even to the dead."

Laine paid no heed to the insult, her focus fixed else-where. "She doth rest in the great hall," she said, and handed him the torch, "Go forth, and I shall remain here to keep watch. We sense the witch hunter's presence drawing near."

Raum was taken aback, "A witch hunter? I know of no such presence in the kingdom."

"The bastard of the white witch," Laine lowered her voice as if speaking of him would draw him closer. "He is a merciless killer, taking the lives of our sisters with-out a second thought. And now, the omens doth scream out in warning, foretelling that he doth hunt us all."

Again, Raum could barely disguise his pleasure but having witnessed the battle himself enabled him to hide his pleasure. He despised the coven and if it were not for fear of Mora's power, he would kill them all himself. "Then by all means, remain here at watch." *Maybe when he comes, he'll cut you down first*, he thought as he ac-cepted the torch that Laine offered.

The two vampires crept down the shadowy, forebod-ing corridor, the darkness swallowing them whole as they delved deeper into the castle's abyssal depths. The black walls seemed to close in around them, the air thick with the weight of centuries and the echoes of past atrocities.

"When this is over and we've broken free from the Mora's clutches," Raum murmured to Jaret, his voice low and full of malice, "remind me to track down this witch hunter."

"You would seek to avenge the coven?" Jaret que-ried, his voice laced with confusion.

"No, my son," Raum scoffed, his eyes alight with a

dangerous glint. "Such formidable prowess and deadly talents must not go to waste. I'll reward him with immortality, an honored place amongst us."

"But the witches will not take kindly to this."

"What witches?" Raum gave a devilish laugh that sent shivers down Jaret's spine. "If all goes according to plan, they'll be nothing but ashes by the end of the night. But if not, we'll have our own hunter to deal with the problem."

As they ventured deeper into the bowels of the castle, the sense of foreboding grew stronger with each step. The air was thick with the stench of decay and death, and the ancient stones seemed to whisper secrets of terror and despair. Finally, they reached the great hall, and the sight that greeted them was one of pure nightmare.

Mora lay before them, her body stretched out on a wooden table as if in a funeral procession. But she was not at peace. Her eyes were open and unseeing, her face twisted in a rictus of fear and pain. Thick quilts had been placed underneath her, but they offered little comfort against the cold, hard surface. The room was dimly lit by flickering candles, and the remaining witches were positioned in each corner, swaying back and forth with thuribles in hand, filling the air with the acrid smoke of burning incense. They mumbled incantations in low, guttural voices, their words twisted and distorted by the echoes of the castle. As Raum approached, the witches began to wail loudly, their voices rising in a crescendo of mourning and despair, as if to underscore the true horror of the scene before them.

"She is dead?" Raum asked, his voice tinged with

a hint of malice. He knew the answer already, for his preternatural senses had already told him the truth. He could feel the faint flicker of her body heat, and the slow, steady beat of her heart. He was disappointed.

The witches, their eyes filled with tears, looked to him with hope and desperation. They had called upon him in their hour of need, hoping his vampire blood could heal their dying mistress.

Raum suppressed a smirk, secretly relishing the sight of Mora's impending demise.

"I yet live," Mora responded weakly and extended her hand toward him. "Come hither to me."

Raum stepped to the side of the table and looked upon her. She was a grotesque sight to behold, her once powerful and regal presence now reduced to a pitiful, rotting form. Her skin was a sickly grayish-blue, flaking away in patches to reveal the bones and tendons beneath. Her eyes were dull and clouded, the light of life all but extinguished. Long gray hairs had fallen from her head and lay in clumps on the table where she rested her head and on the floor beneath the altar. The stench of death and decay filled the room, making it hard to breath. In her left upper shoulder, the offending arrow remained, its poisoned tip still embedded deep in her flesh, spreading its deadly toxins throughout her body. The blackened streaks radiating outward from the wound were a grim reminder of the poison's deadly progress, the flesh around it was rotting and putrid. There was no doubt that she was on the verge of death.

Raum was shocked by her appearance, but rather pleased to see her in such a condition. When he had goaded her into attacking Isabel without delay or forethought, he had hoped that she would put herself in harm's way, this outcome was far beyond what he could have hoped. Mora had underestimated her adversary's abilities, and now she was suffering the fatal consequences of her arrogance.

The irony of the situation was not wasted on Raum. The boy, who was supposed to be nothing more than a sacrifice in Mora's grand scheme to restore her youth and power, was now the very instrument of her demise. The very seed she had sown had blossomed into the thorn that pricked her downfall.

Mora lay before him, twisted and rotting, like a macabre trophy of his own treachery and ambition. He couldn't help but feel a sense of satisfaction and triumph as he stood over her, relishing in the knowledge that he had played a crucial role in her downfall. The bitter taste of victory was sweeter than any elixir of immortality.

"I must have the dark blood," Mora spoke, her voice barely audible and her eyes pleading.

Raum stood there, relishing the sight of Mora's downfall. He would have preferred to have remained there for however long it took for her to waste away in death. But as the poison worked its deadly magic, as he saw the agony contort her face, a seed of pity sprouted in his heart. After all, it was she who had given him the gift of immortality. He owed her for that at least. Perhaps, he thought, he could use his blood to ease her suffering and in doing so, gain her favor and freedom for his clan.

He examined the wound again. It was clear that Mora was beyond saving. But out of a sense of obligation and for prudence, he decided to make a show of trying, in case by some miracle she did survive. And in the event that she died, he wanted to make sure Laine and the remaining coven would not blame him for it.

Raum's eyes roamed over Mora's body, taking in the grotesque sight of her decaying flesh that had been eaten away to reveal the bones beneath in some spots. The stench of rot and death hung thick in the air, making it hard for him to breathe. He knew that even the power of his blood would not be enough to heal her mortal flesh.

"Dark Mother," he said, his voice low and grave, "I'm afraid the most my blood can do is to ease your pain, but to heal you is beyond my power." The pain and desperation was plainly visible on her face, and he knew that death would be a mercy for her. "If you wish, I can end your suffering and put you out of your misery." He offered her the kindness of a peaceful death, but the final decision was hers to make.

"No, death will not take me this day," Mora said weakly, her voice barely audible. "'Twas your hand that has failed and brought me to the brink of destruction. This mortal shell is wilting, but the power it contains remains strong. Do not mistake the weakness of my flesh for vulnerability, I wield power even in death. Retribution will fall upon you and your children." Her eyes were filled with anger and her words full of threat.

"I will do what I can," he said, his voice as cold as the witch's heart. The fleeting compassion he had felt for her was now a distant memory, replaced by a deep-seated contempt.

"Why has the arrow not been removed?" He barked

at the witches, his anger simmering just below the surface. "Left in place, it continues to poison her like a venomous snake."

"We have tried to remove it," one of the witches stammered, her voice trembling with fear and frustration. "But she is in too much pain, and the arrowhead will not dislodge, as if it were fused to her very bones."

"Sit her up," he commanded, his voice ringing with authority. The witches quickly obeyed, lifting Mora's fragile body so that she was in a sitting position. She let out a soft cry of agony as they moved her, her head lolling forward and her breath coming in ragged gasps.

Raum approached Mora with a sense of callous detachment, his only concern being the removal of the arrow. He firmly grasped the shaft of the arrow and with a warning to Mora, "this is going to hurt," he brutally shoved the arrow through her shoulder. The crunch of bone and the anguished scream that ripped from her throat was music to his ears. Without hesitation, he grasped the arrow from behind and with a swift tug, pulled it through her back, eliciting another scream of pain. The witches recoiled in horror at his actions, but he paid them no mind, his focus solely on the task at hand.

"Lay her back down now," Raum commanded, his tone firm yet measured. The witches carefully lowered Mora's frail body onto the table, her moans of pain filling the air as they did so..

Raum's eyes were locked on the arrow, taking in every detail of the intricate craftsmanship of the iron and silver arrowhead and the symbols engraved onto the arrow's shaft. He could feel the weight of destiny in his hands as he considered the prospect of using it to eliminate Mora with a single strike to the heart.

But with that move, he knew would come with dire consequences. The coven of four witches stood only a few steps away, their eyes fixed on him, waiting for him to make his next move. He could feel their power emanating from them, and knew that if he were to strike, they would strike back with all their might.

Raum was certain of his own strength and abilities, but perhaps his confidence was misplaced. Though he had only been a vampire for two decades, the witches he faced were ancient beings, with centuries of experience and power behind them. He couldn't help but wonder if he was underestimating their abilities. Even if he could defend himself, his companion Jaret was still a fledgling vampire, his powers untested and fragile. Jaret would be no match for the witches' wrath.

Mora's warning still rang in his ears. "Do not mistake the weakness of my flesh for vulnerability," she had whispered, her eyes locked with his. "I wield power even in death."

Who knew what kind of power Mora still possessed, even as she edged closer to death.

Raum's heart pounded as he frantically searched for a way out of the predicament, his mind racing with possibilities, each one leading to either victory or defeat. The tension was palpable as he stood there, the deadly arrow in hand, one move away from determining their fate. He couldn't help but consider the possibility of sacrificing Jaret, his son in the dark blood, in order to rid himself of the powerful witch Mora. But ultimately, he knew he couldn't bring himself to do it. Jaret was his blood now, born of his dark power, and he couldn't risk bringing about his death. With a deep breath, Raum made his decision, he tossed the arrow aside and prepared for whatever lay ahead. The weight of the moment was heavy on his shoulders as he knew this decision could be a fatal one but his love for his child was stronger than his hatred of the witches.

He turned his attention to Mora, how to save her rather than killing her. He bit into his wrist and held his arm over her open wound so that the blood dripped down into it. He watched closely for the flesh to respond, but there was nothing. The tissue around the wound was dead and though his dark blood was powerful enough to sustain life, it could not resurrect something already dead.

"The wound does not mend," he pronounced after a few moments. He withdrew his arm and licked the bite on his wrist so that it immediately healed. He was both surprised and relieved that there was no change in her condition. If his blood cannot heal the wound then she would surely die.

"'Tis a powerful curse that plagues me," Mora gasped, her body wracked with pain. "I must taste the dark gift."

Raum walked to a nearby table, picking up the chalice that had held his blood many times before. He unsheathed his dagger, preparing to open his wrist once again.

"No," Mora said, her voice barely audible. "A mere cup will not suffice. To survive this night, I require not just the blood, but the life force of a vampire."

For centuries, Mora, like many black witches, had consumed small amounts of vampire blood on a regular basis to sustain her own life and heal injuries and illnesses. But this wound was not a typical injury; it was a fatal curse. It could not be healed so easily. In dire circumstances like this, when a small amount of blood could not work, a much larger sacrifice was required. Mora needed not only the dark blood, but also the life essence of a vampire. She needed his life force.

"You would demand my own life to save thine?" Raum asked, his voice trembling with shock and horror.

"Not you, my most trusted advisor," Mora replied, her eyes flitting around the chamber. "But one of your own must be offered up."

"I cannot sacrifice the life of one of my children. They are born of my blood, my legacy."

"Then you would condemn me to death," Mora said, her voice growing weaker.

"I cannot sacrifice one of my children any more than you would sacrifice one of your sister witches," Raum replied, his voice filled with conviction.

Mora let out a bitter laugh, coughing as she did so. She raised her hand and pointed across the chamber. Suddenly, the arrow that had been pulled from her shoulder and discarded earlier, flew through the air with the force of a bowstring, striking one of the coven witches in the chest. She burst into flames, leaving nothing but ashes where she had once stood.

"I value no life above my own," Mora said, her gaze fixed on Raum. "As should you. Sacrifice thyself or offer one of your own."

As Mora's words hung heavy in the air, the remaining three witches cowered back in fear, their hearts pounding in their chests. The reality of the situation was becoming clearer with each passing moment, and the gravity of the sacrifice required was not lost on them.

As Raum watched Mora unleash her deadly magic, a shiver of fear ran through him. He could see the raw power emanating from her, even as she lay dying. He realized that his assumption of her impending demise was a grave mistake, and his apprehension grew as he felt the weight of her desperation bearing down upon him.

Raum realized too late that he had underestimated her strength and by not plunging the deadly arrow into her black heart when he had the opportunity was a grievous mistake. He struggled for a means to appease her, to save himself and his son from her judgment. Fortunately, fate had dealt Raum one final hand, and he knew that he could not keep it hidden any longer..

"Last eve we found the girl you seek," Raum spoke with trepidation. "A virgin who conceived in violence. She is heavily with child and close to giving birth. Surely, she will be the one to save you."

"Are you certain this is the one?" Mora demanded, her eyes boring into Raum's. "Where is she? Bring her to me now."

"She is as I described," Raum lied, "Found in a small village on the border of York. She's already on the road and will be here in three days' time."

"Three days!" Laine screeched as she entered the chamber. "Our mistress hath not three days! I'll dispatch my sisters to fetch her, and they shall bring her hither within the hour."

"You'll terrify her," Raum said, his voice dripping with sarcasm. "Being picked up by a group of witches like a field mouse in an owl's talons. She'll die of fear or harm the baby trying to escape."

"Then she'll arrive kicking and screaming if need be," Laine snarled.

"Then why not just rip the baby out of her along the roadside?" Raum retorted.

Mora raised her hand to silence their bickering. "My sister speaks truly," she said. "I will not survive three days to see the girl's arrival, but neither can we risk harming the child. The girl must come to us willingly for the magic to work."

"Indeed, she shall come willingly," Raum stated, glancing briefly at Laine. "But only if she is not frightened."

"Then bring her with haste. But I must have the dark blood this night, or I am lost."

With a wave of his hand, Raum summoned Jaret forward, and he advanced with hesitancy in his step. The young vampire had never before been in the presence of Mora and her coven, and the atrocities he had already beheld had filled him with a dread beyond measure. As a newly turned vampire, with his powers still in their infancy, the scene before him was a foreign and terrifying landscape.

Offering his blood to Mora was a rite of passage for each vampire. The rite served as a symbol of her dominion over the vampire clan. Once the vampire's offering was completed, he was accepted into the fold and placed under the Mora's protection. Thereafter, whenever Mora needed the dark blood, it would be up to Raum to decide which of his children would provide the offering. Tonight, this was more significant than the usual rite of passage. Mora desired more this time than a small chalice.

"Together we will both share our blood. Surely, that will suffice to preserve your life until the maiden arrives to make you whole again."

"'Tis not the dark blood I require, but the life force within it. Thy blood has not healed my wound and I continue to waste away. To take me from death's reach there must be a life for a life. That is what is required."

"There must be another way," Raum protested, desperate to find a solution that would not involve Jaret's sacrifice. But Mora was firm in her demands. She lifted her hand and pointed to the young vampire, her voice commanding. "You will give yourself to me."

Jaret looked at Raum in terror, his eyes begging for his dark father to rescue him from this fate.

"No, you will not have him!" Raum shouted defiantly, standing between Mora and Jaret.

But Mora was unyielding. "Sisters," she said, her voice cold and commanding, "collect my offering."

The witches descended upon the young vampire, Jaret, with a fierce determination. He fought against them with all his might, but despite his efforts, the coven's power proved too great. Raum tried to intervene, but before he could, Mora waved her hand and an invisible force cast him from the room, the heavy wooden doors slamming shut behind him, locking him out.

Raum could hear Jaret's screams from within, and with a roar of fury, he threw himself against the door, pounding and battering it with all his might. He flung his body against it desperately, trying to break through, but even under his immense strength, the door would not budge. His cries of frustration and anger filled the air as he realized he was powerless to save his child.

Beyond the locked doors the coven witches overpowered Jaret, holding him firmly in place as they forced him to his knees. He struggled against them, his muscles straining with all his might, but despite his own supernatural strength, he was unable to break free. It was not just their physical strength that held him captive. It was their dark power that kept him bound, rendering him helpless.

He cried out for Raum in terror as one of the witches brought a dagger to his throat, while the others helped Mora to stand. They removed her robes, revealing her emaciated and decaying body. Her sagging, leathery skin was marbled like a corpse, chunks of flesh hanging from her bones and the wound in her shoulder wept black puss.

She looked upon the trembling vampire with a twisted smile and a look of hunger in her eyes. With a quick nod to the witch holding the blade, the sacrifice began.

In one swift stroke, the hag drew the blade across the vampire's throat and blood gushed into the awaiting basin. Jaret continued to struggle, his vampire blood keeping him alive even when a mortal man would have already died. The witch struck the blade across his throat repeatedly; hacking at the flesh, brutally chopping until his head was completely severed from the body. She held the head above the basin until the blood ceased to flow, then tossed it across the floor. Once the last of the blood drained from the vampire's body, they tossed it to the side as well. A moment later, the vampire's lifeless remains began to melt into a mess of sludge.

Immediately, the witches dipped their hands into the basin and began to massage the blood over Mora's gray flesh, painting her from head to toe. When she was completely covered in the blood, Mora raised her arms outward and began to chant a spell.

"Sevan yecht valam," she cried out as if she were pleading with a hidden spirit. She repeated the incantation over and over, and with each refrain her voice grew stronger and her stature more robust. Finally, she picked up the basin, raised it to her lips, and drank the remaining blood.

With his vampire son's cries for help ringing in his ears, Raum continued battering the heavily bolted chamber door, his preternatural senses on high alert. The smell of spilled blood filled the air, and he could hear the beat of Jaret's heart fading away. The pain of his companion's death was like a physical blow to Raum, as if it were his own child that had been taken from him, for in the vampire world, Jaret was just that - a son of Raum. With a heavy heart, Raum's struggles came to an end as he heard the final beat of Jaret's heart. He sank down to the floor, his hands bloody and torn from pounding and scratching at the door in a desperate attempt to save Jaret. Realizing his failure, he curled up against the stone wall and sobbed uncontrollably.

Hearing the sound of the heavy door unlock, Raum stormed into the chamber, shoving aside the coven witches as if they were nothing more than mere nuisances. As he fell to his knees beside the pool of disintegrating remains of his beloved Jaret, tears of grief streamed down his face. He paused for a moment of sorrowful reflection, his heart heavy with the weight of his loss. But as he rose to his feet, the fire of rage burned brightly within him, and he strode towards Mora, who now seated on her throne, her body naked and glistening with the blood of his kin.

Despite her apparent strength and recovery, the wound from the arrow was still clearly visible, still seeping with the black ooze of infection. And in that moment, Raum knew that he would not rest until he had avenged his fallen son.

She saw him looking at the wound. She raised her hand and lightly touched it. "Still it does not heal. By this time tomorrow, it will spread again, and by nightfall will require another sacrifice to hold death back."

Raum was overcome with anger and hatred. Abruptly, he clinched his fist and hit Mora with his full strength in the face. The witch flinched only slightly from the blow. He hit her again, then again, but to no avail. She remained undaunted. He prepared to strike her again, but as he swung, she caught his fist in her hand and held it.

"'Tis enough," she said calmly and clenched her hand around his, the bones in his knuckles snapping under the pressure. He cringed from the pain until he was on his knee, only then did she finally release her grip.

Raum clutched at his broken hand for a moment as the fingers once again straightened and the fractures healed spontaneously.

"You took my son's life, stole his immortality, just so you could live one more night," rage still filled him. "You shall have no more of our blood!"

"Do you take me for a fool?" The witch bellowed at him. "'Tis thy failure to deliver the maid and her unborn child that brought this consequence. Thy son's blood is on your hands. Until she is brought to me, one of your children will be taken each night to sustain my life."

Raum came to the crushing realization that by concealing the girl, he was just as culpable for Jaret's death as the witches. He had tried to stall and postpone, hoping that Mora would succumb to her injury, but it had only led to the loss of his own son. He realized that if he had plunged the cursed arrow into Mora's heart when he had the opportunity, it would have been a more merciful outcome. Now, it was clear that Mora intended to punish him for his failure to deliver the girl and she would do so in the most devastating way possible.

"As a comfort, know that once I have the girl and the spell is done, it will be centuries before I will have need of the dark blood again."

Though Mora had imbibed the vampire blood, she remained mortal, the passage of time only slowed to an excruciating crawl. The blood gifted her an extended life, but she knew she was not exempt from the clutches of old age, destined to face mortality like any other human.

Yet, her ambition knew no bounds. She sought a spell, a dark and forbidden ritual that required a young girl and her unborn child. With a sinister plan in mind, Mora envisioned shedding her own mortal shell and stealing the infant's life force, thus bestowing upon herself the gifts of prolonged youth and vitality. No longer would she age in mere years; instead, she would bask in centuries of unending existence, an allure beyond the grasp of ordinary mortals.

This twisted prize of eternal youth was the driving force behind Mora's actions. There was no limit to what she would do to attain it, no matter how wicked the path she tread. The innocent girl and the unborn child were mere means to an end, as she ventured forth with unwavering determination, embracing the darkness that consumed her soul.

Her heart was cold and black, devoid of compassion, and she felt no qualms about the consequences of her malevolent desires. In her relentless pursuit, Mora had forsaken her humanity, casting aside any semblance of moral restraint.

The ultimate goal loomed on the horizon—centuries of stolen life force, perpetuating her existence until she would need to repeat the sinister ritual once more. No remorse held her back, for she was consumed by the allure of eternal life.

In her world, where the boundaries of morality blurred into shadows, Mora's dark tale unfurled. A haunting symphony of malevolence guided her actions, driving her closer to the culmination of her sinister ambitions. "With each passing day, the price you must pay grows greater," Mora declared, her eyes narrowing with suspicion as she sensed Raum's intentional procrastination. "You will bring her to me, and only then will our pact be fulfilled. But know this, Raum, your debt to me will never be fully paid."

Mora let out a chilling laugh, relishing in the power she held over him. "I have bestowed upon you immortality, and with it, eternal servitude. As long as the dark blood flows through your veins, as long as you walk this earth, you and all thy children belong to me. *Forever.*"

"Be damned, witch!" he thundered, his anger reaching a boiling point. "A life for a life! 'Tis your own words! You gave me immortality, but in return, you took it from my son. The scales are balanced, my debt is paid. I will fulfill my end of the bargain and bring you the girl, but mark my words, if you ever speak my name or seek me out again, I will consume thee with fire."

Mora sneered at him, her power radiating off of her in waves. "You dare to threaten me? I could snuff out your existence and that of your spawn with a mere thought. You belong to me!"

He stood tall and met her gaze unflinchingly. "Kill us if you must, we will be free of you one way or another. But know this, harm me or my clan and the maid you so desire will be ripped to shreds."

She took a moment to weigh her options, her mind racing as she considered the ramifications of her next move. She knew Raum all too well. His unbridled anger and his relentless pursuit of vengeance were all too clear in her mind, and he was not one to make empty threats. He would fight to his dying breath rather than submit and accept defeat.

"As your wish," she finally relented, realizing there was no reason for this struggle of wills. "Once I have the woman and the spell is cast, I will have no need of you or thy children. Deliver the girl and you may go free."

"I'll have your word, or the girl dies," he warned her, his voice low and dangerous.

"Aye, I give thee my word," she replied coolly. "But there is one more thing you must do. You must give me a vial of thy blood, for future use."

"For what purpose? So you can cast a spell on me?"

"No, my dear," she replied with a sly smile. "I would not waste such a valuable commodity for mere amusement. You, of all people, know its true purpose."

Raum knew all too well the true purpose of the blood. Though it may take centuries, someday she would once again need the dark blood to sustain her. The vial would be used by Mora to create a new vampire servant, a blood source to fend off death. He also suspected that Laine and the remaining witches would seek the dark blood as well. As long as he and his family were free of the coven and not the ones feeding their blood thirst, Raum would willingly fulfill her request.

"Then so be it," Raum declared, his voice resolute.

"Our deal is sealed," Mora said. "But be warned, if your brood defiles the girl in any way, she will be worthless to me. Her blood must be untainted and the child pure. If not, your children will pay the price."

"Do not worry. If she is the price for our freedom, then I will guard her with my life."

"As well you should. And Raum, I would have the girl at sunset."

Raum, dipped his head in agreement.

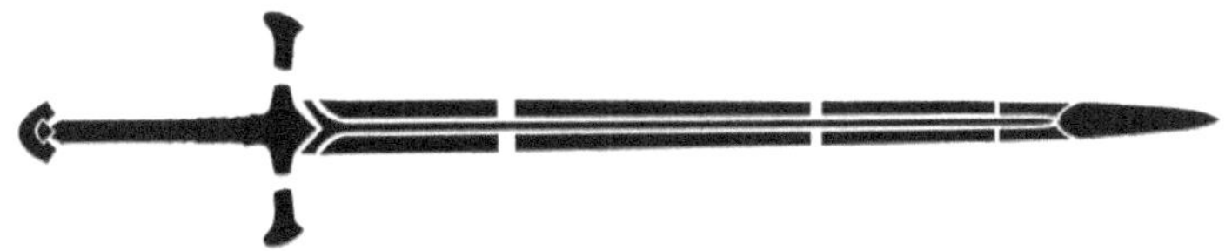

CHAPTER 8

The Redcap Goblin

As the night air grew colder, Drustan added more wood to the crackling fire. He gingerly picked up his clothing, which he had laid out to dry. With relief, he found that they were now toasty warm and ready to wear. He quickly slipped into his garments, returning to his spot by the wall. Wrapping his cloak tightly around himself, he allowed himself to sink into the comforting warmth of the fire.

He couldn't take his eyes off the mesmerizing dance of the flames, his lids heavy with exhaustion as sleep slowly crept up on him. It had been a grueling day, and he welcomed the chance to rest. But just as he was on the brink of slumber, the snap of a twig jolted him awake, sending his heart racing. Was it just the fire's crackling embers or something more ominous lurking in the darkness? He scanned the shadows, but saw nothing out of the ordinary. Shaking off his unease, he leaned back against the wall and lost himself once again in the mesmerizing glow of the fire.

Just as he had settled into a comfortable slumber, a

sharp crack echoed through the woods. Alerted by the sound, he jolted awake and quickly rose to his feet, unsheathing his sword with a swift motion. His eyes scanned the darkness, cautiously searching for anything out of the ordinary. He knew this was not the gentle crackling of the campfire.

With measured steps, he approached the trees, peering into the inky blackness. But there was nothing to be seen. He remained poised and ready for attack, listening intently to the forest sounds. Then, the words of the Bean Nighe came to mind: *When the fire rages and the woods crack, guard thyself, he's at thy back.*

With a sudden realization, he whirled around, and found himself facing an eerie and enigmatic figure. It was a short, gnarled old man, with long, tangled brown hair and a matching beard that hung in knotted disarray. His eyes were red and piercing, and his fat little fingers ended in sharp claws that looked like talons. Drustan was taken aback by the strange creature before him, studying him curiously. He noticed that the old man wore heavy black iron boots and a red cap, the latter of which was dripping with blood. At first, Drustan thought the dwarf had been injured, but then he realized the blood was not coming from the old man's head, but from the ominous red cap.

One crown of gold and the other of red. Blood for vengeance or blood for his head. The haunting melody of the washerwoman's song finally reveals its dark secrets to Drustan. With a shock, he realizes that the creature before him was the infamous Redcap goblin, the monster of legend his mother warned him of as a child.

Amidst the desolate remnants of ancient castles, The Redcap lurks, a malevolent specter, eager to ensnare unwitting wanderers who dare trespass into his domain. Swift as a lightning bolt, his enchanted iron boots grant him an unparalleled speed, leaving no chance of escape for those who cross his path. With merciless precision, he strikes when his prey least expects it, launching himself upon them in a frenzied assault. The Redcap revels in his savage spree, staining his cap with the life essence of those unfortunate enough to fall under his curse.

Its thirst for blood is insatiable, driving the Redcap to kill again and again in order to sustain its power and longevity. The Bean Nighe's warning rang clear in Drustan's mind - *run and die* – run from the thing and face certain death. It appeared the only hope to escape this monster's grasp was to face it head on, but legend states that no one has ever lived to tell the tale of facing the Redcap.

Drustan leapt back just in the nick of time to feel the wind from the Redcap's pike whisk by his hair as the spear's tip narrowly missed him. A grin swept across the dwarf's face as the two hunters watched a lock of Drustan's hair float to the ground, having been cut by the sharp blade of the pike.

Drustan raised his sword just as the goblin lunged at him again. The two weapons clashed in a shower of sparks as Drustan expertly blocked each attack. The Redcap kept coming, swinging and stabbing wildly, but Drustan stood his ground, using his sword to parry each thrust with grace.

The Redcap was relentless, and Drustan was struggling to keep up with the persistent attacks. He frantically searched his mind for a way out, trying to recall any stories his mother had told him about the deadly creatures. But all he could remember was the grim fate that befell those who encountered the Redcap - none survived.

Just when all hope seemed lost, a glimmer of an idea sparked in his mind. He remembered the warning from the Bean Nighe: *his crown ye must take*. "That's it!" He declared aloud. With renewed determination, Drustan realized the key to defeating the Redcap was its bloody cap.

Filled with newfound determination, Drustan squared off against his assailant. The Redcap lunged once more, but this time, instead of parrying the attack, Drustan seized the pike's shaft and exerted all his strength, yanking the goblin forward. In a sudden twist of fate, the two adversaries stood side by side. Looking up, the Redcap found Drustan towering above, wearing a smug smile of satisfaction. With lightning speed, Drustan snatched the blood-stained cap from the creature's head. The Redcap emitted a howl of fury, but it was an exercise in futility - its destiny had been irrevocably sealed.

Unsure of what would happen next, Drustan didn't waste a second. He bolted away at full speed, his heart pounding in his chest. But as he ran, he noticed something unexpected - there was no sound of pursuit from the goblin. He slowed down, his curiosity getting the better of him and cautiously glanced over his shoulder. What he saw made him stop in his tracks. The Redcap was motionless, frozen like a statue. Its pike was still extended, its head looking up. Drustan stood there, staring in disbelief.

With caution, Drustan approached the frozen Redcap, his steps slow and steady. He circled the goblin, observing its still form. As he drew nearer, he noticed a
change in the creature. Its skin was turning pale, aging
before his very eyes as life drained from its body. He
gazed down at the red cap in his hand, now noticing it
too was losing its vibrancy, the once-rich color fading
away like a dying ember.

"What is this?" Drustan mumbled, seeing blood all
over his hands that had dripped from the cap. It was more
of an observation than a question, so he was surprised to
receive an answer.

"'Tis the blood of the ones who came before thee."

Drustan was gobsmacked to hear the goblin respond.
He jumped back, his sword flashing as he prepared for
another brutal attack. But, to his disbelief, the Redcap remained frozen in place, as if suspended in time. Drustan
cautiously lowered his weapon, leaning in to get a closer
look at the dwarf's face. He was horrified to see the look
of pure malice etched on its features.

"You did speak, didn't you?" Drustan whispered, his
voice trembling. He wasn't sure if the thing had actually
answered of if it was some trick of his own mind.

As he studied the thing, the Redcap's eyes flickered
to life, fixing upon Drustan with an unblinking gaze. Despite its rigid, immobile form, it seemed to be following
Drustan's every move, watching him with malevolent intent. Drustan recoiled, feeling as if he was being hunted
by a monster that should have been dead.

"Aye, you asked, I answered," the Redcap replied.

Drustan looked at him with even more curiosity. Moments ago the thing had all intent on murdering him, but now it seemed to be ready for a conversation.

"Why did you attack me? What have I done to provoke you?"

"'Tis what I do. I need thy blood for my cap," the goblin replied. "Now, will you give it back so that I may go about my business?"

"Go about your business? And what is your business? How do I know you won't just try to kill me again?"

"Killing trespassers is my business. To use thy blood to color my cap."

Drustan laughed involuntarily. "That is not the best answer to give if you want to gain your freedom. Why would you speak so plainly?"

"I have no choice, you hold my cap."

Drustan looked at the cap curiously then back at the goblin. "You have no choice," he repeated the goblin's words with realization. "You must answer my questions because I have your cap?"

"Aye. 'Tis my curse."

"Why have I never heard of this? In the stories I was told, there was no mention that the Redcap would be compelled to answer my questions if I held his cap." Drustan was pondering the question aloud, again not intending for the goblin to answer, yet it did.

"Because no one has ever captured a Redcap goblin's cap before this moment."

Drustan straightened up with pride. "So, I am the first to defeat a Redcap goblin?"

"'Tis so."

"And you are bound to answer my questions, and answer truthfully?"

"Aye," the Redcap answered. "Will you let me go now?"

"That depends on how you answer the next questions I ask."

"Ask what you will and I shall speak truly. I can tell ye of thy future and the past if that is what you desire."

"I know my past already," Drustan replied in amusement. "As for my future, why would I trust you with that? You didn't foresee that I would steal thy cap, so I doubt your ability to see the future."

"Because the future is every changing, as a result of your thoughts and actions. When you started to believe you could prevail, your fate was no long in my hands but in thy own."

"Aye, I see what you mean. Still, why tell me of my future when I make it myself?"

"Then what do you seek?" The Redcap asked.

Drustan did not hesitate about what question to ask the goblin. He knew what information was most important to him at that moment.

"Tell me little man. What do you know of Mora the witch?"

"That she is a witch," was his simple reply.

"Do you know where she lives?"

"Nay, I know nothing about this Mora other than what you have just told me yourself. That she is a witch."

"That wasn't very helpful. You don't know of her?" Drustan was surprised. He assumed every foul creature knew all the others; that there was some sort of guild or at least some shared knowledge.

"I know her not. I remain in these woods and have no contact with any other living being, except those I kill."

"Then what good are you to me? Your knowledge of the world is as worthless as your foresight."

"None at all," the goblin answered truthfully.

Drustan chuckled at the goblin, amused that the creature had no choice but to indict himself and expose his own evil guilt with his answers.

"Tell me now. If I give you back your cap and set you free, what would happen?"

"I will be released and once again able to move."

"Ah, that's not the question and you know it," Drustan prodded. "If you are released and free to move, what will you do?"

"I will kill you and use thy blood to wet my cap."

"Well, you understand I cannot let that happen. One more question. If our fortunes were reversed, you in my shoes and I in your iron boots, what would you do?"

"I would run you through with my pike," the goblin responded, his tone reflecting the knowledge that he had just sealed his own fate.

"I suspected as much," Drustan said as he raised his sword high. "Sorry little man, but I can't let you do that."

With a swift blow Drustan chopped off the creature's head and the foul goblin disintegrated into dust before hitting the ground.

Drustan breathed a sigh of relief as he watched the remains of the Redcap blow away in the night breeze. He was about to toss the bloody cap into the darkness, but instead thought better of it. Not knowing the potential power held within the goblin's cap, he didn't want to discard it in the forest for someone or something to stumble upon. So, he tucked it into the waist of his pants and made his way back to his campsite.

He fed the fire with two more logs and watched it roar back to life. Then, he threw the bloody cap into the fire, relishing the moment of victory and relieved to have the thing gone. After ensuring that it was burned away, he finally returned to his resting place against a ruined stone wall.

His body was exhausted, but his mind was still alert. The excitement of the battle still had adrenaline coursing through his veins. He felt empowered and ready to face Mora and her witches.

It had been a day of strange encounters. The first was his encounter with the Bean Nighe and then the Redcap goblin. Each new encounter seemed to progress deeper into the unusual and strange. He wondered what the next day would bring and what extraordinary things he would find as he continued his journey.

Eventually, as the night passed and the fire died, Drustan grew weary. He closed his eyes and fell asleep. There were no dreams of the Bean Nighe or the Redcap. He slept peacefully, dreaming of faraway places, heroic battles, and big-bosomed barmaids in village taverns.

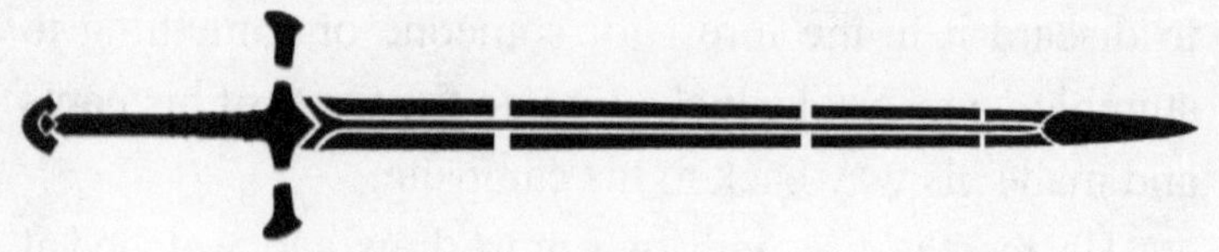

CHAPTER 9

A Father's Confession

In the cover of night, Raum stealthed through the darkness towards a dense thicket that guarded the entrance to a cavern. With a flick of his wrist, he pushed aside the overgrown branches and stepped through the rocky threshold. This secluded lair was where the vampire clan made their home, nestled in the side of a hill at the edge of the forest. They had chosen this location for its concealment and proximity to several villages and farms which were for now their hunting grounds.

As nomads of the night, the vampires were always on the move, never staying in one place for too long. Over-hunting an area would draw attention, so they roamed from one location to the next in search of fresh prey. Caves were their preferred dwelling, but they also made use of abandoned farmhouses and forgotten fortresses. Once they settled into a new place, they would feed on the unsuspecting villagers for several weeks before moving on to avoid detection.

Raum's clan, his cherished offspring, had been eagerly awaiting his return, fervently hoping for news of the witch's downfall. Seven sets of eyes, once eight, now haunted by the loss of Jaret at the hands of the witches, converged on Raum as he entered the cave. The room fell silent, as the tension mounted and Raum stood still, as if frozen in shock. His sorrow was palpable, and his clan could feel it weighing down on them like a heavy blanket. Raum strode towards the fire seeking its warmth before making his way to a towering rock that rose from the cave floor. He climbed atop it, crouching like a stone gargoyle, surveying his clan from his elevated perch, still silent, still stoic.

"Master," the vampire Byron finally broke the silence. "Where is our brother, Jaret? Did he not accompany you to Mora's castle?"

"He is gone," Raum growled. "She took him."

"What do you mean she took him?"

"She took him!" Raum bellowed. "The sickening hags took him!"

The vampires backed away in fear and cowered under his gaze. He turned silent, mournfully contemplating, but only for a moment. He looked at the confused and fearful expressions on his children's faces, and his temper softened. He realized that the loss of Jaret was a blow to them as well. They were Jaret's brothers and sisters and his loss would be greatly felt by each of them.

"They killed him," Raum repeated in a low defeated voice. "They drained him and used his blood in one of their rituals, so that Mora might live another night."

"How dare you let this happen?" Cailin, a fiery and impassioned female vampire, stepped forward, her eyes blazing with anger. "Jaret was our brother, our own blood! Your son!"

Cailin's heart was heavy with grief over the loss of Jaret. She had taken a special liking to him, seeing him as a younger brother, and had taken it upon herself to show him the ways of the vampire world. The thought of Jaret's untimely death left her feeling hollow and empty.

Raum let out a thunderous roar and rose to his feet, his eyes blazing with fury. "Allow? Allow?! I had no say in the matter! The witch took what she wanted, and there was nothing I could do to stop her. As she draws closer to death, her power only grows stronger and more unpredictable."

"You led him there like a sheep to the slaughter?" Cailin seethed. "You promised to protect him. You should have done so with your own life!"

Raum jumped down and in a flash had his hand around Cailin's throat lifting her into the air. "You dare speak to me in such a manner," he growled and exposed his teeth like a wolf. "I should rip your head off for your insolence."

"Do it," she spat, a fierce glint in her eye. "I'd rather face death by your hand than be a sacrificial lamb for that vile witch!"

Raum's eyes narrowed as he tightened his grip on her neck, causing her to cough and gasp for air as she desperately tried to pry his hand away. But he only tightened his hold, squeezing her throat with deadly force.

"Father, stop!" Byron cried out, his voice fraught with fear as he grabbed Raum's arm in a desperate attempt to save her.

Raum spun around, his gaze dark and deadly as he

bore down on Byron, ready to unleash his wrath upon them both.

"Father, I beg of you," Byron implored, his eyes wide with fear and his voice trembling. "She speaks from the shattered remains of her heart. Have mercy and forgive her."

Raum treasured Byron above all his other offspring, choosing him as his closest confidant and the son to stand by his side. In moments when Raum's temper boiled over, only Byron had the power to calm the storm. In that fateful moment, he stood fearless, using his soothing voice and wise words to quell his father's rage. Raum's grip on Cailin's neck was loosened, saving her from certain death.

Cailin crumpled to the floor, choking on the remnants of her nearly fatal struggle. But even as she struggled for breath, her eyes blazed with a fierce, indignant fire. With a single, fiery glance, she confronted Raum, her eyes blazing with a righteous wrath that spoke volumes about her unbreakable spirit.

Despite facing death itself, Cailin refused to back down, rising from the ashes of her near-defeat to challenge her master again. "And what price did your extract as payment for our brother's? How was he avenged?"

This time, it was Byron who stepped forward, his voice rising like a tempest as he bellowed, "Silence!" With a powerful blow, he struck Cailin, sending her tumbling to the ground. "I will not intervene to save thee a second time," he declared, his voice ringing with authority.

Cailin lay stunned on the floor, her mind reeling in

shock. Byron had long been the voice of reason in their family, the calming force that soothed their rage and brought peace to their troubled hearts.

"Do you think you are the only one who mourns our brother's loss?" Byron roared. "We are all consumed by grief! Don't bring more upheaval to our clan with your reckless anger."

The cavern was shrouded in silence as all eyes turned to Raum, waiting for his next move. It was a moment of penetrating tension, as everyone held their breath and braced for what Raum would reveal next. An explanation? A recounting of the events at Mora's castle? There was more he had to say, and his children waited in silence.

The silence was broken by the solemn rumble of Raum's voice, filled with a grief that shook the very foundations of the cavern. "My anger runs as deep as any man's when it comes to these witches. But, we must not be hasty. Mora's power, even as death hangs over her, is too great. We have underestimated her strength as well as her desperation."

"Will she survive, O Mighty One?" implored one of the children, desperate for a shred of solace.

"Though she hangs by a mere thread, she possesses the power to endure and shall," came the fateful reply, causing a chorus of murmurs to rise from the clan.

"Listen well, we have made a pact with Mora, a vow that once her curse is cast, she will never again feast on our blood and we shall be free from her grasp forever," Raum proclaimed, his voice echoing with newfound hope. "I have found the instrument of her deliverance.

An innocent, pure maiden who now carries a child within her. I will deliver this woman to Mora, and in return, she has promised us freedom."

"Her word is truth?" Byron challenged, skepticism fixed in his voice. "Can we trust that she will uphold this agreement?"

"She will for a time, for with this unborn child, she can reclaim her youth and live for centuries to come. Then, she will have no further need of our blood," Raum explained.

"But what of the others? Laine and the coven. Will they not demand our blood tribute in their quest for youth?" Byron pressed on.

"The coven is all but crushed, seven of them lie dead by the hand of a witch hunter and another at Mora's own hand. Only Laine and three others remain. It was the witch hunter who inflicted mortal wounds upon Mora, and even now he comes for them. If he does, he could be our instrument of revenge."

"And if he fails?"

"If he fails, we are no worse off than we are now," Raum stated. "But there is a chance he may weaken her enough for us to strike."

"You have said Mora lies on her deathbed. How much weaker must she be before we act?" Cailin pressed on. "Instead of making deals with this witch, let us destroy her now; once and for all."

"Then go forth and face her! March to her fortress and bring her down!" Raum challenged, his voice rising in anger. "I stood beside her deathbed, watching as she withered away before my very eyes. Flesh dripping away from her bones. Yet with a wave of her hand, she cast me out, trapping me outside the chamber as my own son cried out in terror, begging for me to save him."

Cailin was silent, suddenly aware that she was speaking hastily and out of anger at the loss of her brother. If her father was unable to stand against Mora, then she knew she would be powerless as well.

"She is still too powerful," Raum lamented. "And even if Mora dies, we must also deal with Laine. She is as potent and deadly as her mistress. We must wait and watch for our opportunity. Our time will come, but for now, we obey. And when the time is right, we will take our revenge."

"We follow thee, Master," Byron said and the other vampires nodded their consent. "We will do as you command."

"And you Cailin? Where do you stand?" Raum confronted her. "If you so wish, you are free to go your own way. But if you do, go quickly and go far from my sight. There will be only one clan hunting in my highlands."

Cailin bowed at the waist before him. "I stand with you, father."

"Very well," Raum said. "Where is the girl?"

"The one who is with child?" Byron clarified.

"Aye! Where is she?"

"She is at an inn in the village," Byron answered.

"Send two of our brethren to guard her," Raum instructed. "Be certain that she remains safe and unseen. The witches do not know we have her, they believe she is still on the road. I want to keep it that way, at least for tonight. Maybe luck will be with us and the hunter will

146

kill Mora before moonrise tomorrow."

Byron nodded then turned to two of his vampire brothers and sent them on the mission.

"And what of the family?" Byron questioned. "The man, woman and child we took from the road. What would you have us do with them?"

"Bring them before me," Raum ordered.

Seized on the roadside as Mora had commanded, the family whom Sibby had aided were dragged before Raum for his judgment. The man and woman were beaten and bruised, having been sport for the vampires while they impatiently awaited their master's permission to feed. The child clung to his father's leg and all three trembled in fear, sobbing before Raum.

"Why does the witch Mora despise you so?" Raum questioned them. "What have you done to incur her wrath?"

The couple clung to each other, sheltering their child between them. They sobbed uncontrollably but did not respond to Raum's inquiry.

"Well? Speak!" Raum's voice boomed and echoed in the cavern.

"We know of no such witch?" The man ventured to answer.

"Please, have mercy on us! For the sake of our child!" The woman cried and threw herself at Raum's feet.

"Silence!" Raum responded, then went back to his questioning. "You do not know of this evil hag? Withered and gray she is. Known by the name of Mora?"

"We know of no such woman," the mother cried.

"Why would she seek to curse a child for no reason,

and then order the slaughter of a helpless family?" Byron asked Raum.

"Because she can," Raum answered coldly. "She takes pleasure in the suffering of others."

"Then what of them?" Byron asked. "Mora has demanded their deaths."

"No! Please! I beg of you!" The woman pleaded. "Have mercy! I will gladly give thee my life, but please spare my child!"

"Please sir! We have done no harm to this woman," the man fell to his knees before Raum and pleaded. "If we have caused her injury, then take my life if you must. But please spare my wife and son."

Raum looked at them emotionlessly. He cared nothing for the humans and felt no compassion for them; he considered them little more than food. He was unmoved by their pleas and to a degree was even disgusted by their pathetic begging. However, it was again Byron who interceded on their behalf and stirred him to compassion.

"Father, you have lost your own son and I have lost a brother. The sorrow and grief of this night is unbearable. Let us have mercy, at least on this family who has already suffered greatly."

"Their suffering does not move me to mercy."

"I plead not only for their suffering, but for my own," Byron spoke, placing his hand gently upon Raum's shoulder and gazing deeply into his eyes. "Please father, grant me a glimpse of kindness this evening. If not for their sake, then for the sake of my own troubled heart."

He studied the pleading faces of the mother and father, and then he looked at the young boy with his face buried against his father's chest. He considered the situation for a moment. Raum truly felt no compassion for them, but he did feel the pain in Byron's plea. For the sake of his favorite son, he relented.

"Set them free," Raum finally sighed.

"What?" Cailin spoke up. "Are we to not feed now?"

"Go and find your meal in the nearby village if you must," Raum answered. "But these people are to remain untouched. If Mora wishes them dead, then I wish them to live long and prosperous lives."

"Bless you, my lord! God bless you!" The man groveled before him.

Raum looked at the man with contempt, as if the blessing he pronounced was instead an insult. To Raum it was as such, because he knew that God had forsaken him the moment he received the dark gift. God had nothing to do with him any longer, nor did he have any purpose with their Christian ways. So as the man heaped his blessings, Raum's heart hardened again.

"Your god does not bless us; he has condemned us to hell!" Raum growled at him. "I am your god now and I will give you my blessing!"

Raum seized the man by the collar of his shirt and forced him to his feet. He looked him in his face as the poor man cowered before him. "Bare your throat to me!" Raum demanded.

"Please, good sir! He meant no harm!" The woman cried out, grabbed her son, and pulled him close so that the boy would not see what was happening. "I beg of thee!"

"Bare your throat," Raum ordered again, "or watch

while your woman and son suffer in your place."

"Father …" Byron tried to intercede again but Raum would have none of it.

"Bare your throat!" Raum growled. "I will not ask again!"

The man reluctantly turned his head to the side. Tears streamed down his face as he took what he suspected would be one last look at his wife and child.

Raum took a moment to appreciate the muscular throat and watched the rapid pounding of the man's pulse beneath the smooth skin. Then, he plunged his fangs deep into the waiting flesh.

The man cried out in pain as the vampire bit into his neck, but he did not fight; rather he accepted his fate in exchange for the lives of his wife and child. Raum resisted his own thirst and drained only a small amount of blood from his victim. It was not the blood that he desired, but the purpose of his bite was to infect the man with the dark curse.

Raum withdrew after a moment and licked the blood from the man's throat, allowing his saliva to heal the wound. Then Raum bit into his own wrist and opened a vein so that blood flowed freely from the wound. He raised his arm to the man's mouth.

"Drink!" Raum thundered, as he forced the man's lips to his bleeding wrist. The man struggled against Raum's iron grip, but it was to no avail. The crimson liquid gushed into his mouth, filling him with the corrupting essence of Raum's dark curse.

As Raum withdrew his arm, the man crumpled to the ground, retching and choking on the foul taste of the blood. But Raum merely laughed, his lips curling into a sadistic grin as he licked the two puncture wounds on his wrist, sealing them shut.

The pack of vampires erupted into fits of cackles, reveling in the latest addition to their family - a doomed soul forever bound to the thirst for blood. Raum had claimed another victim, sinking his fangs deep into the man's neck and infecting him with the deadly venom.

But Raum was not content to simply let the venom run its course. He desired the man to taste his blood, so that the dark curse would consume him entirely, leaving him yearning for more.

"Once you have shed this mortal coil, and the thirst grips you like a vice, come find me," Raum declared, his voice carrying like a boom of thunder. "You will know me as the god who has truly blessed you with eternal life."

He then turned to Byron. "Escort your new brother and his family to the road, so that they may find their way home," he commanded.

With a deafening roar, Raum summoned his clan. "All of you, be gone! Feast on your victims and bring me no more news tonight."

Byron's heart ached as he guided the man and his family away from the vampire den. He knew that the man was doomed to die, to be resurrected as a monster thirsting for blood. And yet, he was grateful that the woman and child would be spared - at least for now.

As they reached the edge of the road, Byron paused. "You must go on alone from here," he told the woman. "Take the boy and follow the road to the village, and you will find respite before returning home."

"But my husband," the woman pleaded.

"He is dying, and soon he will become like those in the cavern," Byron replied, his voice heavy with sorrow. "A ravenous beast thirsting for blood. You must walk away, leave him in my care, or he'll tear you and your child apart, along with anyone who cares for him."

Tears streamed down the woman's face as she clung to her son, her heart breaking at the thought of leaving her husband behind. But Byron was resolute. "Go," he commanded. "I will do what you cannot. He will find peace."

With a final, longing look, the woman took her son and ran toward the road, disappearing into the darkness. Byron tenderly lowered the man to the ground and watched as he slipped in and out of consciousness. When the moment was right, he drew his dagger and plunged it deep into the man's heart.

"Rest, my brother," Byron whispered. "Your family is safe."

CHAPTER 10

Raum's Dark History

The fire crackled and danced in the cavern, casting an eerie glow on Raum as he brooded over his thoughts. He had been lost in his musings for what seemed like hours, his mind consumed with the witches and the need for retribution. The silence was only broken by the sound of Byron's footsteps as he returned from his task of escorting the young family away. He sat down beside his father, his eyes downcast, weighed down by a heavy heart.

"You are angry," Raum observed, breaking the stillness.

Disappointment and sadness weighed heavy on Byron's voice as he responded, "Aye."

"These humans are not like us. Do not waste your pity on mere animals."

"Would you treat them with any less dignity than a stray dog? Kicking them merely for existing?" Byron countered. "Though they may be our sustenance, must we treat them so brutally? They are the roots of our existence; they are our origin and deserve respect."

Raum sneered at the mention of dignity. "I kept my word and spared them, did I not?"

"No, you did not. You infected the father, intent that he would turn on his own wife and child in a bloodlust," Byron accused. "You sentenced them to a painful death. It would have been kinder to simply take their lives this night."

Frustration marred Raum's features. "Kill or spare, make up thy mind!"

"Do as you please, I shall not try to change your black heart anymore," Byron replied resolutely.

Their conversation fell into silence, the tension between them palpable. Raum lacked any empathy towards humans, viewing them simply as prey. Compassion and mercy were weaknesses he could not afford. If he were to consider humans as anything more than animals meant for slaughter, it would completely shatter his beliefs and challenge the very foundation of his existence as a predator. He might begin to question his actions and the morality of feeding on innocent lives. He could not risk that self-exploration.

Byron, in contrast, held tight to his humanity, a beacon of emotion amidst a sea of indifference. He felt the tides of sorrow and compassion with a depth unmatched by any mere mortal. His hunting was a delicate dance, each step calculated and measured, with only the most deserving of death deemed worthy of his feast. Yet even in the moment of the kill, he extended a mercy few could imagine, lulling his prey into a trance of peace before the final draw of his fangs.

"These mere mortals and their feeble gods," Raum

spat, his disdain cutting through the stillness.

Byron remained wordless, the tempest of emotions still roiling within him.

"No hunt tonight, then?" Raum inquired, trying to ease the tension with a false calm.

"No," Byron replied, his voice heavy with sorrow. "I have lost my taste for it."

The silence descended once more, the animosity between them a tangible force.

"I took the father's life," Byron spoke at last, breaking the quiet. "And granted freedom to the mother and child."

Raum raised a quizzical brow, his gaze turning to ice. "You would defy me?"

"I claimed what was given to me," Byron retorted, his voice resolute. "You promised mercy and then delivered condemnation. I only sought to rectify the injustice done."

"You tread dangerous waters, that is either brave or foolish," Raum warned, his voice low and dangerous.

Byron withdrew into a meditative silence, his gaze fixed upon the flickering embers. Raum gazed upon Byron, lost in his own thoughts, a flicker of concern crossed his mind. He feared that the widening divide between them would grow into an unbridgeable chasm, tearing them apart forever. He shook his head, trying to dispel the gloomy thoughts, but they persisted, a constant reminder of the fragile bond they shared.

He pondered on the thought that he should strive to comprehend and embrace Byron's viewpoint, even if it did not align with his own emotions. Perhaps, he should make a conscious effort to be more patient and accepting of Byron's humanity, for if he didn't, the divide between them would only widen with each passing moment.

Raum weighed the option of offering an olive branch in the form of an apology. He understood that acknowledging his wrongs could potentially mend their relationship and mean the world to Byron. However, when it came down to actually uttering the apology, Raum instead elected to shift the conversation and hold onto hope that the disagreement would simply fade into oblivion.

"You and your brethren wonder why I do not challenge Mora?" Raum diverted the conversation.

Byron answered, the sadness still heavy in his voice, yet grateful for the shift in topic. "I cannot fathom your motives, yet I hold faith in your judgment."

"If only your kin shared your trust," Raum sighed.

"Aye, Cailin," Byron nodded. "She is grieving, she and Jaret had grown close."

"Ah, I was unaware," Raum said with a hint of surprise.

"They bonded swiftly."

"'Tis well that he is gone, then," Raum stated coldly, "our kind is not meant for love, it is a weakness to have such fragile emotions within our clan."

"Then I suffer from that same frailty, for I love you," Byron proclaimed.

Raum let out a heavy sigh. "Then you are as foolish as your sister."

Byron kept quiet, his gaze fixed on the flickering fire. He felt certain that Raum was not as heartless as he portrayed himself to be, but there was no use in delving deeper into the topic. He loved his maker and believed that he was loved in return, although he never expected those feelings to be verbalized.

Silence descended upon them once more, an unspoken disagreement lingering in the air like a thick fog. Raum sighed heavily, desperate for a way to bridge the divide between him and Byron, to offer solace in his grief and to find solace himself. With a heavy sigh, he spoke up, his voice a low rumble in the quiet.

"Have I ever told thee of the day I was reborn, the moment of my resurrection?"

Byron's eyes flicked towards Raum, a flicker of interest in their depths. "Nay, thou hast not.'"

"I have never shared it with another soul," Raum confessed.

"Thou hast never shared anything of substance with me," Byron replied with a hint of bitterness.

'That is not true, my son. We have had many conversations," Raum countered.

"Aye, we have shared many words. We have spoken of my life and my history, but of thyself, you have only shared thy name," Byron said with a wry smile.

Raum returned the smile, his eyes twinkling in the firelight. "Then let us change that this night. What would you know of me?"

Byron leaned forward, his curiosity piqued. "Begin at the beginning. Tell me of thy resurrection."

"The more you learn of me, the less you will like the person you call father," Raum cautioned.

"Your past is the past. I know who you are, but not the road you traveled to get here," Byron smiled back.

"Tell your story."

"Not long by our standards, but in human years, I believe it has been nigh on two decades," Raum mused.

"Two decades? I thought you were the eldest among our kind," Byron said with a hint of surprise.

Raum let out a deep, throaty laugh. "Thy brethern believe me to be ancient. But in the grand scheme of things, I am but a newborn babe. There are those who have roamed this earth since its creation, and it is whispered that even the father of our kind still walks among us."

"And what of the one who granted you the gift of immortality, the sire who birthed you into darkness?"

Raum's expression softened as he delved into memories. "The one who passed on the dark blood...it was Mora, the same witch who torments us now," he said in a voice barely above a whisper.

"Mora! But how could that be? She is not one of us. She lacks the ability to bestow the gift."

"Indeed," Raum replied with a cryptic smile. "Mora's kind is not meant for the immortal embrace of the dark gift. They walk a different path, a path steeped in the shadows of the arcane and the mysterious. But in her cunning, Mora saw the opportunity to extend her life, to continue her reign of terror, and she sought me out to make the bargain.

"So how did she do it? Was it by a curse or spell?"

"A single vial of blood, the harbinger of immortality, lay before me. Its source, shrouded in mystery – she claimed it to be the blood from the father of our kind, personally handed to her by his own blood-stained hand, or maybe it was just the ill-gotten elixir of another hapless vampire fallen under her evil spell? Regardless of its origin, the cunning witch offered it to me as a currency, in exchange for a deed most foul. The promise of everlasting life, for a single act of unspeakable evil. To me, it was a fair trade."

Raum's gaze lingered on Byron as he sought any hint of judgment in the vampire's expression. But all he saw was a glimmer of curiosity and interest in the story. Feeling encouraged, Raum continued.

"Mora is ancient, with a history spanning hundreds of years. Though not human, she is still mortal, susceptible to the ravages of time and the eventual touch of death. When I first met her, her once youthful form was already withered with age. But she had a plan, a dark spell that would renew her youth and extend her life for centuries to come."

"Why didn't she just take the dark blood herself?" Byron asked, puzzled. "Wouldn't she have gained everlasting life and stay forever young?"

"Witches are different from us," Raum explained. "Their mastery of black magic transforms them into something more, something not quite human. So, while the dark blood can sustain their life, it won't bring them back from the dead."

"So, a witch can never become a vampire, not even through the blood or the bite?"

"There are ways, but why would a witch bother? They can live for centuries using their magic and a vampire's blood. Mora, however, seeks something different. We are the living dead, but she desires true eternal life.

To be ageless, youthful, and above all, fully alive."

"The nature of our existence eludes me," Byron confessed, not understanding the difference. "Are we not eternal and breathing?"

"Vampires walk a fine line between life and death. We are the living dead. We awaken from slumber, only to inevitably fall once more. Bound to the shadows, unable to bask in the sun's warm embrace. Mora, however, craves a different kind of immortality. She yearns for the simple pleasures of mortality – the taste of food and drink, the warmth of the sun on her skin, the possibility of bearing offspring."

"So she seeks to live forever, but as a mortal."

"Indeed," Raum nodded. "But for her wish to come true, she needs a very powerful spell. One reserved for only the most powerful witch. A spell that requires rare and unique ingredients."

"The expectant mother!" Byron exclaimed, finally piecing together the puzzle. "That's why she wants her."

"Precisely," Raum confirmed. "The spell requires the life of an unborn child, born of violence and conceived in deceit. The mother must be pure and untouched, known to no man before or after the act of conception. And when her time comes, the child must be taken from the womb, still unborn, and the life force taken."

"But what does this spell have to do with your resurrection? Bryon began to realize the depth of the unspeakable pact Raum had struck with Mora. "You bargained to find the unfortunate maiden who was with child."

"Alas, if only it were so straightforward," Raum sighed with regret. "As I hath mentioned, the elements for the spell are a rare find. Mora scoured the land for years without success. Each passing day brought her closer to the embrace of death. In a frantic act of desperation, she devised a plan to bring forth the necessary components herself.

"And that was when she found me. I was a Viking warrior, one among many who sailed from the north to wreak havoc and destruction upon these lands. Our acts of conquest had earned us infamy and we struck terror in the hearts of the people. But one fateful day, the king's army ambushed us. My brotherhood was decimated, and I was among the few survivors."

"It was then that Mora entered my life. I saw her as a withered and feeble hag, residing on the fringes of a village, and I thought her an easy conquest. But she proved to be more cunning than I anticipated. She ensnared me and revealed her true identity as a witch. She offered to make me invincible and grant me immortality in exchange for a pact."

As the story unfolded, Byron felt a growing sense of foreboding. Raum's revelations were painting a picture of a sinister and troubled past. "What did you do, Father?" he asked, his voice filled with concern. "The weight of this deed seems to be bearing down on you. Speak it aloud and ease your burden."

"I was to gather my remaining men, and we would set upon a farm house and the family that lived there. We were to slaughter the whole family except for the young daughter. Then, I was to forcibly take the girl and fill her with my seed."

Bryon hung his head in despair, his voice barely

above a whisper as he muttered, "An innocent girl, unknown to the world, carrying a child born of unspeakable violence."

"Yes, I was paid to father the child that Mora required for her dark magic."

"And what happened? If Mora is still withered and old, she never cast the spell."

"I upheld my end of the deal, and the girl indeed carried the child that Mora sought for her dark magic. My reward was given, and I savored the dark blood that fateful night. Mora held onto the girl for months, eagerly awaiting the moment when she could lay her hands on the unborn baby and cast her spell. But fate intervened and before Mora could complete the ritual, the girl fled into the countryside, never to be seen again.

"So, you have a mortal child. Born of your blood, just as I was."

"The child was born of mortal flesh, but my only aim was to possess the dark blood, nothing more."

The story was not yet finished. Byron felt the weight of Raum's words, like a leaden anvil crushing his chest. He sat in stunned silence, grappling with the enormity of the tale just told. A mortal child born of Raum's blood, conceived in violence, and yet left to disappear into the world.

As Byron contemplated their conversation, the mysterious figure known as Raum emerged as an enigma. Prior to his resurrection, Raum had kept his life's details hidden, shrouded in secrecy. With no known background, lineage, or even a complete name, he tightly guarded his secrets. Yet, unexpectedly, he chose to entrust Byron with his deepest revelation, instilling in Byron a profound sense of honor.

Now, Byron grappled with questions. Why did Raum choose to share this tale? Was he seeking advice or simply opening up for once? Could his disclosure be a quest for absolution following Jaret's death, or an attempt to find clarity in his relationship with Mora? These questions churned in Byron's mind like a tempest, leaving him disoriented and dizzy.

At last, he mustered the courage to speak. "Why are you revealing this to me?" Byron asked, his voice barely above a whisper.

Raum's eyes met his, and in their depths, Byron saw a flicker of something he could not quite name. Regret? Remorse? Resignation? Whatever it was, it was gone as quickly as it appeared.

"Because, my dear Byron," Raum said, his voice as cold and hard as a winter's night, "You are the only one I trust. And it is time for you to know the truth about me and my past."

"So is this the reason you do not challenge Mora," Byron finally asked. "Because she gave you the dark gift and is therefore your mother."

"No, my son, there is no blood bond between Mora and myself. She is merely a witch and it was not her blood that sired me, but the blood of another. It is her raw power that holds me at bay. The knowledge of what she can do to you and your brethren is what prevents me from challenging her. I do not fear for my own safety, but for yours. We cannot stand against her, not yet."

"If not now, when shall we?"

"Alas, it may be beyond our capabilities," he added, his voice heavy with defeat. "For she has delved deeper into the abyss of the black arts than any before her. Death may claim her yet, or the hunter who inflicted her mortal wound may return to finish the task. But these are slim hopes, indeed."

Byron, however, was not so easily discouraged. "What of the white witch? Has she not proven herself to be a formidable adversary against Mora? Perhaps we could forge an alliance, united in our quest to defeat the coven."

But Raum was quick to dampen his son's enthusiasm. "Do not be fooled, Byron. No white witch would offer our kind aid. And this witch, in particular, would revel in my downfall."

"What do you mean, father?"

"Swear to me, son," Raum demanded, his voice becoming low and grave. "Swear on your life that you will never reveal what I am about to tell you."

"I so swear, father," Byron pledged, placing his hand over his heart. "On my life and honor, I vow never to betray your trust."

"This white witch, the one that Mora hates so; she is the girl from the farmhouse, and the witch hunter is the child she delivered."

Byron was initially struck with disbelief, rendering him momentarily speechless. However, the overwhelming curiosity pushed him to find his voice and express his astonishment, "The hunter who wounded Mora, the one with the power to challenge the coven, is... is he truly your own blood?"

"Aye, that he is," Raum confirmed, his voice low and filled with dark intent.

"What is your plan then? Will you reveal yourself to him?"

Raum let out a dark, mocking laugh. "You are still so naive, my son. Do not be so quick to trust."

"But he is your son," Byron pressed. "Surely you would wish to know him?"

"You are my son," Raum thundered, his eyes blazing with ancient power. "He is the spawn of a woman I once wronged, a woman whose family I took from her. I doubt he would receive me with open arms." Raum's voice was cold and unforgiving. "I have no doubt that, given the choice between aligning with me or with Mora, they would see me dead before they offered me their hand."

"Aye," Byron reluctantly admitted. "Your tale gives me no reason to believe otherwise."

"Right now, we have no choice but to do as Mora commands," Raum declared firmly. "We will wait and hope this hunter makes a move against Mora and her coven soon. We'll observe as they tear each other apart."

"And if Mora emerges victorious?"

"If she does, she's promised to spare our lives and let us go our separate ways after completing her spell and restoring her youth," Raum answered, his voice as unyielding as steel.

"Do you trust her word?" Byron asked, studying Raum's face for any sign of deceit.

"I don't," Raum replied coolly, his eyes as icy as the underworld. "But I do believe that once her spell is cast, Mora will have no further need for us."

"No further need for us," Byron echoed, feeling a shiver run down his spine. "That gives me little comfort, father."

CHAPTER 11

The Shellycoat

Drustan was jolted from slumber by the most delicious fragrance. The smoke from the smoldering embers blended with the savory aroma of sizzling fish, a delightful scent he couldn't ignore. With blurry eyes, he gazed upon his campsite in amazement. The fire that should have long since gone out still blazed with life, casting a warm glow in the cool forest air. He rubbed his chin, trying to recall if he had risen in the night to tend to the fire, but his memory was foggy. Then there was the fish, a succulent meal that he certainly didn't remember catching or cooking himself. There was someone else in the forest with him.

"Hello?" he called out, his voice echoing in the stillness. "Who's there?"

There was no answer.

Drustan approached the fire, warily scanning the surrounding trees, feeling as though he was being watched. Despite the eerie feeling, the enticing aroma of the fish was too much to resist. He shrugged, sat down beside the fire, and enjoyed the gift, pondering the mystery of who could have left it for him.

Once he was finished, he stood up and once again looked around the forest. "Thank you for the fish," he called out, but still, there was no response. "I'll be on my way now," he announced, before setting out once more along the winding riverbank, his sights set on the north.

The riddle of the fire and the fish followed him, as he kept his wits sharp, searching for any sign of his mysterious benefactor. The sound of rocks tumbling from the riverbank echoed around him, a haunting reminder that he was not alone, yet try as he might, Drustan could not catch a glimpse of his stalker.

Midmorning found him in a sun-drenched clearing near the river. The dappled shadows of the trees gave way to the warm embrace of the sun, lifting Drustan's spirits and renewing his energy. He stood there, basking in the golden rays, letting the peaceful surroundings soothe his weary soul. The river flowed beside him, its melody a balm to his troubled spirit, as the scent of the pine trees filled his nostrils. He breathed deeply, taking in the moment, feeling his troubles slip away.

For a moment, Drustan was at peace, but as he opened his eyes, the strange sensation of being watched returned. He spun around, searching for the source, but saw nothing but the shimmering river and the trees that surrounded it. He shrugged it off and continued on his journey, the beauty of the forest filling his heart with a sense of wonder.

As the day wore on, the forest grew denser and the shadows grew longer. The riverbank narrowed, and Drustan found himself walking along a thin path, with the rushing water on one side and towering trees on the other. The rustling of leaves and the chirping of birds were the only sounds that broke the stillness.

He was enjoying his hike and had all but forgotten about the strange sensation of being watched when, as he ascended a small embankment, a tree branch suddenly swooped around slapping him hard in the chest and knocking him on his back into the water.

"Faugh!" Drustan bellowed as he emerged from the chilly river, shivering in the autumn breeze that was made even colder by the shadows of the forest. As he looked back at the treacherous tree branch, he realized that it was not just a chance encounter, but a well-planned ambush. The tree branch was cunningly set with a snare made from gnarled vines, a crude trap that Drustan had fallen victim to.

Drustan stood still, his senses on high alert, as he listened for any signs of his attacker. His eyes darted back and forth, searching for the source of the noise. "Who's there?" he challenged, his voice resounding through the forest. "Show yourself! Come forth and face me, be you man or beast!" he roared, his hand clutching the hilt of his sword.

The sounds of rustling leaves and snapping twigs, echoed from upriver, spurring Drustan into action. He gave chase, sprinting through the forest, his heart pounding with excitement and adrenaline. But just as suddenly as the sounds had started, they stopped.

Drustan skidded to a halt, panting for breath, and gazed around the clearing for any sign of movement. "Who's there?" he called out again, his voice filled with authority. Yet, the only reply was the gentle bubbling of the river and the distant cooing of a wood dove.

With a scowl, Drustan's hand returned to the hilt of his sword. "You won't hide from me," he growled, his voice filled with determination. "I'll find you, whoever you are." He stood motionless, listening intently for any sounds that would betray the presence of his attacker.

Despite the silence that met his challenge, Drustan finally released his grip on his sword with a weary sigh. "Run, you spineless coward," he growled, his voice echoing menacingly through the forest. He scanned the area, but it seemed that the troublemaker had fled.

He unpacked his bow and quiver, emptied the water that had accumulated inside and checked their condition. While the bow and arrows appeared unscathed, he couldn't shake the worry that the water might have impacted their potency or enchanted qualities. Only a trial run on a witch would reveal the truth.

Drustan reached into his pack and savored the familiar taste of a piece of jerky he had procured at the tavern. The wrapping was still dry, a welcome reprieve. He took a hearty bite of the savory, dried meat and carefully wrapped the rest, ready for later.

With a determined step, he set off once more along the riverbank, his destination set firmly to the north. Suddenly, a branch came crashing down, sending him tumbling to the ground once more. Dazed and disoriented, Drustan lay there, gathering his wits and assessing the damage. As he regained his composure, he heard the telltale crunch of footsteps approaching. With a stroke of genius, Drustan feigned unconsciousness, waiting for the mystery figure to draw near.

And then, from the corner of his eye, he saw the culprit; a short, squat creature, no taller than Drustan's knees, with a body covered in gleaming, iridescent shells that clacked with each movement. Its face was ghostly pale, almost translucent, and had the elongated, amphibian appearance of an overgrown tadpole. Strands of tangled, seaweed-like hair crowned its head, while its thin, spindly limbs ended in razor-sharp claws. Despite its menacing appearance, Drustan was more intrigued than frightened. After all, he had already encountered witches, a sluagh, a Bean Nighe, and the Redcap. Why would a giant frog in a vestment of seashells raise an eyebrow?

Drustan cautiously stood up, taking care not to make any sudden movements that might startle the creature. It tilted its head, watching him intently with its large, bulbous eyes, but made no move to attack. Instead, it let out a series of soft, clucking noises.

Drustan approached the strange creature with a mixture of wonder and apprehension. He extended a trembling hand, reaching out to touch the shimmering shells that covered its body. The creature remained still, permitting Drustan to examine it. The shells were smooth and cool to the touch, like polished pebbles from a riverbed. He ran his hand over the creature's back, marveling at its singular appearance.

He knelt down to get a better look at the creature. With its elongated amphibian face, seaweed hair, and sharp claws, it was easily the most grotesque thing he had ever laid eyes on. Yet there was something undeniably fascinating about it. "What sort of creature are you, little one?" Drustan whispered, both intrigued and bewildered by this mysterious, water-dwelling faerie.

The creature responded with a series of strange bubbling and popping sounds. Drustan cocked his head to one side, trying to decipher the creature's response. It was like nothing he had ever heard before, a symphony of bubbles and pops, like the song of an underwater stream. He extended a hand again, offering it to the strange being. To his surprise, the creature didn't shy away but instead tilted its head and jutted out its own hand, as if mimicking his movements.

"Can you understand me, little guy?" Drustan asked, crouching down to look more closely into the creature's eyes."

A wide, toothless grin spread across the creature's face, and without a moment's warning, it suddenly delivered a fierce kick to Drustan's groin. He crumpled to the ground in agony, clutching himself, as the creature erupted into peals of gleeful laughter.

"Did you understand that?" the creature laughed in a childlike voice before scampering away upstream, its shells clacking as it went.

Drustan writhed on the ground, clutching himself in pain, as the creature's maniacal cackles echoed in the distance. Through the haze of his anguish, he couldn't help but question what had transpired. Had this mischievous being truly just toyed with him for its own twisted amusement?

Struggling, Drustan rose to his feet, still tender in the aftermath of the brutal kick. The creature had vanished upstream, leaving Drustan to nurse his wounds and simmer with wrath. He clinched his teeth, pushed aside the pain, and started to make his way upstream in pursuit of the elusive stinkard.

Drustan continued to track the creature for some time, but to no avail. It seemed to have vanished into thin air. Exhausted, he eventually relented and slowed his pace, assuming the strange being had grown tired of its sport and retreated. He was relieved but a part of him was hoping to still encounter the creature one last time and have the opportunity to kick it right in the shells for good measure.

Drustan felt a wave of relief wash over him as he emerged from the forest onto the sprawling plain. The north road lay before him, just a few steps away, and he hastened towards it with renewed energy. Stepping onto the dirt path, Drustan cast a final glance over his shoulder at the line of trees, feeling grateful to have left the treacherous woods behind. The open plain offered easier navigation, and he could rest assured that he wouldn't cross paths with any sinister creatures bent on his demise.

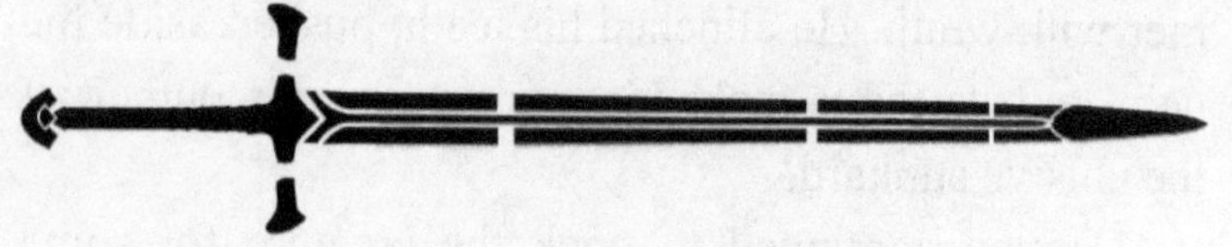

CHAPTER 12

Three Wishes and a Kiss

As he journeyed forth, Drustan's thoughts were once again heavy with the recent revelation about his father and the circumstances of his birth. The truth had shaken him to the very core, leaving him with a sense of disbelief and profound sadness. He had always believed himself to be the son of a hero, only to find out that he was the product of a brutal act of violence and rape. The once-proud connection to his roots was now tarnished with shame and dishonor.

His anger towards the evil witch who had orchestrated such a cruel plot boiled within him. He yearned for justice for his mother and, above all, revenge. The retribution he sought was not just for Sibby, but for himself, as he aimed to punish the witch for stealing away his pride and leaving him with shame and guilt. This quest for revenge was not just about punishing the witch, but also proving himself to his mother and the world.

In the depths of his heart, Drustan came to realize why his mother had lied to him all these years. She had wanted to spare him the shame of his true origins, but her actions also revealed her own feelings of guilt and shame. The possibility that his mother had viewed him with disdain his entire life left him feeling angry and hurt. He hated her for lying to him and hated her even more for finally telling him the truth. A part of him wished that she had never revealed the truth and that he could have lived his life in ignorance.

As the sun approached its final descent, Drustan found himself at the threshold of another forest. The trees were towering monoliths, their twisted branches stretching skyward like bony fingers, and their trunks, blackened by the passage of time, stood like ancient sentinels guarding the secrets within. The leaves, ablaze in autumn hues of rust and red, whispered ominous warnings to all who dared enter.

With a sense of foreboding, Drustan instinctively knew that he stood before the Caledonian Forest, a vast and ancient woodland steeped in legends and magic. It was here, amidst the whispers of faeries and mystical creatures, that he believed he would find Mora, the witch who held the answers he so desperately sought. He steeled himself for the trials to come, for he knew that the journey ahead would be fraught with danger and the unknown.

As the last rays of sunlight melted into the horizon, Drustan felt a chill run through his bones. Before him stood the Caledonian Forest, a place where magic ran deep and the veil between the mortal and mystical worlds was at its most fragile. He hesitated, his thoughts haunted by the recent encounter with the Redcap and the knowledge that the moment of the Between Time was closing in.

The Between Times, whispered of in folklore, were not just transitions between beginnings and endings, but sacred thresholds to otherworldly realms. Dawn, with its fiery fingers streaking the sky in a brilliant display, marked the end of night and the birth of a new day. Noon, when the sun blazed in its full glory, held a tranquil stillness and potent energy, signifying the sun's zenith before its descent. Sunset, when the moon claimed the heavens with its graceful silver light, and midnight, the witching hour. Each of these moments possessed an air of mystery and enchantment, where the barrier between worlds grew faint, and mystical creatures freely traversed the realms.

His mother, being one of the cunning folk, warned him of the dangers of being in the woods during the Between Times and especially after nightfall. With a weaver's skill, she spun tales of horror, of malevolent faeries and other fell beasts that haunted the dark, dense woods once the sun dipped below the horizon. He had already tasted their wrath on his journey, but she warned him that the most dangerous hour of all was the Between Time at dusk.

Having recognized the truth in his mother's chilling tales, he decided it would be best to remain outside the boundaries of the Caledonian woods for the night. He would set up his camp on the outskirts of the forest and at the break of day he would awake refreshed and renewed and ready to face the challenges ahead.

Drustan cast aside his pack and provisions, shed his weapons and sat down seeking refuge beneath a gnarled tree just as the sun touched the horizon. He intended to rest for a spell, to gather his waning strength for the task of igniting a warm fire, but slumber claimed him swiftly, pulling him into the depths of dreams. Just as the veil of sleep enveloped him, a child's voice, fearful and anguished, rent the stillness and jolted him to alertness.

He rose to his feet, momentarily dazed, questioning if the cry had been but a figment of his imagination. The forest was shrouded in an eerie stillness, but then, there it was again.

"Help me!" the voice cried out from the shadows.

Drustan scanned the surrounding glade, attempting to place the source of the cries. He advanced towards the trees with wary steps, listening closely to the stillness for the child's voice.

"Hail!" he yelled. "Where are you, young one?"

"Here! I am here!" the voice replied, the fear palpable in its tone. "Please, help me!"

"Where?" he called back, scanning the underbrush. "I cannot see you!"

"Here! I am hear!"

He pressed forward beyond the verdant boundary and into the ominous embrace of the woodland, each footfall carrying him closer to the source of the desperate pleas.

"I'm here!" the voice was close now, so close that Drustan felt as if the child was just beyond his grasp.

And then he stumbled into a deep pit, cunningly concealed by broken branches, fallen leaves and pine needles. He hit the bottom with a dull thud leaving him momentarily breathless. He groaned, not only from the pain of his fall and the bruising he sustained, but also from his own foolishness at being tricked again by what he suspected was that foul frog faerie wearing the shells. He thought he had left the creature far behind on the riverbank, but it seemed it had continued to follow him.

He remained still for a moment, taking stock of the toll on his body. Finding no fractures, he struggled to his feet and brushed the dirt from his attire. Above, he heard the jeering laughter of children, cruel and taunting.

"You find that humorous, you vile slug?" he bellowed, scanning the walls of the pit for any means of escape.

Two diminutive figures suddenly appeared at the lip of the pit, their tiny, ethereal wings pulsing with a dragonfly-like hum as they gazed down upon him with mirth and merriment. One was a female, the other a male, both no larger than sparrows, with eyes that shone like beacons of emerald green, and tresses of shining gold that danced in the wind. Though their faces were those of cherubs, there was a hint of mischievousness that lurked within their expressions, a telltale sign that they were not to be trusted.

Drustan peered at the tiny figures with a wary eye, for he had anticipated facing the squat, frog-like entity that had plagued him of late, not this new affliction. Yet as he gazed upon the tiny beings, he knew with a certainty that they were faeries, unlike the ones he had encountered already in his quest. His mother's tales spoke of such creatures, and now, finally, he beheld a true faerie with his own eyes, a sight he had never before experienced.

"Thou art pretty!" The female faerie shyly exclaimed as she gracefully fluttered down into the pit. She circled

Drustan, admiring his every feature with a gleam in her eye. But just as quickly, she soared back up to the rim of the pit, making sure to keep a safe distance from the man below.

"Don't talk to it!" the male faerie warned.

"Why not? It can't hurt us," the female replied, tossing her golden locks over her shoulder. "It's down there and we're up here."

"We don't know that. It could be a warlock, or a monster of some sort," the male said, his eyes wide with concern.

"Not a warlock!" The female gasped, dramatically clutching at her chest. "Or perchance a monster?"

"I'm just a man," Drustan stated, trying to reassure them. "I mean no harm."

"It looks like a man, and speaks like a man," the male faerie observed, creeping forward but still keeping a wary distance. "But it reeks of a wet cat."

"Gross! We loathe cats!" The female squealed, erupting into peals of laughter.

"I am not a cat," Drustan retorted, his ire mounting.

"It's too large to be a cat," the female pointed out, cocking her head to one side. "Maybe it's a donkey?"

"I am not a donkey!" Drustan roared, his voice trembling with anger.

"A bear, mayhap?" The female taunted, her eyes alight with mischief.

"By the god's teeth!" Drustan bellowed, throwing his arms up in despair. "I am a man, can you not see that?"

"I think it's a man," the female confided to the male faerie. "Donkeys and bears don't curse like that."

"But why is it here?" The male wondered aloud, gazing back and forth between Drustan and the female faerie.

"I do not know," she replied with a shrug. "Maybe you should ask it."

"Why have you come?" The male hovered a little closer, courageously querying. "Do you seek to bring us harm? To steal our magic?"

"I have no intention to harm," spoke Drustan with a voice steady as the mountains. "I am on a quest and seek thy aid to get from this pit, then we may converse as friends."

"We shall leave him be, sister," spoke the male faerie, Tyree.

But the female faerie, Aster, floated down for a another close look. "I am fond of him, Tyree. Let us release him."

"Beware, Aster, for they say these creatures bite," warned Tyree. "They eat faeries."

"That is not true! Fear not, fair maiden," Drustan assured her. "I shall not cause thee any harm."

"I am called Aster," said the faerie, "and that is my brother Tyree. Pray, what may I call thee?"

"Drustan is my name," he replied.

"A name as fair as thy face, Drustan," she said with a smile, her cheeks blushing bright pink afterwards. "If I release thee, dost thou swear to cause no trouble?"

"Aster, have no dealings with him," Tyree again cautioned. "Thou cannot trust a man."

"I swear on God's bones, fair Aster, that I shall cause thee no harm," Drustan pledged.

180

Aster hesitated, a playful glint in her eye. "Thou dost speak much of oaths and curses, Drustan. Perhaps I should leave thee be."

"Forgive me, kind maiden," Drustan implored. "But I am trapped and in need of thy aid. I shall be more gentle in my speech, if that is thy desire."

"Very well, Drustan," she said with a nod. "But thou must promise to cause no trouble and speak with gentleness."

And with a swift motion, Aster departed from the pit, disappearing into the mists. Yet, in but a moment's time, she returned, her form now that of a comely maiden, clutching a rope of vines. She kept a firm hold on one end, and cast the other down to Drustan. And with quick fingers, she secured it to the trunk of a nearby tree.

"Climb, if you will," she declared.

Drustan tested the rope's strength before he began his ascent. And when he was finally free from the depths of the pit, he shook the dirt from his clothes and faced the two faeries, who now stood before him the size of children.

"Your appearance is pleasing," she spoke in a coquettish manner. "Are all men as tall and well-formed as thyself?"

Drustan replied, a hint of pride in his voice, "Nay, not all."

Her bold fingers roamed over his biceps and face, as she inspected him like a prize horse at market. Drustan felt discomfort at her attention.

"I've encountered larger men," Tyree said with a shrug. "And many who were more comely."

"Forgive my brother," she apologized. "He has a distaste for humankind. But I find you exquisite, Drustan."

"I suppose I should thank you," Drustan said, pushing away her wandering hands.

"We are faeries of the Seelie Court," Tyree proclaimed. "What brings you to our forest?"

"I seek someone," Drustan stated. "Possibly you have knowledge of her whereabouts."

Aster walked around Drustan and looked at him closely, again touching his shoulders, his back and finally checking the firmness of his rear.

"Please!" Drustan jumped in surprise. "You are being a little too brash for one so young and so offended by a swear."

Undaunted, Aster persisted boldly. "Do you have a mate?"

"Aster, enough!" Tyree growled.

"I was saying, I am searching for a woman," Drustan continued.

"I am a woman!" Aster proclaimed with glee, puffing out her chest.

"No, I seek a particular woman," Drustan corrected. "A witch."

"There are many witches in these lands," Tyree replied, a hint of suspicion in his voice. "Do you seek a sorceress of light or a dark witch?"

"She is a dark one. Her name is Mora."

At the mention of her name, both faeries spat upon the ground in revulsion.

"I see you are familiar with her," Drustan noted, his eyes narrowing.

"I told you, Aster!" Tyree shouted. "You should have left him in the pit! He consorts with the evil witch from the Between."

"I consort with no one, I assure you."

"We know of the witch you seek. She has killed many of our kind and stolen their magic," Aster answered. "Why do you search for such an evil creature? Are you one of her men?"

Drustan straightened, his jaw set with determination. "Nay, I am no servant of hers," he declared. "She has caused harm upon my family and I will stop her, no matter the cost. I only wish to protect those I hold dear."

"And so you seek to slay the witch?" Tyree asked, a hint of amusement in his voice.

"Aye," Drustan replied, his hand straying to the hilt of his sword. "That is my purpose. To discover if she has succumbed to her wound, and if not, to bring an end to what I have started."

Aster gaped in disbelief, her eyes growing wide. "You...you are the hunter they whisper of, the one who dealt a mortal blow to Mora and drove her coven back to their stronghold?"

Drustan stood like a towering oak, his shoulders squared and his chest swelling with pride. "Aye, that I am," he declared, his voice laced with determination. "And not a moment shall pass where my quest for Mora's demise falters, for I shall persist until either she draws her final breath or I succumb to the tides of fate."

Tyree merely sneered, unimpressed. "Foolish mortal. If this be true, then you have only served to anger her further. Your foolish quest will be the death of you."

"Do you know for a certainty that she yet lives?" Drustan queried, his brow furrowed.

"Her maleficent power still looms over our world," Tyree replied solemnly. "Can you hear any revelries, any songs of rejoicing for our liberation? Nay, for all the Fae can sense her wickedness. She still draws breath."

"Then inform me, how may she be defeated?" Drustan pressed.

"Thou knowest how. Though ancient and potent, she remains mortal," Aster said. "She can be felled by blade, or by fire, or any other weapon that can strike down a mortal man."

"She will surely succumb to her wounds as any living being," Tyree added, "but you will never approach close enough to strike such a decisive blow. And if you wound her, she shall heal once more. The deed must be done in one swift, true strike."

"Then show me where she is," Drustan implored, his voice growing forceful. "You spoke of her having taken the lives and magic of your kind. Then aid me in vanquishing her."

"We cannot risk getting involved," Tyree declared, a note of finality in his voice. "If thou should fail, she will come for us."

"She comes for us regardless," Aster countered. Turning back to Drustan she explained, "She has us trapped here in this mortal world, unable to return to our faerie realm. To go home we would have to pass through her realm and risk capture."

"Then please, aid me in this," Drustan implored. "Help me to destroy her for both our sakes."

"Maybe we could offer some assistance," Aster said, against Tyree's protests.

"Aster, no!" Tyree bellowed. "This is not allowed. I'll have no part in this."

"Then go, Tyree!" Aster spat.

"Perhaps I will! I grow tired of this human's bluster and boasts, anyway."

"Good riddance!" she yelled as Tyree transformed back into his winged faerie form and flew away. "We do not need thy help," Aster muttered before turning back to Drustan. "To slay the witch, thou must strike her down like any mortal. She cannot be left wounded, lest she heal and strike again. Take off her head or burn her, and she shall surely die."

"But how do I get close enough to do so?" Drustan asked.

"Ah, there lies the rub," Aster sighed. "She'll not let down her guard. How did you wound her before?"

"I shot her with an arrow," he replied.

"Then you should do so again, but next time, make certain that she doesn't escape."

"Do you know of any weaknesses she may have? A means to distract her or catch her off guard?"

"She is too clever for trickery. And no doubt she will not underestimate you a second time," Aster replied. "My suggestion is that you do not pursue this path and instead run and hide."

"I do not run, nor will I hide," Drustan scolded.

"I suspected as much. You are too big and too brave. Then I'm sad to say you will likely die."

"That's it! That's all you have to offer!"

"Only my condolences," Aster snickered.

"I thought you wanted to help!"

"Aye," the faerie looked at him thoughtfully. She walked around him examining him from head to toe. After a moment, she grinned sheepishly and said, "I will help you then. I will grant you three wishes to aid in your quest. But there is a price."

"And what is that price?"

Aster's eyes dropped to the ground and she twisted and turned her foot in the dirt like a nervous child. "A kiss," she answered.

"A kiss?" Drustan laughed. "That's it, a kiss?"

"Not just a little peck on the cheek. I mean a real kiss — on the mouth." She turned her head slightly, looking away with a blush.

"I would be happy to pay such a price in a few years," he laughed again, "but you are a mere child. You are too young to be kissing a grown man."

"A child!" She stamped her foot in a huff. "I am a grand faerie of the Seeley Court, not a child! I am 325 years old! If anyone is a child, it would be you!"

"Oh, I beg your pardon then."

"As well you should, witch hunter," she replied with a haughty tone, but her bashful demeanor quickly returned. "So, will you pay the price?"

"A kiss, that is all?" Drustan asked with a raised brow.

"Indeed, just a kiss," she replied with a shy smile.

"In that case, I shall give it with great delight."

Drustan pondered the offer she presented. He had little to his name besides his bow, a quiver of witch-slaying arrows, and a well-worn sword. He was a man on foot, wandering aimlessly through the forest.

"Anything I desire?" Drustan asked with a thoughtful expression.

"Anything within my power to grant," she said. "Know this before ye make your wishes. even a faerie's magic has limits. I cannot raise the dead, for once the spirit has left the body it is beyond my power to restore it. Nor can I alter past events, for what has been done cannot be undone. But within these limits, I shall do what I can to aid thee. Choose thy wishes wisely, for once they are granted, they cannot be undone."

"Then, I would ask for a horse," he stated firmly. "I request a mighty steed to carry me forth on my journey. Let the beast be of strong limb and stout heart. Equipped with a saddle and bridle, it shall be a fitting companion for a warrior such as myself. "

As soon as the words left his lips, a rustling in the woods caught his attention. He spun around to see a magnificent gray stallion, complete with saddle and reins, emerge from the trees and approach him.

"Magnificent," Drustan marveled. "Is he really for me?"

The horse walked directly up to Drustan and nuzzled against him affectionately. Drustan patted him on the side of his neck in return.

"He is thine. His name is Ghost," she snickered slightly. "He will serve you faithfully. Now, what is your second desire?"

Drustan considered carefully, but he did not have to ponder the question for very long since his only armament of value was his bow and arrows. The sword he carried was beaten and dulled, having been used as a practice sword for many years. Though it had served its purpose against the Redcap, the blade was blunted and offered little value without the use of brute force. He needed a sword, well made with a sharp blade to fight at close quarters.

"Well?" Aster pressed and began to tap her foot impatiently.

"A sword," he announced. "One made by a master smith, its blade honed sharp and true. Sharp enough to cut through the neck of the foulest witch."

"Then let it be so." Aster plucked a gnarled branch from the forest floor and offered it to Drustan. "Behold, Drustan, the sword I present to thee! Its blade is as sharp as a dragon's tooth, yet as light as a feather in thy hand. The steel is of the finest quality, forged by the hands of skilled craftsmen in the Seelie Court. It is a sword fit for a warrior such as thyself and shall serve thee well in battle."

The hunter took the branch in hand, bemused. And in that moment, the twisted wood transformed, its bark melting away to reveal a scabbard and sword of exquisite craftsmanship.

Drustan's eyes widened as he grasped the weapon's golden hilt, drawing the blade from its sheath with a hiss. He held it aloft, testing its weight and balance, marveling at the sharpness of its edge.

"Truly, a masterwork," he praised. "And deadly, I'd wager."

"'Tis none sharper."

188

With a nod of approval, Drustan replaced the blade in its scabbard, laying aside his old sword with a wistful sigh. He fastened the new weapon to his belt with pride, ready for whatever challenges lay ahead.

"And your final wish, witch hunter?" Aster asked, tapping her foot impatiently.

"Slay the witch, Mora," he spoke with a chill in his voice and a firm determination.

Aster laughed loudly at him. "Silly mortal, if I had the power to do so, I would have vanquished the witch myself long ago. But alas, as a wee bonnie faerie, my abilities have their limits. Though I can weave enchantments and cast spells, I cannot change the path of fate. Tho' the outcome is still unknown, 'tis thy destiny is to face Mora and her coven. I am sorry, but I cannot alter the course of destiny. Make another wish."

Drustan weighed his choices with caution. He had but one final wish and it had to be of great significance. Despite Aster's growing impatience, marked by her tapping foot, he finally made his decision.

"I wish ye to guide my steps on this journey and illuminate the path to Mora's lair. This wooded expanse presents a formidable challenge, for the dense foliage and tangled underbrush threaten to ensnare and confound even the bravest of men. Aye, they say the Black Keep lies at the heart of the forest, but which way is that? One unfamiliar with these woods, such as I, could easily lose his way. "

"Aye, I see thy plight, for this forest is a labyrinth, easily confounding even the most seasoned of hunters. Its depths can easily bewilder those unaccustomed to its ways. Tho' the leaves are falling, the canopy is still so thick as to obstruct the sun's guidance, and the stars at night are but a mere glimmer amidst the shroud of darkness. 'Tis a formidable challenge indeed."

"So you will be my guide?" Drustan asked.

"Art thou daft?" Aster laughed. "Absolutely not! I would sooner lead thee through the underworld than venture to Mora's fortress!"

"Seems ye have made some bold claims about yer abilities, yet everything seems to be beyond thy power. Methinks ye have over-promised." Drustan said sternly. "Methinks you're not such a grand faerie after all."

"Don't be such a stinker," Aster snapped. "I can grant thy wish by other means, without having to step foot in that cursed place."

She extended her closed hand, then opened it to reveal a shiny disk in her palm. "Here, this can be your guide."

Drustan took the object she offered, examining it with wonder. It was a golden disk with a small arrow, pointing steadfast in one direction, no matter how he turned it. Upon its surface, a depiction of a hag riding a broomstick, etched in delicate detail at the top of the disk.

"What manner of trinket is this?" he asked, perplexed.

"'Tis called a compass. It is the only one of its kind in this land."

"And what does a compass do?"

"Unfurl the compass before thee, and let its arrow guide you towards the wicked witch Mora. Follow the path it sets for you, and thou shalt reach her castle - a dark fortress of black stone, standing alone and forgotten in the forest. But beware, brave hunter," Aster warned. "Her castle is guarded by witches and evil creatures. But the compass will not steer you wrong, it will lead you to your destiny."

Drustan turned the compass this way and that, watching as the arrow danced. "The arrow points east, not north," he said, eyebrows knitted in confusion.

"To the east," Aster confirmed, "and there you shall find what you seek."

"But others have claimed the witch's keep lies in the north, in the heart of the forest," Drustan countered.

"In the heart of the forest, aye, but that heart lies to the east," Aster declared. "Have faith in the compass, brave hunter. It will not steer you wrong."

"Aye, I'll trust it," Drustan said, still uncertain, but unwilling to dispute the faerie. "And I thank you for these gifts, kind Aster."

Gifts! 'Tis not gifts! 'Twas a bargain struck and now the price ye must pay," she said, her voice dripping with portent.

"Aye, I haven't forgotten," he smiled.

"Then now give me my kiss." She closed her eyes, puckered her lips and stood on her tiptoes waiting.

Drustan smiled at her childish innocence and was somewhat uncomfortable at the thought that she appeared so young. He wondered if maybe he was taking advantage of the situation and her innocence.

"Well?" She asked impatiently and opened one eye to look at him.

He stepped to her and with his hand swept her golden hair away from her face. With a gentle touch he placed his hands on her arms, leaned down, and softly pressed his lips to hers. Her lips were supple and tasted like honey, and the scent of fresh flowers filled the air around her. After a moment, he stepped away and looked at her angelic face.

Her eyes opened, and with a tone of disappointment and anger, she asked, "Is that all you have to offer? A mere peck?"

Drustan was taken aback, "Are you not pleased?"

"If that's all you have to give, then no wonder you have no mate," Aster said in frustration. "You kissed the horse more passionately than me. That was no kiss! I want a real kiss!"

Drustan was a little embarrassed by her impetuous behavior, but now his masculinity had been stung. He was determined he was not going to disappoint her. After all, this was not only a matter of his masculine pride; it was indeed a debt he owed.

He took her in his arms and pulled her tightly against him. Looking deeply into her green eyes, he slipped his hand around the nap of her neck and the other arm around her waist. Then he kissed her again. This time deeply and with passion. A few moments later, he released her and stepped back.

She swayed as if intoxicated, swooning from his fiery kiss. Clearly, his masculinity had been proven beyond question. She opened her eyes and blushed bright red as she looked at him. Then without warning, she transformed into her original faerie form and took flight, giggles spilling from her lips as she flew away.

Drustan couldn't help but grin as he beheld the faerie's fading form, swallowed by the growing shadows of the forest. He felt a sense of pride and satisfaction, not only for the bargain he had struck, but also for the unmistakable impact of his kiss upon the faerie.

He took hold of the reins of his new steed, Ghost, and walked back to where he would set his camp. His steps were filled with a prideful, self-assured gait. His gaze was locked upon the wandering needle of his compass, marveling at its erratic movement with a naive curiosity. The sun had disappeared behind the distant mountain and night was at hand. It was time for him to make his rest. In the morning, he would continue his journey, guided by his trusty compass and the strength of his new mount, until he reached the walls of Mora's castle. There, he would discover if she still lived, and if fate was kind, he would bring an end to the mission he had begun.

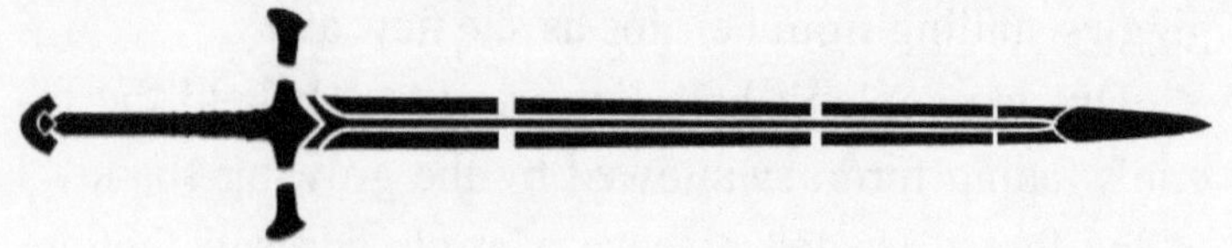

CHAPTER 13

The Ritual of Rebirth

It was the stroke of midnight when Mora, garbed in robes of scarlet velvet, made her way into the moon-kissed courtyard of the castle, attended by the remnants of her coven. A day had passed since the slaughter of Jaret the vampire, whose blood they had used to stave off her impending demise. Yet the dark power of his blood, combined with her magic, was failing. The wound in her shoulder wept anew, the black ichor staining the plush fabric of her robes, as the streaks of poison from the arrow spread once more through her veins. Her shoulder throbbed with pain, a dire reminder that if she did not perform the ritual or find another vampire to sacrifice, death would claim her soon enough.

She paced anxiously around the wooden altar that had been assembled in the center of the courtyard. Its surface was crafted from rough-hewn planks, and beneath it lay a pile of kindling, arranged in a manner that could only signal one thing: a funeral pyre. The torches that dotted the ground flickered and danced, casting an orange glow over the scene, while a blazing fire pit in the

194

center of the courtyard illuminated the enclosure with its bright, flickering light.

After a quarter century of planning and searching, her long wait was almost at an end. A quest born of the cruel advance of time, a reminder that her mortal body was not immune to the ravages of age. Despite her mastery of the dark arts, she could only slow the pace of her decline, not stop it entirely. The lines on her face grew deeper, the once-smooth skin now creased with wrinkles, her hair turning from raven black to white as cotton. Realizing that her spells had reached their limit of power over the march of time she began preparations for the ritual of rebirth, a rite that would restore her youth and power.

Her coven had been tasked with finding the rarest of all the ingredients needed for her ritual, a suitable vessel to bear her reincarnated form. But the elusive commodity proved difficult to find. Time, that unrelenting thief, was closing in, stealing her youth and power with each passing day. And so, she decided to take matters into her own hands, manipulating the conception and hatching a diabolical plan for the young maid, Isabel.

Fate had never been a friend to her, it seemed. Despite all her careful planning and the help of Raum, all was not as it should be. Isabel, once a student of the dark arts under her tutelage, had betrayed her in the cruelest of fashions. With a swift hand, she had taken the child that was key to the ritual, the child that would bring her the rebirth she so desperately sought, and fled into the night.

The decades of planning and searching had all been

for naught. Her body grew weaker, her magic faded, and her desperation deepened. The winds of fate continued to conspire against her, leaving her to wander in a world where her once boundless power was now but a shadow of its former self. The darkness was closing in, threatening to swallow her whole.

And yet, despite all that, she refused to be defeated. Her thirst for power and youth burned like an flame within her, a flame that would not be quenched. One day, she would have what she so desperately desired. For in the end, she would not be undone by the fickle whims of fate.

And so it was, two decades later, as Mora lay upon the brink of death, that Raum, long-sworn to her service, would finally fulfill his purpose. A mother and child, rare and precious, the key to her rebirth, would be brought to her. The past, with its memories and regrets, would be cast aside, a thing to be discarded and forgotten. And in their place, Mora would rise, a being of youth and power, free from the grasp of time, reborn in all her glory. The darkness that had once threatened to consume her would be but a fading memory, and in its place, the light of her rebirth would shine bright and strong. For Mora, nothing could stand in the way of her will, not even death itself.

Raum arrived at the courtyard, where Mora and her coven of witches had assembled, leading a young woman heavy with child. He lingered at the entrance, wary of venturing too close to the cackling hags and their dark magic after having witnessed Jaret's fate. The girl hesitated at his side, gazing fearfully at the gathered hags. With a gentle nudge, he directed her towards Mora, and she advanced, her eyes darting around the eerie surroundings until she stood before the crone. She hesitated once more, casting a glance over her shoulder at Raum, who offered a reassuring nod.

She trusted him, this foolish girl. He had worked diligently to build that trust. He had come upon her one night, wandering lost and despairing. He had intended to feed upon her, but when he saw the swell of her belly, he hesitated. Not out of any sense of decency, for he had none. The thought of killing a woman with child held no revulsion for him. He merely wondered if this might be the one Mora sought.

He began his seduction, weaving a web of deceit and false promises. Night after night, he met her in secret, playing upon her desperation and offering comfort for her situation, promising love and salvation. She had fallen under his spell, lured by the false whispers of love and safety. He had crafted a mirage of kindness and compassion, playing upon her vulnerable state, until she was ensnared in his trap. But Raum was a master of deceit, telling her that he was from a wealthy family and that his father would never accept a marriage if she carried another man's child.

The girl was once again distraught, and hated her unborn child even more than she had previously. It was then that Raum offered a solution. He told her of Mora, and that she was a witch who could end the pregnancy. Once the baby was gone, there would be nothing standing between them. They could return to his home and be married.

Hopelessly in love, and desperate to be free of the

baby, the girl agreed. She was to return to her home and wait for Raum to make the arrangements. When the time was right, Raum assured her that he would send his servants to bring her to the village where he would be waiting.

The foolish girl had placed her faith in a monster, and now she would pay the price for her naivety. The thought of it brought a wicked grin to Raum's lips, as he reveled in the power he held over her.

Now, standing in the courtyard she was nervous, yet she had no misgivings about her decision, nor reservations about ending the life of the child she had felt moving inside her. Her only concern was for what pain she might experience in the process, and how quickly she would recover so that she and Raum could marry.

"Approach, my dear child," Mora crooned, her wrinkled hand extended toward the young woman. "Let me gaze upon thee with these tired eyes."

With uncertain steps, the girl drew near, until she stood before the hag.

"What is thy name, sweetling?" Mora asked, her hand reaching out to stroke Abi's auburn tresses.

"Abi, ma'am," she replied, dipping into a nervous curtsy.

"Such beauty, such grace," Mora marveled. "And what brings thee to my doorstep?"

"Raum," Abi stammered, clutching her belly protectively. "He said you could help me."

"Indeed, he did," Mora nodded sagely. "But first, thou must tell me thy tale. I've had too many a maid brought here, against their will, by cruel men. Thou must speak it from thy own lips, that thou come of thy own accord, with a will unbroken."

"It is my choice," Abi declared, her voice firmer.

"And what is it ye seek?" Mora probed, her eyes like black pits, drilling into Abi's soul.

"He said you could rid me of this ... this ..." Abi whispered, rubbing a hand over her swollen belly, "this unclean spawn."

"Aye, my sweet little dove," Mora spoke with sinister glee. "But why do you seek such a thing? A child is oftentimes a cherished gift for a young couple."

"This is not our child, nor a gift," Abi retorted with bitterness. "It is a curse upon me, an abomination that I wish to be rid of, so that I may be with my true love."

"Oh, my dear child! Such a trying circumstance you find yourself in, but how can you call an unborn babe an abomination? Such words wound the very essence of motherhood."

The girl hung her head in disgrace, glancing towards Raum who lingered in the darkness at the entrance.

"Fear not, we shall not judge thee," Mora whispered, placing a hand upon the girl's cheek, forcing her to look into her eyes. "We merely seek the truth. Tell me, young one, how did you come to be in this state?"

"I was wandering through the meadow, alone," Abi revealed, her voice trembling with the memory. "I didn't see him at first, he must have followed me. But then I spotted him lurking amongst the trees, observing me. I thought he was playing a cruel game, so I approached him." She faltered, pausing as the terror of the event flooded back to her.

"You are safe, my dear. Tell me what happened?" Mora coaxed.

"He grabbed me and began to grope me … in places," she again whispered in embarrassment. "I tried to push him away, but then he tore my dress. He threw me to the ground and forced himself upon me."

"Ah, the wretched fate of this innocent lamb," Mora spoke with a sorrowful, yet electric voice. "But, I must know, why did you not run from this stranger when you first saw him lurking in secret?"

"'Twas no stranger, my lady. It was my own father who committed this foul deed."

"The betrayal," Mora sighed, her voice trembling with a mixture of empathy and excitement. "It cuts deep, oh so deep. To be beset upon by the one who should have shielded thee, who should have kept thee from harm. Such a cruel, cruel blow."

Mora swiveled her gaze towards Laine, who stood but a stone's throw away. "Sister, did thou hear the lamentable tale, the sorrow of such a misfortune?"

"A merciless blow of fate, indeed," Laine concurred, her voice rough with feigned sorrow, mirroring Mora's artful display of empathy.

"And tell me, little one, has another man taken advantage of thy youthful innocence, before or after this monstrous occurrence?" Mora continued.

"No, there has been no other."

"Oh, my sweet, innocent child," Mora said, her voice rich with pity. "If banishing this unborn curse is truly your heart's desire, then fear not, for we shall make it so."

Mora guided the girl to the wooden altar and helped her up on it. "Lay down, my dear, and soon this dreadful situation will be put behind you."

With obedient fear, Abi lay back and watched as the coven witches descended upon her, swiftly tying her arms and legs to the altar. Her fear and alarm were palpable, and she turned to Raum for comfort, but instead, she was met with his emotionless, frigid gaze. The witches held her firmly in place despite her struggles.

"What are you doing? Why are they tying me?" Abi cried out, her voice shaking as she pulled against the ropes.

"This may be painful, my little Abi," Mora replied with a dry, almost cruel tone. "We cannot have you writhing about during our work."

As the witches secured her restraints, Mora withdrew a gleaming dagger from the folds of her robes. She held it aloft, silently reciting incantations with moving lips, producing no sound. As she spoke, the witches roughly tore Abi's clothing from her body, revealing her distended abdomen. The girl screamed in terror as she finally understood the danger she faced. The coven began to chant in unison, ignoring Abi's pleas for mercy.

"Please, let me go!" Abi screamed, desperately trying to break free. Yet no one paid her any heed. "I've changed my mind, please! Raum, make them stop!" she cried, looking to him with pleading eyes, begging for his intervention. But to her horror, she was met with his blank, unfeeling expression, as he turned his back on her and walked away, leaving her to face her fate alone.

With an icy heart, he left the young woman behind,

feeling not a shred of mercy or remorse for the horrors he had inflicted upon her. Instead, only a sense of deliverance washed over him, as his debt to Mora was finally paid in full.

The taste of fear sat upon his tongue like a mouthful of bile, a noxious brew that threatened to choke him even as he strode from the castle. This night, Mora might no longer want for his vampire blood, at least not for centuries to come, but he knew all too well the dangers that still lurked in the shadows. The witch had not earned her reputation for nothing, after all. He had no illusions that she would willingly give up her thirst for power, nor could he be certain that the coven witches would not seek to prolong their own lives with his dark blood. In his mind, there was no true victory, only a momentary reprieve from the unceasing threat that Mora posed to his kin.

As he made his way through to woods headed back to his lair, Raum was consumed with thoughts of his fallen son Jaret. The burden of his loss lay heavy upon him, a weight that would not lift. No longer bound to Mora's will, his mind turned towards retribution. He burned with a desire for vengeance, an unquenchable thirst for Mora's blood.

With the completion of the ritual, Mora may regain her youth and vigor, but Raum was not so easily defeated. He was immortal, with endless time to plan and execute his revenge. The fires of his hatred burned bright and would not be extinguished until Mora was destroyed, body and soul.

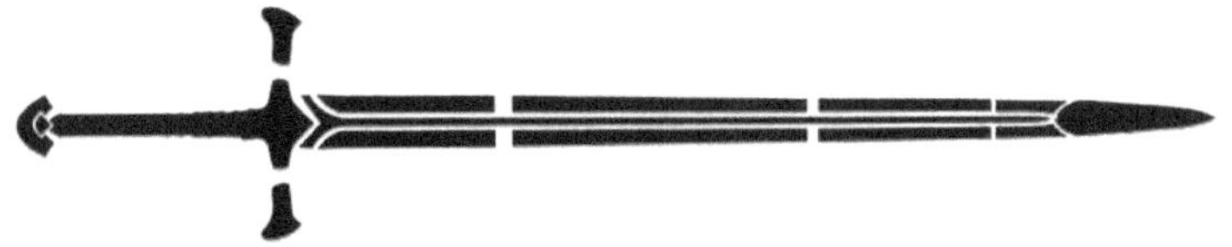

CHAPTER 14

Hornswoggled

Roused from slumber by the gentle touch of the morning sun, Drustan awoke to find himself bathed in a warm golden light. He felt a sense of purpose stirring within him, and he rose to his feet, ready to continue his quest. His gaze fell upon the magnificent sword, a gift from the faerie of the night before. Its smooth surface shimmered in the sunlight, and Drustan ran his fingers over its glistening surface, marveling at its beauty. It was the most magnificent weapon he had ever seen, a sword fit for a hero.

His old sword rested on the ground, dull and rusty compared to its magnificent successor. For a moment, Drustan considered leaving it behind, but the memories it held were too strong. He remembered the years of training with his stepfather, Rowan, and the lessons he had learned. With a touch of reverence, Drustan collected his old sword and secured it to his backpack, a symbol of the journey he had taken thus far and the hero he had become.

With a glint of determination in his eye, Drustan

reached into his backpack and withdrew a piece of jerky. He bit down on it, savoring the salty, smoky flavor as he prepared to continue his journey. He turned to his magnificent stallion, another gift from the faerie, Aster, and lovingly patted its neck. The animal was strong and regal, its muscles rippling beneath its shimmering coat.

Drustan then gazed upon the magical compass that Aster had given him, a symbol of hope and guidance on his quest. The needle was unwavering, pointing in the direction where the darkness of evil lay and the wicked witch awaited. The sun caught the golden edges of the compass, casting a warm, shimmering glow upon Drustan's face.

He was filled with a sense of purpose and courage, knowing that he was not alone on his journey. With the magic of the compass guiding him, the strength of his stallion beneath him, and the blade of his sword on his side, Drustan prepared to set out into the unknown, ready to face any dangers that lay ahead and bring an end to the evil that threatened his family.

With fluid movements, Drustan hoisted himself upon his magnificent steed, his heart ablaze with pride and fierce determination. As he braced himself for the journey ahead, he gazed upon the face of the magical compass. The needle spun and pointed towards the east, yet Drustan couldn't shake the nagging feeling that something was amiss.

He looked up to the sky, where the sun was slowly climbing higher, and then back down at the compass. "This isn't north," he murmured, turning in circles, alternating his gaze between the compass and the sky. The men in the village had spoken of Mora's castle lying to the north, and the faerie Aster had whispered that it was nestled in the heart of the enchanted forest, also to the north. Yet the compass pointed towards the east.

Perplexed and uncertain, Drustan sat atop his mount, wondering which path to take. Should he trust his own instincts and head north, or follow the guidance of the magical compass towards the east? He couldn't fathom the discrepancy, unless perhaps there was an easier route that the compass would lead him towards, or some unseen obstacle blocking his direct route to the north.

"What do you think, Ghost?" Drustan asked his horse, who nodded its head and neighed in response, before ambling forward into the dense forest, turning towards the east.

With a heart ablaze with uncertainty and a thirst for adventure, Drustan allowed Ghost to guide him deeper into the unknown. The beat of the horse's hooves was a mesmerizing rhythm, as if the earth itself was beckoning Drustan to his fate. The air was thick with the musky perfume of pine and oak tree sap, and every breath Drustan took was an elixir of enchantment.

As they ventured forth, the forest was a kaleidoscope of sensory delights. The dappled light filtering through the canopy of branches was a mesmerizing play of light and shadow, casting an eerie beauty upon the forest floor. Drustan's hand was firm on the reins, his heart pulsing with excitement and trepidation.

With each footfall, his horse carried him closer to his fate, a sense of awe and wonder creeping over him, a foretelling of something greater at work. Drustan was unwavering in his determination, to follow the path set before him, no matter where it might take him. He was on a pilgrimage to confront his destiny, and as Ghost's strides took him deeper into the enchanted forest, Drustan felt himself becoming more deeply ensnared in the spell-binding magic that surrounded him. He was where he was meant to be, and not even the fiercest tempest or malevolent entity could stop him from facing his fate head-on.

Drustan's insides churned with an overwhelming sense of dread, a fear that was fed by the mysteries that lay ahead of him and the mystical beings he had already encountered. But Drustan was not one to let fear consume him. He understood that a wise man knows how to harness the power of fear, to turn it into a weapon that sharpens his mind and quickens his reactions. He saw fear not as a hindrance but as a driving force, one that could push him to greater heights of bravery. For Drustan knew that without fear, there can be no courage. So, he did not shy away from it, but instead, he embraced it, using it as a guiding light on his journey towards bravery.

Despite his inexperience in the ways of the world, Drustan was filled with a confidence bordering on arrogance, ready to face both the unknown and the feared witches. Each step of his journey only served to strengthen his resolve and feed the fire within him.

Drustan and his steadfast mount, Ghost, came upon a formidable barrier of thorns and undergrowth that would not yield to their passing. Despite Drustan's valiant efforts to guide Ghost around the obstruction, the horse remained steadfast, its hooves digging into the soft earth as if it refused to be swayed. Drustan knew that they could not turn back now, not when their quest hung in the balance, and so he made the brave decision to dismount and clear a path with his trusty sword.

He unsheathed the magnificent weapon, its gleaming blade catching the rays of light filtering through the leaves overhead. With a fierce determination, Drustan swung the sword with all his might, slicing through the dense undergrowth like a scythe through wheat. But with each successive blow, the sword grew heavier and heavier, as if some unseen force was sapping its strength. The weight of the sword became a burden upon Drustan's arms, and he was soon straining with the effort of lifting it.

And yet, he refused to give in. He swung the sword again and again, sweat pouring down his face as he battled against the unseen magic that sought to hold him back. And then, with a final, resounding clang, the sword was wrenched from his grasp, crashing to the ground with a thud. Drustan stared in disbelief as he gazed upon the inert weapon, its blade buried in the earth as if it were rooted there.

Drustan dropped to his knees in near exhaustion, his chest and shoulders heaving to catch his breath. "What manner of sorcery is this?"

With a fierce determination, Drustan set about retrieving his sword from the thicket where it had fallen. He gritted his teeth and summoned all his strength, using every ounce of his might to drag the weapon from the earth. The sword was heavy, as if it had been forged from lead, and he was forced to use every ounce of his energy just to budge it from its resting place. But even then he was not deterred, for he was a warrior of great courage and determination, and he would not let a mere weapon best him.

Finally, with a triumphant shout, he managed to wrench the sword free, the sound of its release ringing out through the trees. He staggered back, panting for breath, as he gazed upon the weapon. It was a magnificent piece of craftsmanship, its blade shimmering as it lay on the ground. But as he reached for the hilt, he was met with a terrible surprise, for the sword had grown even heavier. It was as heavy as a boulder, and he could not lift it.

He studied the sword, his eyes scanning its length, searching for any signs of curse or enchantment. And as he gazed upon the weapon, he was filled with a sense of foreboding, a premonition that something sinister was afoot. He knew that the sword had not simply become heavy by chance, for the magic that surrounded it was palpable, as thick as the air he breathed. And as he considered the thicket that surrounded him, he could not help but wonder whether it too was enchanted, designed to keep him from his quest.

He cast his wary gaze upon the thicket, and saw that his path was almost cut. A little longer he would have a passage through. With a fierce determination, he reached for his old, reliable sword, drawing it from his backpack with a swift motion. The familiar hilt felt comforting in his hand, and he felt a surge of confidence as he approached the thicket once more. With a roar, he began to cut away the brush, his blade flashing with deadly grace as it carved a path through the tangled vines and thorns.

Drustan attacked the remaining brush with a ferocity born of exhaustion and frustration. With each stroke of his trusty sword, the tangled vines and thorns fell away, until at last the path before him was clear. He sheathed his blade with a sense of relief, feeling the weariness of his work settle deep into his bones.

But even as he trudged back to the place where the sword that Aster had given him lay, Drustan knew that his trials were far from over. For as he reached for the enchanted weapon, he was met with a cruel reminder of the magic that surrounded it. The sword was still as heavy as a boulder, its weight defying his every attempt to lift it from the ground.

In a rage he kicked at it. Drustan's foot connected with the cursed sword, sending a jolt of pain rocketing up his leg like he had kicked the very foundation of the earth itself. The truth of the situation hit him like a ton of bricks, the sword was beyond his control, a nightmare made of steel, taunting him with its inaccessibility. He turned away from the bewitched weapon, his heart heavy with defeat, and made his way back to the faithful Ghost.

"What could that have meant?" Drustan muttered to his horse, as he pondered the implications of the enchanted sword. Was that the faerie's cruel game or the manipulative hand of Mora. "It's all your fault, you stubborn beast," he added as he prepared to mount Ghost, "we could have easily gone around."

With a sense of relief, Drustan mounted his trusty steed, Ghost, fully expecting a uneventful ride through the forest. However, as soon as his body settled into the saddle, he was met with a startling reality, as the horse reared up in a fit of madness. Snorting and squealing with an animalistic fervor, Ghost was soon galloping through the dense trees at a breakneck pace. Drustan was left clinging desperately to the saddle, dodging the whipping branches and ducking under low-hanging boughs as the horse charged forward, its once-tame demeanor completely consumed by the grip of crazed insanity.

Drustan was at the mercy of the horse's wild will, with each hoofbeat echoing like a clap of thunder, urging them forward with a reckless abandon. Through the forest they raced, a tempest of horseflesh and man, until they burst into a sun-dappled clearing, where the shimmering expanse of a freshwater loch lay before them. The horse's pace quickened, lured by the dark and mysterious waters.

Drustan fought with the reins, his hands grappling frantically, trying to regain control over the horse. But the stallion was not to be restrained, and with a ferocious determination, it charged towards the loch, its hooves pounding the earth with a relentless rhythm. The wind howled past them as they rode, each step bringing them closer to the unknown, to what lay beneath the dark waters.

"Whoa, boy!" Drustan shouted, but his words were lost in the rush of wind and the pounding of hooves. He could do nothing but hold on tight and pray that they both emerged from this dizzying, wild ride unscathed. The power of the horse and the pull of the dark loch combined to create a force that threatened to overwhelm them both, and all Drustan could do was surrender to the ride and hope that Ghost would soon tire and calm down again.

But the stallion showed not signs of slowing and instead ran faster and faster the closer it got to the water's edge.

With a mighty splash, the stallion dove headlong into the loch, sinking deep into the dark and murky waters, pulling Drustan down with him. Desperately, Drustan fought to free himself from the saddle, swimming with all his might back to the surface. Treading water, he shivered in the icy cold, his mind whirling with confusion and uncertainty. Why had Ghost become so uncontrollable, why had he recklessly plunged into the loch? Drustan searched the waters, turning in every direction, but there was no sign of the stallion. The horse had vanished, somewhere deep beneath the dark murky waters.

A voice, fraught with alarm, cut through the tranquil air and reached Drustan's ears. "Get out of the water, lad!" it cried, its tone leaving no room for doubt. "Make for the shore!"

The urgency in the voice sent a shiver down Drustan's spine and he scanned the shoreline, searching for the source. Peering through the shimmering veil of the loch, Drustan caught sight of a figure on the shore, a dark and looming presence that appeared to be a dog standing upright on its hind legs, its eyes fixed on him. The sight was unearthly, filling Drustan with a deep sense of unease and sending his heart racing.

And then, from the dark, inky depths of the loch, something emerged that shattered all Drustan's perceptions of reality. It was Ghost, his once-majestic stallion, now twisted and transformed into a grotesque apparition, a nightmarish vision of horror. The once-sleek and shining coat of the horse was now coated in sickly green scales, its hide mottled and moss-covered, while the shape of its body was now more reminiscent of a diseased amphibian than a horse. The head of the beast remained, but the ears were gone, replaced by empty holes that hinted at an abyssal void. Running the length of its long, slender neck were gills, fluttering in the water like the fins of a fish.

"Ghost?" Drustan was filled with alarm as he gazed upon the creature before him. The magnificent stallion that had been gifted to him by the faerie Aster had been twisted and corrupted, transforming into a monstrosity from the blackest depths of the loch. He could not tell if the beast before him was truly his beloved Ghost, or a spawn of darkness conjured from the loch to drag him to a watery grave.

"No!" Drustan yelled as the creature lunged forward, its mouth agape with jagged teeth bared.

The voice from the shore shouted again, "Get away from it!"

But Drustan was already in the creature's grasp, dragged under the water as its transformed front legs, now spindly tenacles ending in sharp claws, tightened around him. He thrashed, desperate to break free, but the monster was relentless, pulling him deeper and deeper into the icy depths of the loch. Drustan fought with all his might, knowing that if he didn't escape, the devilish beast would surely claim his life.

Drustan clutched desperately for his sword. But in

the midst of the fray, the weapon was wrenched from his grasp and disappeared into the dark, forbidding depths. Panic surged through him, but he fought back with all his might, having enough wits about him in the confusion to seize an arrow from his quiver and plunge into the beast.

The battle was a nightmare of flesh and fury. Drustan plunged the arrow into the monster's neck again and again, his arms growing heavy and his chest aching for air. Despite his resistance, the beast dragged him deeper and deeper into the water, the darkness of the depths closing in around him like a shroud. His vision blurred and consciousness slipped away, but he fought against the impending darkness, determined to vanquish his enemy even as he drew his last breath.

With a final burst of strength, Drustan plunged the arrow deep into the beast's neck, feeling the surge of triumph even as the water rushed into his lungs. He convulsed and choked, his body writhing in its death throes as the world around him faded to black. Yet, even in the face of certain death, his mind remained strangely calm, surrendering to the embrace of the water as the beast's lifeless tentacles finally released him from their grasp. Together, the warrior and his enemy sank into the murky depths of the loch.

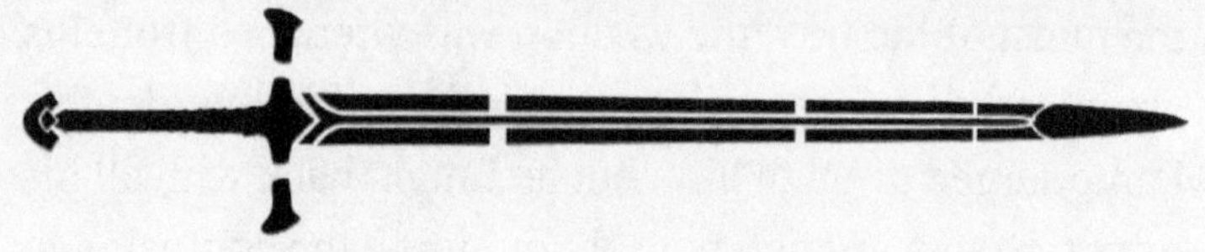

CHAPTER 15

Saved by the Wulver

When Drustan awoke, he thought he had been transported to the afterlife. He lay on the shore, surrounded by the soft, cloying mud, coughing and retching water from his lungs. The howling of the autumn wind echoed over the loch like the wail of a banshee, its icy touch gripping him as he trembled and shook, his body overwhelmed by weakness.

With his vision clouded, Drustan struggled to take in his surroundings, seeking any sign of the monster that had brought him to this place. But all he saw was a dark, shapeless form kneeling beside him, and in his confusion, he fought against it, believing it to be the beast that had once been his horse, returned to claim him once and for all.

"You're safe, lad," the indistinct figure assured him. "Take deep breaths. That's it, slow and steady."

As the comforting voice washed over him, Drustan felt his fear and confusion dissipate. He collapsed back into the mud, his breathing slowly returning to normal.

He rubbed his eyes, attempting to clear his vision, and as his sight sharpened, he was met with a shock that nearly made him bolt upright.

Before him stood a creature unlike any he had ever seen. Towering on two hind legs, covered head to toe in thick, brown fur, it was a being of both man and beast. Its long snout was lined with menacing canine teeth, and its eyes, golden brown and piercing, watched him with a mix of curiosity and caution. It wore pants, but no shirt or shoes, leaving its powerful arms and hands fully exposed. This was no man - it was a towering, speaking wolf-beast, and Drustan could not help but scuttle away in fear.

"Fear not, young lad," spoke the creature, his deep voice rumbling like the thunder that trembled the Highlands. He shook his shaggy coat, sending droplets of water flying, before fixing his gaze upon the Drustan. "For 'tis I who delivered thee from thy watery grave."

"What manner of creature art thou?" Drustan managed to ask, his breaths coming in short gasps and coughs as he continued to expel water. "A werewolf," he answered his own query, though his conclusion was flawed.

The creature let out a low, rumbling chuckle. "Nay, good sir," it spoke. "Though I can see how thou hast arrived at such a conclusion. I am, in truth, a wulver."

"A wulver? What is a wulver? Are you a faerie of sorts?"

"Nay," he laughed again. "Wulvers are … well, like me. Werewolves are like you, but can turn into like me. And faeries are a whole different thing all together."

Drustan gazed upon the beast with a furrowed brow, seeking to comprehend its words. "I see," he said, though his confusion was evident. Yet, despite his confusion, the soothing tone of the wulver's voice served to calm his nerves.

"Simply put, a werewolf is a human that can turn into a wolf, a pretty mean one at that. We wulvers do not change our form, we are always just as you see me now. Most of us are kind and gentle, we make no trouble when none is started."

He extended his hand to help Drustan to his feet. "Can you stand now? Best climb out of that cold mud before you freeze in it."

Drustan's heart wavered, caught in the grip of doubt, as he questioned whether he could place his trust in the immense, wild creature standing before him. Yet, as his gaze delved into the depths of the wulver's eyes, and he pondered the tenderness in its voice, a glimmer of assurance kindled within him. The realization struck him that this formidable creature could have effortlessly snuffed out his life while he lay defenseless, yet it had refrained. Perhaps, just perhaps, this enigmatic being harbored no ill intentions toward him - at least for the present moment. Taking a resolute breath, Drustan reached out and clasped the proffered hand, hauling himself up from the mire, his muddied boots skidding on the slick earth.

"My name's Gib," the wulver said, its voice rich and warm as a summer day.

"Were you enchanted?" Drustan asked, still wary. "Are you a man transformed into a wolf, or a wolf transformed into a man?"

The wulver's deep laughter filled the air. "Did you inhale too much of the water? Or do you simply not pay heed?" Gib asked, his eyes twinkling. "I am just a wulver. This is who I am, just as my father was, and his father before him. Have you never heard of my kind?"

Drustan shook his head, the beads of water in his hair catching the light like diamonds. "Not that I can recall."

"Well, I suppose 'tis no surprise. Not a lot of us left, and we mostly keep to ourselves and do not bother people. We may look like wolves, and our build is like a man; but we are neither and we are both. We are just wulvers. Some could say that men walk and are built like a wulver, and wolves have heads and faces like us. Depends on whose perspective you are speaking from."

"I guess so," Drustan stammered. He was still confused by the bestial appearance of the wulver combined with its disarmingly cheerful disposition and chattiness. "Well, Gib, I'm grateful for your help."

"Ah, I only saved you from the water, but you saved yourself from a most ghastly fate," Gib said, patting Drustan on the shoulder with a warm smile. "To have faced the beast and lived to tell the tale is a triumph in and of itself. May I inquire as to how you found yourself in such dire straits?"

"I cannot say for certain," Drustan stammered, still trying to make sense of the surreal encounter. "I was mounting my horse and all of a sudden, it turned wild. The next thing I knew, we were thrashing through the woods. Next thing I know I was in the loch being pulled under by... that thing. It was my horse, but it had transformed into a monstrosity beyond description."

"Ah, but that was no horse, my friend," Gib said with a knowing nod. "I would wager that if you have never heard of a wulver, then neither are you familiar with the kelpie."

"No, I cannot say that I am," Drustan admitted.

"A most diabolical creature it is," Gib continued with a tinge of disgust. "It lurks in the lochs and deep rivers, waiting to ensnare the unsuspecting. In its guise as a gentle steed, it lures victims onto its back and then, once mounted, drags them into the water to reveal its true form. If one is fortunate, they are drowned before the beast begins to eat. Once the kelpie has feasted, there is naught left but a trail of entrails along the bank."

"That is a grisly fate," Drustan whispered, feeling a chill run down his spine. "I am forever in your debt for coming to my rescue."

"I am simply glad to have been of assistance," Gib replied. "I have been hoping to rid this loch of the kelpie for some time now. Its presence puts the fish off, you see. And may I inquire, where did you come across this... horse?"

"It was given to me by a faerie," Drustan said, still trying to make sense of it all. "Along with a sword that proved to be too heavy to lift just when I needed it most."

"Ah, those mischievous faeries!" Gib huffed and spat, his disdain for the elusive creatures palpable. "Beware, my friend, for they are nothing but sly tricksters and deceitful cheats. Though, occasionally, you may come across one with an ounce of honor, the vast majority of them are vindictive and malevolent imps."

"Should my path ever cross with that vile snake

again," Drustan's voice shook with seething fury, "I will grasp her and squeeze her till she pops like a grape." He curled his hand into a tight, trembling fist, his anger a palpable presence in the air around him.

"And what of the third gift?" Gib inquired. "She bestowed upon ye a horse and a sword, but the faeries always offer three gifts."

"Aye," Drustan replied with a nod, as he delved into the depths of his pocket to retrieve a gleaming disk. "This was the last of her gifts," he said, handing the compass over to Gib with a hint of bitterness. "I felt an unease about it from the start, but I chose to ignore it."

"What is this trinket?" Gib asked, turning it over in his hands.

"That," Drustan huffed, "is a good question, considering the horse and the sword were nothing but empty promises. The fiend claimed it was something called a compass, one that would guide me in the direction I needed to go."

Gib turned the compass from side to side, observing as the arrow steadfastly pointed towards the loch, no matter which way he turned. "It seems you have reached your destination," he chuckled. "It points directly to the loch."

Drustan took back the compass and looked at it, his anger rising as he saw the arrow indeed pointed towards the water. "That malicious little harpy," he growled, clenching his jaw. "If I ever get my hands on her, I will pluck the very wings from her back." He thrust the compass back into his pocket, his body trembling with frustration.

Gib gave a humorless laugh. "Easy there, lad. Don't let your anger consume you. It's what they want, after all."

As the wind grew stronger, Drustan's shivers only intensified, wracking his body with unrelenting force. He pulled his cloak tighter around himself in a desperate attempt to fend off the chill, but the wind tore through the wet material as if it were made of gossamer. His clothes were drenched, clinging to his skin and adding to the cold that gnawed at him from within.

"You must get dry, or risk succumbing to the cold," Gib warned, his voice deep with concern. "I will take you to my cottage, where you can warm yourself by the fire and hang your clothes to dry. Stay as long as you need, and share my table if you like. Only then, when you are rested and ready, should you continue on your journey."

Drustan nodded, grateful for the offer. He looked around for his backpack and weapons, only to realize with a heavy heart that they, along with all his supplies, were now resting at the bottom of the loch. "All is lost," he moaned.

"Sorry to say I saw no sign of your belongings in the area. They have likely sunk to the depths of the loch."

"It could have been worse," Drustan sighed with a shrug. "I could be down there with them."

"Truly," Gib intoned with a nod of his shaggy head. "Your mere existence is a testament to your luck. Now, let us hasten to my humble abode, lest the bitter chill of this day cause your flesh to turn an unsightly shade of blue."

With a subtle nod, Drustan followed the wulver as he retrieved his fishing pole and tackle box from the shore. The two then set off, their pace quick as they traversed the dense woodland towards Gib's cottage.

"Pray, what name do you go by, young one?" Gib queried.

"My sincerest apologies," replied Drustan. "I am known as Drustan."

Gib mused on the name, his brow furrowed in thought. It was a name that resonated with him. As they continued on their journey, Gib's pace slowed until he came to a sudden halt.

"Drustan!" he proclaimed with a voice that boomed through the trees. "Could it be that you are the eldest son of one known as Sibby?"

"You know my mother?"

"Ah, yes, the name of Sibby the Wise is a legend throughout the land," Gib intoned with a knowing nod. "She is a gentle soul, steeped in the ancient ways, a mistress of the arcane arts practiced by both the Picts and the Druids. How can it be, then, that her own offspring remains ignorant of the wulvers and the dangers posed by malevolent kelpies? I am shocked that she has not seen fit to impart her wisdom upon thee more fully."

"I am but a sorry excuse for a student, I fear," Drustan replied with a shrug of his broad shoulders.

"Nonetheless, thou must be made aware of the perils that lurk beyond thy doorstep," Gib scolded, his tone laced with concern. "Thou must learn to distinguish friend from foe, and above all, never trust a faerie."

"My mother has indeed imparted some knowledge

upon me, but I have little inclination for magic," Drustan admitted. "I find greater satisfaction in the tension of a bowstring or the heft of a steel blade, rather than dabbling in the mysterious arts."

"You must heed the words of thy mother," Gib implored. "For not all battles are fought with weapons, and not all foes can be defeated with steel. Seek out her wisdom and embrace it, for it may prove to be thy greatest defense against the dark forces that threaten thee."

"Your words hold truth, and they echo those of my mother," Drustan replied with newfound respect. "I am beginning to understand the value of her teachings."

To Drustan's relief they were only a short walking distance away from Gib's abode, a sturdy hut constructed of rugged logs and sealed with earth to keep out the biting winds. As Drustan stepped inside, he was greeted by a scent that caught him unexpectedly. The interior was odorous with the musky fragrance of animals, not unpleasant like excrement, but rather rich and earthy, like the pelt of a great stag. The space within was neat and orderly, a single chamber with a small table and chair in one corner, and a pile of straw in the other that served as a bed. Stacked against one wall were boxes and wooden chests, the repositories of Gib's personal belongings. Near the bedding, a fireplace crackled and smoked, the embers pulsing with a rosy glow.

Gib tended to the fire, tossing more wood upon the blazing logs, until the flames danced high and bright. From a trunk, he withdrew a blanket and offered it to Drustan. "Set your clothing to dry and wrap yourself in this and sit by the fire, to drive the chill from your bones," Gib urged.

Drustan eagerly stripped off his wet garb and wrapped himself in the blanket, settling on the earthen floor beside the roaring hearth.

"Are you hungry?" Gib asked.

"I cannot bother you. You've done too much already."

"'Tis no bother, laddie."

Gib opened a chest and took out a plate, then from another chest he took out some dried fish that had been salted and wrapped in paper to keep. He put the fish on the plate and handed it to Drustan then sat down across from him in front of the roaring fire.

"I am grateful," Drustan accepted the food and began to devour it. He was famished. He had not eaten since the night before, and now his own food supply was lost either scattered in the woods or in the dark waters of the loch.

"Don't choke on the bones, laddie. I've plenty more if you like." Gib was pleased to see him eating. Wulvers love to fish, more than anything else; and they are very good at it. As a result, Gib had boxes of salted and dried fish on hand and was happy to have a guest to help relieve him of the bounty. In fact, wulvers were famous for sharing their catch, frequently leaving fresh fish on the windowsills and doorsteps of the poor or infirmed.

"Pray tell, what brings you so far from thy home? Your family has crops, and 'tis plentiful fishing and hunting in the area. Why have you strayed so far?"

"I am searching for someone."

"Ah! A wife?" Gib presumed. "You are at the age when you should be thinking of a family."

"Nay, I seek an evil witch."

"Careful, my boy. Sometimes those can be one and the same," Gib laughed.

"It is a true witch I seek. She attacked our home and threatened my family. I will take her life before she can do any more harm."

"Laddie, what do you know of witches? You were bested by a faerie and almost eaten by a kelpie. Do you think you will fare any better against a witch?"

"I have already killed many of her coven," Drustan replied in defense. "And I killed a Redcap goblin just two nights past. I believe I can handle myself well enough."

"A Redcap! Laddie, no one can kill a Redcap," Gib challenged. "You cannot run from one. You cannot hide from one. 'Tis no way to escape a Redcap."

"I did not run nor hide. I fought him and won."

"And how did you accomplish such a feat?"

"I took hold of his cap and, like a stone, he froze in place," Drustan said with a smirk. "And with one swift blow, I severed his head from his shoulders."

"He froze?" Gib asked, surprised. "I had no idea that would happen when his cap was removed."

"Aye," Drustan confirmed relishing the opportunity to share his story. "And did you know that when you claim a Redcap's cap, he must answer any question truthfully?"

"No," Gib replied, his tone filled with wonder. "That's a valuable piece of information to have."

"The Redcap claimed he could answer any question about the past, present, or future," Drustan continued. "But when pressed, he had no answers. And considering his situation, I couldn't trust his ability to foretell the future anyway." Drustan chuckled good-naturedly.

"Ah, so it seems I have underestimated your prowess as a warrior," Gib said with a hint of surprise. "And may I inquire, what is the name of the witch you seek?"

"Mora," came the simple reply.

"Mora!" Gib exclaimed, his face contorting in revulsion as he spat on the ground.

"That seems to be everyone's reaction."

"Indeed, it defiles my tongue to utter such an evil name," Gib declared, his tone stern. "I must say, you possess either immense bravery or a startling lack of sense to pursue such a malevolent witch. Regardless, it is a perilous quest, if not a foolish one."

"You know of Mora," Drustan said, his tone filled with determination. "Where can I find her?"

"I cannot in good conscience aid you in this quest," Gib replied, his voice stern. "Sending you to Mora is like leaving you in the clutches of a kelpie. At least the kelpie would have drowned you before gnawing on your bones; Mora will have no such mercy."

"She may already be dead," Drustan said, his expression serious. "I shot her with an enchanted arrow designed to kill witches. She was wounded and dying when I last saw her, but I must know if she still lives so I can finish what I started."

"Beware," Gib warned. "Some creatures are even more dangerous when they're wounded. That's especially true with witches. Their bodies may be broken, but their power remains strong."

"I hope she's dead before I reach her," Drustan said,

a note of fear creeping into his voice. "But reach her I must."

"Does your mother know about your plans?" Gib asked, his tone skeptical. "Does she know you are taking on such a dangerous journey?"

"Yes," Drustan replied firmly. "I left with her blessing."

"I find that hard to believe," Gib said, his eyes narrowing. "You wouldn't lie to the one who just saved your life, would you?"

"I speak the truth," Drustan insisted. "My mother consulted the spirits, and though reluctantly, she sent me on my way."

"If your mother, one of the truest of the cunning folk, sent you on this journey, then I'll help you, too," Gib said, his tone resigned. "All of us forest dwellers owe a great debt to your mother. And to be honest, we'll all be better off without the evil Mora."

Gib rose from his seat and tossed another log into the roaring fire. As he stood, he snatched two more of the salted fish from the wooden box on the table and placed them in front of Drustan, who eagerly began chomping on the dried seafood.

"Tell me, young Drustan," Gib spoke, "what was the name of that faerie that hornswoggled you?"

"Aster," Drustan replied, his mouth full of food.

"Ah, yes. I know of her. A mischievous little sprite who always causes a ruckus, but she's mostly harmless," Gib chuckled.

"She nearly got me killed," Drustan protested. "I wouldn't say her antics are harmless."

"It is true, the little ones often don't understand the weight of their pranks. They are not used to dealing with humans and the danger that their tricks can pose."

"If I ever cross paths with that little hellion," Drustan growled, "I'll show her what real harm is. I'll crush her under my boot like the annoying pest she is."

"I gather that. You'll crush her like a grape; pluck out her wings, and so on. No need for any of that. I can handle her and get what is owed to you," Gib assured him. "Aster is one of the Seeley Court. They are, for the most part, honorable and will not break their word when it is given. Tell me, these were not truly gifts were they? They were wishes. What did she ask of you in exchange for these three wishes?"

"Nothing of value," Drustan replied with a shrug.

Gib raised an eyebrow. "Nothing? No bargain, no trade, no payment?"

"Well," Drustan hesitated, "there was one thing, but it was nothing really." He didn't consider the kiss to be a significant part of the deal, even though it was the only thing Aster had requested.

Gib's eyes narrowed. "And what was this 'nothing' you gave her?"

"A kiss."

"A kiss? That is rather odd. You are a handsome young buck, but even so, three wishes for a simple kiss does not sound like a fair deal. No wonder she toyed with your wishes and turned them against thee."

Drustan felt his hackles rise at Gib's dismissive tone. He may have downplayed the kiss himself, but he didn't appreciate Gib doing the same. "I wouldn't say I'm the world's greatest kisser," he retorted. "But she seemed insistent and was pleased with the outcome."

"Is that so? Tell me, laddie, and speak the truth. Surely, a handsome lad such as you, and one at your age, has kissed a girl before.

"Of course," he answered crossly, offended that Gib would think him to be so naïve of the world. However, upon reconsideration he realized that he had only kissed his mother and sisters on the cheek or forehead. The fact was that they lived a good distance from the nearest neighbor and even farther from the village. Being in the company of an attractive woman near his own age was a rare event.

"You mean, really kiss a woman," Drustan hedged. "The way a man would kiss a woman?"

"Precisely," Gib laughed loudly. "As a healthy young man, have you ever felt an attraction toward a girl and kissed her on the mouth; as thy father would kiss thy mother?"

"Well, not really," he admitted. "Since you put it that way. There are very few women of interest close at hand."

"I suppose not."

"What does that matter," Drustan asked. "She seemed to be satisfied when I gave her the kiss. To speak truly, she swooned."

"She swooned you say? Then my suspicions are right. It matters because you did not give Aster just an innocent kiss. You gave her your first kiss."

"My first kiss?"

"Aye, thy first true kiss," Gib's voice filled the air

with a sense of reverence. " For every man and woman, this moment be but once in a lifetime. The first true kiss is a spell woven by fate, a memory that shall linger with thee until the end of thy days. Thy gift to the maiden Aster was a powerful one, and the reason she did swoon. Such a bargain must be entered with full knowledge and its terms must be honored."

"The thought of a mere kiss holds little weight in my mind," Drustan scoffed. "Had she fulfilled her part of the deal, I would not be burdened with this regret."

"Maybe not now as a youthful lad with so much life before you, but thy first true kiss is something that you remember forever. It happens only once in a lifetime. One day, you will understand the importance of that."

"It matters not," Drustan said dismissively.

"Nay, it matters a great deal," the wulver countered. "When you have rested and your belly full, we shall journey to The Ring of Brodgar. That is where the troublesome Aster can often be found, when she's not harassing unsuspecting travelers."

"What is The Ring of Brodgar?"

The Ring of Brodgar is an ancient and sacred site of the Druids," Gib explained. "Its standing stones are thousands of years old and it's one of the places where the faeries converge when they enter this realm."

"So what's the point in seeking her out if you won't let me crush her underfoot?" Drustan asked skeptically. "As for the first kiss, tis hard to unring that bell."

"It's true that finding Aster is of little consequence," Gib admitted. "But our true objective is to locate the king of the Seeley faeries, King Jorin. He will not tolerate this affront and will ensure that justice is served."

And so, once their clothing was dry and Drustan had recovered from his near drowning, the two set out to find the faeries. It was a short hike from Gib's hut to the Ring of Brodgar, the ancient circle of massive standing stones. Here, according to Gib, was where the faeries gathered to spend their days playing games and pulling pranks on each other.

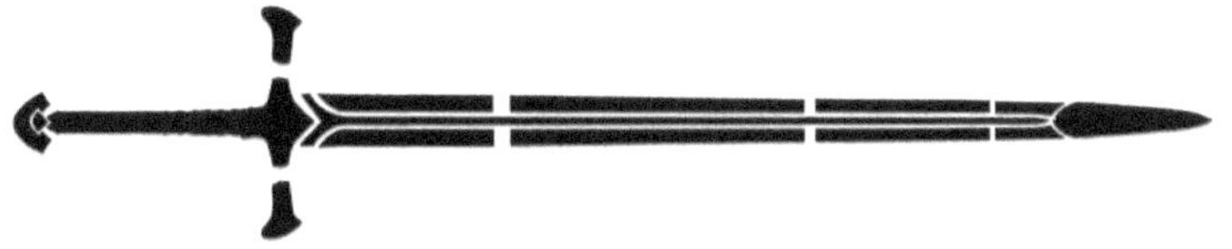

CHAPTER 16

The Ring of Brodgar

As he followed Gib through the misty moors, Drustan couldn't help but feel a sense of awe and wonder. This land was so much different from his own home, it was dark and brooding and an air of mystery hung over the land.

Suddenly, the thick fog parted, revealing a vista that left Drustan stunned, one that he would carry with him until the end of his days. Before him stood the Ring of Brodgar, a monument to the magnificent might and mysterious magic of the ancients. Colossal stones, weathered by centuries of exposure to the elements and the passage of time, formed an awe-inspiring circle, as if arranged by some celestial force. He felt as if he were standing before the entrance of a holy shrine, and could not help but experience a deep sense of reverence for the ancient beings who had crafted such a marvel. Their voices, lifted in hymns and songs of worship, seemed to resound through the ages, echoing all around him.

Drustan approached the stones with reverence, his steps measured and deliberate, feeling the weight of history press down upon him with every step. Drustan felt the power of the stones seep into his very being, a testament to the potency of the ancient magic that still lingered there.

This was a place of immense power, where legends were born and where heroes could draw upon the strength of their forebears. Drustan was aware that he stood upon hallowed ground, and that realization filled him with humility.

And so he made a solemn vow, there in the Ring of Brodgar, to always remember the magic and mystique of this place, to always draw upon its power in moments of need. Standing within the circle of stones, Drustan was awed by the grandeur of the site, yet he saw no signs of the Fae. But he knew in his heart that if they had a gathering place, this would be it, a place where their magic and power were at their strongest.

"Magnificent is it not?" Gib broke the silence that had enveloped them..

Drustan turned to Gib, his eyes shining with wonder. "It is indeed," he said in awe. "I feel as if I have been transported to another world, one steeped in magic and mystery. To think that the hands of mere mortals could create something so grand, so beautiful, is beyond comprehension."

Gib nodded in agreement. "It is a testament to the ingenuity and creativity of our ancestors."

"I see why the faeries would favor such a place, but where are they?' Drustan asked. "'Tis no one here,."

Gib placed a finger to his snout, signaling for Drustan to keep silent. "Patience, my friend," he replied, his voice a hushed whisper that hung in the air like a delicate veil. "We are being watched. The Fae will reveal themselves in their own time."

Gib opened the leather pouch that he carried over his shoulder and pulled out a tin whistle. It was a small musical instrument made of a hallow pipe with finger holes for making notes. He placed one end of the pipe in his mouth and blew, making a high-pitched sound. Then he began to cover some of the finger holes to make various notes.

Satisfied with the tones, he took the whistle from his mouth and spoke to Drustan. "Faeries love music and dancing. Make no sudden moves and they will come."

Gib put the tin whistle back in his mouth and began to play a quick and festive tune. Drustan was pleasantly surprised by the wulver's musical skill, and as the music filled the air, he found himself tapping his foot and nodding his head back and forth to the lively rhythm.

As the melodious notes of Gib's tin whistle filled the air, the faeries, who had been hiding behind the stones and in secret nooks, began to peek out from their concealed places. Slowly, they emerged, their delicate bodies weaving in and out of sight as they cautiously approached the source of the music. As Gib continued to play, their intrigue turned to delight, and before long, they were engaged in an impassioned dance, clapping and twirling to the beat. The music came to an end, and the faeries flocked around Gib, their glittering eyes eagerly anticipating more.

"Greetings, my cherished faerie friends," Gib beamed at them, his voice filled with warmth.

"Oh, won't you grace us with more of your enchanting melodies?" A faerie beseeched, its words reverberating through the air, embraced and echoed by the chorus of eager voices surrounding it.

"I would be delighted to, my dear," Gib replied, "but first, I must complete my quest. Where is the one known as Aster?"

"She fled into the forest as you approached," one of the faeries informed him, pointing towards the nearby trees.

Gib turned to Drustan, he spoke softly, "She most likely recognized you, my friend. But do not fret, we shall retrieve what is rightfully yours."

At that moment, a small faerie descended gracefully upon the ground before them, his piercing eyes trained upon Gib. "Why do you seek Aster?" the small faerie inquired.

Gib bowed his head respectfully, "Your Majesty, may I present my companion Drustan. Drustan, allow me to introduce His Majesty King Jorin, ruler of the Seeley Court."

Drustan was taken aback, he felt a great sense of honor to be in the presence of royalty. He bowed deeply before King Jorin, "It is an immense privilege, Your Majesty."

King Jorin gave a nod with his head, a warm smile gracing his features. "Any friend of Gib is always welcome in the Seeley Court. Now, what has our Aster done this time?"

Gib sighed, the weight of the situation heavy upon his heart. "Your Majesty, the treachery that has transpired is a most lamentable one. My friend Drustan entered into a fair agreement with the one called Aster, she deceived him to gain something of great value, and then, with her deceitful heart, broke that contract, thereby sullying the honor of your court."

King Jorin raised an eyebrow in inquiry, directing his gaze towards Drustan. "Is this so?" "

"Indeed, Your Majesty," Drustan confirmed.

"And pray tell, what was this great treasure she swindled from you?" The king questioned further.

A blush crept upon Drustan's cheeks at the embarrassment of making such a big fuss over a simple kiss.

"Well, speak lad," the king pressed.

"'Twas a kiss," Drustan answered in a muffled voice.

"A kiss?" Jorin chuckled and the faeries all laughed among themselves.

"But Gib quickly interjected, his voice filled with ominous undertones. "Your Majesty, 'twas no ordinary kiss. This was Drustan's first kiss. Unaware of the value of such a gift, Aster took advantage of his innocence and he agreed to grant it to her in exchange for three wishes. He honored his end of the bargain, but she deceived him, nearly causing him to lose his life through her treachery."

The laughter died down and the king's demeanor shifted, his face becoming serious. "A first kiss, you say? Such a thing is not to be taken lightly. The consequences of a broken contract involving such a cherished rite of passage can be dire."

The faeries erupted into a chorus of hushed whispers, their eyes wide with disbelief. The very air seemed to grow heavy, as though a storm was gathering on the horizon. Such was the weight of this situation, for all knew that the ways of the Fae were not to be trifled with.

In the world of the faeries, trickery and theft were commonplace. Yet a bargain was a sacred thing, and all knew that an agreement made must be honored. But this, this was something greater still. The first kiss was a magical thing, a gift beyond measure, and to steal it or deceive another for it was an affront not only to the one wronged, but to the entire Fae Kingdom.

King Jorin was visibly disturbed by the news. With a flick of his wrist, he shed his faerie form and took on the appearance of a grown man, his long black beard twitching with thought. He settled himself upon a stone beside Drustan, his piercing gaze trained upon the young man. "Tell me, lad," he said in a deep, rumble of a voice. "What was this bargain you struck with Aster?"

Drustan recounted the events of his encounter with Aster, relaying the moment he stumbled into the pit, and how she promised him three wishes in exchange for a kiss. He explained how the wishes had gone wrong, and how she had betrayed the agreement. The telling was a source of embarrassment for Drustan, not just for the deception he had fallen victim to, but also for the admission that he had never kissed a maiden before Aster.

"By the gods," the King said in disbelief, "you are a fine, strapping young man. Is it truly the case that you have never kissed a woman before Aster?"

Drustan blushed deeply, feeling defensive. He stammered defensively, "It's not like women grow on trees where I'm from."

"But a handsome young fellow with broad shoulders

and full head of hair such as you could have your pick of any woman," Jorin continued pressing the issue. "Surely they do not grow on trees, but do they hide under stones? Are there no women in the place where you are from?"

The cackles of the faeries filled the air, each one a sharp stab of ridicule aimed at Drustan. He hung his head, feeling the sting of embarrassment and anger.

This whole ordeal over a 'first kiss' was starting to become too much for him to bear. He couldn't grasp the significance of it all and that only added to the humiliation he was feeling.

"I'll be fine on my own," he muttered, his voice low and bitter. "I'll take this as a lesson learned. The Seeley Court's faeries can't be trusted and don't keep their word."

King Jorin cleared his throat, a touch of regret in his tone. "Do not judge us as a whole based on the misdeeds of one rogue faerie. Aster's actions have brought shame upon us all. We of the Seeley Court hold ourselves to a higher standard and always honor our bargains, even those that are ill advised and made in haste."

"Apparently not," Drustan retorted, his voice sharp and indignant. "Aster betrayed me, and yet you and your court find humor in it."

"Despite our unfortunate amusement at the circumstances, we shall not tolerate this transgression," the king declared, his voice carrying an air of authority. "Aster's actions nearly cost your life, Drustan, and thus, it is my decree that she pay the ultimate price. Aster is sentenced to death."

There was a collective gasp from the gathered faeries, and Drustan felt a pang of pity for Aster. Despite her mischievous ways, he understood that she was only being impish and was not intent on killing him. At least, he hoped that was the case.

"Your majesty, I implore you, do not make such a severe judgment," Drustan implored. Though he had threatened to take matters into his own hands, he did not wish to bear the weight of her death on his conscience. "I do not desire to have her blood on my hands, nor to have the fate of her life be a burden upon my soul."

"Very well," the king replied, his voice softening. "By your plea, her life shall be spared. Yet, she must still be held accountable for her actions and pay the consequences. Aster has brought shame upon the Fae, and she shall be banished from our court."

The other faeries began to whisper at the king's pronouncement. To be banished from the Seeley Court was a heavy punishment almost as severe as death. Nevertheless, using deception to steal a first kiss and then make the crime worse by dishonoring her bargain, those were severe offenses calling for the harshest of judgments.

"I regret that it is not within my power to restore what she stole from you, but if you wish, we can fulfill Aster's commitment to you."

"That is all I ask, your majesty," Drustan replied. "It was a fair bargain provided I am given my due."

"Then you shall have it," King Jorin pledged. "What were thy three wishes?"

"A horse outfitted for adventure, a gleaming sword with a deadly edge, and direction's to the wicked witch Mora's lair. But, if it pleases Your Majesty, Aster's trickery has also cost me my bow and quiver of enchanted arrows which now rest at the depths of the loch, irreplaceable," Drustan spoke with a hint of sorrow in his voice.

King Jorin looked at the young man with intrigue. "Mora's castle, huh? What prompts a daring lad like you to embark on such a dangerous quest and confront that evil witch?"

Drustan's reply was matter-of-fact. "To put an end to her reign of terror, and bring peace to this land," he said with determination.

"Ah, if that is your quest, then I shall ensure you have everything you need to succeed," King Jorin declared. He addressed his faerie subjects. "Fetch the swiftest and strongest steed in all the realm, bedeck it with the finest saddle and bring it to our brave friend Drustan. Seek the assistance of our elfin cousins and procure him the finest blade, along with a bow and quiver filled with arrows. And do not forget to provide him with a flask of wine and dried meats for sustenance on his journey."

The King clapped his hands loudly, twice. "Hurry, hurry, my brethren!" he commanded, and in a twinkling, a flutter of faeries were on their way to fulfill his orders. He called out after them, "And if you happen to cross paths with Aster, convey my judgment to her."

Drustan thanked the King for his generosity, to which King Jorin replied, "'Tis not an act of kindness, but an obligation of honor. You will receive what is rightfully yours. I regret that I cannot replace your enchanted arrows, but I can offer you this token as compensation for your troubles."

The King, with regal grace, undid the clasp of the

glittering necklace from around his neck and presented it to Drustan with a flourish. "Behold, my dear friend," he said, his voice low and filled with mystery, "a wondrous gift from the mystical realm. This is a Faerie Stone, a shimmering gem of legend, a symbol of the magic that flows through our world like a river."

Drustan had heard of such stones only in the whispered tales passed down from his mother, tales of a gem so rare and precious that it was sought after by those who longed to possess its magical power. And now, here it was before him, its fiery ruby depths encased in silver and suspended from a delicate leather cord.

The King continued, his voice soft and full of enchantment, "Wear this Faerie Stone, and it will render you invisible to the denizens of the spirit world. It will grant you passage where others cannot go and unlock secrets hidden from mortal eyes."

Drustan gazed upon the Faerie Stone in awe, marveling at its beauty and the powerful magic it contained. He felt a shiver run down his spine, for he knew that this was a gift beyond measure, a treasure of untold value.

"So, a witch cannot see me?"

"Witches are living creatures whose eyes will see thee as plainly as I do now. But some things the witch conjures, as well as, spirits, demons and other beings not of this mortal world ... to them you will pass undetected," Jorin said. "But this stone is more importantly a key. It will open the Faerie Door to thee, so that you may enter and leave the Faerie Realm at will."

"The Faerie Door?"

"Aye. There are places throughout the land, mystical

places that are passages between the world of man and the world of the Fae. When the door is open during the Between Times, anyone may pass between the worlds. But with this stone, you may open the passageways and pass through at will."

"Where are these passages?" Drustan looked at the stone curiously.

"You will find them at the stone circles and the henges, and the most important one is the Faerie Door. To open the passage simply hold the stone in your hand and focus your thoughts, the door will reveal itself and open to thee," King Jorin explained. "But you must use the stone with great caution. In the olden days, the Faerie Door was the passage directly between our two worlds, but that was before the Between was made."

"I've heard of this dark realm, the Between. What is it?"

"'Tis the realm that separates the world of man from the world of the Fae. Before, there was only a thin veil like a curtain that separated the realms. But that was before the evil came. Mora. She used her magic and the power she drained from many faeries and expanded the veil into what has become the Between. It is a dim and hopeless world, where evil dwells."

"Then I will use it wisely. I am grateful for your gift," Drustan said as he slipped the rope over his head and around his neck.

"Now play, my dear wulver friend," the King commanded, his voice ringing with merriment. With a leap, he sprung into the air, clicking his heels together in a joyous display. "While we wait, let us be merry! Play us a tune, good Gib, and let us drink wine and dance to our heart's content, in celebration of our new ally."

Gib obliged, striking up a lively and cheerful melody, as the King and his faerie subjects twirled and spun within the ancient stone circle, their laughter ringing out like the sweetest of music. And before the sun began its descent, the faeries returned with a swift and sturdy steed, along with all the supplies and weapons they had promised.

Drustan offered his thanks to the King, his heart overflowing with gratitude. "Your Majesty, I am forever in your debt for your kindness. But there remains one more wish," he said. "What of the way to Mora's castle?"

King Jorin smiled, his eyes twinkling with mischief. "Fear not, my friend. Simply follow the setting sun, and you will come upon a small hill. Cross over it, and on the other side, you will find Mora's castle, her home when she walks in this world."

"Farewell, brave hunter," the King said, bowing with grace. "May may the winds of magic always be at thy back."

"And to you, Your Majesty," Drustan replied, with a bow of his own.

In a twinkle, the King and his faerie subjects transformed into their ethereal forms and flitted away into the forest, their laughter and songs lingering in the air.

After a moment of silent reflection, Gib declared in a resolute voice, "Drustan, I cannot leave you to undertake this perilous journey alone. Your quest to defeat Mora is a noble one, and it serves us all to see you succeed. I will remain at your side."

"Gib, your bravery humbles me, but it is too dangerous," Drustan replied, a mournful note in his voice. "You
have already done so much for me, I could not bear the
thought of putting you in harm's way."

"I cannot sit idly by while you face the unknown,"
Gib protested, his fists clenched.

"My dear friend, 'tis easier for one to slip undetected through the shadows. The presence of another would
only draw the gaze of our enemies, and I must be free
from distraction to carry out my mission. I cannot risk
being preoccupied with your safety. This is the best way,
my friend."

"Farewell then, my friend," Gib said, his voice heavy
with emotion.

"Your kindness and friendship are beyond measure,"
Drustan said, his eyes shining with gratitude. "I do not
know how to repay you."

"Your safety and victory will be payment enough. If
you rid us of this malevolent force, we will be forever in
your debt. So go with care, my friend."

"Until we are reunited," Drustan said, his heart filled
with hope for their next meeting.

Drustan mounted the horse and urged it forward with
a click of his tongue and a gentle flick of the reins. He
galloped into the thicket of trees, leaving Gib behind.
The wulver watched as his human friend vanished into
the distance, his heart heavy with worry. Although they
had only just met, Gib felt a deep bond with Drustan and
a strong urge to protect him.

Despite Drustan's youth and bravery, Gib could see
that he was ill-equipped for the dangers of the dark for-

est. From being tricked into kissing a faerie to taking a wild ride on a kelpie, Drustan's inexperience and naivety put him in constant peril. As he sat on the ground and whined, his eyes fixed on the spot where Drustan had disappeared, Gib worried that his friend would be in grave danger once he reached Mora's castle.

Gib raised his head and howled, his mournful cry echoed through the forest, piercing the stillness like a beacon. The wulver was resolute, he would not abandon his newfound friend to the dangers that lurked ahead. He stood tall, his fur rippling in the gentle breeze, his eyes bright with determination. The way of the wulver was to protect and care for those in need, and Drustan was in need of his help.

Gib took one last longing look at the direction where Drustan had vanished and then set out, his powerful legs propelling him through the underbrush, his senses sharp and alert. He would not rest until he had found Drustan and brought him back to safety.

CHAPTER 17

The Beauty in the Tower

The evening had descended upon the land, and the silver moon was making its ascent into the sky, casting a haunting glow over the rolling hills. As Drustan crested the final rise, he was greeted by the ominous sight of the castle, its silhouette towering high against the backdrop of the night sky. The stone walls were black as coal, stained by the ravages of time, and appeared to be almost sentient with malevolence. A section of the castle had crumbled to ruins, the stones lying in a jumbled heap, a testament to the ages that had passed. A faint flicker of firelight shone through the openings in the stone walls, providing evidence that the castle was not completely abandoned, and that life still persisted within its confines. The castle's foreboding appearance left Drustan confident that this was the location he had been seeking. This was the seat of power for the infamous Mora, and its dark presence filled him with unease.

The dilapidated state of the fortress evoked memories of the ruins where he had crossed paths with the

Redcap just a few nights prior. With utmost stealth, he dismounted his trusty steed and securely tethered its reins to a bough of a nearby tree. Grasping his sword with a firm grip, he crouched down in the thicket, his senses keen and alert, ready to face any danger that may lurk in the shadows. He surveyed his surroundings with a vigilant eye, wary of another vicious Redcap or worse lurking about. He remained still, blending in with his surroundings as he kept watch, his keen ears attuned to the slightest rustle of leaves or snap of a twig.

With his sword at the ready, he scanned the area for any signs of Mora's sentries, and braced himself for any creatures she might have summoned to protect her lair. He lightly brushed his fingers against the faerie stone that hung from a leather cord around his neck, seeking comfort in its supposed power to conceal his presence from any and all of Mora's conjurations. He silently prayed that the stone would work its magic, and shield him from detection as he approached the ominous tower.

He remained hidden and motionless for a long while, silently observing. Seeing nothing unusual, he finally began to advance toward the castle, creeping stealthily through the trees until he was able to view the entrance, expecting at any moment to see guards or some unspeakable horror lurking in the shadows. And yet, as he drew closer, he saw that there was no one there to challenge him. No beasts or soldiers to keep him from entering the castle. He felt a moment of relief, but it was quickly replaced by a sense of foreboding. Something was not right.

With sword in hand, he stepped inside, his footsteps

echoing through the musty halls. The stench of rot and smoke hung heavy in the air, and he could smell the unmistakable odor of burned flesh. He kept to the shadows, edging his way deeper into the castle. As he rounded a corner, he saw the flicker of a torch, and he stopped, pressing himself against the cold stone wall, his eyes fixed upon the courtyard ahead.

The enshrouding darkness of the inner courtyard was disturbed only by the eerie glow of two figures squatting on the ground. As Drustan approached, he could make out the gnarled and withered forms of what appeared to be two crones, part of Mora's coven. Their backs were turned to him as they delved into the smoldering ashes before them, searching for something. He scanned the area for any other threats, and then approached the witches, his movements slow and silent.

The closer he got, the stronger the acrid stench of burned flesh grew. The source of the smell was revealed as he approached the pile of ashes: a blackened, skeletal figure, barely recognizable as a once-living being. The witches were bent over the scorched remains, meticulously cutting off the fingers of the skeleton for use in their dark rituals. The sight was nauseating, a chilling reminder of the depravity that lay within the walls of Mora's stronghold.

Drustan raised his sword, the blade gleaming ominously in the flickering light of the smoldering ashes. With a roar, he brought it down, striking the first witch with deadly force. Her head tumbled into the ashes, leaving behind a trail of smoke and gore. The second witch, however, was not so easily defeated. With a piercing scream, she lunged at Drustan, her talon-like fingers reaching for him like the claws of a beast.

Drustan stumbled back, losing his grip on his sword as he fell. The witch was on him in an instant, strangling him with her powerful hands, her sharp nails digging deep into his flesh. Despite his best efforts, Drustan couldn't break her hold. He swung at her with all his might, landing punches on her jaw, but she only tightened her grip, laughing with manic glee as she choked the life out of him. It was a battle of strength and will, with the outcome hanging in the balance.

The witch laughed in hideous satisfaction as Drustan began to weaken, his face turning dark red as her hands constricted around his throat. He hit at her again and again with his fists, but it was to no avail. He felt himself fading, his life draining away. Then suddenly, something knocked the witch off him.

Drustan staggered to his feet, coughing heavily as he prepared to confront the witch again, but when he turned, he saw her on her back with Gib on top. Her arms and legs were flailing wildly as the wulver tore at the hag's throat like a rapacious wolf. After a moment, the witch's arms fell limp to the ground and she ceased her fight. Gib remained motionless, his canine jaws locked tightly around her neck until he was certain the crone was dead. Finally, he released his grip and stood upright, the fur on his face soaked with the witch's blood. Without a word, he removed his ax from the pack that was slung over his shoulder and chopped off the witch's head.

"Can't take any chances with these witches; always take off the head," Gib said then wiped the blood from both his face and his ax on the hem of the witch's robe.

"Gib! What are you doing here?" Drustan was a mixture of emotions at the sight of his friend. He had warned Gib not to come, but now he was grateful for his presence. If Gib had listened to his demand, Drustan would be the one lying lifeless on the ground instead of the witch.

"I couldn't just sit idly by, I thought you might need my help," Gib said.

"I told you not to come, but I can't deny that I'm glad you're here. You've saved my life once again," Drustan said, still feeling the remnants of the witch's grasp around his neck.

Gib looked at the deep nail marks and patted Drustan on the back, "'Tis a flesh wound. You'll be alright."

Drustan rubbed his neck, "Thanks to you. That skinny old hag had the strength of an ox."

"You'd do well to remember that, Drustan. The witches may seem frail, but they are deadly creatures. Their strength is not of this world."

"Believe me, it's a lesson I won't forget anytime soon," Drustan added, still in awe of the witch's supernatural strength.

Gib looked at the burnt human remains in the ashes. "Who do you think it was?"

"Hard to say. Maybe one of the witches, or even a human sacrifice," Drustan replied. "Could be Mora, succumbed to her wound and this is her funeral pyre."

"Let us hope, but I doubt we will be so lucky."

As they entered the castle, Drustan and Gib made their way down a dimly lit hall until they reached a large chamber, the flickering light of countless candles illuminating the room. In the center stood a wooden bier, upon which lay a shrouded figure.

Stepping cautiously forward, Drustan reached out and slowly pulled back the cloth, revealing the face of the deceased. "I was wrong," he muttered. "It's not the one outside. It's her. Mora the witch."

Gib leaned in, examining the lifeless figure. What he saw was a shocking sight, the body was like an aged and decaying mummy, with wrinkled skin clinging to bones and ligaments visible through the tattered flesh. The teeth were yellow and jagged, the eye sockets empty and hollow. It was a gruesome sight that would haunt him for some time to come. "Are you sure that's her?" He asked as he cringed and turned away.

"Aye," Drustan replied firmly. "I'll never forget her face."

"And you're sure she's dead?" Gib whispered.

Drustan lifted his sword, ready to strike. He kicked the platform, and then quickly recoiled. There was no response. Slowly, he pressed the tip of his sword to the hag's side and then gave a quick jab, piercing deep into the flesh.

"Well, she looks dead to me," Gib proclaimed with a hint of delight.

Drustan raised his sword and slammed it down hard to sever the witch's head from the body. "As a wise man told me, don't take any chance," he said with a wink. "Always take off the head."

"Then 'tis over. Thy family is safe and the world is free of this evil."

"The thought of her coven's continued existence troubles me," Drustan contemplated. "Her coven is broken, but someone remains to have prepared her body for the pyre. We must root out any remaining members and ensure that their evil deeds come to an end."

"Agreed," Gib replied. "There is another witch, Laine, who is said to be just as wicked as Mora. If she still lives, then Mora's death will have been in vain."

"We will leave no stone unturned in our search," Drustan declared. "None of Mora's minions will be allowed to escape justice."

As he spoke, Drustan's gaze landed upon a towering pile of firewood stacked near the bier. Without hesitation, he grabbed handfuls of dry tinder and cast it beneath the wooden platform where Mora's body lay. He then upturned a nearby oil lamp, drenching both the wood and the deceased witch in its flammable contents. Finally, he plucked one of the flickering candles from its holder and tossed it onto the pile, igniting the pyre in a whoosh of flame. The orange and yellow inferno crackled and danced, casting a warm, sinister light over the chamber.

"I will search the castle for the remaining witches," Drustan said. "I cannot ask you to risk yourself any further."

"You do not need to ask, nor do I await approval."

"Then let us finish this," Drustan nodded his consent. "When I arrived, I saw the flicker of light from the highest tower. Perhaps we will find our quarry there."

Cautiously they made their way down the shadowy corridor, their footsteps muffled by the thick carpet of dust that covered the floor. As they approached a staircase, they looked at each other, steeling themselves for what lay ahead. They slowly climbed the steps, the stone walls closing in around them as they ascended higher and higher. When they finally reached the top of the tower, they hesitated for a moment, bracing themselves for the confrontation to come.

With a deep breath, they rounded the corner and were suddenly face to face with two witches. The crones were just as startled as Drustan and Gib, but they quickly recovered, their screeches echoing through the tower as they lunged forward, brandishing their knives.

Gib hurled his ax towards one of the witches, the blade striking its target and embedding itself deeply into the hag's forehead. She fell to the ground, lifeless. The second witch continued her attack, swinging her weapon wildly as she charged towards them. Drustan swung his sword and nearly missed her neck, causing her to retreat in surprise.

She checked to make sure she was unharmed and, upon recognizing Drustan from their attack upon Sibby, she hissed "The hunter!"

Drustan advanced, his sword at the ready, but instead of confronting him, the witch transformed into a plume of black smoke and disappeared down the staircase like a sudden gust of wind.

"She's escaped," Drustan shouted. "We need to go after her."

"We must," added Gib, "That was the one known as Laine, she is the witch I warned you about."

"However," Drustan pointed to the door, "there may be more pressing issues at hand. I can see light coming from beneath the door and there is movement from within."

Gib nodded in agreement and the two approached the door, weapons at the ready. Gib gingerly turned the doorknob, but it was locked.

"Who's there?" a female voice called out from inside the room. "I know someone is there. Please, help me!"

Gib and Drustan looked at each other with a touch of uncertainty.

"Open the door and reveal yourself," Drustan commanded.

"'Tis locked! I am a prisoner," came the reply, her voice trembling with fear. "Please let me out, I beseech thee, before they return."

"What say you?" Drustan turned to Gib, his eyes seeking counsel. "Is it a trick?"

"It may be so. Whether 'tis a trap or not, we still need to get inside. Either we rescue whoever she may be, or she is a witch and we must kill her."

"Truly," Drustan said and sheathed his sword. "Stand back, away from the door," he shouted to the woman. He took a few steps back then charged at the door with all his might intending to break it down. He slammed hard against the heavy wood but the door did not yield.

"By God's bones!" Drustan groaned and backed away from the door clutching his shoulder in pain.

Gib couldn't help but chuckle in amusement. Drustan and Gib exchanged glances, both filled with a touch of levity.

"Allow me," Gib said, a glint of determination in his eye.

He stepped back, then charged forward with all his strength, launching himself at the door. With a mighty leap, he kicked the door with both feet. The door quaked, but still it held fast. Gib landed on the ground with a thud, groaning as he picked himself up. "By the gods!" he cursed.

Drustan shook his head, a wry smile on his lips. "Not so funny, is it?" He smirked.

"Our foe seems to have chosen her fortress well," Gib said. "We must find another way inside."

As the pyre below sent plumes of smoke spiraling up the staircase, Gib and Drustan struggled to keep their breaths steady.

"Curse our haste," Gib breathed ruefully, "We should have waited until we were out of the castle to set the blaze."

Drustan's eyes surveyed all around, sharp and determined. "There must be a key," he declared with a fierce urgency.

Gib delved into the witch's robes, while Drustan scoured the surroundings. Suddenly, a triumphant cry echoed through the chamber as Gib exclaimed, "Aha! I have found it!" The key, tied to the witch's waist with a slender cord, was now clutched tightly in Gib's grasp. With purpose, he broke the cord and hastened to the door, his ax at the ready to defend against any malicious intent.

He unlocked the door and pushed it open, but instead of the evil hag he expected, he beheld a fair maid, shivering with terror.

"Come!" he growled, his voice a roar, as he swept the damsel into his arms and bore her from the smoke-filled chamber.

Together, they descended the staircase, choking on the acrid smoke, until at last, they stumbled out into the fresh air, all three collapsing onto the earth, drawing in deep, sweet breaths of relief.

The young woman looked at Drustan and Gib, her eyes shining with gratitude. "Thank you, gentle knights," she spoke in a voice as pure as a mountain stream.

Drustan was immediately struck by the young woman's beauty. He had never seen such a delicate and flawless creature, whose grace and charm defied description. She was not the kind of work-hardened woman he was accustomed to seeing in the villages near his home. This girl was beguiling. He stared at her, speechless.

Adorned in robes that billowed like ethereal clouds, she donned a pristine white ensemble that trailed gracefully behind her. Her skin, as flawless and radiant as alabaster, bestowed an otherworldly glow upon her presence. Fiery red tresses flowed in undulating waves, reaching the small of her back with an enchanting allure. Yet, it was her vibrant green eyes, shining like gemstones, that ensnared Drustan's every thought. They held him captive, their piercing gaze bewitching him entirely. In an instant, this mesmerizing young being had entered his world, unannounced and unexpected, weaving a spell that left him thoroughly captivated.

Being a wulver and immune to the charm of humans, Gib remained unfazed by the girl's beauty. With a gruff tone, he asked, "What's your name, miss? How did you end up in the witch's tower?"

"My name is Etta," she replied, her voice soft and

demure. "The witches had me locked in the tower, a prisoner with no escape."

Gib's brow furrowed in suspicion. "Why were you held captive, Etta? What did the witches want with you?"

Etta looked down, her eyes clouded with fear. "I do not know, sir. I was simply taken one day and locked away in the tower."

Gib pressed on, unwilling to accept her answer. "How long have you been there?"

"Time was an elusive, unyielding companion within the tower's walls, and I was powerless to gauge its passage," Etta murmured in response to Gib's inquiry, her voice fragile and uncertain.

Gib's eyes narrowed, his suspicions growing. He glanced over at Drustan, but found his companion completely entranced by Etta's beauty, staring at her with wonder and awe.

"Drustan," Gib muttered, nudging him with his elbow. "Drustan!"

Drustan shook himself from his trance and stammered, "I am Drustan."

Etta smiled back, a blush spreading across her cheeks. "I am grateful to you both, for your bravery in rescuing me."

"'Tis my honor, my lady," Drustan replied, his eyes never leaving hers.

As Drustan and the mysterious girl locked eyes, Gib looked on with a storm of conflicting emotions. Despite his friend's enamored state, he was filled with frustration and unease. For all they knew, this beguiling stranger could be a disciple of Mora, the harbinger of darkness.

Yet, Drustan appeared completely entranced, willing to trust her story solely based on her stunning visage. Gib worried that his friend's infatuation would lead them down a dangerous path akin to his romp with the kelpie.

"Farewell to this accursed place," Gib declared with a resolute voice, his eyes scanning the surrounding darkness, wary of any dangers that may yet lurk within its shadows. "Who knows what malevolent forces may yet slumber within its shadows."

Together, the trio made their way back to where Drustan's steed awaited. With a tender strength, Drustan lifted the young girl, Etta, up onto the horse, seating her sidesaddle, before leading the horse forward, his steps in perfect sync with Gib's.

"My friend," Gib whispered to Drustan, his voice a low murmur, "I am beset with unease. I cannot shake the feeling of foreboding that has settled upon me."

"And why is that?" Drustan queried, a smile playing at the corners of his lips as he shot a quick, longing glance back at Etta.

"This girl, Etta. There is something amiss with her," Gib continued, his gaze flicking briefly in her direction. "There is something not right about her story, her manner, her very being."

"I see nothing of the sort. She has been through a great deal, it is only natural that she would be a touch bewildered."

"Bewildered, perhaps, but she showed no fear, not even a blink when encountering a wulver such as myself. Do you not find that strange?"

"Mayhap she has seen the likes of thy kind before,"

Drustan countered, "or mayhap she has seen sights in the coven's tower that would send shivers down the spine of the bravest warrior."

"But that is precisely my worry," Gib replied, his voice low and cautious, "For the likes of witches and their dark sorcery are not to be trifled with. And if this lass has indeed seen such horrors, how can she be untouched by fear?"

Drustan shot Gib a look of annoyance, unable to contain his growing frustration with the wulver's suspicion. "Thou art too quick to judge, my friend. She has suffered much at the hands of the coven, 'tis not uncommon for one to be left in a state of confusion and disorientation. And as for her lack of fear, mayhap she is a fierce warrior herself, one who has faced her demons and conquered them."

Gib snorted, "Or mayhap she is simply hiding her true nature, waiting for the right moment to unleash her dark powers upon us."

"Nay," Drustan shot back, his voice rising in defiance, "I will not believe that this fair maiden is anything but pure and true. Look at her, she is an angel, a beacon of light amidst the darkness. And I will not let thy unfounded fears taint what I know to be true in my heart."

"Ah, love is blind," Gib said, his voice laced with a hint of sarcasm, "And so is lust. It makes one vulnerable to the tricks and manipulations of a cunning sorceress."

"If it will silence your grumbling for a while, then fine. I will tread carefully until we know more of her circumstances."

"Very well," Gib said, his tone softening. "I shall

keep my peace, for now. But do not say I did not warn thee, my friend. Wulvers have a keen sense about these things, and something about this lass simply does not feel right."

Drustan said, his hand straying briefly to the hilt of his sword. Fear not, my friend. I've faced far greater terrors than a fair maid."

Gib's eyes narrowed, his voice low and menacing. "But none more dangerous than a woman with a seductive smile and a heart full of deceit."

Gib stopped and took a moment to look around. "We should rest here tonight. We have put a good distance between us and the witch's castle and 'tis still a long way back to my cabin. We can continue on our way at sunrise."

"Come, my lady. We make camp for the night." Drustan took her by the waist and lowered her gently to her feet. The two stood face to face for a moment as Drustan stared longingly down into her eyes and she gazed up into his.

"Get some firewood, lad!" Gib barked at Drustan, breaking the spell.

Drustan was momentarily dazed, caught in Etta's gaze.

"Drustan!" Gib yelled again, this time with more impatience.

"What?" Drustan finally replied, tearing his eyes away from Etta.

"Firewood!" Gib repeated, his annoyance growing. "Or are you planning on keeping warm some other way this evening?"

Drustan blushed and Etta quickly turned away in embarrassment.

"He does not care for me," Etta spoke as if Gib's disapproval hurt her.

"Do not mind him," Drustan reassured her. "He means well, but he does not know how to behave with people."

"Drustan! Wood!" Gib called again.

"Back soon," he said and gave her a quick smile.

Wood was plentiful that time of year with the dried and broken branches littering the ground; so, it was only a short time before they were warming themselves by a roaring fire. Drustan had brought the food supplies that the Faerie King had given him so they had plenty to eat and their bellies were full. Once they finished their meal and were settled around the campfire, Gib resumed his interrogation of the beautiful Etta.

"Tell me, lassie," Gib started. "How did you come to be a prisoner in that tower? You said you were taken, from where might I ask?"

"I know not, sir. It seems I have always been locked in that room. I remember no other place," she replied.

"I do not understand. You do not remember how long you were there, nor do you recall how you got there?"

"I speak truly, sir. As long as I can remember, I was there."

"And how long do you remember?" Gib continued prodding. "A moon? A season? A lifetime? How long?

"It must have been horrible," Drustan interrupted. "Did they mistreat you?"

"I was held against my will, and never allowed to

step outside. That was their only true cruelty. Otherwise, they did not treat me unkindly."

"Again, I ask?" Gib continued impatiently. "How long do you remember? Surely you must have some sense of time, if you have any sense at all."

"Gib!" Drustan snapped. "Can't you see she has been through a very traumatic experience?"

"I take no offense," Etta said gently. "I understand your concern. I do not know how long I was there. The days became weeks, then the weeks turned to months. I lost all sense of time."

"Did they tell you their purpose? The reason for your captivity?" Gib continued to press for information.

"Nay, sir. They offered no explanations." She replied then gave a dreadful look. "Please, I have told thee all I know. May we not speak of this anymore?"

"Of course, my lady," Drustan replied and glared angrily at Gib. "'Tis over now, there is no reason to fear."

"But you do not seem to have been affected by your terrible circumstances beyond your terrible memory. I see neither lingering fear nor signs of distress. Why is that?" Gib pushed again.

"I did not fear for my life, only longed for my freedom," she replied.

"That's enough. Let her rest," Drustan insisted. "We can speak of this tomorrow."

"May I ask one more question?" Gib asked but did not wait for permission. "Have you ever seen a creature like me?"

"I can say that I have not," she answered thoughtfully.

"Yet, you look at me with no curiosity. Why is that?"

"I do not understand, sir. Should I see thee as an oddity or as something to fear?" She seemed confused by his question. "Are all men not as the two I see before me?"

"I am no man, lass. I am a wulver. Have you never heard nor seen my kind before?"

"No, you are my first," she answered then turned to Drustan. "Nor have I seen any man before this night. I must admit I am rather pleased. I did not expect men to be so tall and strongly made, and so pleasing to the eye."

"Not all men are as tall and strong as I." Drustan squared his broad shoulders proudly and smiled.

"Nor as humble," Gib smirked. "Well, I suggest we get some sleep so we can get an early start tomorrow."

"I am not really tired," Drustan said. "I believe I will stay awake a while and stand watch. After all, there's still a witch on the loose."

"Then wake me in a few hours and I will relieve you," Gib said. "You will need to be rested, so we can get an early start tomorrow."

Drustan nodded his agreement. He removed his cloak and wrapped it around Etta. "Take my cloak and stay near the fire; it will get chilly during the night."

"But what of you," she asked as she lay down on the ground and covered herself. "Will you not be cold in the night air?"

"I will be fine, my lady."

"Are you certain? I would not sleep well thinking you would be cold."

"Good grief," Gib snapped as he curled up on the ground close to the campfire. "Take the horse's blanket and both of you stop the chatter."

"Get some rest," Drustan softly told her.

Within a few moments both Gib and Etta were sound asleep. Drustan gathered his bow and his quiver of arrows and sat with his back against a tree so that he could keep guard over his sleeping companions. He watched them as they slept. They were both curious to him, but in very different ways.

Gib was unlike any creature he had seen before with his half-man, half-wolf physique. He exuded a daunting aura that would strike fear in the hearts of the bravest of men. Yet, despite his fearsome appearance, his soul was kind and gentle. He was a selfless friend, willing to give everything he had to those he held dear, even if they were strangers.

Etta, on the other hand, was an enigma in her own right. Drustan had seen many women from the nearby village that possessed a certain beauty, but Etta was unlike any woman he had seen before. Where he came from, the women were stout and toughened by hard work and a difficult life. Etta, on the other hand, was soft and delicate like a flower. Her skin was pale and supple like that of a newborn baby and her frailty was as pronounced as her beauty. She was delicate like Aster, but where Aster was child-like, Etta was a sensual and vibrant woman.

Drustan, a young man of nineteen years, had known the desires that all men his age feel, yet due to his isolated dwelling, far from the villages, he had yet to partake in the carnal pursuits of adulthood. During his travels to the nearby villages, he had encountered many women, and many others who had come seeking the counsel of his mother, yet never had he known the intimacy of which so many of his peers were already well acquainted.

The women of the village, though fair in appearance, were not enough to quench Drustan's thirst for companionship, for he sought a more personal connection than that which a simple meeting in passing could provide. And then there was Etta, who was unlike any woman he had ever beheld. Her delicate form and porcelain skin were in stark contrast to the sturdy women he was used to, and her beauty left him entranced.

Drustan was enamored with this mysterious woman, and his mind could not help but ponder the origin of her captivity and the loss of her memories. He did not share Gib's suspicions, but instead felt pity for the poor soul who was lost and alone in the world. Drustan was eager to trust her, not because of her credibility, but because her beauty had bewitched him.

Drustan could not fathom that a maid as pure and guileless as Etta could be harboring any wickedness within her. After all, witches were foul hags, twisted and ugly in both visage and spirit. There was no way that his Etta could be one. It just wasn't possible.

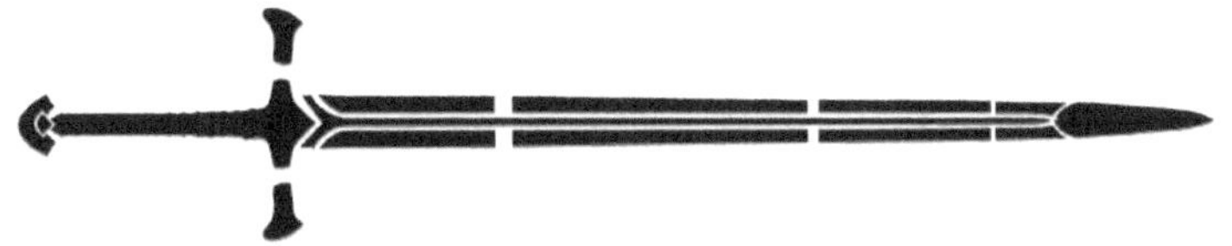

CHAPTER 18

Beguiled and Bewitched

With the dawning of a new day, Gib and Drustan roused themselves from slumber, eager to embark upon their journey. Meanwhile, Etta slumbered on, blissfully unaware of the stirrings of the world around her as the remnants of the campfire flickered weakly in the morning light.

As Drustan tended to his mount, his eyes lingered upon the sleeping form of Etta. Longing and desire filled his gaze, much to the frustration of Gib. Though he held no ill-will towards the young woman, Gib could not help but feel concerned. He desired nothing more than to see Drustan find happiness and love, but with Etta, he could not shake the feeling of unease.

She offered no answers, no explanation for how she came to be trapped within the tower of the witch. No information about her origins or her true identity. And every time Gib pressed for answers, she merely batted her lashes and cast a beguiling smile at Drustan, who would then plead for her to be treated kindly, to not be subjected to questioning.

Gib's contempt for her grew with each passing moment. She was, by human standards, a beautiful creature. Too beautiful, in fact. Her hands were soft and unblemished, never having known the toil of a hard day's work. Her skin was unmarred, pure and white, never having been exposed to the sun's harsh rays. He could not decide if she was a pampered princess, unused to the trials of life, or some unnatural creation conjured forth by the witches. Either way, it troubled him deeply that Drustan, despite knowing nothing of her, was so readily enamored and blinded by her beauty.

Gib and Drustan had barely spoken to each other since they left Mora's castle, both men were focused on Etta but for completely different reasons. Though they had not discussed their plans, both understood that their journey had not yet ended. Although Mora was dead and her coven destroyed, the evil witch Laine had escaped. She was the most powerful of the coven witches, almost as powerful as Mora herself, so to be truly safe they had to find her. She was too dangerous to be left alive; and if given the opportunity, she would no doubt seek revenge against them.

"What do you intend to do with her?" Gib finally asked. "She cannot come with us."

"What are we supposed to do, just leave her alone? We must find someplace where she will be safe."

"'Tis a nunnery in the south, not too far from here. We can take her there."

"A nunnery?" Drustan grimaced. "We might as well take her back to Mora's castle and lock her in the tower again as to leave her in such a place."

"The nuns are kind and care for those in need, they would keep her safe."

"They would want her to convert."

"Aye, now I see your reluctance," Gib said as he realized the nature of Drustan's lack of enthusiasm for the nuns.

"What do you see?"

"You do not want to take her to the nuns because you are afraid she might become one."

Drustan finally stopped staring at Etta and turned to face Gib. "And what is wrong with that?" Drustan responded. "So I am interested in this girl. I find her attractive and desirable. Is that such a horrible thing?"

Gib laughed. "Nay. I suppose 'tis nothing wrong." He stepped close and gently placed his hand on Drustan's shoulder then looked him directly in the eyes. "I just want you to be cautious. Think about where we found this girl and the circumstances. We know nothing of her, and according to her account, she knows nothing of herself. For all we know, she could be a witch."

"She is no witch."

"How do you know? You gaze at her like a moonstruck calf, seeing naught but breasts and curves. Pray tell how you know she is not a witch, so that I too may rest at ease."

"She's just not, Gib." Drustan sighed with frustration that they must again debate the matter.

"We do not know who, or what she is. If not a witch, she could be a wood nymph or some other creature conjured up by the witches to seduce men and drag them to her forest lair."

"That would not be such a bad fate," Drustan laughed and gave a wink.

"Maybe she is human and innocent as a newborn babe. She could easily be already betrothed to another, or even married," Gib suggested. "I'm just saying; do not fall for this girl, or any girl, until you know who she is."

"Alright. I hear your words."

"You hear me, but do you listen?"

"I hear you," Drustan murmured grudgingly.

Unnoticed by the two companions, Etta had awakened and sat quietly listening to their conversation.

"I do not wish to be a burden to thee," she finally spoke up. "I will go to the convent."

"You're awake," Drustan said sheepishly, embarrassed that she had heard their discussion. "I hope our words did not offend you."

"Your friend speaks true. Though I find you to be very gallant and pleasing to the eye, even I do not know who I am. It would be better that I go to the nunnery until I can remember my history and where I belong."

"As we embark on our journey to the convent, we shall pass through a handful of villages along the way," Gib spoke in a measured tone. "Mayhap, one of these hamlets will spark a memory within you or someone might know of your past."

Etta nodded, a flicker of hope in her eyes.

Drustan stepped forward, his voice ringing with confidence. "Fear not, my lady. As soon as we have located the last wicked witch, I shall hasten back to retrieve you. If by then you have not regained your memories, you shall come with me to my home. My mother, a wise woman, will guide you back to the path of your true life. Together, we shall find the answers you seek."

Etta's eyes shone with gratitude as she smiled warmly. "You are too kind, sir. I shall offer prayers for your safe return and successful mission."

Gib snorted, his wolfish features twisting into a wry grin. "Aye, aye, you are a kindly lad indeed. Now that we have reached an agreement, I suggest we be on our way."

Etta looked down demurely, "But first, I must excuse myself for a moment of privacy."

Drustan cocked his head, confusion written all over his face. "Privacy, my lady?"

"To attend to my personal needs," Etta said softly.

Gib barked out a laugh, clapping Drustan on the arm. "She needs to relieve herself, lad. Not all is meant to be done in the open like us simple folk."

Drustan looked abashed, realizing his ignorance. "Of course, my lady. Pray, do as you must."

With a gracious nod, Etta turned and walked towards the surrounding woods, seeking the privacy she needed.

Gib turned to Drustan, his eyes flashing with concern. "What's gotten into you, son? Were you dropped on your head as a babe?"

Drustan shot him a confused look. "What are you talking about?"

"The girl may be a sight for sore eyes, but you cannot just bring her into your family home without knowing anything about her past. Have you lost all sense of caution?" Gib warned, his voice filled with mistrust.

"You are too mistrusting, my friend," Drustan replied, standing firm in his conviction.

"I am mistrusting? 'Tis a fine observation coming from one who was tricked by a faerie and taken to swim with a kelpie," Gib quipped. "Think with your head boy, not your loins. Do not allow your youthful cravings to cloud thy judgment."

"You speak truly. So, let us not go through this again. I need not trust Etta, because I trust my mother's wisdom. She will know what to do."

"If it is your mother's wisdom that will be the judge, then I will defer to her. But, promise me that you will get word to Sibby, and seek her council before taking this woman to your home unannounced."

"Do not worry, I will."

While the two companions prepared for their journey, Etta ventured deep into the heart of the forest where she would be shrouded by the trees and lost from view. In a secluded glade, far from the campsite, she paused. With a steady hand, she took a broken tree branch and made a circle into the soft earth, adorning its circumference with arcane symbols etched in dirt. Raising her arms to the sky, she called out to her deities in a voice that echoed like a clarion call.

"Sei malac tome ra, torre boldre unra ped," she intoned with commanding power.

As she spoke, the earth within the circle stirred, at first a faint tremor, but soon growing stronger until the ground churned and boiled like a cauldron. Undaunted, Etta stepped into the vortex, sinking into the earth as if it were quicksand.

Meanwhile, in the great hall of Mora's castle, a rumbling could be heard, a dark aperture materializing. A black orb of utter darkness, a portal to the void, appeared in the center of the room. From the depths of this void, Etta emerged, as if stepping through a door. In quick strides, she crossed the room to a wooden chest filled with vials and bottles.

"Ah! This will do nicely," she whispered to herself, holding two vials of glowing blue liquid up to examine them.

But she was not alone in the castle, as she had thought. Suddenly, a familiar voice spoke, bristling with disapproval.

"What game dost thou play?" Laine seethed.

Startled, Etta spun around, ready to strike, hissing like a serpent. But when she saw the witch who addressed her, she relaxed. Instead of responding, she returned to her search through the chest.

"Our sisters are all dead," Laine declared, her voice heavy with mourning. "We are the last of our coven."

"We expected as much," Etta replied, with a shrug of indifference. "The hunter took nothing that we were not prepared to give."

"And yet thou dost travel with our enemies," Laine continued, her tone growing darker. "Why dost thou not slay them and be done with it?"

"Plans have changed," Etta said, her voice tinged with a hint of malice. "This witch hunter is the son of Isabel. I will make him my instrument of revenge."

"You mean you would have him as thy paramour?" Laine spat, eyes flashing with anger. "We had agreed upon a swift execution, yet thou wouldst spare his life and make him thine own? Thou art a fool!"

Etta's laughter echoed through the chamber, a sound both cold and mocking. "We agreed to naught, Laine. I am the mistress here, my word is the only law. How dare you question my judgment. Obey my command, or suffer the same fate as thy dear sisters."

Her words were like poison, and Laine took a step back, bowing in submission to Etta's authority. She knew all too well that the young Mora, reborn in Etta's form, would not hesitate to follow through on her threat. It was always Mora's plan to eliminate the coven witches, leaving only the two of them to rule supreme.

For Mora, the coven was a burden, a group of wrinkled hags hindering her return to youth. Laine had agreed to Mora's selfish plan, hoping to receive the coveted ritual of rebirth in exchange for her loyalty. Together, they would bask in the extravagance of their newfound youth.

But Laine's acceptance was wrought with reluctance. She did not wish to bring about the coven's destruction, but feared that refusal would lead to her own demise. Mora was not one to tolerate dissent, and if defied she would surely refuse to secure Laine's rebirth, leaving her to rot.

"Forgive me, mistress," Laine apologized. "I do not question thy wisdom."

"See that you do not!" Etta snapped. "Now, take the Faerie Stone and go to the Between to prepare for our arrival. When I call to you, open the doorway, so that I may bring the handsome Drustan home this night."

"As you command," Laine replied. She bowed at the waist and then hobbled out of the chamber.

Etta took the two vials that she had taken from the

chest, her fingers brushing against the cool glass as she carefully placed them into the bodice of her dress. She hesitated, her eyes lingering around the dimly lit chamber as if in a final farewell to the place that had once housed her treasures. And then, with a deep breath, she stepped back into the black portal and was back in the woods within the circle she had drawn in the dirt.

She took the two small vials from her bosom, their glass facets reflecting the sunlight as she carefully removed the stoppers. And with a quiet reverence, she poured their contents together onto the ground, watching as the mixture seeped into the soil.

Suddenly, there was a stir. A sprout pushed up from the earth, its stem slender and green as it twisted and turned towards the sky. It grew at an alarming pace, its leaves unfurling as it became a twisted vine that reached for the heavens. In mere seconds, it had become a small bush, its branches reaching out like gnarled fingers.

And then, a single branch bore a cluster of delicate white blooms, while the rest of the bush remained barren. From the blossoms came small round buds that swelled into plump, purplish-black bilberries, each one a picture of perfection with not a blemish to be seen. Etta reached out and plucked the fruit from the branch.

She picked each berry with care, her fingers sticky with juice as she collected the last of the fruit. And as the final berry was plucked, the entire bush crumbled into dust and fell to the earth, leaving behind only a faint memory of its existence.

Etta held the bilberries aloft, their dark, glossy beauty glimmering like gemstones in the sunlight. And in that moment, she knew that she held in her hand the key to unlocking a terrible power, a power that she would wield with care and caution.

Back at the campsite, Drustan had begun to worry. Etta had been gone quite a while.

"I should check on her," Drustan said. "She may have gotten lost."

"Give her a few more moments," Gib answered. "Women are different from men, it takes them longer. They can't just undo their codpiece and be done with it."

"I am well aware that women are different, Gib," Drustan said and rolled his eyes. "I wasn't born yesterday."

"No, but you had your first kiss yesterday so I would imagine you don't know much about women."

"Give it a rest. Besides, your cabin didn't exactly have a woman's touch. How much experience have you actually had with the fairer sex?"

"Not as much as I would like," Gib chuckled. "But I have sired four litters with 19 pups in my lifetime, so I suppose I know a thing or two about females."

"Nineteen!" Drustan was surprised and impressed. "Then why do you live alone? Where is your family?"

"Those who are left are scattered across the land. Most of my kind, including my children, have been killed by hunters and terrified villagers. Then there are the wolves. Wolf-kind has killed many wulvers out of fear."

"I am sorry to hear that, Gib. I should not have asked."

"'Tis no concern. Wulvers are not like humans, when

wulver pups are mature enough to hunt and fish on their own, they go their own way. We do not have packs like the wolves. We are loners."

"Still the loss of your family must be difficult. I am sorry that happened."

Gib did not want to discuss it further. He had intended to tease Drustan, but instead found himself on a sad topic that he wanted to leave behind.

"Maybe it would be prudent to check on the girl," the wulver said. "We should soon be on our way if we are to reach the nunnery by nightfall."

Drustan gave the wulver a resounding pat on the back and gathered his sword before venturing into the verdant depths of the forest in search of Etta. Yet, as he delved deeper into the wild, his heart grew heavy with worry, for there was no trace of the girl to be found.

"Etta!" he cried, his voice echoing through the trees, but there was no reply. Fearful that she might have wandered too far and become lost, Drustan pressed on, his eyes scanning the surrounding terrain for any signs that might hint at her whereabouts.

And then, there she was, a distant figure hurrying away from him, her movements harried and uncertain.

"Etta! Over here!" he shouted, his voice resounding with urgency. But she seemed not to hear him, continuing on her hurried escape. Undaunted, Drustan ran after her, pushing his way through the thickets and brambles, determined to reach her side.

"Etta!" he cried once more, his voice resounding through the forest. Yet she remained unfazed, fleeing deeper into the heart of the woodland, her form gradually disappearing from sight. Undeterred, Drustan raced after her, his voice ringing out her name with every step.

Finally, as he crested a rise, he saw her in the distance, standing still as if she were waiting for him. With renewed vigor, he sprinted towards her, his heart pounding in his chest from the exertion of the chase.

As he reached her side, he was breathless, his chest heaving from the pursuit. Yet to his surprise, Etta was serene, her breathing even and her demeanor calm. *What manner of trickery is this?* Drustan thought to himself, gazing upon the girl in wonder.

Etta, did you not hear me calling?" Drustan asked, his voice betraying his confusion.

"Drustan! I was momentarily disoriented and had wandered astray," she answered, her words ringing with a hint of unease. Yet, despite her explanation, her nervous behavior only served to heighten Drustan's suspicion. With her hands hidden behind her back and her body language exuding a sense of caution, he couldn't help but wonder if there was something more to her story.

As Drustan's eyes scanned the surroundings, they were captivated by an extraordinary sight—a mystical rock formation that seemed to embody the essence of an ancient stone doorway. Nestled amidst towering trees and embraced by a vibrant tapestry of moss, this natural marvel exuded an irresistible air of enchantment.

Fashioned from weathered granite, the surface of the formation bore the intricate etchings of time's passage. Gentle undulations and delicate patterns revealed the mark of ancient forces that had shaped it over countless ages. From earthen browns to mossy greens, the rock's hues blended harmoniously with the surrounding landscape, as if seamlessly integrated by nature's hand.

One couldn't help but be drawn to this extraordinary spectacle—a seemingly ordinary rock formation that, through the eyes of wonder, transformed into a gateway to the realms of imagination. Drustan's heart quickened with anticipation, for he sensed that passing through this natural doorway might lead to untold adventures and mysteries waiting to be unraveled.

"What manner of structure is this?" he wondered, his curiosity piqued. "What is this place?"

"'Tis called Clachan na Sith, the Faerie Door," she answered. "They say that during the Between Times, it will open and allow men to pass into another realm."

"The Between. Its very name stirs dread within me, for I have been warned of its dangers time and again. We should not tarry here."

He took her by the arm and started to lead her away, but instead she resisted, her hand clasped tightly and suspiciously behind her back.

"What is it that you hide thus?" he asked, his gaze piercing.

"A gift for thee, sweet knight," she whispered, a hint of mischief in her voice.

"Surprises do not sit well with me. Show me what you conceal."

"Fear not, my lord. Close thine eyes," she said, her laughter ringing like chimes.

He heaved a heavy sigh and impatiently closed his eyes to humor her.

"No peeking," she insisted.

"I do not peek."

"Now, open your eyes."

And when he did, Drustan saw what lay before him, a stunning offering of plump, ripe berries, their sweet fragrance filling the air.

"Bilberries?" he said with wonder, a smile spreading across his face. He cast his gaze about the barren landscape, searching in vain for any hint of verdant growth. Bilberries, with their rich purple hue, were a rare delicacy, found only in the moist highlands during the fleeting days of early summer. Yet here they were, out of season and beyond their time, amidst the bleakness of late autumn.

"Where did you discover these, on the cusp of winter's grasp?" he asked, his tone filled with disbelief.

"Yonder, over the distant hill. They were the last of the season."

He looked at the cluster in her hand and marveled at their perfection, realizing the unlikelihood that they could have survived the chill of the coming winter. Yet, this was Etta who had found them, it was fitting that she would happen upon such perfection and beauty.

"Taste them, my love," she urged. "I plucked them just for you."

"Nay, they are yours to savor," he replied, his heart overflowing with gratitude. "You found them, they belong to you."

"Please, my lord," she implored, her eyes shining with determination. "Allow me to present you with this humble offering, as a token of my gratitude for all that you have done."

With a gentle hand, she plucked a few of the plump bilberries from her palm and placed them upon Drustan's tongue. The moment he swallowed, his expression changed, confusion clouded his eyes as his mind became muddled. He stared at Etta, entranced, as she offered him more of the mysterious fruit.

"Take these," she whispered, the melody of seduction lacing her voice as she bestowed upon him another generous offering of the mystical bilberries.

In that instant, his resolve crumbled and he was overcome by an insatiable longing for her. With the fervor of his desire he swept her into a ravenous embrace. He ravaged her body with kisses, his hands mapping the contours of her curves as if they were the secrets of the universe. He moaned out his cravings, a symphony of yearning, "I want you, now!"

The spell of the enchanted fruit consumed him, erasing all other thoughts, leaving only an all-encompassing obsession with Etta. Gib, Laine, his family, all became a distant memory, fading away into the mists of his mind. He was now Etta's, body and soul.

She led him toward the stones of the Faerie Door, her eyes twinkling with the thrill of conquest. Drustan followed her willingly, his purpose now solely to be with her, to bask in the glow of her love.

"Drustan!" A voice, now foreign to him, echoed through the clearing. But he remained steadfast in his trance, his gaze locked upon Etta, his heart thudding with a drumbeat of desire.

It was Gib's voice that echoed through the woods.

He had trailed after Drustan, sensing something was off about Etta's mysterious disappearance. Due to his reservations about her story and suspecting her motives, Gib felt it was his duty not to leave his friend alone with the enigmatic girl. The wulver tirelessly scoured the forest in search of any trace of his lost companions, until he finally came upon them. To his shock and disappointment, he found Drustan succumbing to his carnal desires, ignoring Gib's previous warnings.

As he was about to discreetly retreat and avoid the awkward scene, he saw Etta take Drustan by the hand and begin leading Drustan through the Faerie Door. It was then that Gib realized her true intentions, and called out in alarm, "Drustan! "Drustan!"

Gib cried out in despair as he sprinted towards Drustan and Etta, his heart pounding with fear for his friend. He had warned him about the dangers of being around Etta, but it seemed his words fell on deaf ears. With each step Gib took, he felt his hopes slipping away, until finally he reached the stone door that led to the world of the Between. But it was too late, the passage was closed and Drustan was gone.

Driven by an overwhelming urgency, Gib reached the door with a desperate determination. His powerful paws lunged at the stone structure, his claws scratching at the unyielding surface in a frenzied attempt. He darted back and forth between the stones, searching for any crevice or opening, his fervor driving him to discover a path through. Yet, despite his relentless efforts, the passage remained resolutely closed, thwarting his every attempt.

A sense of defeat washed over Gib, his heart heavy with sorrow. He lowered himself to the ground, his gaze fixated upon the ancient stones that stood stoically, unmoved by his anguish. Whimpers and mournful whines escaped his lips, their melancholic notes hanging in the air, a lament for the loss of his companion to the mysterious and treacherous creature that was Etta.

Gib's spirit was burdened, his soul entwined with grief and longing. The air seemed to carry the weight of his sorrow, echoing his lamentation through the silent expanse. With every whimper, he mourned the cruel fate that had separated him from his dear companion, an ache that pierced deep into his being. But even in his darkest hour, a flicker of determination remained, a glimmer of hope that perhaps, one day, the ancient stones would reveal the path he sought—a path to reunite with his lost companion and bring an end to the sorrow that enveloped his heart.

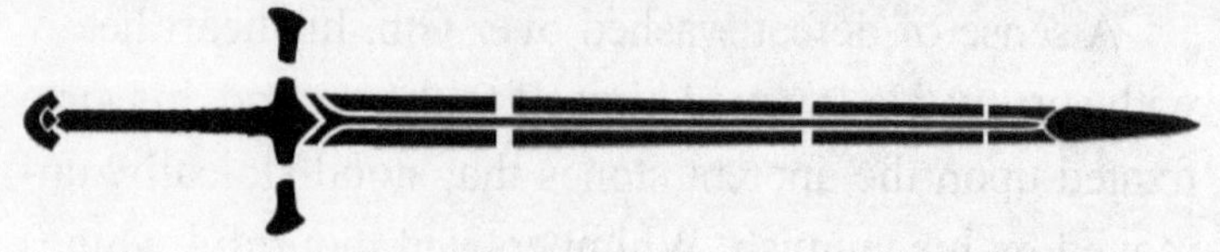

CHAPTER 19

The Twilight World of the Between

Drustan sat perched on the edge of the window in the bedchamber he shared with the alluring Etta. Their shared home was an imposing citadel, a magnificent palace set atop a hill and gazing down upon a valley dotted with a shimmering black lake. From his vantage point, Drustan gazed out at what he believed to be the entire world, with endless miles of rolling hills, lush fields, and towering forests stretching from horizon to horizon. He thought to himself that this was exactly as it should be, with Etta by his side and the world bowing down at his feet bowing in homage to their love.

He looked at the distant horizon lit by the breath-taking orange glow from the rising sun; or maybe it was the sunset. He tried to remember. Was it the dawn whose light brought the promise of coming day, or was it dusk and the fading light of the setting sun? He pondered the question for only a moment then let it go as if time was meaningless now. Sunrise or sunset, neither was a matter of concern in his blissful world. He was in paradise, deeply in love with the beautiful Etta and spending all his time making love, drinking wine and eating the finest cheeses and fruits as they lay together in their bed.

It did not seem odd at all to him that he would not know if it were dusk or dawn, nor did he fret that the sky had neither sun nor moon, just only hints of both. The reality was that Drustan had lost all track of time because there actually was none in this world. To him it had been only hours since he and Etta had arrived at the castle, but in truth, it had been weeks. Day after day, he had sat on that same window ledge, staring out into perpetual twilight, watching for a sun that neither rose nor set but simply lay hidden beyond the horizon.

In this place, time stood still. There was neither day nor night to measure the passage of time, only the unfulfilled promise of both. The red and orange sky where Drustan looked and marveled was always so, colored as if by the fading sun. Yet, on the opposite horizon, there was a bright yellow glow as if at any moment the moon would spill over the mountain. The sky above was starless and grey, seemingly waiting for the first star of the evening to appear; or, perhaps it was the sun that the sky awaited. Such was the world of the Between, a place trapped between light and dark, a border between two worlds.

None of this strangeness affected Drustan, nor concerned him as unusual. To him it was not odd; it just was. He was bewitched and nothing mattered to him beyond Etta. The passage of time did not matter, nor did the reality of the world around. The reality was that it all was little more than an illusion. The sweet wine he shared with his beloved was in fact only water. The cheese and fruits were in truth pieces of stale bread. The opulent surroundings in his bedchamber were nothing more than a straw bed on a bare stone floor in a cold tower. In fact, rather than being Etta's lover and mate, he was Mora's prisoner; yoked by her magic as soundly as if he were bound in shackles.

Had he known of his true circumstances, it would have made little difference. His only thoughts were of his beloved Etta, and he would have followed her into hell rather than be separated. With a single taste of the hexed berries, he became her captive, a slave whose chains were physical lust and obsession, and whose jail was the bed they shared.

Bewitched by a powerful spell, he was blinded to everything in the world except to the one who cast it. Though he had not forgotten his family or his own past, those memories were completely foreign to him as if they belonged to someone else. Those thoughts no longer held any meaning or emotional connection to his life. His past was a distant memory with no more attachment than a story he had heard in childhood. Etta was his world now, and no one could distract his attention from her.

In the deepest part of his mind, Drustan understood who Etta truly was. She was the evil witch Mora, transformed into this beautiful young creature he now adored through some dark spell. Still, that realization was unimportant to him and did not distract from his devotion to her. Although in his mind he knew the truth, he could not fully understand its significance, nor could he process the knowledge; or, perhaps he just didn't care to. His mind may have known the truth, but it was his heart

284

and his carnal lust that were in control.

Etta stirred from her sleep and turned to see Drustan sitting at the window. She observed him intently, appreciating the magnificence of his nude body and his physical perfection. At that moment, he seemed more like the statue of a Norse god than a mere mortal man. Were anyone to see him there, they would think him to be in thoughtful contemplation, but she knew that was not the case. He was thinking of her, else he was thinking of nothing at all, mindlessly looking out into the distance, waiting for her to arise and give his life meaning.

She should have been quite pleased with her handiwork. The eldest son of her mortal enemy was under her power, willing to give anything she asked, willing to do anything she wanted. She could even order Drustan to kill his mother and his entire family, and he would gladly do so to please her. In time, she would give that order, but for now, she was satisfied just having him under her spell. She should have been well satisfied with herself, but instead she felt strangely incomplete. She enjoyed having Drustan as her lover; she was actually growing quite fond of him, and that was the basis of her feelings of discontent.

He was a strikingly handsome man, lean but powerfully built; and despite his lack of experience, he proved to be a great and passionate lover for her. Having lived the last several centuries as a decrepit old hag, the physical pleasure Drustan provided was invigorating and addicting. Just as he was completely and mindlessly under her spell, she was falling under his; succumbing to his charms and the physical pleasures he offered. She found herself beginning to care for him, trying to please him; even considering the possibility of having his child.

It was her own attraction to Drustan that fueled her discontent. She began to entertain the idea that his emotions for her were not solely the product of the potion, but rather a deeper truth. Could it be that he could love her, unencumbered by magic's hold? She remembered their first encounter, prior to the curse of the magic berries, and the way his eyes had beheld hers, ablaze with passion. It was evident that he was drawn to her, even before the spell had taken root. As the spell made him lavish his affections on her, she became convinced that even without the enchantment, he would love her. It was these thoughts that made her leave the chamber door unlocked; this confidence that made her allow him to move freely about the castle. It was her own growing affection for Drustan that began to weaken her power over him.

Etta eased lightly from the bed where she lay, and softly crept toward him so not to disturb his thoughts. Just as she was upon him, he spun around and grabbed her. He wrapped his arms firmly around her and pulled their nude bodies tightly together.

She giggled happily and pretended to struggle against him. "What are you doing? Let me go, you voracious brute!"

"What do you want me to be doing?" He laughed playfully and spoke in a deep sexy voice. He swept her off her feet and carried her back to bed. As he settled beside her, he propped himself up on his elbow, gazing deeply into her eyes. The soft glow of the firelight illuminated their faces, creating an intimate atmosphere. He took a moment to admire her beauty and to bask in the moment, knowing that this was exactly where he was meant to be. He reached out and took her hand, entwining his fingers with hers, feeling a sense of contentment wash over him. They lay there in silence, enjoying each other's company and basking in the warmth of the moment. He leaned over and kissed her passionately, but after a moment, she reluctantly pushed him away.

"I must get up and dressed," she stated. "I cannot spend my entire life in this bed."

"And why not?"

"I have things I must do. Plans to make. A house to run."

"You have servants for those things," he protested, but obediently began to climb back out of bed. "Besides, look at the sky. The day is at an end."

"No, my beloved. 'Tis the sunrise," she insisted knowing that he would accept whatever she suggested as the truth. "I must have an early start; there is much work to be done."

"How can I help you? I feel as if I have done nothing but eat, sleep and make love."

Had she not been so captivated by Drustan and so self-assured she would have realized that he had just revealed the first sign that her power over him was fading. He had voiced his restlessness and his growing boredom with the status quo. Though his passion still burned for her, he was beginning to realize that love was not enough. Rather than be alerted that this was a sign her spell was losing its hold, she was instead pleased that he wanted to help.

"'Tis all you need to do, my love," she smiled and began donning her robes. "Eat to keep up thy strength so you can continue to make love. But if you must, take a walk around the grounds. Explore the castle. You do not need to sit in this room all day awaiting my return."

"I will find something to do," he answered and grabbed her for another embrace. "But for the moment, why not come back to bed; just for a little while."

"Nay, stop tempting me." She pulled away and slapped him playfully on the bare butt. "Get yourself dressed and do something besides sulk in this room."

Not ready to give up, he grabbed her again and roughly pushed her against the stone wall. He took her by the wrists, stretched her arms up against the wall, and held her in place.

"Should I force myself upon you," he growled in a deep threatening voice. "Make you my captive and bind you like a slave? Then ravage you like the savage Norsemen do their women."

She was tempted by his offer, but she had too many pressing matters to attend to rather than indulge in such pleasures. She pushed him away gently and insistently. "You can be the conquering warrior this evening when we have more time. But for now, I must tend to my duties."

"As you wish then," he said and gave an exaggerated frown.

She gave him a long goodbye kiss, then disappeared out the chamber door.

Drustan donned his garments as he gazed out the window, taking in the breathtaking view of the orange horizon. Despite living in a world where the sun never truly rose nor set, he acknowledged that it was indeed dawn, as Etta had advised him. However, as he gazed at the sky, a sense of unease settled deep within him. Something seemed amiss, as if he was missing a vital piece of information, like a forgotten memory or a word on the brink of recall. For a moment, a realization stirred within his mind, telling him that something was wrong, that this was not right.

But just as quickly as the feeling had come, it was gone. Drustan dismissed it and decided to explore the castle until the sun rose higher in the sky. He would then venture out into the grounds and possibly go hunting in the nearby woods with his bow.

In the depths of the council chamber, just off the main hall, sat a room stripped of all adornments. The only feature of the bleak space was an elongated table surrounded by chairs, where Etta presided over the meeting. To her right sat Laine, while on the opposite side, facing Etta, stood her two generals, Dok and Krob.

The generals, like the majority of Etta's army, were once faeries, but they had been corrupted and twisted into the monstrous beings they now were. Their skin was rough and gray, covered in moles and warts, with long pointed noses and coal black eyes. Bald and bereft of any hair, even their eyebrows and lashes were absent, rendering them even more grotesque. They were a far cry from the graceful faeries they once were, and now served as Etta's generals in the goblin army of the Between, commanding the forces of evil.

Etta's gaze bore into the two goblin generals as they

stood before her. "What news do you have for me?" she demanded.

Dok stepped forward, a hint of nervousness in his voice. "Our army stands ready at the border, ready to storm the Faerie Realm."

"And the gate?" Etta asked, her tone turning icy. "Is it open?"

Krob shifted uneasily, "The passage remains locked tight, mistress. The faeries' magic is proving formidable."

"We are making progress," Dok interjected quickly. "The barrier cannot hold much longer."

Etta's eyes blazed with anger. "You'd better open that gate, or I'll have your heads on pikes. Get out of here, and don't return until the way is clear."

The goblins hastened to obey, bowing and backing out of the room. Etta turned her attention to Laine. "And what news do you bring from the mortal world, sister?"

Laine leaned back in her chair, a sly smile on her lips. "Our goblins art scouring the forest for any rogue faeries that may be hiding there. 'Tis only a matter of time before they have all been rounded up."

"None of them can escape!" Etta roared, her voice echoing through the room. "What about the wulver?"

"He knows the forests too well," Laine reported. "He's still out there, evading our soldiers and attacking them from the shadows."

"I don't want him captured," Etta snarled, slamming her fist down on the table. "I want him dead."

"It shall be done," Laine promised.

"Is there anything else?" Etta asked, her eyes piercing Laine's.

"Good sister, I am full of worry," Laine started uncertainly. "This man thou hast taken to thy bed...he is the son of thine enemy, and a witch-killer. He hunted and killed our sisters, and he once sought thy very life. Keeping such a peril alive is not wise."

"You question my judgment again?" Etta said, her eyes flashing with anger.

"Verily, in this matter I must," Laine replied, standing firm. "Dost thou not share thy bed with the one who would slay us? I fear thy emotions clouds thy judgment."

"I have no emotions for this man," Etta said, her voice icy. "He is under my control, as weak and harmless as a mouse. He is nothing more than a toy for my entertainment, a momentary distraction for my pleasure."

"A distraction indeed! A distraction from our goals. Our generals are preparing for battle in the Faerie Realm, and this witch hunter's mother, who is our deadly enemy still lives while her child shares thy bed. Hast thou given any consideration to our plans for the mortal world? You should win the favor of the King of Alba instead of dallying with the offspring of a savage and a common witch who yet poses a threat to us!"

Etta glared at Laine, "Take heed of what you say, Laine! Your boldness has gone too far. Have you forgotten the end that befell our sisters?"

Laine held her ground, her voice stern and unwavering. "Take care with thy words, Etta. Do not turn thy only true ally into an adversary."

Etta was incensed by Laine's impudence, but she acknowledged that the witch was speaking the truth. Laine was the one who stood by her side when the Between was created, and together they devised a plan to control both the mortal and Faerie realms. Making an enemy out of a witch who was nearly her equal wouldn't benefit Etta, at least not at this moment. In the future, Etta would need to deal with Laine and eliminate the only witch who could potentially pose a threat to her rule. But for now, she would maintain their friendship.

Etta took a deep breath and instead of escalating the argument, she decided to calm herself down. "I will take thy council under consideration, sister. Let us not argue between ourselves."

"Then wilt thou rid us of that man? This hunter?"

"In time, but not yet. He has his purpose. Soon, we will have to face Isabel again. I would see her face when her son stands by my side and he himself will deliver her into my hands."

"Then thou dost not heed my word, but will continue this dalliance," Laine said with contempt.

"As I said, I will consider your council. Nevertheless, for now, he amuses me. And he will prove useful in the war to come."

Laine rose to her feet and gave a slight bow towards Etta. "Then that is thy judgment. I pray we shall not have to bear the burden of that decision," she said and then angrily stormed from the room.

As Drustan wandered the stone halls of the castle, he peered into chamber after chamber, searching for something that might pique his interest. But every room he investigated proved empty and uninspiring. After what felt like hours of aimless wandering, he finally made his way down to the main floor of the fortress.

It was there, as he turned a corner, that he collided with Laine. The old crone was rushing down the hall with an air of urgency, fleeing from her meeting with Etta. The two of them bounced off one another, startled, and Drustan found himself face to face with the haggard witch.

Though he had seen Laine lurking through the halls of the castle on many occasions, the sight of her this time stirred something within him, a vague memory that ran much deeper than just her physical appearance. He knew her, or felt like he did, yet the feelings of hatred and disgust that he had for her were as strong as ever, even though he could not place why he felt such loathing.

The realization hit him like a thunderbolt, but just as quickly as the memory came, it was gone, leaving Drustan to ponder the strange sensations that had just overtaken him. He shook his head and tried to push the thoughts aside, determined to continue his exploration of the castle and the surrounding lands.

"Out of my way, filthy swine!" She snarled at him in fury, blaming him for being the source of her growing rift with Etta.

"Forgive me, my lady. You were downwind and I did not smell you coming," he taunted in jest, but the fact was that he could not disguise his disgust for her any more than she could for him.

"Go back to thy room, pig!"

"Don't you have some chamber pots to clean, or wings to pluck from butterflies?" He shot back.

"Thy humor is boundless," she scowled. "I see thy

purpose now, thou art the court jester."

"Though I do so enjoy your wit, or at least the half you have to offer; I seek Etta. Have you seen her?" Drustan asked.

Laine pushed by him and started to walk away without responding, but then she hesitated. An idea suddenly crossed her mind. If Etta refused to see the danger that this mortal posed for them, maybe it was necessary to show her.

"Thy mistress is in the bowels of the castle," Laine said deceptively. "Thou may find her in the dungeon."

"The dungeon? Are you certain?" Though he had never stepped foot in the place, he imagined it to be dark and dreary.

"Verily," she said with a sly grin, "thou shalt find her there, if thou hast the courage to venture into the depths of the castle."

Laine's tone was almost inviting, as if she were daring him to take the challenge. Drustan couldn't help but wonder why Etta would be in the dungeon, but he knew he had to find out for himself.

"What is she doing there?"

"Verily, she converses with the new captives. Ye should seek her out. I am certain she would feel more secure in the company of a valiant man such as thyself, rather than be in such a loathsome abode unaccompanied."

Drustan was concerned for Etta venturing into the dungeon unescorted. "She's alone! How do I get there?"

"Proceed along yon passageway and thou shalt come upon a stairway leading down to the dungeon. Take hold of one of the torches from the wall, for the path is dreary and extends far down into the bowels of the castle."

"I thank you for your aid," Drustan said and hurried down the corridor.

"'Tis always my pleasure to help the young master," Laine snarled.

"If you truly wish to help," Drustan shouted back, "go to the sewers and take a bath. Thy stench offends even the rats."

Laine continued on her way, but no longer was she in a fit of anger. She walked briskly with a smile playing on her lips, rather pleased with herself knowing what Drustan would find when he reached the dungeon and the trouble that would ensue.

When Drustan arrived at the end of the corridor, he came to the staircase as Laine had said. He grabbed a torch from the wall, the flickering flames casting eerie shadows on the wall as he descended the long dark stairway into the underbelly of the castle. The air grew colder and damper with each step, until finally he found himself in the dungeon.

"Etta!" Drustan shouted into the dark, echoing tunnels. "Hello? Etta?" But there was no response, only the deafening silence of the blackness.

He walked down the corridor past several rooms fitted with iron bars.

Drustan surveyed the dark and ominous dungeon with a mixture of curiosity and apprehension. He wondered what manner of dangerous creatures lay locked away in these cells. He approached one of the cells, holding his torch aloft, and peered inside.

"Hello? Is anyone in there?" he called out, his voice echoing through the silent tunnels. "Rise and shine!" But his calls were met with only silence, as the blackness seemed to swallow up any response.

He was not disappointed to find the cell was empty. Despite the eerie stillness of the dungeon, he pressed on, driven by a mixture of curiosity and a sense of obligation to find Etta. He paused at another cell and looked inside again, there was nothing. The place seemed to be completely abandoned.

"Etta!" He called out, still there was no response. It was becoming clear that Laine intentionally lied to him and was playing a cruel joke. Nevertheless, since he was already there he decided to continue to explore the place and see what strange torture devices he might find. He continued down the hallway and came to another cell. Again, he stopped and peered inside. This time he was startled to see movement in the darkness.

"Who's there?" Drustan demanded, his voice ringing through the dark cell. He held the torch high, illuminating the chamber as he approached the bars. But instead of finding the answer he was searching for, he was met with darkness and a whisper of voices in the shadows.

"Etta, is that you?" he called out, his voice tense and shaking. "Show yourself, or I'll tie you to the rack and have my way with you."

A voice emerged from the darkness, "Eww!" followed by hushed whispers.

As Drustan approached the cell, his heart quickened, anticipation coursing through his veins. The dim light cast mysterious shadows, concealing the shapes that adorned the back wall. With each passing moment, his eyes adapted, revealing a sight that piqued his curiosity. Suspended from hooks were peculiar objects, swaying gently in the stillness. His mind raced with questions. Were they birdcages, or something entirely different? The answer eluded him, fueling his intrigue.

He strained to see inside, but the light was too dim and the objects too far away. He couldn't quite make out what was inside, but he was determined to find out.

"What is that?" He asked himself aloud.

He looked around the hallway and saw a set of keys hanging on a nearby hook. With a quick, sure hand, Drustan retrieved the keys and hastened back to the cell. He fumbled with each key, trying it against the iron door, until he finally found the one that fit. With a loud, haunting creak, the door swung open, and Drustan stepped inside.

Slowly, cautiously, he scanned the cell, his heart pounding in his chest, searching for any signs of danger. But there was no one there. He approached the birdcages, and leaned over the first one. To his amazement, he saw a tiny, winged creature cowering in the back. It was a faerie, dressed in moss-green clothing, its eyes wide with fear.

"Please! Don't hurt me!" The faerie begged, its voice a soft whisper.

"Fear not, I mean no harm," Drustan said, his voice gentle and soothing. "What crime have you committed to find yourself in such a place?"

"We committed no crime. The witch, she holds us prisoner to steal our magic."

"We?" Drustan gazed around the room, taking in the sight of the faeries, each one confined within a cage of iron like captive birds.

"Drustan?" A voice came from a cage nearby, and he moved closer to see who had spoken. In the flickering torchlight, he saw the face of a female faerie, her hair golden and her cheeks rosy. He knew her, yet the love spell had clouded his memory, leaving only a vague recognition.

"How do you know my name?" he asked, his voice hushed.

"I am Aster. You know me, do you not remember?"

"Aster?" The name echoed in his mind, ringing with a faint familiarity. A nagging sensation in his gut told him that she was someone he should know, a face from his past that had once held meaning for him.

"Yes, I am Aster. Please, open the cages and set us free."

"I cannot," Drustan replied, his voice resolute. "I do not know what crimes ye have committed, I must speak with Etta first."

Aster's voice became insistent. "You're not still angry about that kelpie thing, are you? It was only a joke."

I know not of this kelpie," Drustan growled, his eyes narrowing. "Regardless, I cannot open your cage. I must speak with Etta first."

"Don't leave us here, Drustan! Please!" Aster begged, her voice shaking with urgency. "Etta is an evil witch! She is the spirit of Mora reborn."

"You're wrong," Drustan shot back, his voice firm. "Etta would never harm anyone. She is a kind and loving woman. I must speak to her about this."

"Drustan! Listen to me!" a new voice rang out from one of the cages. Drustan quickly held up the torch, illuminating the face of an older, bearded faerie.

"This woman you call Etta," King Jorin declared, "she is not who you think she is."

"And who are you?" Drustan asked, his voice tense. "Do I know you?"

"I'm King Jorin," the faerie replied. "Think, boy! Try to remember. You know me, you know us!"

"I do not remember you," Drustan said hesitantly. "This one called Aster, she does seem familiar, but you and the others, I cannot place."

"'Tis a spell!" Jorin declared to his fellow faeries. "The witch has him under her power."

"What witch do you speak of?" Drustan's voice was dismissive as he replied.

"Etta is not who she presents herself to be," King Jorin warned. "She is the evil witch Mora, reborn into a new body."

"It matters not what name she goes by," Drustan said, his eyes blazing with passion. "She is my love, my heart, my everything."

"You are under her spell," Jorin declared. "This woman, this witch, is your mortal enemy. You have hunted her and sought to destroy her, and now she holds you captive."

"I will not listen to these fabrications," Drustan spoke sternly. "I may not know the crimes you have committed, but I am certain you are here for a reason. And here you shall remain."

Drustan turned to leave, but Aster's voice stopped him. "Drustan, wait! I have proof that she is a witch."

"I will hear no more of this," Drustan refused.

"Please!" Aster implored. "You once gave me something, 'twas precious and unique, unlike any other in the world. Let me show it to you. It will prove that Etta is a witch."

Drustan was struck with a sudden, electric sensation of familiarity as he gazed upon Aster. A flash of recognition swept over him, a shiver of déjà vu that set his heart ablaze with wonder. Could it be that he did indeed know her, but had simply forgotten in the maze of time?

"And this gift you speak of, what might that be?" he asked, his voice a husky rumble.

"Thy first kiss," she whispered as if she were betraying a secret, her eyes gleaming with hope.

He roared with laughter, his rich baritone echoing through the dungeon. "My first kiss? You want to give me back my first kiss?"

"Aye," she replied, unperturbed by his mirth. "The first kiss is a moment of pure magic, where time stands still and the world fades away into the background. You gave me your first kiss. Allow me to return it to you, and it shall break the wicked spell cast upon you by the witch and restore your lost memories."

"You want to kiss me and break a spell?" Drustan laughed again. "How does one give back a first kiss? It's like trying to unstitch the fabric of time."

Drustan was right. There was no way to take back a first kiss and no way to return one, short of turning back time itself. Aster's goal was not to undo that which was already done, but to use the magic of the first kiss to break the spell he was under. The first kiss held powerful magic, powerful enough to restore Drustan's memory and free him from his enchantment.

"What harm could it bring?" King Jorin encouraged. "'Tis only a simple kiss."

"Maybe he is too shy and has yet to become a man," one of the faeries taunted in an effort to prod him on.

"Just as I thought, he is afraid of girls," another continued the teasing. "Or maybe he only likes kissing boys."

"'Tis enough, you pack of imps!" Drustan shouted. The faeries' plan had worked; he hated to be taunted.

He then turned back to Aster. "One kiss? That's all."

"Just one," she smiled.

"So be it. Give me this so-called first kiss and I will be on my way."

He leaned over and pressed his lips to the bars of Aster's cage. "Well?" He asked impatiently.

"This will not work; the iron bars — faeries cannot touch iron. You need to open the cage and let me out."

"Nay, I see your game," Drustan said. "You are trying to trick me. I will not let you out."

"'Tis no trick! You know that faeries cannot touch iron. Besides how can we kiss with you being so big and me so small? I must change to human size."

"I told you so," a male faerie once again teased. "He is afraid of girls."

"Shut up!" Aster yelled at the other faeries in order to boost Drustan's ego. "Drustan is a brave hero and fears nothing! You'll see."

"I wouldn't bother, Aster." A male faerie spoke up. "He probable kisses like a dead fish anyway."

A female faerie chimed in. "I bet he kisses like a dream," she swooned. "Look at those soft full lips, and that chiseled jaw."

"Enough!" Drustan looked around and contemplated the situation. The faeries knew exactly how to play to his ego and he was falling for their scheme.

"The keys to our cages are hanging over there. Next to the door," Aster encouraged once she realized he was wavering.

"There is no *our*, just you. The others remain locked."

"Whatever you say," Aster readily agreed.

"Alright, but no tricks," he warned as he fished a set of keys from the wall. "Try something and I will swat you like a fly."

With a clinking of metal against metal, Drustan tried several keys until he found the right one to open the cage door. In an instant, Aster emerged, soaring out of her imprisonment and blossoming into a petite young woman. With a touch as gentle as a summer breeze, Aster's fingers caressed Drustan's cheeks as she pressed her lips to his. In a moment that felt eternal, she stepped back and watched as the magic embraced him and his memories of the past came rushing back.

Drustan's knees buckled as he was consumed by the deluge of confusion and disorientation. He muttered words of bewilderment, "Where am I?"

King Jorin's voice boomed with the force of a storm, "You are in the castle of Mora, in the realm of the Between."

Drustan's eyes widened with disbelief, "Mora? She's dead. I saw her. I burned her body." But as the words left his mouth, he felt a creeping realization wash over him. The memories came flooding back, every treacherous moment that had transpired in the weeks leading up to this very moment. He felt a wave of nausea as the depth of Mora's deception was laid bare before him.

"'Tis truly Mora. She transformed herself through a powerful black spell," Jorin explained. "The fair maiden you call Etta, 'tis a new body but is indeed the same evil witch that rules the Between."

"But I have … we were …" Drustan stammered. "I have been with her. We have lain together."

"Ewww," Aster said and spat repeatedly on the floor. Then she began vigorously wiping her lips with her hands. "Stop saying stuff like that. I'm getting sick."

"'Tis no time to waste," King Jorin urged. "Open the cages and let us escape this prison while there is time."

Drustan opened Jorin's cage and once outside the king immediately transformed to the size of a man.

"Free the others," Drustan instructed and handed Jorin the set of keys. "I will deal with Mora and end her life once and for all."

"No, she is too strong here. The Between is her domain and it is from here that she draws her power," Jorin replied. "We must flee this place and return to the world of men. Here in the Between, she is all powerful. We must draw her into the mortal realm where she is vulnerable. We can face her there."

"I have been warned that she cannot be killed in the mortal world, and now you tell me neither can she be killed in this one," Drustan objected. "No one is immune to death."

"You do not understand, my human friend," Jorin said. "This is her world. She created it and she is invincible here."

"What do you mean she created it?"

"The Between is of her doing. Centuries ago, there was no realm between the mortal world and the Faerie Realm. The Between was merely a thin veil betwixt our two worlds, and we faeries could pass easily from our world to thine."

"Then she came," Aster interjected with contempt.

"Aye, she used her magic to create a barrier between the two worlds. At first, her purpose was to trap faeries who tried to cross between the two realms. She would capture our kind and drain them of their magical powers. Then pervert them into something vile and evil."

"Why would she do such a thing?" Drustan asked. "If Mora is powerful enough to create a whole world what would she need with your magic? I mean no disrespect but it seems you faeries are pretty lacking when it comes to usable magic."

Aster abruptly slapped Drustan hard across the face. He was stunned not only by the fact she had slapped him, but also by how forceful the blow was.

"Aster!" King Jorin exclaimed, his tone disapproving.

"He asked for it," Aster replied haughtily, her voice ringing with the power of the faeries. She turned her gaze upon Drustan, her eyes blazing with a mystical fire. "Know this, mortal," she said in a voice like the rush of a summer wind, "we faeries are magic! We are not mere conjurers of spells and weavers of charms like witches and sorcerers. Our very essence is suffused with magic, a magic born from the wild and untamed forces of nature."

"My apologies," Drustan said as he rubbed his stinging cheek. "I meant no insult."

Aster's tone quickly turned from anger to demure gentleness once again. "You are forgiven," she smiled sheepishly then added in a sharp tone, "but do not utter such blasphemy again."

"Aster speaks true, although somewhat inappropriate in her behavior," King Jorin continued. "Faeries are not just born of magic, we are magic incarnate. That is why Mora has hunted our kind. She steals our magic and takes it unto herself. That is how she has grown to be so powerful. That's how she made this twilight world of the Between."

"Then I will finish the job I set out to do. I will kill her. Not just for my world but for yours," Drustan proclaimed.

"Listen carefully, young Drustan," Jorin cautioned, his voice stern and serious. "Attacking Mora in this realm is a fool's errand. She reigns supreme here as a goddess. But if we venture into the mortal world, we may have a chance to defeat her where she is vulnerable."

"Witch, goddess, hag," Drustan shrugged, a fearless glint in his eye. "It makes no difference to me. I've yet to come across any being that can survive without a head."

"Beware, Drustan," Jorin warned once more, but the young man was resolute.

"I'll stay here and continue to play the role of her

devoted lover. When she lets her guard down, I'll strike and sever her head from her body," Drustan declared. "Now, you must flee this place at once. If I fail, she'll likely come after you. You must be ready."

"Remember, Drustan," Jorin added with a grave expression. "If you do succeed in killing Mora, her magic will die with her and so will this world. The Between will be no more. You must act quickly and head toward the orange sky, for there lies the path back to your world. Do you still have the Faerie Stone I gave you?"

"Aye, I do." Drustan pulled the leather string from his pocket and showed the stone to Jorin.

"Very well. When you reach the door, if it is a Between Time, then it will be glowing and you will see into the mortal world as clearly as if you were looking through a window. Simply pass through."

Drustan put the leather string around his neck and tucked the Faerie Stone inside his shirt. "And if it is closed, and not at the Between Time?"

"Then you have the means to open it. Take the Faerie Stone from around thy neck and grasp it tightly in the palm of your hand," Jorin instructed. "Focus your thoughts on the doorway and the passage will be open to you."

"I understand," Drustan replied. "Now free your fellow faeries and be on your way. I must return before Etta notices I am gone."

Once the cages were opened and all the faeries freed, both Jorin and Aster returned to their small winged forms and joined the others as they flew from the dungeon and out of the castle.

"Godspeed, my brave friend," King Jorin said a final goodbye as he flew away.

"And to you as well!"

Aster hovered in front of him briefly; she flew closer and kissed him on the cheek. Then she darted away and disappeared down the dark corridor.

Drustan quickly exited the cell and locked the door behind him, making the dungeon seem undisturbed unless there was a close inspection of the cell. Then, he made his way back up the steps into the main castle and back to the chamber that he shared with Etta.

As Drustan stepped into the chamber, the true reality hit him with the force of a spell unbroken. The world he had lived in under Etta's, or rather Mora's, enchantment was a mere mirage, a phantom woven from the magic of her witchcraft.

What he once believed to be a sumptuous chamber of soft beds with linen covers, grand art hanging from the walls, and every luxury one could desire, was now revealed to be a much humbler abode. The bed was simple straw, draped in rough wool blankets, the walls bare and unadorned, the furnishings plain. The table where he had dined was now stripped of all delicacies, save for a few moldy crumbs of bread and a carafe of water.

A laugh, small and involuntary, escaped Drustan's lips as he took in the true state of his surroundings. Etta's bedchamber, stripped of its illusions, was no grander than the humble life Drustan had always known. And in a strange way, he found the reality more comforting, more suited to his nature, than the fantastical world Etta had spun around him.

In that moment, Drustan was consumed by a burning fury and overwhelming regret. He was plagued by the question of how he could have been so thoroughly fooled by the illusions before him. The realization that he had fallen under Etta's spell was a source of deep shame and anger. While he could have easily blamed the enchanted bilberries she had presented him, the truth was that he had already been bewitched by her charms long before he took a single bite. His own common sense should have told him that something was amiss, that the alluring woman before him was not what she appeared to be. He was incensed with himself for failing to see the warning signs, for blindly accepting the tempting bilberries that grew in the dead of autumn's forest. The thought of his own foolishness was enough to make him want to lash out in self-reproach.

"By God's teeth," he cursed aloud as he recalled that moment, "it was the beginning of winter. Any fool would have known those berries were bewitched."

Then Drustan was struck with the memory of his wulver companion, Gib. He realized that he had been so blinded by his infatuation with Etta, that he had been rude and dismissive towards Gib's warnings about her. He felt a pang of shame as he imagined Gib's thoughts of him as a foolish and gullible individual. If only he had listened to Gib, he could have swiftly taken down Etta and prevented the chaos that now threatened the existence of two worlds. Instead, he was so entranced by her captivating beauty and the allure of her ample bosom, that he had disregarded the obvious signs that something was amiss. Now, the future of entire realms hung in the balance as a result of his carelessness.

Drustan approached the wooden chest near his bed and lifted the lid to reveal a dagger Etta had bestowed upon him as a gift. He gazed upon it with wonder, marveling at its beauty, unchanged from when she had first presented it to him. The blade shimmered in the dim light, its steel harder than the hardest stone, and the golden handle was bedecked with glittering rubies and diamonds, just as he remembered. He had anticipated discovering a dull, ordinary knife, unfit for a common peasant, yet here was the one true object in a world of illusions. Was it possible that Etta had intended to offer him a sincere and heartfelt token? He was left to ponder on this mystery.

With the dagger tucked securely in his boot, Drustan gathered his sword, bow, and quiver of arrows, laying them out upon the small table before him. Then, with a heavy heart, he seated himself upon the windowsill and waited for Etta's return.

He gazed out into the Between, a world of perpetual twilight where the moon and sun seemed to dance along the horizon, never fully rising or setting. He remembered how many times he had sat in that same spot, without a second thought to the strangeness of this unchanging sky. How foolish it all seemed to him now, as the veil of illusion lifted from his eyes. He could only curse himself for his own naivety, for allowing himself to be lured into this false reality created by Etta's bewitchment.

Hours passed. He paced the floor impatiently. He was more anxious than nervous, eager to put an end to Mora's evil. There was no fear in him, no doubts of what he must do. His only concern was that if he failed, his faerie friends, his family and two worlds would all suffer the consequences.

As the moments passed, Drustan became increasingly anxious at Etta's absence. The thought crossed his mind that she may have discovered his scheme, and that she would not return to their chamber. He considered the possibility of seeking her out himself, but as he gathered his sword and bow, ready to depart, the door to the chamber creaked open, and in stepped Etta.

Her eyes fell upon the weapons that Drustan had laid out on the table, and she inquired, "What is this?"

Drustan forced a casual smile and lied, "I thought I'd go hunting. I thought you might appreciate some venison for dinner."

Etta raised a curious brow, "Hunting? 'Tis no need. I will have the servants fetch whatever you desire."

"It's not sustenance that I seek, my love," he replied, his hand resting on the hilt of his sword, "but the thrill of the hunt."

Etta unfastened her robes and let them drop to the floor revealing her body to him.

"If it is sport you seek …" she said tauntingly. "Then bring yourself to bed."

Despite her alluring physique, he couldn't bring himself to look at her without being reminded of the withered and grotesque hag she once was. The sight of her was difficult to stomach and he struggled to keep a neutral expression, forcing a fake smile onto his face. "It is a very tempting offer, but I feel the need to get out and breathe in the fresh air," he lied.

Etta's gaze narrowed upon him. She was puzzled as to why this passionate lover, who couldn't get enough of her earlier, was now turning her down. Something was definitely amiss and she could see it in his eyes.

"You seem different, my love. Is everything okay?" she asked with suspicion.

"Of course." Drustan realized that his sudden change in demeanor had not gone unnoticed. Despite this, he maintained his facade, hoping to keep her from realizing that the spell had been lifted. He summoned a comforting smile. "I can always go hunting later, or maybe even tomorrow," he suggested.

Etta's suspicion melted away and she resumed her lighthearted demeanor. She approached him, her naked form pressing against his. Gently, she ran her fingers through his hair and pushed him back until he was seated on the bed. Kneeling before him, she set to work untying the laces of his shirt.

"Let me take care of your needs for a change," she cooed and began to run her hands over his bare chest.

While she was distracted, Drustan eased the dagger from the top of his boot. The handle was cold in his grasp, a promise of retribution.

"What is this?" She asked, seeing the leather rope and Faerie Stone that dangled from around his neck.

"A means of escape from this den of evil," Drustan growled and plunged the dagger into her side.

Etta howled in pain, stumbling back from the strike. Her hand clutched at the weapon, disbelief etched upon her face.

He stood and advanced upon her as she tried to back

away. He wrenched the knife from her flesh and spat his accusation, "I know who you are, Mora!" In a swift motion, he slashed the blade across her throat. Blood spurted over his chest from the gushing wound as she sank to her knees, clutching her neck as the blood continued to spurt between her fingers.

And then, suddenly, she laughed. A crazed, maniacal laughter that chilled Drustan to the bone. He stumbled backwards, fear flooding his veins. He had plunged the blade into her heart, had watched her blood spill forth from the wound he had inflicted upon her throat. And yet, she still stood.

"I must commend you, brave hunter, for finally coming to your senses. In fact, I am a little surprised you were able to break my spell." She smirked as she rose to her feet. Blood continued to pour from the wound. "I'm amused! You thought you could kill me! Here, of all places!"

She laughed hysterically and as she did, blood bubbled and sprayed from the gash in her throat. "Well, my lover, unfortunately for you, you're not as clever as you are handsome."

With a flick of her hand, she sent Drustan flying towards the stone wall, where he collided with a sickening thud. The echoes of his impact reverberated throughout the chamber. She repeated the gesture, and he was thrown against the opposite wall with such force that his head slammed into the rock, leaving him dazed and unsteady.

"Tell me," she demanded, her voice cold and menacing. "What gave me away? How did you break the spell

I cast upon you?"

Drustan stood tall, a smirk tugging at the corners of his mouth. "The dungeon," he answered with satisfaction. "I saw the prisoners and I set them free."

Her expression changed, her eyes wide with shock. "You foolish, foolish man," she sneered. "They will never escape the Between, nor will you."

"It's too late," Drustan countered, his voice filled with defiance. "Hours have passed, and the faeries have already crossed over into the mortal realm, beyond your reach."

With a howl of fury, Etta flipped the table with a swipe of her hand, sending Drustan's sword skittering across the stone floor. But he was quick, and he seized the blade, lunging at her with deadly intent.

The sword connected with a sickening thud, slicing through Etta's neck with ease. Her head hung precariously by a mere sliver of skin and muscle, but as she fell to the ground, writhing in pain, she lifted her hand and with a flick of her wrist, sent an invisible force hurtling into Drustan.

He slammed against the stone wall with bone-shattering force, collapsing to the ground as the wind was knocked from his lungs. But Etta was not defeated. With a fierce grip, she steadied her head and, before Drustan's eyes, the bones and tissues began to knit back together, until she stood once more, whole and unbroken.

Drustan was still stunned by the physical impact of hitting the stone wall, but seeing Etta able to rejuvenate and reattach her head made him fight through the pain to get back to his feet. Quickly, he was able to retrieve his bow along with a single arrow from the quiver. He drew back and let the arrow fly. It sunk into Etta's chest, but she did not flinch from the wound; instead, she yanked it out of her and dropped it to the floor.

"What? No more magical arrows? You must to do better than that," she laughed. "You are in my world now."

Drustan felt a cold grip of fear clutch his heart as he gazed upon the unearthly might of the witch. His pride had blinded him to the true extent of her power in this realm, and now he realized the terrible mistake he had made. Memories flooded back to him of boasting to his mother of never having encountered a being capable of surviving without a head, only to be cautioned against his arrogance. The bitter taste of defeat filled his mouth as he acknowledged his own conceit had led to his downfall. The bow fell from his fingers, clattering against the stone floor, as he stood in stunned silence.

"Guards!" Etta screamed.

Two of her gruesome goblins entered the chamber.

"Bind his hands!"

One of the guards grabbed Drustan and held his arms behind his back while the other bound him with rope.

"Gather my guards and find the Faerie King!" She turned back to Drustan, "As for you, you enjoyed your little visit to my dungeon so much; you should spend more time there."

"I would rather be in the pit of hell than in your bed," Drustan growled.

Etta scowled at him. "Then so be it! After of few days in the dark, when your belly is empty and your lips are dry and cracked from thirst, then you will throw thy-self on my mercy!"

"I will die first!"

"If that is your desire!" She turned to her guards and ordered, "Lock him in the darkest cell and then throw away the key. If he would rather die in my dungeon than reign at my side, then I will not deprive him of his fate."

As the guards forcefully whisked Drustan away, their steps echoed through the corridor. Laine, stood there with an air of self-satisfaction as Drusan was dragged past her. Her lips curled into a smug smirk, relishing the sight of his downfall. As they locked eyes during that fleeting encounter, she reveled in his moment of despair, savoring the bitter taste of his defeat.

Upon entering Etta's bedchamber, a satisfied gleam danced in Laine's eyes. She couldn't contain her delight as she turned to Etta. With an infectious glee, she ex-claimed, "I've always harbored doubts about him, you know. Now, look at him! He has proved me right beyond measure."

"Be careful with your words, sister," Etta warned sternly. "This is not the time for gloating."

"I bring news from General Dok," Laine continued, ignoring Etta's caution. "The gates to the Faerie Realm have been breached, and your army is ready to invade."

"Tell them to hold their positions," Etta commanded. "I have other plans."

"After months of effort to break through the magical barrier, you want them to wait?" Laine asked in disbelief.

"King Jorin and his followers have fled into the mor-tal world," Etta explained. "Their capture is of utmost importance. I want his head on a rope when our army marches into the Faerie Realm, as a symbol of our victory."

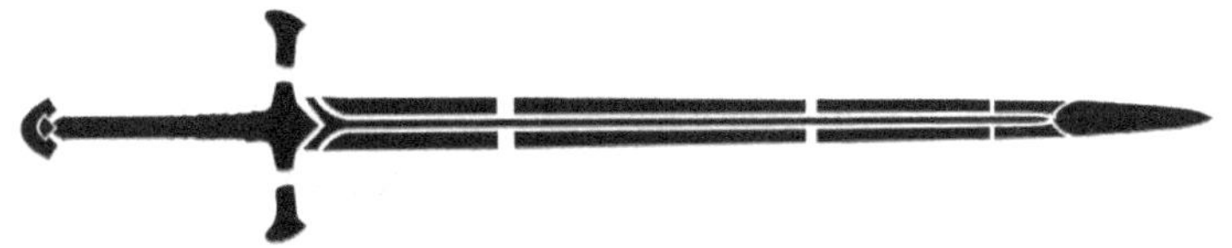

CHAPTER 20

Aster to the Rescue

And so, Drustan was cast into the depths of the dank and desolate dungeon. The chill of the stone floor seeped into his bones as he leaned against the rough, unforgiving wall. The guards, obedient servants of Etta, had followed her commands with ruthless efficiency. They had brought him to the farthest reaches of the dungeon, thrusting him into a cell of darkness where no glimmer of light could reach him. The final sight he beheld was the silhouette of a goblin, as it plucked the key to his prison from its ring and shoved it into a vest pocket. By now the key undoubtedly lay at the bottom of the loch, never to be seen again.

Once the guards had left and taken the light of their torches with them, the dungeon cell was pitch black. There were no shadows, no hints of light. He had waited for his eyes to readjust, fully expecting his surroundings to eventually come back into focus, at least slightly, but there was nothing. He was in complete and total darkness. He sat and listened to the silence, contemplating his situation. Somewhere in the corners of the dungeon,

he could hear the movement of rats, and it sent a shiver
down his spine. He wondered how he would escape, or
if he even could before the vermin came to gnaw at his
fingers and toes in the darkness.

In the depths of the cell, there was only one path
to freedom — through the door. The walls and floor
were hewn from solid stone, offering no hope of escape
through burrowing. Drustan rose, his hand trailing along
the stone, searching for the door. With a desperate burst
of energy, he threw himself against it, hoping to break it
open, but it was to no avail. The door was crafted from
iron, its weight unchanging, and no amount of force
would move it. Drustan sank back to the stone floor,
acceptance of his fate settling over him. Unless Etta
had mercy on him, he would spend the rest of his days
trapped in this cell, doomed to a slow and lonely death.

Trapped in the darkness, Drustan's thoughts turned
to his loved ones, haunted by the fear of what may become of them now that he had failed in his mission. He
had not only fallen short of killing the evil witch, but
had only served to rouse her wrath further. The weight of
his failure weighed heavily on him, knowing that Etta's
wrath would soon be directed at his mother and siblings.
Instead of saving his family, his bravery had only sealed
their fate. He was wracked with guilt, for his desire to
prove himself as a hero had only led to tragedy. His heart
ached with sorrow, his eyes yearning to release the tears,
but he was too proud a man to allow himself the comfort
of such a release.

Hours of solitude in the darkness had passed, when
a faint glimmer of light shone through the tiny window

in the cell door, capturing Drustan's attention. In a heartbeat, he was on his feet, peering out into the distance, his
eyes fixed upon the source of the light. The light grew
brighter and closer, and Drustan's heart raced with uncertainty. Was it one of the guards, returning to end his
life and grant him a merciful release? Or was it the wicked Etta, coming to revel in his suffering? Either way,
Drustan knew that this was his one and only chance for
escape. If the one who approached were to open the cell
door, he would have to act quickly and strike without
hesitation, in a desperate bid for freedom.

Drustan pressed himself against the wall, melting
into the shadows as the bright light outside the cell door
grew stronger. He strained his ears for any sound of footsteps, but the silence was deafening. The dazzling light
reached its zenith outside the door, bathing everything in
its brilliance.

Suddenly, a voice whispered, "Psst... are you in
there?" Drustan remained motionless, unsure who was
addressing him in such hushed tones. "Drustan," the
voice repeated, "where are you?" It was a female voice,
one that he suddenly recognized.

"Aster? Is that you?" he whispered back.

"Indeed, it is I!" she exclaimed, her voice resonating
with a profound sense of relief. Gracefully, she slipped
through the narrow window of the door, effortlessly entering the confines of the cell. Her presence infused the
space with a radiant glow, casting a luminous veil upon
everything in sight.

Drustan's eyes widened in shock. "Aster, you're...
glowing."

She smiled, her body pulsating with light. "Of course I am," she replied, shifting into her human form and maintaining her brilliant glow. The dungeon cell was now ablaze with light, dispelling the shadows and darkness.

"What are you doing here? You should have made it to the Faerie Door. Did something happen to prevent your escape?"

"We reached the door, and the others passed through unscathed," Aster replied, her voice steady and resolute. "But I couldn't abandon you. I felt a pull, a calling, to ensure your safety."

"You should not have come back," Drustan scolded. "Mora … or Etta …." he stammered as he struggled for what to call her. "That vile witch is on a rampage. You have put yourself in great danger."

"I could not abandon you," Aster insisted. "Consider it a debt repaid."

"I may still be trapped here forever. The door and bars are iron, and the key to the lock is likely gone forever."

"Ah, the bane of all faeries," Aster sighed, a hint of frustration in her voice. "Iron bars and doors that block our way. But do not lose heart," Aster said, her voice ringing with encouragement. "I may not be able to unlock the door, but I have the power to free you from this cell. That is, if you will trust me."

Drustan hesitated, memories of Aster's past deceit clouding his thoughts. He scanned the dimly lit cell, searching for any other means of escape, but found none. He was faced with a choice: to place his faith in the faerie trickster, or to spend the rest of his days in this stone prison.

"I will trust you, Aster," he said with a noticeable lack of enthusiasm. "But no tricks, pranks or jokes."

"I promise. I have learned my lesson, cross my heart," she assured him and with her finger traced an X over her heart.

"So, what do you have in mind?"

"First, I have troubling news," Aster stated. "Mora prepares to invade the Faerie Realm. If she does, Drustan, she will enslave my people. She will have all the magic of every faerie at her command and she will be unstoppable, even in the mortal world."

"But faeries have magic too. Can your people not resist her? Do you have no defenses or means to fight?"

"The enchanted seals of the Faerie Kingdom have kept her horde of goblins at bay for many a year. Yet, she has only grown in power, and her army now stands at the brink of breaking through the magical gate and spilling into our realm. Though we shall defend our kingdom with all our might, her strength within the Faerie Realm is equal to that in the Between, and the goblin horde is too great in number. If she breaches our barrier, I fear our defeat shall be certain."

"Then we cannot allow her to pass through into the Faerie Realm. We must stop her now."

"But what is there to do? Do you truly believe you can kill her?"

"Aye, we can lure her into the mortal world," Drustan proclaimed. "If that is where she is vulnerable, then that is where she must be."

"The gate to our world is all but collapsed and her army stands ready. She will not abandon the invasion so easily."

"Aye, she will. I know her ego well. Once she finds I have escaped she will pursue me, I'm sure of it. She will stop at nothing to chase us down. I will lead her through the Faerie Door and into the mortal world where we will kill her. But first, I must get out of this place. How do you intend to accomplish that feat?"

"Offer thy hand," she beckoned, her voice a sweet melody.

He obeyed, placing his hand in hers, and felt an electric jolt course through him.

"Now, inhale deeply," she whispered. "Ye might feel a trifle uncomfortable at first. A little itchy."

"Itchy?" he queried, his gaze scrutinizing hers. But before he could ask more, he felt his body convulse and itch with fervor. The walls and door began to stretch, soaring upward to tower above him, while the room appeared to broaden and expand. Then, he realized it was not the room that was growing, but he and Aster that were shrinking. And then, in a brilliant flicker of light, he found himself minuscule, in the very stature of a faerie.

"Aster! What is this mischief?" He shouted, fearing that he had once again been tricked by her.

"'Tis only one way out of here," she said and pointed at the small window of the door. "Think that you could squeeze through that otherwise?"

He remained skeptical but he did see her logic. If the door would not open, then the only path to the outside was through the small window; and, as a man, his foot wouldn't even fit between the bars much less his whole body. "So now what? How do I get from way down here to way up there?"

"Use your wings, silly" she said and fluttered her wings so that she lifted off the floor and hovered slightly above him.

"My wings?"

Drustan felt a surge of amazement as he gazed upon the appendages that had sprouted from his back. Never before had he laid eyes upon such magnificence. The wings were delicate, nearly translucent, and reminded him of the delicate wings of a dragonfly.

He spun around like a dog chasing its tail, trying to catch a glimpse of every angle of his newfound wings. It was almost as if he was caught in a whirlwind of disbelief, each rotation making the reality of it all sink in deeper.

"How do I use these things to fly?" he asked, unable to peel his eyes away from the marvelous new appendages.

Aster's gentle voice broke through his thoughts. "How do you make your legs to walk? Just move them," she instructed. "Think of them as an extension of yourself like your arms or legs."

Drustan took a deep breath, steeling himself for the unknown, and began to tentatively flutter his wings. To his immense surprise, he felt himself rising off the ground, his body suspended in the air as if weightless. The thrill of flight coursed through him, and he felt a newfound sense of freedom and power.

"That's amazing! Now, how do I control where I

fly?"

"How do you decide where your legs will take you when you walk?" She replied impatiently.

Drustan thought about it briefly then cautiously began to fly a little to one side, then to the other. Before long, he could fly around the cell, changing from one direction to another with little effort. As his comfort increased, he picked up his speed and zipped around the cell confidently.

"I think I could learn to like this!" He said excitedly and began to turn and spin and flip around in mid-air.

"It is rather magnificent is it not?" Aster giggled and clapped her hands excitedly as she watched him flying. "Now, follow me! We must be on our way."

With graceful ease, Drustan and Aster glided through the narrow window between the iron bars and emerged into the dimly lit corridor. Ahead, Aster took the lead, her wings beating steadily as she guided the way up a spiraling stair. Up they went, higher and higher, until they finally emerged into the heart of the castle and through the first opening to the outdoors they encountered.

Once outside in the open air Drustan paused, hovering in the sky as he gazed back at the dark looming castle tower. His eyes drifted to the top of the tower where he could see the flickering of firelight in Etta's chamber.

"You go ahead and I will catch up. I must make sure she knows of my escape and draw her pursuit to me," Drustan said.

"I will wait for you at the Faerie Door, do not tarry long. 'Tis well past the between time so you must use the Faerie Stone for us to pass."

Drustan removed the Faerie Stone from around his neck and handed it to Aster. "Take this and wait for me. If I do not catch up shortly, you must go through without me."

"I will wait," Aster said as she took the stone from him. "Do not be long."

Aster flew toward the orange horizon while Drustan ascended into the sky, flying high up along the castle wall until he came to the window of the bedchamber where he had sat many times before. He peered into the room, confirming it was empty, before darting inside.

He found his sword and using all his strength lifted it up and stabbed it into the bed that he and Etta once shared. With a fierce glint in his eye, he then grabbed an oil lamp from the nearby table and shattered it onto the floor. The oil spread, quickly igniting and sending flames throughout the room..

As the smoke filled the chamber and seeped out into the hallway, the sounds of shouting and the approach of guards could be heard. When the goblin soldiers finally entered the room, Drustan was waiting for them, hovering in the air with a smirk on his face and his pants pulled down. They looked at him in shock, momentarily frozen and unsure of what action they should take as Drustan began to urinate on Etta's bedding. Before they could react, Drustan pulled up his pants and flew out the window laughing hysterically as he went.

When he caught up with Aster at the Faerie Door, he was still laughing; picturing Etta's face when the guards reported his actions. It seemed quite humorous to him in a spiteful sort of way, and he wondered about it. This feeling of mischievousness was odd for him, and he imagined that along with the faerie wings he had also received a dose of the faeries' propensity for pranks. Regardless of the reason, he was rather pleased with himself knowing that Etta would be outraged.

"Does she follow?" Aster questioned.

He turned to look at the castle looming behind him in the distance. Black storm clouds were gathering over the tower and bolts of lightning flashed furiously from the center of the dark storm.

"Most definitely she does," he laughed. "We might need to get out of here quickly."

Together, they hovered before the stones that formed the Faerie Door.

"Here," Aster said and handed him back the necklace with the Faerie Stone. "'Tis yours, you do the honor."

Drustan took the Faerie Stone and clutched it tightly within the palm of his hand just as the king had instructed. Immediately, the Faerie Door began to glow and the mortal world became visible. He heard the storm raging behind them, getting closer by the moment; thunder and lightning violently filling the sky. He looked back, and in the distance, he saw riders on horseback rapidly approaching. In the air above the soldiers, there was a large black reptilian creature that resembled how he thought a dragon would be; conceivably, in this world, maybe it was one. Whatever the winged creature was, Drustan knew instinctively that it was Etta herself, transformed by her fury into a dreadful flying monster.

He grabbed Aster by the hand and chuckled in amusement at Etta's tantrum. "Time to go," he smirked and together the two flew through the doorway, leaving the murky gloom of the Between world behind them, and emerging into the bright sunlight of his own world.

Once he was back in his own realm Drustan suddenly found himself falling. Abruptly, he hit the ground and rolled some distance, hitting stones and scraping through tree branches as he tumbled across the earth. When he came to a stop, he had taken a thorough thrashing and had multiple scratches and bruises.

"By God's bones!" He groaned, and realized he had lost his wings and was once again his full human size. "What happened?"

"Sorry," Aster giggled. "I should have warned you, once we entered the mortal world, you would return to your human self."

"It would have been nice to know that beforehand," he grumbled then climbed to his feet and dusted himself off. He looked over his shoulder briefly at where his wings once were and then pursed his lips with disappointment. "Too bad. I sort of liked those wings."

Looking around he could tell it was early afternoon. The sun was still high overhead and was just beginning its descent. It would be hours before sunset. He looked back at the Faerie Door and saw that it was once again only stones.

"You made it, my friend!" King Jorin said excitedly as he emerged from the cover of some brush.

"Aye, thanks to Aster. She rescued me from certain death in Etta's dungeon."

"Aster! Today you have proven yourself worthy of the Seeley Court!" Jorin proclaimed happily.

Aster transformed into her human form and bowed low before the king. "Thank you, your majesty."

"Can Etta use her magic to open the doorway?" Drustan asked.

"Only the magic of the Between Time or a Faerie Stone will open the doorway between the worlds," King Jorin answered.

"Any chance she has a Faerie Stone?" Drustan asked.

"Undoubtedly. She moves between the worlds with ease, no doubt she has secured one of her own."

"I think not," Aster said. "If she had the means to open the doorway, she would be upon us by now. She was really catching up fast."

"'Tis true, she's pretty irate right now," Drustan admitted. "If she had the means to open the door, she would most likely have done so already. That means we have until sunset to prepare for her arrival."

"So, she follows you? You are certain of this?" Jorin asked.

"No doubt. She is really having a tantrum."

"Then we must ready ourselves," Jorin declared. "We must lure her deep into this world, but make no mistake; she will not be taken down easily. We must be prepared for a fight to the death."

CHAPTER 21

The Wrath of a Scorned Witch

Etta was furious when she learned of Drustan's escape and she was even more enraged that he had defiled the bed they had shared. It was an insult that rocked her to the very core, even more hurtful than when he plunged a dagger into her side and tried to behead her. For some odd reason she could have forgiven him for his attempted murder, in fact, she planned to do just that. She had hoped that being isolated in the darkness Drustan would come to his senses and he would see the benefits of remaining by her side. She even believed that he would eventually grow to love her without the use of magic. However, to befoul the bed that they had shared, the bed where they had made love, that act was an affront to her as a woman. It was an unforgivable offense.

He had insulted her at the deepest level that a man could insult a woman, and she felt violated by him. She wanted to punish him and to see him suffer as she now did. She summoned her guards and although her goblin army was prepared to invade the Faerie Realm, she called them back. She was determined to use all her resources in pursuit of Drustan and the spiteful faeries that had aided him in his escape.

She went to the burned-out bedchamber to see with her own eyes the evidence of his sedition. When she saw the damaged room, the scorched walls, and the ashes that was once their bed, she was as heartsick as she was angry. For the first time in more than 700 years, tears fell from her eyes. Wise men fear the wrath of a woman scorned, but the pillars of hell itself quake in the face of a witch whose affection is rejected. Anger filled her and the Between World was shaken to its foundation and her fury gave rise to a huge storm which manifested in the sky above the castle.

Etta ran to the open window and dove out into the twilight, and as she fell downward, she was transformed into a huge dragon with black glistening scales, broad wings and a long serpent's tale. She flew around and over the castle, screeching so vociferously as to frighten her own soldiers as they drew near returning from the border of the Faerie Realm.

The dragon Etta led her army to the Faerie Door, but when they arrived Drustan and the faeries had already passed through and the doorway was closed. The army stopped unable to continue their advance, while overhead Etta shrieked in anger and frustration as the storm continued to rage with bursts of thunder and lightning.

With a swift descent from the sky, Laine gracefully swooped down, riding a broom as she pursued Etta. Landing softly on the ground, she alighted from her airborne perch. Following closely behind, the colossal dragon, Etta, plummeted from above, causing the earth to tremble with a resounding thud. In a mesmerizing display, the dragon underwent a stunning transformation, morphing back into its youthful human form, revealing the young Etta once more.

"They escaped through the door," a soldier informed the two witches.

"'Tis not a Between Time," Laine said. "They must have stolen the Faerie Stone."

"You think?" Etta screamed in frustration. "He had the stone around his neck, I should have taken it when I had the chance."

In a fit of wrath, she thrust her finger toward the soldier; In an instant, a bolt of lightning shot forth, obliterating the goblin where it stood, leaving nothing but dissipating smoke in its wake. The remaining soldiers recoiled in fear, shrinking back instinctively from the awe-inspiring power she possessed.

"Calm thyself, mistress," Laine insisted. "Let him run. They cannot go far enough that we will not find them. Then the hunter will feel thy judgment."

"And what of the faeries?" Etta demanded. "King Jorin and the others?"

"The gate to their realm has fallen but for the faeries to escape to their world they would have had to pass through your army. They did not go there. Their only means to escape was to have entered the world of men."

"Good. Then they will all be together. We will wait here and when the sun sets we will march through and crush them."

"Why pursue him now?" Laine's tone betrayed her

frustration at Etta's continued obsession with Drustan. "The gate to the Faerie Realm has been broken, yet ye have brought thy army hither to chase a man and a handful of rogue faeries. Let us invade the Faerie Realm now, and pursue this mortal another day."

"May the Faerie Realm be cursed!" Etta's voice resounded with seething fury. Her declaration echoed through the air, carrying the weight of her rage. "Drustan shall not escape my wrath. He will pay for the heinous insult he dared inflict upon me. I will ensnare him, place him in chains, and force him to witness the utter destruction of all that he holds dear."

"This mortal has addled thy mind, just as I forewarned," Laine spoke with a sneer. "We must away to the Faerie Realm, as we had planned. Do not let this human cause thee to veer from our path."

"He is the spawn of my greatest adversary, and he dared to defy me, just as his mother did!" Etta roared. "I shall see him bow before me, begging for mercy."

"And what will thou gain from this foolish pursuit?" Laine retorted. "He shall not bend his knee to thee, nor shall he serve thee willingly. This hunter shall bring naught but death if you continue down this road."

"He is mine," Etta declared, her voice filled with determination. "He was brought forth at my bidding and I shall claim what is rightfully mine. He shall love me, or face the consequences of his defiance."

"Love?" Laine sneered, a harsh laugh escaping her lips. "It was not love that brought him to thy bed, 'twas a spell. Thou art a fool, Mora, to believe that the son of Isabel could ever love thee. Do you plan to poison him with enchanted berries until he is but a mindless oaf?"

"Either love, or fear. It does not matter to me. He will obey. His mother will see him at my side, and he will murder his own family at my bidding."

"You must resist this. This obsession poisons thy mind and clouds your judgment. He has defeated you before, and when you have passed into the world of man you will be vulnerable," Laine warned. "Thy arrogance will lead us to destruction."

"He may be free of my spell, but he will never be completely free of my power." Etta laughed hysterically. "He will not harm me, even if he could."

"You are crazed if you truly think so. Was it not he who attacked ye in thy chamber? Was it not this same lover who stabbed ye in the chest then tried to take off thy head? He will try again, and if you are in the mortal world when he strikes, he will succeed."

"He will not stand against me. I carry his child. To destroy me, he would murder his own flesh and blood. Who would be the monster then?"

"This cannot be so!" Laine gasped, her voice trembling with shock. She had already been distressed by Etta's descent into madness over her obsession with Drustan, but this new revelation was a blow beyond compare. If Etta was indeed with child, then Drustan was undoubtedly the father, and all hope of steering her away from this madness was lost. Drustan had a hold over Etta that could not be broken, and the father and especially the unborn child would become the center of her world, while the plans Laine and Mora had so meticulously crafted would fade into oblivion. Laine would no longer be Etta's confidant and ally, but instead, she would be seen as a mere threat.

"So, this is why you seek the hunter with such desperation!" Laine accused, her voice ringing with fury. "You have betrayed our purpose. We stand at the brink of ruling both the mortal and Faerie realms, but you betrayed our coven, and now, ye have betrayed me, to become a mother; to be bred like a cow for this mortal."

"Enough of thy wretched tongue!" Etta shouted. "You are either my ally or my enemy. Choose now, sister, and choose carefully for your next words may be your last!"

Laine remained silent for a moment and did not respond. She realized that in Etta's eyes she was not an equal but rather her servant. It would not be long before her mistress would consider her a potential rival and move against her. Laine realized with a heavy heart the truth that Etta would never keep her word to initiate the rite of renewal, for fear that the allure of her youthful beauty might prove too great a temptation for Drustan. Despite the bitter taste of betrayal that lingered in her mouth, she held her tongue, masking her treachery behind a veil of false loyalty.

"I shall remain at thy side," Laine spoke with false devotion, her mind already spinning with scheming and deceit. "Thou hast my fealty," she proclaimed, knowing full well that the one she had once called ally was now her sworn adversary.

Beyond the mystical portal of the Faerie Door, Drustan stood amidst a throng of ethereal beings, the very essence of magic and sorcery. Together they huddled, their voices low and urgent as they plotted and planned their defense against the looming shadows of darkness that threatened to engulf their realm.

King Jorin, with regal bearing and a voice as resolute as the mountains themselves, addressed his subjects. "The hour of reckoning draws near, the next Between Time approaches and with it, the opening of the Faerie Door. Our fate hangs in the balance, and we must choose our path. Shall we cower and flee, or shall we stand tall and face the witch, with the fire of our conviction burning bright? Know this, my friends, if we do not gather our courage now, if we do not make a stand, then all that we hold dear shall be lost forever."

Tyree, spoke out, concern imprinted upon his features. "The witch commands an army, and her magic is beyond compare. How can we hope to vanquish her?"

King Jorin's eyes gleamed with determination. "We shall find a way. For it is not the size of our army, nor the strength of our magic, but the courage in our hearts that shall see us through. We fight not just for ourselves, but for all that we hold dear. This, my friends, is the time to show the true mettle of our spirit."

Drustan's piercing gaze fell upon the Faerie Door, its towering frame seeming small in comparison to his stature. "The door shall be their greatest bane," he declared with a cunning smile. "Its slender width shall hamper their advance, for only two or three may pass through at a time. And so, we shall not be overwhelmed by their multitude, but only confronted by a modest detachment of their forces. This door shall be our ally, and we will use it to our advantage."

King Jorin nodded in agreement. "Indeed, a valiant few may defend the passage and repel their charge. Our foes shall not pass."

Aster raised a note of concern. "But what of the witch? Was it not our intent to lure her through the door and into our realm?'"

Drustan's smile faded, replaced by a fierce determination. "Fear not, my friend. The witch shall come, drawn by the call of her own desire. She is arrogant and spiteful. If she remains true to her nature, she will be at the head of her army and lead them through the doorway. Once she has passed between the stones we will move to block the remainder of her soldiers from advancing."

"And once you have her here, what are you to do with the witch?" A gruff voice boomed. "It is she who must bear the brunt of our assault, for when Mora, the Witch Queen, falls, so shall her dark army crumble to dust."

All eyes turned to the source of the voice, and there stood Gib. For weeks, he had lingered near the threshold of the Faerie Door, observing and awaiting the return of his comrade. And today, upon his arrival to keep his customary vigil, he was met with a most welcome sight.

"Gib! My faithful friend!" Drustan exclaimed, joy welling in his heart. He embraced the wulver, slapping him on the back with a hearty clap. "You are a welcome sight! He greeted the wulver with a warm hug and patted him on the back.

"I feared the worst for you," Gib said. "What happened?"

"'Tis a long story," Drustan replied. "But let us just

336

say that your suspicions were right about Etta. I suppose I owe you an apology."

"No apology is necessary, laddie. I saw her take you through the Faerie Door and I found the hexed berries upon the ground," Gib said. "But I knew you would find your way home again."

"Alas, it seems the shadow of misfortune still haunts me," Drustan sighed. "Beyond the Faerie Door waits a horde of goblins, baying for blood with Etta at their helm."

"And what, pray tell, is our strategy against this witch?" Gib asked, his voice firm with determination. "What of the enchanted arrows that brought Mora to the brink of death? Surely, they must be of use to us once again?"

"Ah, my dear friend, those arrows lay at the bottom of the loch, claimed by the kelpie," Drustan replied with regret. "They were the handiwork of my mother and father, crafted with great care and skill. To replace them would take many days to travel home and more to return. Sadly we do not have the time. Yet, I did heed the teachings of my mother. I know how to defend myself against the magic of a witch. If we can but weaken her enough, I am confident I can close in and deliver the fatal blow. Then, and only then, shall this nightmare come to an end."

"And how do you intend to get close enough to do such a thing?" Jorin asked. "Even if we are shielded from her power she can manipulate the world around us. She will be very dangerous no matter what our defense."

"We must first guard ourselves from her magic. Can

you find salt? Lots of it," Drustan questioned. "We must fill our pockets with salt and spread it over as much of the ground as possible."

"I can bring several bags of salt from my hut," Gib replied. "I use it to preserve my fish."

"Your majesty, you once provided me with a magnificent sword. Unfortunately, I had to leave it behind in the Between."

"Say no more," Jorin interrupted. "I can replace it easily."

"Can you find one of iron, or a blade that is coated with silver?"

"Faeries do not deal in iron, but I'm sure we can plate a sharp sword with silver for you."

"And a bow and arrows?" Drustan added.

"Of course. Sadly, I cannot offer any of the enchanted arrows fit for killing a witch, but they will be straight and well balanced."

"Then we will make do. If we can weaken her enough to get close, then I will take off her head and we will burn the body," Drustan said.

"This plan is very fragile. It all depends on hurting a witch who can command the elements. We will be lucky if we survive long enough to see the evening star," Gib said gloomily.

"We can still run. Hide in the forest or flee north to the coast," Tyree suggested. He was clearly reluctant to engage in this battle.

"Wulvers do not run," Gib snapped.

"Nor will I," Drustan affirmed. "We cannot avoid a fight, and we know that with each day Etta grows more powerful. This day, right now, is our best hope."

"I know you are afraid, my fellow fae," King Jorin spoke gravely. "But we cannot hide from this threat. While we were captive in the Between, I learned of a dire plot. One that I hoped not to burden you with, but now you must know. Our world, the Faerie Realm, will soon fall."

"What?" The faeries gasped collectively.

"What has happened?" Asked Tyree.

"While I was prisoner I heard the witches. They spoke of invading our world and enslaving our kind. They have been using dark magic in order to break through the barrier that protected our realm; and I now sense that barrier has fallen."

The faeries gathered around closely, listening to their king. They mumbled and gasped in disbelief at the news.

"If we do not draw Etta into this world and kill her. Our kingdom will fall. Our people will be enslaved, and our children will be slaughtered to feed her hunger for power."

"We cannot allow this to happen!" Tyree shouted and the others concurred. "We must fight her here, tonight!"

"What's our current headcount of fighters?" asked Gib.

"Twenty," replied the king. "With you and Drustan, we stand at twenty-two. When the Between was formed, many fae were trapped on this side of the barrier between the worlds. There are many still in the forests and among the stones who are eager to fight for their return home. We will send out scouts to find any others who may come to our aid."

"We must muster every able body willing to fight," advised Drustan. "From what I saw before we stepped through the doorway, there were thousands of soldiers marching with Etta."

Jorin addressed faeries, "Go into the forest, the rivers and everywhere our brethren may be. Tell them their king beckons they join our cause. Look for elves, trolls, and any of our faerie cousins. Entreat that they join us or share our fate should Mora win."

The group of faeries obeyed and flew off into the woods in search of reinforcements.

"As for Etta, we must insure that she enters this world but does so without the support of her army," Drustan reminded the king.

"There's a possibility that we could separate Etta from her troops," Jorin spoke, deep in thought. "But the thought of doing so worries me."

"If there's a way, we have to take it," Drustan demanded.

"The plan is that when Etta comes through, we'll close the Faerie Door, effectively trapping her on this side, while her army remains stuck in the Between."

"Then you must do it! Keeping her soldiers from entering our realm gives us a better chance to defeat her," Drustan emphasized.

"Drustan, if King Jorin closes the Faerie Door," Gib warned, "it cannot be reopened. It will remain shut forever."

"Aye, 'tis true," King Jorin said with a touch of sadness. "As the Between Time passes and the door closes, that's when we can permanently seal the passage and close the Faerie Door for good."

"But what of the other doors? You said that there were other doors at other places. What is to stop Etta from coming through one of the other passageways?"

"When we seal the Faerie Door, it will close them all," Jorin answered.

"Then what of you?" Drustan asked. "What of Aster and all the others? How will you get back to your own world?"

"We will not. We will be trapped here."

"Then we must find another way. I cannot ask you to make such a sacrifice."

"Indeed, it is a decision that weighs heavily upon us," Jorin spoke, his voice carrying a solemn tone. "But let us face the truth. We have been ensnared within this realm for countless years, held captive by the relentless curse of Mora's Between World. The path back to our homelands has become fraught with perils, making the journey a treacherous one. The doors to the Faerie Realm have been firmly sealed, a measure taken to safeguard our kind from the sinister machinations of Mora. This earthly realm has become our dwelling for nearly two centuries, and yet the mere thought of forsaking the Faerie Realm fills my heart with a profound sorrow."

"And what of her army left behind?" Drustan queried. "Will they not march against the Faerie Realm?"

"Without Etta's guidance, they shall be disarrayed and powerless to launch a united invasion. There's also some that believe when Etta dies, so will the Between." Jorin replied. "But, we must not forget the risk this would pose to this world of men. If Etta is allowed to live, trapped here in this realm, she shall be a menace to all that is good and just."

"If she lives," Drustan pointed out. "We must make sure she doesn't."

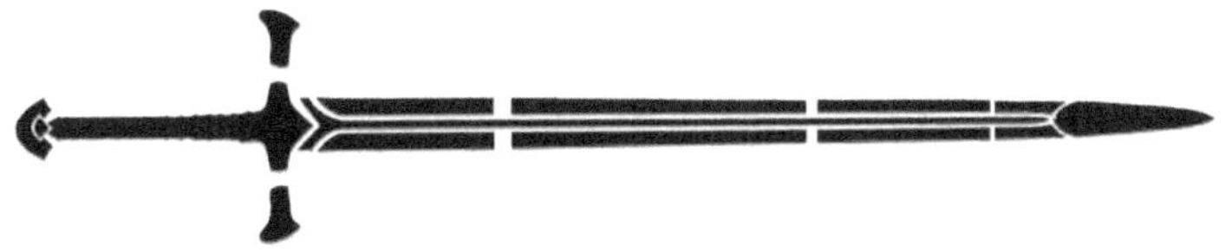

CHAPTER 22

Laine's Betrayal

"Our mistress summons thee back to the castle," Laine said to the goblin soldier standing guard at the Faerie Door.

Having several hours before the Between Time and the opening of the doorway, Etta had permitted her soldiers to rest while she returned to her castle to wait out the delay. One guard had been assigned to watch the door, simply because it seemed prudent to do so in the event someone used a Faerie Stone to pass from the mortal world back into the Between.

"I am under orders to remain here, my lady. Leaving my post would mean my death."

"The mistress herself hath summoned thee to the castle. Refusal shall also result in thy death," she warned him.

"That makes no sense. Why would the mistress place me here and then summon me back?" he persisted. "I apologize, my lady, but I cannot abandon my post."

With a heavy sigh, she flicked her hand in his direction and he exploded into a shower of bloody droplets. "I tried to be kind, but ye were not amenable."

Laine reached into the pocket of her robe and retrieved a small trinket. It was the Faerie Stone, the one she had suggested to Etta that Drustan had stolen, allowing him to escape. She had kept the magical stone hidden, anticipating the moment when Etta would become uncontrollable, and she would need to escape from the Between.

She glanced around to make sure no one was near. Satisfied that she was alone, she clasped the stone tightly and approached the Faerie Door. The darkness between the stone shimmered and transformed into a brilliant and sun-filled view of the mortal world. She stepped through the door and found herself faced with the swift advance of Drustan and his furry friend, the wulver.

"It's Laine! She must not escape!" Drustan cried out, his voice ringing with determination as he raised his gleaming sword to the sky. In his wake, Gib brandished his battle ax, ready to strike at a moment's notice.

But Laine remained steadfast, dropping to her knees and crying out, "Peace! I come in peace!"

Drustan and Gib, caught off guard by the sudden surrender of their foe, stood over her, their weapons at the ready. Yet, Laine remained resolute, her voice steady as she repeated, "Peace! I come in peace, and I bring news.

"What trickery is this?" growled Gib, suspicion written across his face.

"I come bearing no ill will," Laine answered calmly.

Drustan stepped forward, his voice ringing with authority. "How did you pass through the portal?"

Laine slowly extended her hand, revealing the glittering Faerie Stone. "Mora thought thou hadst taken her Faerie Stone," she explained. "And in her moment of distraction, I saw my chance and claimed it for myself."

"Are there more?" Drustan pressed on, his eyes narrowing. "Does Mora have another key?"

"Nay, this is the solitary stone," Laine declared. "If there were others, she would have pursued thee here herself. Now she must await the moment of Between before she can cross the barrier."

Gib's eyes burned with curiosity. "What brings you here, crone? What is your intention?"

"I offer thee aid against Etta," Laine replied, her eyes shining with a fierce determination. "For her tyranny knows no bounds, and it is time that we stand together to defeat her once and for all."

"You lie," Drustan replied. "You are cut of the same cloth as Mora. You would no more betray your queen than you would betray yourself."

"She is not my queen," Laine snapped angrily. "We were to be equals, but she has set herself above me. Soon she will look upon me as her rival and turn to destroy me, just as she plans to destroy thy mother who stood against her."

Drustan lowered his sword. "Stand up and do not make any false moves or my friend will plant his ax in your skull."

Laine rose to her feet and both Drustan and Gib took a step away to maintain a safe distance.

"What aid do you offer us? And why should we trust anything you say?" Gib asked. "Speak now and give me a reason not to cut you down where you stand."

"My words are only for the hunter. I will speak only with him."

"Anything you have to say, you will do so to both of us," Drustan replied. "I will not fall for any more of your witch's tricks."

"'Tis not for my own purpose that I seek a private audience, but for thine," she assured him. "My words are of a delicate matter."

Drustan was reluctant to speak with her alone, suspicious that it was a ruse to allow her to cast some spell upon him. He did not fear the witch, but he had learned the lesson about letting his confidence overrule his common sense.

"Let me assure thee," Laine spoke, her voice low and filled with intrigue. "The tidings I bring pertain to the delicate matter of thy exploits in the shadow realm. Yet, if thou art determined to share such private affairs with thy bestial companion, then so be it." The corners of her lips twitched upward, hinting at a sly grin.

Drustan's curiosity was piqued, yet he was shamed at the thought of the potential revelation of his secret moments with Etta, or Mora. He pondered upon his trysts with the witch and realized that these were matters best left undisclosed. If Laine spoke the truth, then he would be able to share the news at his discretion.

"Gib, if you would excuse us for a moment," Drustan finally spoke after much contemplation. Although he harbored suspicion towards the crone, he wished to avoid any embarrassment that might arise from the public discourse of his intimate affairs.

"Don't be a fool!" Gib snarled. "This witch cannot

be trusted."

"Please, my friend, I implore you," Drustan beseeched. "Do not compound my disgrace in this matter."

Gib was hesitant, for he was wary of this ancient crone, but the look on Drustan's face was not to be ignored. He could see the shame that weighed heavy upon his friend's countenance at the mere thought of speaking of such private matters in public. And truth be told, Gib had no desire to hear of Drustan's intimate moments with Mora while he was under her spell. With a reluctant nod, Gib stepped away, leaving Drustan and Laine alone.

"Go not far, just a few paces, that we may converse in secret," Drustan said, gesturing towards the trees nearby.

Gib gave Laine a fierce look before he withdrew, keeping watch nearby. "Try nothing, witch," he warned.

"It will be fine," Drustan promised.

Once they had privacy, Drustan turned his attention to Laine. "So, what is this information you claim to have brought me?"

"Etta intends to capture thee alive," Laine replied.

"For the purpose of torturing me, I presume?" Drustan asked, skeptical.

"Nay, not to be thy captor but rather thy lover," Laine said with a smile.

Drustan snorted. "She must be out of her mind! After all she has done — the murder of my grandparents, the abuse of my mother, the plan to kill me as an infant — there is nothing in this world that would make me return to her bed. So, what is the true reason for your presence here?"

"My purpose is to give thee forewarning. She may

be filled with wrath, but she remains under thy sway," Laine explained. "Thou art her weakness, witch hunter. Thy hold over her is as potent as any spell she might cast. Use it to thy advantage."

"How do you suppose I do that? Should I flash a smile and give a wink when she comes swooping down as a giant serpent to destroy my world?" He spoke sarcastically. Laine's words were making little sense to him. What difference would it matter that Etta lusted after him, how could that possibly offer any advantage?

"Mock if thou wilt, but she is convinced that ye are destined to be her mate. Given a flicker of hope, she will not harm thee and she will hesitate to act."

"Go back to your evil mistress and tell her this deception did not work. I despise her, and I will never be anything more than her sworn enemy. The only pleasure she can offer me is to see her death."

But Laine grabbed his arm. "Wait!" she exclaimed.

"What now?"

"Hold on tightly to thy hatred for her and let that be thy compass. Ye must cling to that hate and see her for who she truly is, the old crone Mora. Hold fast to that truth if ye want to defeat her."

"I know who and what she is," Drustan replied. "There's nothing she can say or do to dissuade me from my task."

"There is something else," Laine said, "a truth that she will use to gain thy favor. She carries thy child."

Drustan felt as if he had been gutted. He could not believe that Etta could be with child. She was a witch, an ancient crone transformed by dark magic into a fair maiden. How could an unnatural creature such as Etta be produce a child?

"This cannot be true. 'Tis a lie!" Drustan insisted.

"She hath told me such and I can sense the life growing within her. Thou hast lain with her for many a night, you know better than any if this could be so," Laine insisted. "Tell me. Is it possible that she could carry thy child?"

"Aye, 'tis possible," he said reluctantly. "If she's transformed and her body appears to be that of a maiden, then there's little room for doubt."

"Then, to slay her, ye must also slay thy own offspring," Laine warned. "She shall seek to use that against thee. Ye must stand firm and be ready to do what must be done to end her life."

The news that he had fathered a child with Etta disturbed Drustan deeply. He was suddenly in a similar situation as his mother when she carried the son of her attacker. The baby was innocent, just as he himself was innocent of his father's wrongdoing. Though the mother of his child was evil, the unborn child, his child, was also an innocent victim. He finally understood the terrible dilemma his mother faced many years ago.

"If this be true, 'tis a saddening occurrence," he said. "I pray that I can do what must be done."

"Thy life and all ye hold dear depend upon it," Laine informed him. "When the time comes, do not hesitate, young hunter. Hold fast and do not be swayed by sentiment for this unholy thing she carries. For this unborn child is as profane and ungodly as she herself."

The witch stepped away and prepared to leave, confident that she had given Drustan the knowledge he needed so as not to be taken unaware. He would be prepared for his confrontation and when Etta sought to distract him with news of their child, being forewarned would help him stand firm and undaunted; prepared for what he must do.

"Now I will take my leave," Laine said. "Mora has enemies in the mountains; others who would wish to see her dead. I will go to them and bid they come to thy aid."

"Why should I believe any of this? You have been Mora's accomplice for centuries; the same blood on her hands is on your own. Why would you wish to help us?"

"As I said, she has betrayed my sisters and soon she will turn her treachery toward me. I and thy mother are her final remaining threats who could challenge her. Etta would have no equal, and no rival to her power. Soon, she will turn against me."

"You understand that once Etta is dead, it will be you that I will hunt."

"Such is the way it should be. Once your task is fulfilled and Mora's existence is extinguished, seek me atop the northern coast, where I wait in solitude," Laine uttered with a defeated and somber voice. "At that moment, I shall bow my head before thy victorious blade, celebrating the triumph ye have achieved. I have endured countless years already, and weariness has settled deep within my soul. Magic, too, shall fade, and beings like me shall be relegated to mere tales and legends, haunting the imaginations of children."

Drustan looked at her, studying her face for any sign of deceit. But he could see only sincerity in her eyes.

He nodded and said, "Very well. But will you not stand against Mora this day? Instead, you would flee like a mouse before a cat?"

"I would live to fight another day," she answered. "If thy plan should fail, then who would be left to oppose her?'

"How very noble and practical of you," Drustan sneered. "Very well, be on your way. Hide in the caves of some faraway mountain. And pray that we never cross paths again."

Nodding her head in solemn comprehension, Laine swiftly transformed into a sleek black raven with a flick of her wrist, gracefully taking to the skies. Drustan gazed after her as she vanished amidst the towering trees, her course set towards the distant hills. The weight of Laine's message lingered within him, a truth he struggled to accept. Deep down, he recognized its validity. A tumultuous decision loomed before him, one that churned his insides with anguish. Could he bring himself to slay Etta, knowing that his own unborn child would be lost in the process? The fate of both the faerie and mortal realms hung in the balance, offering him little alternative. He understood what lay ahead, yet he questioned his own fortitude to carry it out when the crucial moment arrived.

After Laine departed, Gib hesitated before approaching Drustan. With a deep breath, he cleared his throat before speaking, "I could not help but overhear your conversation with the witch," Gib said, his voice rumbling like distant thunder. "What I heard, is it true?"

Drustan's eyes hardened as he turned to face Gib. "What did you hear?" he asked, his voice laced with a warning.

Gib spoke softly, bracing himself for Drustan's reaction. "Etta is carrying your child," he replied, his words hanging in the air.

Drustan's face contorted with anguish as he grappled with a torrent of conflicting emotions. The unexpected news of Etta's pregnancy blindsided him, leaving him adrift in a sea of confusion and uncertainty. A heavy weight settled upon his heart, while his mind became entangled in the potential ramifications of this revelation.

"Gib, what am I supposed to do?" Drustan's words trembled with a mixture of desperation and frustration, his feelings a jumbled mess.

Gib regarded Drustan with genuine concern, fully aware of the gravity of the predicament. "Etta is not one to be underestimated. She will exploit this child as a weapon against you, and you must be prepared."

Drustan's gaze hardened with determination silently vowing not to let her manipulate their child for her own ends. "I will do whatever it takes," he declared firmly, his voice reflecting unwavering resolve. "But if the moment comes when I falter, hesitate, or show mercy, you must spare none."

Gib nodded, his expression conveying understanding and steadfast support. "If the burden becomes too great for you to bear, I will bear it in your stead," he pledged. "I stand by your side, unwavering, through thick and thin."

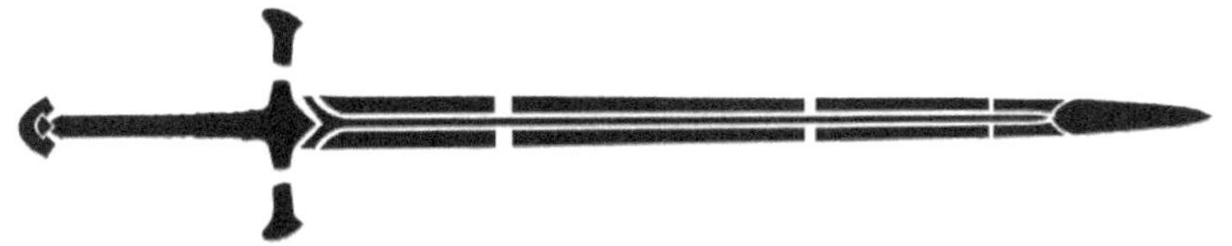

CHAPTER 23

Blood for Blood

With swift and graceful flight, Laine traversed a short distance from the Faerie Door, where she had rendezvoused with Drustan, to the secluded cave where Raum and his clan sought refuge from the daylight. Determination propelled her through the air, as she allowed no obstacles to hinder her mission. The powerful flapping of her wings stirred a gust of wind, causing the tree leaves to rustle below. As she neared the narrow entrance into the cavern, Laine descended from the sky, seamlessly transforming into her human form. Urgency gripped her, spurring her onward into the heart of the mountain, following the perilous path deeper into the murky abyss.

As Laine ventured into the main chamber, where Raum and his clan were gathered, a sense of unease washed over her. In the center of the hollow, a blazing fire illuminated the chamber with a vibrant glow. The vampires stood watchful, regarding Laine's presence with a mix of curiosity and disdain, observing her as she approached.

"Where is Raum?" she demanded in a commanding voice, her eyes scanning the room. "I must speak with thy master."

"Why do you intrude upon my abode, witch, tainting it with your presence?" Raum growled, his voice dripping with contempt. The surrounding vampires nodded in agreement, their disdain evident.

Laine's narrowed gaze scanned the chamber, seeking out Raum's figure perched atop a towering stalagmite that rose high above cavern's floor. She strode forward with unwavering confidence, her sense of urgency palpable.

"She hath betrayed us all," Laine declared, her voice resonating through the chamber. "Surely, ye are already aware of this."

"It matters not to me," Raum retorted, leaping from his perch and landing gracefully before Laine. "I have fulfilled my obligations, and I desire no further involvement with thee or her."

Laine emitted a contemptuous cackle, her lips curling into a sneer aimed at Raum. "Do you truly believe she will release thee and these precious offspring unscathed? She craves thy blood to sustain her youth, and she will rebuild her coven. They shall all partake of thy dark gift."

"I have given her my blood," Raum retorted. "She will make another that will serve her needs."

"She could," Laine conceded, "but she sees thee as her property, just as she sees the son of Isabel as rightfully hers. She will let neither of you go free. In her eyes, you both belong to her!"

"I belong to no one!" Raum snarled, his eyes flashing with anger.

"Verily, as you do say, my lord," she replied and bowed her head respectfully. "Nevertheless, you know that thy freedom will only last as long as she allows. Forever is a long while for two people to share a world and not meet again."

Laine stood her ground, her gaze unwavering. "Mark my words, Raum. She will come for thee and the others, and when she does, there will be no escape. Her thirst for power and immortality knows no bounds."

"Why are you here, witch? You would see me and my clan fight your battle for you? No, we will not."

"And what of thy child? The immortal one whose blood she spilled to live but for only a single day. Shall ye not have revenge for that loss?"

Raum began to circle her, moving like a lion stalking its prey. "What game do you play?"

"I play no games," Laine replied with conviction. "I speak plainly."

"Then what is this? You come here speaking treachery against the one you have called mistress."

"She hath fallen in love with the witch hunter," Laine revealed. "Now, she carries his child. She would have this mortal by her side while we burn in flames."

Raum turned his back on Laine, his eyes cold and unfeeling. "Do you think I care?"

But Laine was undeterred. "You know the hunter, Raum, and what he means to thee."

Raum turned to her, his face twisted in anger. "He means nothing to me," he spat. "Let Mora, or Etta, or whatever she calls herself now, have him. Let her have any lover she chooses. I care not."

The clan emerged from the shadows, their eyes fixed on Raum and Laine. Laine seized her chance, pleading with them to take revenge for her brother's death. "If you desire revenge," she implored, "then the time is now. Etta's army waits beyond the Faerie Door, and the hunter is ready to strike. Will ye stand idly by?"

"The same hunter whom she loves?" Raum mocked. "The same hunter who has fathered her child? That hunter?"

"He would rather see her dead and the bastard child with her," she replied. "He and the Faerie King stand against her. If ye seek revenge for thy brother's death," she turned to look directly at Raum, "thy son's death, then thou must act now. Go to the Faerie Door and stand with thy mortal son!"

"Son?" Cailin repeated in shock, as the others of the clan gasped in disbelief. "Is the witch speaking truthfully?"

Laine's voice trembled with emotion as she replied, "Aye, the witch hunter who stands in thy place against Etta is the mortal son of thy father. He is thy brother."

Raum shrugged, his voice cold and dismissive. "The boy was born of my mortal blood, but I have been reborn. This one they call the Hunter is nothing to me."

"He is thy son!" Laine insisted, her eyes flashing with conviction.

"He means nothing!" Raum bellowed.

The chamber fell into a deathly silence after Raum's outburst, the tension in the air palpable. No one dared to speak, their fear holding them hostage.

After what felt like an eternity, Byron stepped forward, his eyes locked onto Raum with a ferocity that made even the vampire leader flinch. He glared at Raum for a long moment before he spoke, his voice laced with an icy edge.

"He means nothing? This hunter is the flesh of your flesh, and yet he means nothing to you?" Byron's voice rose in anger, and his words echoed through the chamber. "What of Jarit, your son of the dark blood? Did he mean nothing as well?"

Raum's expression turned vicious, and his eyes burned with a fierce intensity as he looked upon Byron. He had grown accustomed to Byron's forward opinions and his calming influence, but now Byron had gone too far. He was directly challenging him in front of the entire clan, and Raum was not one to be so easily challenged.

"Measure your words carefully, son," Raum seethed in a low growl, his voice barely contained. "You are crossing a line that may cost you your life."

Byron sneered and took a step closer to Raum, his eyes blazing with anger. "And now you threaten my life, as if I were nothing more than waste to be discarded."

Raum's eyes flashed with fury as he glared at Byron. "What would you have me do?" he roared, his voice echoing through the cavern with such force that the walls shook. "Send you to your death against the witch? We have finally gained our freedom from Mora, and now you would have us invite her wrath upon us?"

The tension in the room was palpable as the two powerful vampires stood toe-to-toe, their gazes locked in a deadly standoff. The rest of the clan watched in silence, unsure of what would happen next.

Byron's voice echoed through the cavern as he thundered out his demands, fueled by a passion that had been building for years. "I would have revenge for my dead brother, Jarit! I would have the brother, whose face I have yet to see, safe and living in peace! And I would have my father defend his family rather than cower in the darkness of a cave!"

Raum's eyes blazed with fury as he exposed his fangs like a wild animal, and with a guttural growl he launched himself at his son. But to his shock, Byron was ready for the attack, and with a mighty swing of his arm, he sent Raum hurtling across the chamber and slamming into a stone wall. The impact echoed through the cavern, leaving a stunned silence in its wake.

Byron's eyes burned with fierce determination as he stood over the fallen Raum and pressed his foot against his maker's throat. "I will not be silenced," he declared. "I will fight for what is right, for the honor of our clan, and for the memory of Jarit."

Raum struggled to rise, but Byron held him down firmly. "Listen to me, father," he said. "We cannot hide in the shadows forever. We must face our enemies and take back what is rightfully ours."

Raum glared up at Byron, his face contorted with anger and pain. "You dare to challenge me?" he growled. "I am your leader, your father, your creator. You will do as I command or suffer the consequences."

But Byron was unafraid. "I will not back down," he said, his voice steady and resolute. "I will fight for what

I believe in, even if it means challenging you, my own blood."

With his teeth bared and eyes gleaming, Raum snarled with a fierce intensity. "She will kill us all."

"Then let us embrace death and find peace, rather than living in fear," Byron declared firmly.

Despite his fierce resistance, Raum found himself unable to dislodge Byron's foot from his neck. He slowly came to accept his defeat, and the realization washed over him like a wave of icy water. As Raum slowly stopped struggling, sensing his change in demeanor, Byron gradually released his foot from Raum's throat. "Are we settled now, father?" he asked, still poised to strike if necessary.

Raum's eyes burned with fury and his breathing was ragged as he reluctantly nodded, his defeat still fresh on his mind. With Raum's final gesture of surrender, Byron released his father and turned to address the clan.

"Then it is settled," he declared, his voice ringing with conviction. "At nightfall we fly to our brother's aid and pray that we arrive in time to make a difference."

"And what of this one," Cailin asked, pointing to Laine. The question hung in the air, unanswered.

But as the clan turned to him for guidance, Byron hesitated. He was not yet ready to depose his maker and take over leadership of the clan. He looked to his father, in an open display of continuing loyalty he asked. "Father, what would you have us do?"

Raum hesitated, the sting of defeat still fresh and painful. He locked eyes with Byron, uncertain of his own authority to lead, while Byron's calm demeanor left him questioning who was truly in charge.

"Father? What is thy command?" Byron asked again, offer a clear demonstration that Raum was still in charge.

After a moment, Raum regained his composure and spoke to his vampire children. "Perhaps this witch speaks the truth. Maybe it is time for revenge. Blood for blood."

Raum circled Laine, he was hungry for a show of strength and Laine was the obvious target of his wrath. "You were there when they took my son and slaughtered him like a sacrificial lamb for the witch Mora?"

"'Twas not I who took the boy's life," the witch replied, her voice trembling with fear. She looked around nervously, seeing the looks of hatred on the vampire faces now falling upon her. "'Twas Mora who took thy son and no other."

"Were you not the blade she used to strike him down? Did you not hear my son's screams for mercy as his life was drained from him?"

"If it is truly revenge ye seek, then go to the Faerie Door. 'Tis no justice to find here."

In an effortless leap Raum landed back atop the stone perch and looked down at the witch in judgment. The vampire clan had slowly closed in around Laine.

Raum stood atop the stone and addressed the clan. "My children, do you seek revenge?" He pointed at Laine with an accusing finger. "There is your revenge!"

"It was not I who spilled thy son's blood," Laine protested as the group of vampires began to circle her. A sense of panic welled up inside her, as though she were suddenly surrounded by a pack of wild wolves.

The vampires crouched as they moved and began to

make low growling sounds.

"Call them off, Raum," Laine threatened, her voice trembling with fear and anger. "Else, I will turn them all to dust."

Raum leapt down from his perch and seized one of the torches, his eyes ablaze with a fierce determination. "I'm afraid that's not going to happen," he said, holding the fiery torch to a nearby wall. As the flames illuminated the cavern, a series of ancient symbols etched into the stone came into view. Raum lifted the torch higher, revealing that the mysterious markings covered the entire wall and continued onto the ceiling in every direction. "These," he said, with a smug grin, "are binding spells that take away a witch's power." Laine scowled at the sight, her fear and anger mounting with each passing moment.

"I spent years groveling at Mora's feet," Raum declared with a cold, calculated tone. "And in that time, I've learned a thing or two about dealing with black witches. You see, it's important to know how to protect yourself, especially when it comes to binding spells. I knew that eventually, one of you old hags would come calling, spewing your threats. And now, here you are." A wide, chilling grin spread across his face, exposing his razor-sharp fangs.

Laine was visibly shaken by the revelation that she had been tricked and her powers bound. She raised her hand and made a motion towards Raum as if she were casting a spell upon him, but there was no effect. The sigils had done their job and she was powerless. She glanced around anxiously at the vampires.

"Do not do this Raum," she begged. "I have come as an ally."

Raum looked at Laine with a mocking expression. "An ally? A treacherous old crone like you? You came here to threaten and intimidate us. To use us as foot soldiers against Mora. And now you beg for mercy?"

Laine fell to her knees before him, pleading, "Have mercy dark prince! Mercy!"

He turned away from her and leapt back upon his perch overhead. "I offer you the same mercy you showed my son," he roared, then looked upon his children. "Rip her to pieces!"

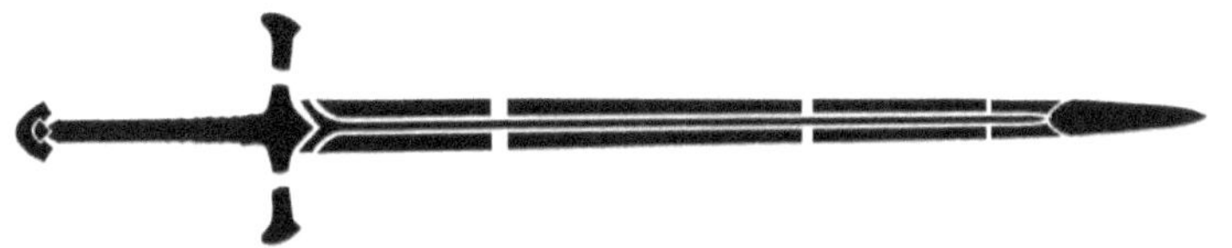

CHAPTER 24

The Final Battle

As the sun descended beneath the horizon, Drustan and his allies gathered before the Faerie Door. Tension hung thick in the air, and it seemed the entire forest held its breath in anticipation. The Between Time was approaching; that enchanted moment when neither day nor night, dusk nor twilight held sway, and time stood suspended between ending and beginning.

They waited, having spent the dwindling hours of daylight preparing for the inevitable: the opening of the Faerie Door and the arrival of the evil witch, Etta, with her army of goblins. In the race against time, they pieced together a hasty, defensive plan, woven together with threads of uncertainty. Yet, Drustan was confident in its solidity.

The plan was audacious and perilous: to confront Etta and her army directly at the doorway, capitalizing on the bottleneck that would hinder the goblin advance. As Etta emerged from the portal, Gib and the faeries would strike, hoping to hold the soldiers off long enough for King Jorin to seal the passage, separating Etta from her army and trapping her in the mortal world where she was vulnerable and could be defeated.

As they waited, Drustan's thoughts drifted to his family, and he took solace in the fact that he had done everything in his power to protect them. Yet, a nagging feeling of regret gnawed at him, and he couldn't help but wonder if he could have done something differently to avert the impending conflict. He analyzed every choice he had made, replaying his journey in his mind. If only he had not made a deal with Aster, he would not have lost his enchanted arrows, the only weapon that had proven effective against Mora. If only he had not been so enamored by Etta when he first discovered her in the castle, he might have recognized her treachery sooner. And if only he had not been so foolish as to eat those cursed bilberries.

Upon reflecting on his journey, Drustan came to the realization that nothing could have been done to improve the outcome of events. However, upon deeper thought, he realized that the situation could have been far worse. Even if he had not been so arrogant as to set out for Mora's castle, Etta still would have been reborn, with her intentions no less dangerous. Her ultimate goal would have been to conquer the Faerie Realm and beyond, but without Drustan's blunders, she would have done so unchallenged. Despite the gravity of the situation, Drustan found comfort in knowing that he and his companions were providing the resistance necessary to oppose her plans.

Having considered all the different possibilities,

Drustan finally dismissed his self-doubt and remorse, acknowledging that only one thing could have changed the course of events: a well-aimed arrow on that fateful night when Mora attacked his family's home. Though it was a bitter realization, he also knew that dwelling on it would not alter the current situation. Thus, he shifted his attention to the battle looming ahead and resolved to do everything in his power to safeguard those he cherished.

With a steadying breath, Drustan filled his lungs with the crisp, cool air of the forest, letting it wash away the clinging doubts and regrets that clouded his thoughts. Though he yearned to rewrite the past and choose a different course, he knew that he was here, now, for a reason. The fates had deemed it so, and it was his duty to face it with all the valor and fortitude he could muster. Destiny had chosen him, and he would meet it with unflinching courage and unyielding strength.

As the sun disappeared behind the mountain, the sky blazed with a vivid orange hue, as if the heavens were on fire. A faint humming sound echoed through the air, growing louder with each passing moment. The Between Time had arrived, and the magical Faerie Door began to radiate with an otherworldly glow, drawing the eye and mind toward its mysterious depths.

"Prepare yourselves," King Jorin's voice called out to the assembled faeries, who stood around the glowing door. Their numbers were depleted; of the 20 who had set out to seek reinforcements, only half returned, and they returned alone. The others had retreated deep into the forest to hide from the impending darkness. The remaining faeries, including Tyree, Aster, and King Jorin, were joined by two elves who had answered the call for help. With Drustan and Gib at their side, they were the last line of defense for the realm. The forest was eerily quiet, as if every living thing had sensed the impending doom and retreated to safety, leaving the defenders alone to face the darkness.

In the face of what appeared to be insurmountable odds, the stalwart band remained resolute, their determination unyielding. The plan they had devised relied not on brute strength or overwhelming numbers, but on cunning and strategy. The Faerie Door loomed before them, a portal between worlds, and their success hinged on closing the door and isolating Etta from her troops. Once that was accomplished then it was up to Drustan to face and defeat the witch.

The group stood frozen in rapturous awe, mesmerized by the pulsating radiance emanating from the Faerie Door. The air surrounding it was a dazzling array of iridescent colors, like the surface of a lake at the height of a fiery sunset. A low, ominous hum filled the air, escalating in volume and intensity with each passing moment, echoing through the forest like the rumble of distant thunder. The threshold of the doorway gradually became translucent, revealing the silhouette of Etta, flanked before her goblin army on the other side, poised and ready to strike as soon as the portal was fully open. Suddenly, the door opened, and the goblins charged forward, surging through the opening in an unrelenting wave.

As expected, their rush through the door was impeded by the narrow width of the opening, allowing only two and three at a time to enter. As soon as they passed, they were taken down by the arrows loosed by Drustan and the elves. Still, they continued to pour through the narrow opening, walking over those who had fallen and pushing the dead bodies aside as they came. The few that did make it through were cut down by Gib and the faeries with their swords.

It seemed that they would succeed in holding back the advance of Etta's soldiers until an unfortunate reality set in. There were more goblin soldiers than Drustan and the elves had arrows. Once the archers were spent, it was not long before the goblins began to push the faeries back, forcing them to withdraw. As the goblins advanced, even more of Etta's soldiers were able to pass through.

"We can't hold them any longer!" Gib cried out to Jorin. "You must close the door now!"

Jorin glanced at the horizon and saw that the orange glow of the sunset was nearly faded. "We must hold them, just a few moments longer! The doorway will soon close; if Etta is to come, she must do so now."

Just as he spoke the words there was a sudden push by the goblins and Etta emerged through the doorway. She entered the mortal world as the last of the orange sunset was fading to deep blue, signaling the end of the Between Time. This was the only time that the Faerie Door could be closed permanently, as the last of the orange twilight passed away.

"Seal the door!" King Jorin called to his fellow fae.

In a moment of anticipation, the faeries shimmered with an ethereal glow, their brilliance illuminating the surroundings. As if guided by a shared purpose, beams of radiant light erupted from their chests, converging upon the stones that composed the Faerie Door. The fusion of magical energy and solid rock brought about a tremor in the earth, causing the stones to radiate with a fiery intensity akin to molten heat. The door frame itself shifted and rumbled, as if responding to the surge of enchantment coursing through it. Then, in an awe-inspiring spectacle, the entire structure erupted into a dazzling burst of light.

In the aftermath of the blinding flash, the Faerie Door revealed its transformation—a stark contrast to its former resplendence. Now, it stood as nothing more than a cold and lifeless arrangement of stone. Though the physical structure remained unchanged, the vibrant aura that once animated the door had vanished completely. Its former allure and enchantment had dissipated, leaving behind a mere oddity of nature—a peculiar stone formation bereft of magic.

"What have you done?" Etta screamed, realizing that the Faerie Door was now sealed and she was banished from the Between world she had created. "You have trapped us here! You will pay with your blood!"

The throng of Etta's soldiers surged ahead, forcing Drustan and his allies to retreat deeper into the woods. Yet, as they did, Etta met the first obstacle set in her path. Drustan had anticipated her advance and erected a series of barriers to slow her down. The first was a wide circle of salt encompassing the area surrounding the Faerie Door. With the aid of Gib's plentiful bags of salt stored in his hut, the allies had salted the earth, invoking an ancient defense passed down from Sibby to ward off witches.

As she stepped upon the salted ground, she cried out in pain and the soles of her shoes began to smoke. Immediately, she backed away and began studying the ground around her, looking for a means to penetrate the circle.

"Drustan! She is held by the salt!" Gib shouted to alert the witch hunter that Etta was vulnerable.

Drustan was locked in battle with two goblins when Gib called to him. Realizing his opportunity was finally at hand, he quickly dispatched the two soldiers and rushed to confront Etta. She backed away as Drustan approached, his sword in his hand ready to thrust.

Etta's voice oozed with seduction, casting a spell over Drustan like a dream. "Drustan, my love," she purred, her words laced with a hypnotic quality. "You would not harm me."

Drustan found himself ensnared by the beguiling cadence of Etta's honeyed words, his mind whisked away to the vivid recollections of their once-fiery passion. The grip on his blade loosened, a fleeting moment of vulnerability taking hold as he became entranced by the piercing intensity of her gaze. Yet, as he stepped across the salted ground, a jolt of awakening abruptly shattered the enchanting hold she had over him.

Etta seized the opportunity presented by Drustan's muddled emotions without delay. "I bear our child, a son. Let us cast aside this bitterness and forge a new world together," she implored.

Despite the forewarning Laine had provided, Drustan found himself momentarily swayed by Etta's revelation.

The knowledge that the child she carried was a boy added an additional layer of distraction, testing his resolve.

In that brief moment of hesitation from Drustan, the witch seized her opportunity with swift precision. Etta's arm extended in a seamless motion, and a nearby sword, abandoned by a fallen soldier, flew into her waiting grasp. With a swift and powerful slice through the air, she inflicted a deep gash across Drustan's chest.

Drustan staggered, aghast, as crimson streams cascaded down his chest. The unexpected strike left him momentarily disoriented, but he swiftly regained his senses just as Etta's blade cleaved through the air once more, its lethal trajectory mere inches from his vulnerable throat.

Undeterred by his wound, Drustan summoned his inner resolve and deftly evaded the imminent danger, his body instinctively recoiling. Etta's relentless assault persisted, her sword a blur of deadly arcs, but Drustan, now composed, met her strikes head-on. With nimble mastery, he skillfully intercepted her blows and retaliated with calculated precision, anticipating her every countermove. The symphony of clashing steel reverberated through the air, bearing witness to the clash of two formidable adversaries, both warriors honed by experience and unyielding resolve.

Etta, despite her diminutive frame, possessed an astonishing amalgamation of speed and power that rivaled any mortal man. Yet, Drustan stood firm, unyielding in his determination. He refused to falter under her relentless onslaught, launching a relentless barrage of his own, forcing her to exert every ounce of effort to deflect his assaults. The battle unfolded in a tempestuous frenzy, each combatant evenly matched, their eyes ablaze with an unwavering resolve to emerge victorious from the chaotic fray.

Soon, the intensity of the struggle began to take its toll and Drustan's grip on the sword handle began to waver. While a master swordsman, his expertise lay in technique rather than endurance in prolonged combat. Sensing his weakness, Etta relentlessly pummeled him with stroke after stroke, causing him to lose his grip and send his sword hurtling through the air. Disarmed and vulnerable, Drustan was at the mercy of the witch as she raised her sword to strike the final blow. But this time it was she who hesitated. She looked at him through the eyes of Etta, rather than as Mora. Her heart momentarily aching from the loss of their passion.

Drustan seized on the moment, and he sprang through the air and tumbled to the ground several feet away. Etta regained her composure along with her anger and charged after him. But as she advanced, she found herself once again standing on the salted earth with pain shooting through her feet and up into her legs.

She screamed in a combination of pain and rage at him and retreated backward. She raised a fire ball in the palm of her hand and flung it at Drustan, but the orb disintegrated in the air as it crossed over the salt barrier. She seized one of the goblins by the arm, "sweep a path through this cursed earth," she ordered. The goblin fell to his knees and began using his hands to dust away the dirt and salt to make a path for her to pass.

Gib grabbed Drustan and began to pull at him urgently. "We must fall back!"

Drustan and his allies fell back, engaged in a relentless struggle as they retreated toward the second fortified boundary they had erected. This magical barrier stood as a last-ditch effort to impede Etta's relentless advance. Fueled by their unyielding determination, the goblins pursued them with unwavering fervor.

The tide of battle began to tip heavily against Drustan's forces. The goblin soldiers who had already breached the barrier proved too numerous to overcome, their ranks overwhelming.

Knowing the futility of their current stand, some of the faeries reluctantly relinquished their swords, their faces etched with fear. With a swift transformation, they shed their mortal forms, their wings unfurling in a desperate bid for freedom. One by one, they ascended into the darkened embrace of the forest, abandoning their fight.

Tyree grabbed Aster and pulled at her urgently. "Aster, we must flee!"

"No!" She cried out. "I cannot leave him!"

"We must!"

Aster surveyed the battlefield, her heart heavy as she locked eyes with Drustan. His gaze was filled with despair, and she knew they had to leave before it was too late.

"Go, Aster!" Drustan shouted, his voice a desperate plea. "I will find you!"

But Tyree was already tugging at Aster's arm, urging her to transform and flee. Aster hesitated, torn between her loyalty to Drustan and her own survival.

With a heavy heart, Aster yielded to Tyree's urging and transformed into her faerie form. Tyree followed suit, and they took off into the forest, the distant echoes of battle fading behind them.

Once he had crossed the second barrier, Drustan turned to see Etta had breeched the salt barrier and was nearly upon them. It was then that Drustan and his fellow fighters accepted the futility of their resistance and seized the opportunity to escape.

"We can't hold them! Everyone retreat!" Drustan yelled.

While Etta and the goblins were temporarily held back by the second barrier, Drustan and what was left of the resistance escaped into the woods. They had gone only a short distance before they could hear the goblin troops once again closing rapidly on them.

"Quickly, this way!" King Jorin urgently beckoned, guiding the group into the mouth of a cavern skillfully obscured behind a dense curtain of brush. Silently, they took refuge within the sanctuary of the cave, their breaths held in anticipation, while the echoes of goblin troops searching the vicinity reverberated through the air. Time seemed to stretch, each passing moment fraught with tension as Drustan and his allies maintained their hushed vigilance.

The group stood poised, their bodies coiled like springs, senses heightened and weapons poised, bracing for the enemy's imminent assault. Yet, as the stillness lingered in an eerie chorus of silence, it seemed that their hiding place had not been compromised. The distant sounds of enemy soldiers prowling nearby were audible, but their presence remained undetected, granting a fleeting reprieve.

Suddenly, the disconcerting symphony of approaching boots grew louder, accompanied by the distinct cadence of the soldiers' voices. Panic surged through the group, realization dawning upon them with chilling clarity — they had been found. An ominous shiver crawled up their spines as they beheld a menacing sight: a viscous, ebony liquid began to seep into the cave, slithering like a malevolent serpent..

Gib's voice rang out, sharp and urgent. "'Tis pitch! They mean to burn us alive!"

The realization dawned on them: their enemies were not attacking because they didn't need to. The goblins intended to use the pitch to burn them out.

"Go back and search for another way out," Drustan whispered urgently. "There may be another passage that leads to the surface."

As panic set in, faeries quickly scattered into the darkened corridors, descending deeper into the mountain in search of a means of escape.

"You have lost. The battle is over." Etta called triumphantly from outside. "Send Drustan out, and I will spare the others."

"Do not do it laddie," Gib warned. "You cannot trust her. She will kill you on sight and then turn this cave into an oven."

"What do you suggest? There are no other options," Drustan replied. "The battle is done, and we have lost."

Drustan stepped toward the entrance and called back to her. "Do I have your word? If I surrender, my friends will go free."

"I will not take their lives. Come forward and kneel, then take thy place beside your queen and all will be forgiven."

Drustan began to walk out, but Gib grabbed him by the arm. "You cannot believe she will honor her word."

"If there is another choice, then I will gladly listen; but clearly, we have lost. At least I will try and save the rest of you."

"We will fight. We will storm out of this cave and we fight to the death," King Jorin declared.

"It will be to the death without a doubt. But, you must live to fight another day," Drustan insisted.

"What is your choice?" Etta called again from outside. "My patience grows weary."

"You have won Etta, I'm coming out," Drustan answered grudgingly. He emerged from the cave and found himself surrounded by Etta's soldiers.

As he stood before her, she regarded him with great satisfaction. "On thy knees," she commanded.

He hesitated for a moment, then reluctantly drew his sword and held it out before him. He paused, accepting defeat he sank down to his knees and laid the sword down at her feet.

"You thought you could defy me," she screamed at him. "I will not be disobeyed!"

With purposeful steps, she approached the source of the streaming oil—a massive wooden barrel—its contents still cascading into the mouth of the cave, where Drustan's beleaguered allies found themselves ensnared. A chilling resolve settled upon her as she lifted her hand

and exhaled a gust, igniting a fiery orb in her palm.

"No, Etta! You swore an oath!" Drustan's plea rang out, laced with desperation.

A derisive laughter escaped Etta's lips, dripping with disdain. "Did I, Drustan? This is the consequence of defiance."

Etta's eyes gleamed with the thrill of power as she prepared to unleash the fiery destruction upon Drustan's allies who were still trapped in the caverns. Oh, how she longed for their annihilation, relishing in the thought of the lesson it would teach Drustan of her unyielding wrath.

Just as Etta was poised to ignite the oil, a sudden disturbance from above shattered her focus. A round object hurtled towards her, falling at her feet with a dull thud. Her eyes widened in disbelief as she gazed upon the severed head of Laine, its lifeless eyes fixed upon her.

"Sister!" Etta gasped, horror gripping her soul as the unexpected sight shook her to her core.

But before she could react, figures descended from the sky with unyielding determination. Raum, Byron, Cailin, and two others stood before her, their weapons brandished and poised for battle.

Etta's rage boiled like an inferno as she locked her gaze on Raum. "What is the meaning of this?" she demanded, her voice dripping with venom.

Raum met her gaze with icy resolve. "She sought our aid, to betray you and fight alongside those who seek your destruction," he responded calmly, his words slicing through the air. "We exacted her life as payment for what you did to my son. But I thought it fitting that you know, that even she turned against you in the end. That you now stand alone."

Etta scoffed, a cruel smile twisting her lips. "Alone?" she laughed, waving her arms around to indicate her army of goblins. "I have all I need."

"But is that enough?" Raum asked, a hint of threat in his tone.

Etta's smug expression faltered, a flicker of uncertainty crossing her face as she absorbed Raum's words. Could it be that her power was not as absolute as she had believed? The realization struck her like a thunderbolt. Laine, a formidable force in her own right, had been brought down by Raum and his clan. Was Etta more vulnerable than she had arrogantly assumed?

Doubt clawed its way into her thoughts, but her gaze swiftly shifted to Drustan, and a sinister grin spread across her lips. "Ah, so you have sacrificed all your blood kin to be slaughtered," she hissed, her voice dripping with malice. "All for the sake of saving your precious offspring."

Confusion and horror etched Drustan's face as he scrambled to comprehend the revelation. "What?" he stammered, rising to his feet. "What is she talking about? Who are you?" His eyes darted between Etta and Raum, desperately seeking an explanation.

Etta didn't give Raum a chance to respond. "Behold, your loving father, young hunter," she cooed in delight. "A son of the dark blood, as handsome and potent as the day he slaughtered your mother's family and claimed Isabel like a savage beast." Her laughter sliced through the air, a cruel, rasping cackle that echoed with wickedness.

Drustan's gaze shifted from Etta to Raum, his expression a mix of shock and disbelief. "Is this true? Are you my father?"

Etta interjected with delicious contempt. "Oh, do enlighten your dear child, Raum. Share with him the nature of his conception. How you tortured his mother, leaving her for dead, all for a taste of dark blood to secure your own immortality."

Drustan's anger burned like the fiery sun as he turned his rage away from Etta and directed it to Raum. He was consumed with fury, the intensity of which could rival the fires of hell. Raum's cruel savagery had ruined his mother's life and, in turn, Drustan's. He was the son of a villain, born of a tainted bloodline, the issue of an evil abomination.

Etta sensed the growing hatred in him and, like a serpent coiling around her prey, she used her dark power to urge him on. Her voice, a mere whisper in the wind, was as soft as silk but as deadly as a viper's bite. "Take thy sword," she hissed.

With a newfound sense of purpose, Drustan picked up his sword and strode forward, his steps echoing like the heavy pounding of a funeral drum. Each stride seemed to bring him closer to the edge of a precipice, to the brink of something that could only end in bloodshed.

The air grew thick with anticipation, each passing moment stretched taut with tension. It was as if the very fabric of time had slowed to a crawl, each heartbeat an eternity in itself. And in that endless moment, Drustan was the eye of a gathering storm, a force of nature that threatened to unleash destruction upon all who dared stand in his way.

Drustan stopped just within striking distance of Raum. The two men locked eyes in a tense and defiant stand-off. Drustan prepared to strike, his sword at the ready, while Raum remained motionless, offering no defense.

With total disgust and hatred, Drustan looked at his father, and then he surveyed the scene around him. The horde of goblins stood ready to unleash destruction on all the creatures of the forest and beyond. To one side, Etta stood with an evil grin upon her lips. He saw the trail of pitch winding its way into the cavern where his companions were trapped. And he saw a group of fanged savages baring their teeth, preparing to rip him apart.

In that moment, Drustan realized the impossibility of his situation. No matter what move he made, the battle was lost. His friends would be burned alive by Etta's hands, his family would be hunted down and put to the sword, and the world as he knew it would crumble under Etta's heel. He was alone and completely without hope.

With his heart heavy and his will nearly broken, Drustan relinquished his sword, letting it fall with a resounding clang upon the unforgiving ground. He refused to succumb to Etta's malicious whispers, for he would not become the monster that Raum was. Amidst the chaos and unfathomable despair that surrounded him, Drustan sank to his knees, his breaths ragged and labored. He had only one last recourse left, and so he raised his arms high to the inky black sky, his voice ringing out in a mournful plea, "Hear the cry of this hopeless and lost soul!"

"What is this?" Etta stood in dismay.

"In utter despair I call upon the cursed and unforgiven dead," Drustan cried out to the darkness. "I call upon the Underfolk. Come! And feast upon this hopeless soul! Come to me ... sluagh!"

Etta looked on in dismay, her twisted plans crumbling before her eyes as Drustan's voice filled the air with power and fury. The very ground beneath them trembled in response, as though the very earth itself was stirred by Drustan's call. And in the shadows, in the deepest recesses of the earth, something stirred. Something ancient and powerful, a force that had long slumbered in the dark.

As Drustan's words echoed through the forest, a horde of creatures began to stir. The sluagh, the black horde, a legion of spirits and wraiths that haunted the edges of the world. They rose up from the earth like a swarm of locusts, their twisted shapes writhing in the darkness. They hungered for the sorrow that filled Drustan's heart, and they thirsted for the blood those who stood in their path. With a terrible roar, they surged forward, their forms blending into a seething mass of blackness and shadow as they filled the sky.

And in the midst of it all, Drustan stood with arms outstretched, his voice ringing out through the darkness as the sluagh fell upon his enemies like a storm. The world was plunged into chaos, but in that chaos, there was a glimmer of hope. A glimmer of redemption.

The sky erupted with a deafening roar of flapping wings, and the horde swooped down upon goblin and vampire alike in a dark whirlwind of teeth and claws. Drustan remained stoic and unmoved as the Underfolk seized Etta, pulling her back and forth between them, tearing chunks of flesh from her body as they vied to take possession of her.

Drustan watched the carnage, unaffected and unafraid, waiting for the moment when the horde would be upon him. Suddenly, he was knocked to the ground and one of the sluagh sat on his chest, pinning him down. Drustan did not fight; he closed his eyes and accepted his fate. The creature spread its wings wide and enveloped him completely within its leathery embrace.

Drustan was unable to move; the creature held him so tightly and pressed to the earth. He felt its hot breath on him and smelled the foul stench of death. From underneath the creature's wings he could hear the screams of the goblin soldiers as they were taken by the horde. He awaited his own fate, but still it did not come. Soon, the beating wings of the horde subsided, and the screams of their victims were no more.

The wings of the sluagh that held him unfurled, and Drustan met the creature's gaze. Its eyes were a striking juxtaposition — one green, one blue — and as he looked closer, recognition struck him like a bolt of lightning. This was the very same sluagh he had saved in the forest.

The creature roared and its throat emitted an odd combination of clicks and grunts, a language Drustan could not comprehend. But he knew what the creature was saying, for gratitude and debt are universal languages, and the sluagh was repaying its debt to Drustan.

The sluagh spread its wings and flew off, joining the horde as they continued eastward in their wild hunt. Drustan stood up and surveyed the carnage. The area around him was filled with broken tree limbs, and bloody pieces of flesh were spattered all around. There were no bodies, no survivors; only he alone remained.

Where there had been soldiers only moments before, now there were abandoned weapons lying in puddles of blood. He walked to where he had last seen Etta, where the sluagh had held her in their grips. She was gone, and what remained was evidence enough that even she did not survive the horde. On the ground lay chunks of bloody scalp with long red hair clinging to the torn flesh. It was finally over. Etta was dead.

Relief flooded his heart at the sight of his friends cautiously emerged from the cavern safe and unharmed. As he approached his companions, he saw the hope and gratitude in their eyes. They knew he was the reason they had survived and they were grateful for his unwavering determination.

Together, they walked away from the battlefield, their footsteps marking a path of triumph and resilience. As they walked, Drustan gazed upward, his eyes fixed on the sky where the first rays of dawn pierced through the lingering shadows. It was a celestial promise, a glimmer of hope that whispered of new beginnings. The weight of victory draped around his shoulders, but he understood that the battle against evil had merely taken a pause.

This hard-fought triumph provided only a fleeting respite in the eternal struggle between light and darkness. The war had persisted for ages, its echoes resonating through time. The tendrils of malevolence slithered through the world, patient and cunning, awaiting their opportune moment to strike. Drustan had witnessed its face, felt its chilling breath on his neck, and understood that it could not be defeated with a single blow.

His journey had bestowed upon him wisdom, revealing the truth that evil lurked in every crevice, beneath the surface of all things. It dwelled in hidden caverns, twisted branches, meandering rivers, and treacherous depths. It lay in wait, ready to ensnare spirits and extinguish hope. Yet, Drustan harbored no fear.

He knew the unrelenting advance of darkness, but his own resolve matched its relentlessness. Embracing his role as The Hunter, he remained steadfast in his vigilance. Cloaked in unwavering courage and an indomitable will, he stood against the encroaching night. His purpose burned within him, a defiant beacon.

The adventure that awaited him would test and shape him, revealing his true destiny. The threads of fate had woven themselves around his existence, inexorably drawing him into a tapestry of mystery and purpose. Drustan recognized that the road ahead would be treacherous, yet he embraced it eagerly, for he was bound to confront the darkness and reclaim the light.

With unwavering resolve and the company of allies forged through fire, Drustan pressed forward. The sun ascended higher in the sky, casting its golden glow upon a world brimming with challenges and secrets.

Destiny's gaze fell upon Drustan, marking him as one of her own. His deeds captured the divine attention, and from that moment on, he would tread a path few had ventured before. This victory was not the culmination of his journey, but its very inception.

Now Drustan's true adventure begins.

www.ingramcontent.com/pod-product-compliance
Lightning Source LLC
Chambersburg PA
CBHW030959190726
48285CB00004BB/1383